THE WITCH'S REVENGE

An Urban Fantasy Thriller (Myth & Magic, Book 1)

S. W. Millar

TAGLINE
PUBLISHING

Tagline Publishing

ALSO BY S. W. MILLar

Myth & Magic

The Thief's Magic # 0.5 (FREE prequel short story)
The Coven's Executioner # 2
The Fury's Vengeance [Novelette] # 3
The Demon's Shadow # 4 (out in May 2022)
More *Myth & Magic* coming soon...

The Witch's Revenge: An Urban Fantasy Thriller (Myth & Magic, Book 1)

Copyright © 2021 by S. W. Millar

All rights reserved

Published by Tagline Publishing

https://swmillar.com

ISBN (eBook): 978-1-915192-01-1

ISBN (Paperback): 978-1-915192-02-8

Cover design by Damonza

Formatted using Atticus

contents

IS THIS BOOK FOr YOU?

This book contains adult themes, fantasy violence, and colourful language. Basically, all the fun stuff. I write using British English. Sound good? Then read on and enjoy!

For Mum. Thank you for passing on your love of reading. Without you, this book wouldn't exist.

"Revenge proves its own executioner."— **John Ford**

CHaPTer 1

The vodka tastes poisonous. It's the same flavour as those words in that letter—a harsh burn with a bitter acidic edge. Unlike that letter though, I welcome this burn. It numbs the dull pain and makes the edges of my mind fizz like a sharp-sweet lemon sherbet dissolving on the tongue.

Dear Henry Stone... We write regarding your application... We regret to inform you...

I slam the empty glass down on the bar, snatch up another shot, throw it back. More burning.

Good.

Burning is good. It distracts me from the pain. I signal to the woman behind the bar and point at the empty glasses. I hold up two fingers.

She collects the glasses and swivels to the row of optics, back-lit in white neon.

A hand clamps down on my shoulder, hard enough to bruise.

I flinch and twist to face Jez.

"Happy birthday, bud. What did I tell you? This place is epic." He shouts over the relentless bass, which punch, punch, punches me in the chest. "The lights are epic, the music is epic, the atmosphere is epic."

I breathe deep through my nose. Cheap, honey-sweet perfume and even cheaper aftershave—heavy with cinnamon and clove—pollutes the air and turns my stomach. Coloured lights waltz across the walls, a dizzying kaleidoscope of blue, green and red. They don't help with the nausea. I shrug Jez's hand away. "Yeah, epic."

"It's so alive, man. Know what I mean?"

I stare at him. We could be brothers—same dark hair, same pale skin, same tall stature. There are two differences between us, though. First, Jez's nose is straight, and mine is slightly crooked. Second, our personalities juxtapose completely. Wasn't always this way, but it is now.

Crowds of people pack the club, mob the bar, ram the tables, and writhe on the dance floor in a mass of tangled limbs.

I fold my arms. "Oh, yeah. It's alive, all right."

"You've got a face like a bag of spanners. What's up with you?"

"Nothing."

"Here you go. Four quid." The woman brings two more shots.

I hand over a five-pound note and she passes me my change.

"That a good idea?" Jez asks. "You've had four already."

I want to tell him it's a brilliant idea, but I'm not in the mood to argue. "You have them, then. I'm going for a slash."

Jez grabs my arm. "This isn't about Oxford, is it? I thought you were over that."

We regret to inform you—

"No." Liar. "It's not about Oxford."

"Bunch of snobby bastards. Who cares?"

I bloody care. I don't say that, though. Instead, I say, "I know."

"Plus, this way, we get to boss post-grad together."

"I know."

"You'll save a packet on accommodation fees, too."

"I know."

They're familiar, these tired lines of dialogue. They should be. We've rehearsed them almost every day since the letter arrived. My undergrad tutor said I should appeal, but I didn't want to make a fuss. The authorities at Oxford had made their decision. I had no choice other than to accept it and move on. Try to move on, anyway.

"Trust me. It's their loss," Jez says.

I force a smile. "Yeah, you're right. Thanks, mate."

He chews at his bottom lip, a sign he wants to say more.

"What is it?"

"Nothing."

"No. Go on."

"It's Sensei Toby."

Fear prickles at the nape of my neck. "I'm not going back."

"I told him that, but he won't let it go."

"He'll have to."

"You didn't stop because of—"

"No. Of course not." Two lies in one night. I'm on a roll.

"Why, then? You never said."

I try to look him in the eye. "I only started doing karate as a kid because Mum and Dad forced me." That part's true. I shrug. "Just wasn't for me anymore. It got stale." And that's lie number three.

He doesn't believe me. I can tell, but he must decide to let it go, because he swipes a shot off the bar and drains the glass. "Find a table when you're done, yeah? And stop thinking about those snobby bastards at Oxford."

"Already stopped." I turn away. The smile slides down my face like a concussed pigeon skidding down a window.

Oxford.

The Masters in Creative Writing.

It's all I've ever wanted, and I'll never have it now.

Happy birthday to me.

I leave the gents, push back into the club, and weave through the crowd. I scan for somewhere to sit, but all the tables are full.

There must be some spare seats somewhere.

A metal staircase climbing the back wall leads to a mezzanine level, which is separated from the club by a thick sheet of glass.

Thank God. It'll be quieter up there.

My temples throb in time to the music, and I need some respite. I fight my way across the dance floor, mouthing, "Sorry," when I step on someone's foot, and, "Excuse me," when I need people to move, and jog up the stairs.

The bold, black lettering on the glass door reads, *The Snug*. I shove the door open, step through and, when it closes behind me, the deafening thump from below recedes to a muffled pulse.

That's better.

The Snug is all low tables, squishy leather sofas and dim lighting.

A single empty table beckons to me from the far corner. I'm halfway there when a flash of colour catches my attention.

A woman wearing a vintage, bright green *Guns N' Roses* T-shirt and black jeans reclines on a sofa with her legs tucked up. She twirls a lock of auburn hair around her index finger while reading a copy of Jim Butcher's *Storm Front*.

I wouldn't normally approach a stranger in a bar, but I'm emboldened by alcohol and embittered by rejection, so I cross to her table. "Enjoying the book?" Riveting opener.

Her eyes remain glued to the page. "Trying to."

"I've read the entire series. Twice."

"Good for you. Too bad I'm fresh out of medals."

Heat rushes up the back of my neck. "Sorry. I didn't mean—"

"What is it with guys? Why can't you take the fucking—" She glances up, breaks off mid-sentence, blinks at me, and says, "Oh."

Oh, is right.

Her eyes are a strange colour, like burnished copper, and a pale silver ring encircles each iris.

Unnatural.

An icy finger trails down my spine. "Uh, cool contacts."

She cocks her head to one side, and her full lips curve into a slow smile, flashing brilliant white teeth. "That's interesting."

My stomach flips. "What is?"

She slides her long, slender legs out from under her and crosses her feet at the ankles. "Never met someone like me before, that's all."

"Someone like you?"

She opens her mouth, closes it again. "Never mind, I'm talking shit. Too much gin. Didn't mean to bite your head off." She picks up a tumbler of colourless liquid and drains it in one, banging the empty glass down on the table. "Wanky day." She chuckles, a low, dirty sound. "Understatement. Wanky year, actually."

"No worries." I know all about that.

Dear Henry Stone... We regret to inform you...

I dig my thumbnail into the tiny knot of scar tissue in the hollow between my collarbones and pick, again and again.

The woman spots me picking, and says, "A problem shared, and all that," gesturing at the seat opposite her.

I perch on the edge of the sofa and point at my chest. "Henry."

"Primrose." She closes her book and places it on the table. "Something tells me you've had a shit year too?"

I have, but I won't tell her that. "What? Oh, no, no. I meant today. It's my twenty-first, but I'm not feeling it."

"Can't have that." Primrose's eyes catch the light and the silver rings around her copper irises glint. "Still, nothing a drink and a dance won't cure."

"I don't dance."

"Then what the fuck are you doing in a club?"

"Says the woman reading."

"Ha ha," she says in a dry tone. "Supposed to be meeting a friend, but she's a no show. You might be better company, though." Her gaze travels down my face and lingers on my lips.

The heat on my neck spreads into my cheeks.

Primrose grins, grabs her book and slides it into the cavernous purple handbag squatting next to her. The strap of a *Daxbridge City University* lanyard pokes out of the top.

"You're a student at DCU?"

"Am now. About to start my post-grad."

"Me too."

Her brow furrows. "You don't sound too happy about it?"

"I—um—I applied to Oxford."

"Didn't get in, huh?"

"No."

Silence sucks all the air from the room and holds its breath.

Eventually, Primrose clears her throat. "What are you studying?"

"Creative Writing."

She rolls her eyes so hard I'm surprised they don't get stuck in the back of her head. "Ugh. You don't want to be the next James Patterson, or Stephen King, do you? Hate to tell you, but it's probably not going to happen."

My mouth sags open.

More toe-curling silence ensues.

Primrose closes her eyes and presses a thumb and forefinger to her eyelids. "I'm such an idiot. Mum's always telling me I was born with both feet in my mouth."

"Don't worry about it," I say, a beat too fast. In fairness, she doesn't know I've read Stephen King's *On Writing* ten times and have a stack of half-polished, dust-gathering manuscripts stashed in a deep, deep drawer. "How about you?"

She drags a doorstop-sized textbook from her bag and holds it up. The words *An Advanced Guide to Criminal Law* emblazon the cover. "Take a wild guess."

My eyebrows crease in mock-puzzlement. "Politics?"

She gives another throaty chuckle. "So, how come—" Her face drains of colour, copper eyes widening as they fix on something over my shoulder.

"You okay?" I follow her gaze.

Not something.

Someone.

A blonde guy in his mid-forties wearing a smart, blood red suit sprawls on a sofa across the room, his arms resting on the back. His long, tapered fingers—piano player's fingers, Dad would call them—caress the brown leather like a spider's legs brushing over bare skin.

Primrose clutches her throat, fingers trembling.

Goosebumps erupt along my arms. "Who's he?"

Her mouth drops open. "You can see him?"

"Of course."

"Shit. I was right. You really are like me."

"What do you—"

"Primrose, it's been a while," a deep, masculine voice says. I jump.

The spider-fingered man stands at my shoulder now. His voice is rough and rich, like burnt toast glazed with honey.

Primrose asks, "How did you find me, Razor?"

His eyebrow quirks up, stretching the puckered scar running through it. "In the usual way. We need a chat, in private."

"I'm not going anywhere with you." She snatches up her bag, stands, and pivots on her heel.

Razor clamps a hand around Primrose's arm. "You'll do whatever I say."

"Get off me."

Fierce heat makes my blood boil. No man should touch a woman like that. I'm on my feet and, before I can stop myself, I grab Razor's arm, my hand clammy with sweat. It's the alcohol again, making me do things I'd never normally do. "Hey. Leave her alone."

Every single muscle in Razor's body stiffens, and he turns his head with deliberate slowness. His gaze travels from my hand to my arm, and up to my face—eyes a shade of brown, so dark they're almost black. "You shouldn't be able to see me."

The skin on my scalp shrinks as if vacuum packed. Razor's wolf-like, his predatory stare freezing me in place.

I can't speak.

Can't move.

Can't breathe.

He yanks his arm back, tearing from my grasp, and seizes my wrist with his nicotine-stained fingers.

I know how to break a wrist hold. Bring my captured hand up to my face. Grab his wrist with my other hand. Squeeze. Twist my hips away. Simple.

Or it should be, but I'm paralysed by fear.

Razor leans in closer. His breath's thick with the potent scent of fruit-flavoured chewing gum and old tobacco. "Word of advice. Don't go looking for trouble. If you do, chances are it'll find you."

Fruit-flavoured chewing gum.

Old tobacco.

We regret to inform you...

I hate that smell. Something heavy drops into my stomach and cold sweat breaks out on my upper lip. All thoughts of escape slam to a halt. "I don't want any trouble."

"Good lad." Razor winks and thrusts me away.

I collapse back onto the sofa.

He tugs on Primrose's arm, dragging her towards a door marked with a fire exit sign. "You're coming with me."

Don't go looking for trouble.

I pick my scar again. I pick until it aches, until the raw skin throbs.

Primrose struggles in Razor's grip, but he's stronger than her. She doesn't stand a chance.

Don't go looking for trouble.

My nail catches a sensitive spot and I flinch.

I want to do something, want to go after them, but Razor's warning pounds a drumbeat against my skull. My breathing comes in shallow gasps. I stagger to my feet and the room spins, my vision blurring. Cheeks blazing, I turn away from Primrose and Razor, and a wave of dizzying heat overwhelms me. I'm going to pass out or throw up. I'm not sure which.

"Let me go, arsehole," Primrose says.

The room snaps back into focus. I spin around as the fire exit door closes.

The other people in *The Snug* wear confused expressions, exchange worried glances, and mutter to each other under their breath. Not one of them moves towards the exit.

What am I doing? Razor's dangerous. I can't just let him take her, let him do God knows what to her. What's the alternative? Stand by and do nothing. I can't do that. It isn't right.

I clench my fists to stop my hands from shaking and stride towards the fire exit door.

CHaPTer 2

A dark, grubby hallway greets me, a grime-coated emergency light casting a feeble glow. Steep stairs lead upwards and pivot at an abrupt ninety-degree angle, and the sound of a scuffle comes from above. A door creaks open and a breath of chilly air blows down the stairs and raises the hair on the back of my neck. The staircase must lead to the roof.

I jog up the stairs, heart slamming against my ribcage, and round the corner halfway up. Then I keep on climbing. The door to the roof's ajar. I halt by the door, and raised voices reach me.

"Tell me what you've done with it," Razor says.

"It's gone." Primrose's voice has lost all of its earlier warmth. "You're never getting it back."

I creep closer, limbs heavy, and peer around the door frame.

They stand at the roof's edge and Daxbridge City sprawls below them, an amalgam of old and new. Squat, sand-yellow domes cower in the shadows of steel-armoured skyscrapers, and thousands of cat-eyed streetlights glare out of the darkness.

"For your sake"—Razor clutches the low metal rail bordering the roof—"I hope that's a lie."

I angle my body to get a better view.

Primrose laughs. "You know me better than that."

"I swear to God, if I don't get my money back, I'll—"

"You'll do what?" Primrose advances on him, the sharp click of her heels echoing off the concrete. "Kill me? Slit my throat, like Finnegan?"

"Yes." The word's quiet, sibilant. "Just like Finnegan."

"I knew it. I knew it was you." There's genuine hurt in Primrose's voice.

My chest tightens and I can't release the breath trapped in my throat. He killed someone. Razor *murdered* someone. My mouth's dry. I want to run, but I'm frozen, unable to move.

"He didn't give me a choice," Razor says.

She cringes away from him. "Of course you had a choice. There's always a fucking—"

"You don't understand. He was on the take," Razor says.

"Liar." Primrose whacks the metal railing, and it rings like a shaken lamppost. "He wasn't a thief."

"He was stealing my gear, cutting it with Christ knows what, and selling it for a profit. Right under my nose."

Gear? Does he mean drugs? I swallow, hard. I don't want anything to do with drug dealers.

"You're talking out of your arse," Primrose says.

"One of my regulars died because of the shit your precious boyfriend was peddling. I found him in the woods, in a ditch. He was bleeding from the eyes."

"Horseshit."

It hits me then. Primrose's boyfriend was tangled up with Razor. She's connected to him somehow, too. Is she a criminal? Why the hell did I follow them up here? I don't know Primrose. Who is she, really? I should leave, but my feet won't budge.

"Believe me, don't believe me, I don't care," Razor says, a hard edge creeping into his voice. "I just want my seventy grand back."

Primrose's answering laugh's high and laced with a note of hysteria.

Razor's fingers twitch. "You think this is funny?"

"I think it's fucking hilarious."

Razor swings his arm up and points his outstretched fingers at Primrose.

The laugh dies on her lips.

"I've given you everything, you ungrateful bitch. I made you. You were nothing without me. A two-bit junkie scraping a living on the streets. I got you clean, gave you money, a new identity, paid your uni fees, taught you magic, and for what? So you could stab me in the back and steal from me."

Magic? Did he say magic? Why would he teach Primrose card tricks?

"I loved him." Primrose's lower lip trembles. "I loved him, you murdering bastard."

Razor's face is set, emotionless.

I hold my breath, not daring to make a sound. If he catches me up here... it doesn't bear thinking about.

When Razor speaks, his voice is quiet, but the sound still carries. "Finnegan knew what would happen if he betrayed me. He paid the price. So I'm only going to ask one more time." His lips press into a firm line. "Where. Is. My. Money?"

Primrose clenches her fists so tight her knuckles turn white. "You'll regret this. I'll go to the MID. I'll tell them everything. You forget, I know where you buried the bodies."

The MID? What's Primrose talking about?

Razor lowers his eyes for a moment. "I wish you hadn't said that." His hand whips through the air, his fingers hooked into claws. He whispers under his breath and slashes his arm across his body in a wide arc, the tips of his fingers glowing red.

Primrose's body jerks. Her hands go to her throat, fingers clasping at her neck.

My pulse beats everywhere—in my neck, in my head, even in my fingertips. What the fuck was that? What did Razor do?

She coughs and shiny red beads well up between her fingers. The rubies drip onto her T-shirt and stain the green material scarlet.

No. Not rubies.

Blood.

My head swims. What the hell's happening?

Primrose's eyes bulge, and she staggers sideways, hip striking the metal railing hard. She hinges outward, from the torso, tilted at an impossible angle. She hangs there, one foot off the floor. A second passes, and another, and another, and then her legs windmill up and over the rail. A flash of copper eyes and lime green fabric. And she's gone.

Without thinking, I race through the door, out onto the roof, and shout her name.

Razor's head snaps round, and the dark pits of his eyes bore into mine. His brow wrinkles, then his expression clears. "You," he says.

My heart migrates to my throat. What do I do? Fight, flight, or freeze? I almost laugh. Fighting's out of the question. Freezing will get me killed. I need to run, and fast.

Razor flicks his fingers, and they glow red again. "*Pedibus nostris.*"

The air snaps, the sound of a flag snatched by the wind, and a heavy pressure settles around my legs. I try to move my feet, but they won't budge. I try again, straining until my muscles ache. What the—

Wait. *Pedibus nostris.* Thanks to my parents' inexplicable insistence I learn Latin, I understand what he said. *Pedibus nostris* translates to *bind him*.

"How—" My voice cracks. "How did you do that?"

A disturbing thought barges its way into my mind. When Razor said he taught Primrose magic, maybe he meant *real* magic. The kind my favourite authors write about.

No.

That's sheer lunacy.

Magic isn't real.

A shiver runs through me, laced with a sharp pang of apprehension.

Is it?

Razor stalks closer, nicotine-stained fingers rising a third time.

I will my legs to move, but it's no good. I'm trapped like a fly in a jam jar. My windpipe shrinks until it's pinhole sized, and black spots cavort before my eyes.

Razor's twelve feet away.

My head spins.

Eleven feet.

Please, God, please. Let me get out of this alive.

Ten feet, and he halts.

Somehow, I find my voice, and my words come out pleading. "Please. Don't kill me. Please."

He coughs, a harsh bark. "You should've stayed downstairs. If you hadn't seen what just happened—"

"I won't tell anyone, I swear. I swear. Please, let me go and I'll keep my mouth shut. I promise. Please."

A crease appears between his eyebrows. "The MID are already building a case against me. It's all circumstantial, but if they find out about this, I'm finished."

"They won't. I don't even know what the MID is. I won't say a word."

He sneers at me. "No. No, I'm sorry. I can't take that risk."

"No, no, no." My insides dissolve.

"I warned you about looking for trouble."

I know then that it's over, and the proverbial curtain's coming down. They say your entire life flashes before your eyes when you're about to die, but that doesn't happen. Instead, a collage of the people I love winks into existence. Mum, Dad, Jez; Jez, Dad, Mum; Mum, Dad, Jez, spinning round and round. A beat passes. Primrose. A woman who'd asked me to dance. A woman who'll never dance again.

Razor's arm sweeps across his body, and he opens his mouth to utter the words I know will end my life.

A metallic crash rings out from the bottom of the stairs. "You back here, bud?"

Jez.

All the breath bursts out of me in a long rush. "Yeah. Up here."

A string of expletives explodes from Razor, vile enough to taint the air. His jaw works like he's chewing something tough and full of gristle. He clicks his fingers. "*Invisibilia*."

I translate on autopilot. *Invisible.*

A shimmer of crimson light—like rippling water—travels from the crown of Razor's head to the soles of his shoes. I can still see him. Maybe it—whatever *it* was—didn't work.

The muffled thump of trainers on carpet travels up the staircase behind me.

Razor snaps his fingers again, and the vice-like pressure around my legs vanishes.

I lift my foot and it leaves the floor.

Jez barrels through the doorway. "What are you doing up here? I've been looking for you everywhere. Why are you standing on one leg?"

"What? Oh." I lower my foot. "I just needed some air, that's all."

Razor says. "You got lucky."

"Don't you dare. Don't speak to me," I retort.

Jez narrows his eyes. "Why? What did I do?"

"Not you."

"There's no one else here."

"Sure." I thrust out a hand, pointing at Razor.

Jez inches back. "Are you okay?"

Razor slides a hand into his inside jacket pocket.

I jerk back.

"Relax." He extracts a packet of cigarettes and shakes them at me. "I'm hardly going to do anything in front of your mortal friend, and risk being witch-bound."

"Witch-bound?"

"What are you on about?" Jez presses the back of his hand to my forehead. "Seriously, bud, are you ill or something?"

I bat his hand away.

"Now he thinks you're mad." Razor pops open the pack of cigarettes, brings it to his mouth and catches one between his teeth. No, not a cigarette—too fat—must be a spliff. He drops the square carton back into his pocket and holds up his index finger. "*Ignis*."

Fire.

A scarlet spark flashes, and a small red flame flickers to life, dancing on Razor's fingertip. He touches the flame to the end of the spliff and takes a deep drag. When he exhales, he blows out three blue-grey smoke rings in quick succession.

The thick, woody-sweet rotten vegetable scent of marijuana coats my nostrils.

"No way." Jez's eyebrows shoot up. "It makes sense now. You're on the wacky tobacky."

"No, I'm not."

He sniffs the air. "Come off it, you sneaky stoner."

I glare at Razor as he expels another smoke ring. "I'm not stoned." Whatever Razor did to prevent Jez from seeing and hearing him obviously doesn't mask odours.

"Yeah, whatever. You reek of weed." Jez waves his hand in front of his nose to underscore his point.

"I—" Wait. Better he thinks I'm stoned than crazy. I adopt what I hope's a dopey grin and duck my head. "Okay. You caught me."

"Wonders never cease." He shakes his head. "You coming back inside, or what? The DJ just started this mad set, and—"

"No."

"Why not?"

This is my chance to get away from Razor, to get away from this club. I can run now, and Razor won't be able to stop me. "I, um, I'm not feeling so good. Reckon that weed was dodgy. I'm just going to go."

"Go? We only just got here."

"Stay, then." I draw my phone out of my pocket.

Two texts from Mum.

Can you let me know when you're on your way back? X

I groan and read the next one.

Have you remembered your birthday surprise? X

Like I would've forgotten. I'm twenty-one years old, for Christ's sake, and she still treats me like I'm twelve. Yet another reason I wish I was going to Oxford—at least I could've put a bit of much needed distance between my parents and I.

Another text from Dad.

Hi, Champ. Do me a favour and text your mum back. You know what she's like with surprises.

I thumb a quick reply to Mum.

Leaving now. Don't stress. You know what Dad's like with surprises.

I bring up my contacts list. "I'm going to call a taxi. You want to split it, or are you staying?"

"Yeah." Jez stuffs his hands deep in his pockets. "We'll split it."

Razor runs a finger across his throat, and mouths the words, "This isn't over."

I turn towards the door. The world tips on its side and I grab the door frame to steady myself. I place one shaky foot in front of the other as I pick my way down the stairs.

Razor's whistling, the tune familiar, but hazy, like a dream. Then it clicks. The *First Cut is the Deepest*. Mum plays the Sheryl Crow version *ad infinitum*. I go cold as I reach the bottom of the stairs and fast-walk through the club—zigzagging through the crowd—and out into the night, Razor's words ringing in my ears.

This isn't over.

CHAPTER 3

M y knees tremble long after the taxi clears Daxbridge City limits. We hurtle along a narrow country lane. The scenery smudges to a blur of brown and green, the multi-coloured sugar skull hanging from the taxi driver's rearview mirror—its grinning mouth mocking me—bounces up and down, but not as fast as my knee. I keep my eyes open, because every time I close them, she's there.

Primrose.

"Your friend looks a wee bit green around the gills," the taxi driver says in her thick Scottish burr, while changing gear. "If he's sick, you're cleaning it up."

Jez glares out of the window. "He'll be fine."

Will I, though? I don't know. My shoulders are up by my ears, and I roll my neck to ease the tension there. I'm picking at my scar again, unable to stop.

"What's up with you?" Jez asks.

"Nothing."

He turns his narrowed gaze on me. "Doesn't look like nothing."

"I'm fine."

"How long have we been friends?"

I shrug. "Forever."

"Yeah. So I know when something's wrong."

"Nothing's wrong."

He snorts, a derisive sound. "I call bullshit."

"Call whatever you like."

Jez sets his jaw. "Say that again." If there's one thing he hates, it's being lied to, and I've told enough lies tonight already.

Guilt gnaws at my stomach. I can't tell him the truth. There's no way he'll believe me. I'm not sure I believe it myself. I don't want to look him in the eye, so I don't. My gaze remains on the road ahead. What does he want me to say? This guy killed this girl by waving his fingers in the air. Might as well fit me up for a straitjacket now. "Just leave it, will you?" I plead.

"No. I won't."

Ugh. He can be such an arsehole.

The taxi driver clears her throat. "Take it down a notch, lads. You're giving me a headache."

Jez ignores her, firing a question at me. "Can you stop doing that? It's annoying."

"Doing what?"

He nods at my scar.

I force my hands to relax, lace my fingers together, and squeeze them hard.

Jez sighs. "Maybe you should..." His words trail off, and he turns back towards the window. "Never mind."

"Maybe I should what?"

"Forget it."

"No. Go on. Say it."

Jez bites the inside of his cheek. "Maybe you should see someone."

"What?"

"Someone who can help you. With the panic attacks."

Fierce heat rushes through me. "Don't know what you're talking about."

"Right." Jez sounds tired. He runs a hand through his thick hair, so that it sticks out at odd angles. "Whatever."

The taxi's headlights gleam off the road sign that says, *Welcome to Aston Parva.*

Almost home. Thank God.

Jez picks at a frayed stitch on his seatbelt. "Well?"

I grit my teeth. "Well, what?"

"Are you going to get help?"

"I don't need help."

Jez's fists clench in his lap. "You can't bury it forever. It's been, what? Just under a year now? I want my mate back. You haven't been the same since it happened. You need to—"

"Shut up. Just shut the fuck up."

A pernicious silence falls.

The taxi driver glances at us in the rearview mirror—flicks her eyes to the road—and back again. "Come on, fellas, I don't need this. I've had a shitty day as it is. I just want to finish my shift in peace."

When Jez speaks two minutes later, his words are slow, like he's explaining something complicated to a dim-witted child. "I get it. You're dealing with some shit. I'll let that go. This time. I'm not trying to make you mad, but you're my best bud, and I hate seeing you like this."

My fingers find the scar again. He wants his mate back? Yeah, well, me too, but that Henry doesn't exist anymore. Not since...

Dear Henry Stone—

No.

That's the last thing I want to think about right now.

I don't respond to Jez.

The taxi pulls up outside Jez's house. He gets out. He doesn't say, "In a bit," or, "See ya," like he always does. Instead, he slams the door and trudges up the drive.

The taxi driver releases the handbrake, and we're off again. "I hear all kinds of things in this taxi. Things you wouldn't believe. Things that would put hairs on your chest. See here, I don't want to pry—not really my style—but, I've got to say this. He's right, you know. Your friend."

I grunt, noncommittal.

"Went through a bad patch myself, after my divorce. Depression, anxiety, panic attacks—the works. It was a dark time, that's for sure. Did a lot I regret." She pauses. "A lot. Bad, bad things."

I lean my head back against the headrest. A thick bank of cloud hides the stars from view and threatens rain.

"Oh, aye." She spins the steering wheel and we glide around a corner. "Tried it all. Mindfulness, meditation, talking therapy. All bollocks. None of it worked. Not one thing."

I bow my head, staring at the back of the passenger seat.

"Only got better when I admitted I had a problem. And boy did I have a problem. There I was, standing in my bathroom with a nose full of coke and a belly-full of whiskey. Caught sight of myself in the mirror, and I'm like, Jesus on a pogo-stick, you need to start standing up for yourself, woman."

I want to yell at her. I want to scream. What the hell do you know! Primrose stood up for herself. Look where that got her. I don't yell. Instead, I pick and pick and pick at my scar until my thumbnail comes away tinged red.

The taxi driver drones on and on and on. "Got a pal who owns a boxing gym in the city. Helped me turn my life around. Well, I say pal. Don't get me wrong. The guy's a bit of a prick, and it's wall-to-wall twats lifting weights and grunting in front of mirrors, but it worked. Never felt better."

Please. Stop talking.

"Not touched a drop of the poison in ages."

Please. Just stop.

"He's got me on this whole *clean living* pile of wank. All avocados, and goji berries, and spirulina. Goes right through me, but it does the job.

Please. God. Stop.

The taxi crunches to a halt on my gravel driveway, and the driver twists in her seat, the ring through her eyebrow shining.

"I could give you his number? Tell him I sent you. He loves me."

Been there, done that. "Thanks. I'm all good."

"Suit yourself, but you're missing out. Nothing like knowing you can beat the shit out of someone. That's six fifty."

I thrust a crisp ten-pound note at her. "Keep the change."

"You sure? I've got—"

I climb out of the taxi, bang the door shut, stumble up the drive. I blink and the afterimage of Razor's glowing fingers burns behind my eyelids.

The car's headlights wash over the cottage's white walls, the engine revs, and the taxi pulls away, but it's all muted.

It's like I'm submerged underwater. Someone squeezes my head in a vice and my breaths are shallow. My heart rate spikes, beating so fast it almost hums. Everything lurches and I stagger sideways. My hands slam into the wall and pain prickles my palms. My stomach folds in on itself and I gag once, twice, vomit gushing between my lips and smattering the flowerbeds. The air's thick with the sour stench of bile and the perfumed, floral scent of roses, a combination that makes my stomach roil even more.

A wild animal bellowing shatters the silence. A low, rumbling wail.

What *is* that?

And then I realise, I'm the one making the noise.

I scream and scream and scream.

A loud click, followed by an even louder creek. The front door opening.

Steady footsteps scrunch across the gravel, and Dad's hand rests on my shoulder. "Henry! What have you done to Mum's flowers? She'll go spare."

"Dad." I tilt my head up to meet his gaze.

He draws back, slides a hand into his pocket, and pulls out a clean handkerchief. "Here, wipe your face."

I snatch the handkerchief, scrub it across my mouth, and straighten.

"What's all the fuss about?"

Quick. Think of an excuse, a lie. "I overdid it with the drink a bit, that's all."

"It would be nice if you could make it to the toilet next time."

"Dad?"

"Yes?"

I want to tell him everything, but how can I? He'll think I'm crazy. "Nothing."

Dad opens his mouth and closes it again. Then he says, "Come on. Let's fetch you a glass of water."

He turns away, and I follow him into the house, the taste of vomit still thick on my tongue.

The front door closes with a soft click. The cottage's soap and clean linen scent embraces me in a warm hug. My muscles relax a little.

Dad paces down the hall, the soles of his shoes tapping on the distressed oak floorboards as he passes his small music room—the top of the piano cluttered with his collection of heavy glass paperweights. "Mum won't be pleased."

"No, I don't suppose she will." I follow him down the hall and round the corner.

Mum stands by the fridge. She's got her back to us, her mobile pressed against her ear. Her hair frizzes out in a wild, tangled mess of black curls, a sure sign of stress. "No, you listen, Kate. Someone had to do something. What did you expect? I couldn't just sit by and watch while—" She breaks off, spins on her heel, spots us "—Kate? I have to go. Henry's home. Fine. Yes, okay, fine. Do whatever you need to do." She hangs up the phone and chucks it on the granite worktop, where it lands with a clatter.

Dad says, "Everything—"

Mum holds up a finger, cutting him off, her hazel eyes boring into mine. "What happened?"

"Drank too much." I walk to the sink, grab a clean glass off the draining board, and fill it from the tap. The light reflects off something shiny in the windowsill. My parents' wedding rings nestled together. Must've taken them off to wash up again.

"You're a terrible liar," she says.

How does she do that? I bring the glass to my lips and take a swig, the water a balm to my dry, burning throat. She knows something's up, and she won't stop quizzing me until she finds out what's wrong. I'm not ready to talk, so I take another sip.

"Stop stalling."

"I'm not," I say, through gritted teeth.

Mum taps her fingers on the worktop, her nails clicking. "What's Jez got you into now?"

"Why do you hate him so much?" I drain the glass and slam it down on the side.

Dad scratches his head. "Mum doesn't hate Jez."

"She does, ever since we were kids. She's always had it in for him."

Mum storms around the breakfast island, locks her fingers around my chin, and tilts my head from side to side. "Your father and I aren't stupid, you know."

Your father. She only refers to Dad as *father* when she's pissed off. I twist out of her grip. "What are you on about?"

"You smell like a hydroponic skunk farm."

"I wouldn't touch that stuff if you paid me."

"Do *not* lie—"

"Yvonne."

"Don't Yvonne me." She rounds on Dad and jabs a finger at him. "If that Jez has got our son hooked on drugs—"

"I'm not taking drugs."

Dad shakes his head. "Maybe we should all take a breath. So, he got high, it's not the end of the world."

Mum clicks her tongue. "It's called a gateway drug for a reason, Nigel. Weed today, heroin tomorrow."

"Oh, for God's sake, why do you always have to overreact?" My voice is too loud, the following silence even louder.

Mum folds her arms. "If it's not drugs, then what is it? And don't say nothing."

I tip my head back and rub my neck. "I can't say. You'll think I'm mental."

Dad's mouth curves into a smile. "Like we don't already."

Mum tuts.

I grin and then think of her.

Primrose.

I taste something sour, and it's not bile this time. "I can't."

Mum fiddles with the silver, crow-shaped stud in her earlobe. "We can't help you unless you tell us what's wrong."

"I—" I pause, the words jammed in my throat. How do I tell them what happened? Where do I even start? A malign thought works its way to the forefront.

Maybe Jez was right.

No. There's nothing wrong with me.

Is there? What Razor did—what I thought I saw him do—can't be real, can it? There's no such thing as magic.

We can't help you unless you tell us what's wrong.

I shiver. Maybe I do need help. I take a deep breath, clear my throat, and start at the beginning. Initially, the words come out syrup-coated, sticking to my teeth. Then faster and faster still, until they gush from me like *Coca-Cola* from a shaken bottle. I tell them everything and, when I'm finished, all's silent, save for the ticking of the clock above the aga.

Mum's face is pale, her lips slightly parted.

Dad wears a concerned frown.

Yeah. They think I'm mad.

Eventually, Mum says, "This woman. Primrose, you said her name was?"

"What about her?" I blink away the image of Primrose's body plummeting from the roof and fight the urge to pick at my scar.

"She said you were like her?"

"Yeah, but I don't know what she meant."

"And when her attacker made himself invisible, you could still see him?"

"Right, but when Jez got there, I swear he couldn't."

"What colour were her eyes?" Dad's expression's the same one he wears when he puzzles over *The Times Crossword* at breakfast—eyebrows tugged low, nose a little scrunched. The only thing missing's the green pencil clamped between his teeth.

"What?"

"Answer the question," Mum bites. She closes her eyes and pinches the bridge of her nose. "I didn't mean to snap, but this is important."

A tingle runs down my spine. This isn't the reaction I expected. "I think she was wearing contacts, but I still don't get—"

"Why?" Dad's eyes are sharp, unfamiliar.

The hair at the nape of my neck stands on end. "Why what?"

"Why do you think she was wearing contacts?"

"Her eyes were this strange colour. Copper, almost, with a silver ring around each iris."

Mum's mouth drops open, and she stares at Dad, eyes wide. "You know what this means?"

"Shit."

A patch of cold sweat breaks out on my lower back. Dad never swears. "What's going on?"

Mum shrieks, punches the air, and whoops. "Yes! Wait until everyone at work finds out."

"One step at a time, Little Crow." Dad says it like an admonishment, but he's smiling.

"Can someone tell me what's happening?" There's a slight tremor in my voice.

Mum scowls at Dad. "You're not excited about this?"

"Of course I am, but—"

"Will you both just shut up." My pulse pounds and the tips of my ears burn. "I watched Primrose die. Razor murdered her, he—"

"Wait." The colour drains from Mum's face a second time. "Did you say Razor?"

My scalp prickles and I nod, my throat too tight to speak.

"What are we going to do?" Mum raises a trembling hand to her mouth and flicks her eyes at Dad.

"You know what to do."

Bile rises up my throat. Why are they behaving like this? It's almost... almost like they believe me.

"No way," Mum says.

Dad's tone's stern. "Make the call."

"Call? What call? What are you guys talking about?"

Mum bites her lip. "I can't."

"It's the only way to keep Henry safe."

"Fine." She stomps back to her phone, snatches it up and stalks from the room.

Someone's packed my head with bubble wrap. "I don't understand. What's going on?"

"I wish we could've told you sooner." Dad taps his foot against the slate-grey quarry tiled floor.

"Told me what?"

"What you need to understand is—"

"Dad. Tell me."

"All right, all right. What you saw tonight—what Razor did—it was magic."

That word again.

Magic.

I make a strange sound. Half laugh, half hiccup. "Don't be stupid."

He erases the space between us in three quick strides and grabs my shoulders. "I'm telling you the truth. Magic is real."

"It can't be. That's impossible."

"It's real. I swear." His grip tightens. "I'm sorry. God, I wish we had time to explain things properly."

"None of this makes any sense."

"I know. I know. Okay, I'm just going to say it. Thing is—your mum and I—we're witches, and you're one too."

CHAPTER 4

"Y ou're mad," I say. "What you're saying's ludicrous."

Dad's eyes flick to the clock, which reads eleven forty-nine. "We don't have time for this. Once you're through your Manifestation, we can—"

"Manifestation?"

"It's what we call it when a witch inherits their magic. All witches Manifest on their twenty-first birthday."

"Hang on? If I don't have magic yet, how did Primrose know about—how did she know I'm a..."

"You can say it."

I take a deep breath. "A witch." The word has a strange texture.

"You'll see."

"What does that—"

Dad grabs my arm and steers me towards the kitchen door. "We have to move, now."

I yank my arm back and scowl at him. "What happens if I refuse?"

"Refuse what?"

"This Manifestation thing, magic, all of it."

"You can't refuse."

"I can do whatever I want." A pretzel-like knot squeezes my chest.

"No, sorry. I mean you literally can't refuse."

Literally.

Can't.

Refuse.

Each word's like a vicious uppercut to my stomach. "What?"

"The Manifestation is automatic. It happens—"

"I know what automatic means." My head spins. This can't be happening, it can't, it can't. "Does—does it always work?"

"Not always, no." Dad's mouth puckers like he tastes something foul. "The chances of a failed Manifestation are slim to none though, thank God."

"I didn't ask for this, and I don't want it."

"You'll feel differently afterwards."

"You have no right to tell me how I'll feel. What about my plans? What about my MFA?"

"Uni will have to wait until we've sorted this mess out."

"What?"

"I'm not saying you can't go. I'm just saying you'll have to wait. Look, Razor won't let this go. He'll come after you. He'll come here. My only concern right now is you. We can discuss everything else once we're sure you're safe."

A wave of dizzying sickness rolls over me, almost dragging me under. "You know him, don't you? Razor."

"I know *of* him." Faint lines crease the skin around Dad's eyes. I'm sure they weren't there before. It's like he's aged ten years in as many minutes.

"How?"

"Now isn't the time. We have to get you somewhere safe."

"Now's exactly the time." My voice is too loud. It bounces off the walls.

He sets his jaw. "Work."

"You're kidding. He works at the bank?"

"Ah."

Sweat collects along the lines on my palms. "Ah?"

Dad looks away. "Your Mum and I don't really work at a bank."

"Then where the hell do you work?"

"We work for the Daxbridge branch of the Magical Investigations Department."

Magical Investigations Department.

Why does that sound familiar?

Wait.

Magical Investigations Department.

MID.

My heart skips a beat. "That's why Razor killed her."

Dad's gaze snaps back to mine. "What do you mean?"

"Primrose said she was going to report Razor to the MID."

"Shit. If only she'd made a statement sooner."

"What are you saying? You and Mum are... what, magical coppers?"

He nods. "Basically, yes."

"And the MID's investigating Razor?"

"Vice has been trying to convict him for years. Razor Finch runs an SOCG."

"SOCG?"

"Sorry. Supernatural Organised Crime Group. Razor and his crew are ruthless. Into drug smuggling, people trafficking, and he's suspected of committing at least a dozen murders. You don't want to get on his nasty side."

I'm picking again. "Bit late for that."

"Don't worry, we'll keep you safe, I swear. You just have to trust us."

I take a step back. "Trust you. You're joking, right? How can I trust you now?"

His eyes flash. "Hey. Mum and I want what's best for you, you know that."

"Do I? You've kept this huge secret my entire life. How's that doing what's best for me?"

"It's not that simple, Champ."

Blood pounds in my ears. "Don't *Champ* me. Looks pretty simple from where I'm standing. You've lied to me for the past two decades."

"We wanted to tell you ages ago."

"Then why the hell didn't you?"

"Because the Second Law forbids it."

"I—" I don't know how to reply, so I opt for a question instead. "What's the Second Law?"

"I promise, we'll tell you everything, but right now, we need to focus on your Manifestation." He seizes my arm and drags me towards the kitchen door again.

I plant my feet and tense the muscles in my calves, and we skid to a halt. "I'm not doing anything until you tell me what The Second Law is."

Dad lets go. "Why are you being so stubborn? You're usually so—"

My cheeks flush. "I'm usually so what, Dad?" What word was he about to use? Passive? Weak?

He sighs. "It doesn't matter."

I cross my arms and wait.

"Fine. The short version, then. The Witches Council governs witches. They set the Laws, and most witches abide by them. When they don't, the MID enforce them. There are Five Primary Laws of Magic, and breaking any of them carries a severe sentence. The Second Law forbids the parents, guardians or other family members of Potentials—witches who haven't Manifested yet—from telling them about magic, to prevent exposure."

My brow furrows. "Exposure? Exposure to what?"

"Manifestation now, explanations later. I provided you with the information you asked for, now come on."

"You can't make me do this."

"Tonight's been difficult for you, but—"

I snort. "Understatement of the year."

THE WITCH'S REVENGE   41

"But. You need to be inside a sealed circle in"—he squints at the clock—"seven minutes. Otherwise, something bad is going to happen."

I tense. "Are you threatening me?"

"What?" Dad screws up his face. "No, of course not. That didn't come out right. When the Manifestation hits, it unleashes a tremendous amount of magical energy. A sealed circle prevents that energy from escaping and harming anyone."

"Harming anyone? You mean like you and Mum?"

"Potentially, yes."

My stomach drops. I might be mad at my parents, but I don't want them to get hurt. "Fine. Where's this circle?"

"I'll show you," he says.

Darkness shrouds the lounge, and the air's close and pungent, reeking of incense and sage and burned things. Someone's shunted all the furniture aside. The rugs that usually cover the floor sit stacked in a corner, and a large white circle, etched in chalk, dominates the bare floorboards. Five lit candles squat at equidistant intervals around the circle's circumference, their flickering, amber-orange glow casting long, wavering shadows on the walls.

My knees tremble as I hover at the lounge's threshold. "What happens now?"

Dad paces across the room, stopping just shy of the powdery white line. "Stand in the middle of the circle. Mum and I will do the rest."

I drift into the circle, careful to avoid the smoking candles and, when I turn to face the door, Mum stands in the doorway.

"Well?" Dad asks her, his voice grave.

"They're on their way." Mum's face is harder than the granite worktops in the kitchen.

"Who did you call?" I ask.

Mum's expression softens a little. "Someone who can help us protect you from Razor."

"You should've told me the truth," I say, my tone firmer than I'd expected. "About witches, about magic, about your work."

"Dad spilled the beans then?"

"I did. He wasn't happy about it, either. Kicked up a right old fuss."

I fold my arms. "I'm still here, you know. You should've told me."

"We couldn't. We would've broken the—"

"Yeah, yeah. I know. The Second Law."

Dad glances at the grandfather clock in the corner. It reads three minutes to twelve. He nods at Mum. "You ready?"

She actually has the gall to smile. She strolls over to the other side of the circle, low heels clicking, and stands opposite Dad. "Ready? I've been waiting for this for twenty-one years. Of course I'm ready."

He smiles back. "Let's get started then."

They pace around the circle's edge, murmuring Latin phrases.

"What are you doing?" I ask.

"We need to seal the circle, so don't move, all right?"

I dig my heels into the floor to stop my knees from shaking.

They chant in low voices. I can't make out the words, but pale blue mist pours from the tips of Dad's fingers, and vibrant yellow vapour flows from Mum's. The effervescent mist caresses the chalk-white line, which absorbs the diaphanous substance until it glows. They pace the circle's edge a second time, and the light intensifies, becoming so bright I'm forced to shield my eyes. One final revolution. The air pressure inside the circle shifts, and my ears pop.

"Now what?" I say.

"Now," Mum says, foot tapping with impatience, "we wait."

CHAPTER 5

A bead of sweat trickles down the back of my neck and soaks into the collar of my T-shirt, and the heady incense leaves me thick and sluggish. I'm picking at my scar yet again. It's eleven fifty-nine now, and the obstinate minute hand refuses to budge. How long can a minute last?

I shift my weight from one foot to the other. Dad said the chances of a failed Manifestation are slim to none, not that it's impossible. Maybe it won't work. I cross my fingers. Please, don't let it work. "What happens if—"

Click.

The minute hand shifts to twelve.

Bong.

The circle enclosing me flashes like lightning, and I scrunch my eyes closed against the brightness. I open them again and a cylinder of white light stretches from floor to ceiling, and I'm trapped in the centre. Knife-edged pain—wicked sharp—slices into my chest. "What the fuck?" I scream.

"It's happening," Mum says.

Bong.

Malign fire spreads through my chest, searing my lungs, my back, my diaphragm. I try to speak, but a strangled croak's all I can manage.

"Stay strong, Henry." Dad's eyes shine. "It'll be over soon."

Bong.

The flames clawing at my chest swell beyond the borders of my ribcage. They singe my liver, blister my stomach, scald my limbs, scorch my brain. I can't count the chimes anymore. The fire, which is everywhere now, threatens to devour me from the inside out. A bear-like roar erupts from my parched throat.

When will it stop?

Make it stop.

Make it stop.

My heart beats, and a ripping sound, like tearing fabric, cuts through the air. The agony's so intense the edges of my vision blur. Without warning, I'm plunged into a vat of freezing water, the fierce heat in my chest extinguished in an instant. The temperature plummets to below freezing. Arctic wind blows through the circle, rising from the earth, whistling across my feet, curling around my legs, and lifting the hem on my T-shirt away from my skin.

"Not long now, sweetheart," Mum says.

I turn my head towards Mum, which takes considerable effort, and narrow my eyes at her. "Easy for you to say."

My heart beats again, but it's too loud, like someone's hooked a portable amp to my chest and whacked the bass up to full volume. My limbs jerk straight out, feet and arms spread wide as if bound by rope. Something lifts the crown of my head until the tips of my big toes skim the floor.

Thud-thud.

A wave of bright green energy shoots from the centre of my chest, blasts outward and strikes the edge of the circle with a burst of static.

The chalk line pulses.

Mum and Dad both flinch and dig their fingers into their temples.

"Strengthen the seal." Dad flings out his hands and flexes his shimmering fingers.

"I'm trying."

"Try harder."

Thud-thud.

Another surge of power rushes out of me, and I grit my teeth against the stabbing pain. The wave of energy smacks into the barrier, and this time, the chalk line wavers.

Mum staggers back a step, regains her balance, and plants her feet. "I can't hold it much longer."

"You have to." Dad's face drips with sweat.

Someone touches two lit matches to my optic nerves. I bellow, and everything goes dark. I can't see, I can't see. Why can't I fucking see?

"Oh, my God. Yvonne, look at his eyes."

My eyes. What's wrong with my eyes?

"Amazing." Mum steeps the word in something like awe.

The sound of a gunshot fires in my head. The world rushes back in glorious technicolour. Everything seems brighter, colours richer, angles more defined. It's as if I'm wearing a pair of high-definition contact lenses.

Thud-thud.

Another energy blast, followed by a clap of thunder and the tinkle-smash of breaking glass.

I'm held in place for a beat of silence, then I collapse to my knees and stinging pain prickles up my thighs. But it's nothing compared to what I've just been through. My sweat-soaked T-shirt clings to my skin and I breathe in short bursts. I glance up, and my mouth drops open. "Oh, shit." I groan.

The lounge is in chaos—the circle broken, windows shattered, walls cracked and furniture splintered.

Mum and Dad are nowhere to be seen.

"Dad? Mum?" My entire body shivers.

"Ugh." What's left of the Chesterfield armchair and the battered console table—propped against each other—shudders apart, and Dad sits up amidst the debris.

Mum staggers through the lounge doorway, her eyes shining, face split into a wide grin. "You broke the circle. That never happens."

I rush to my feet, my pulse still racing. "Are you okay?"

"We're fine." Dad uses the broken chair to haul himself up.

"But—"

"How do you feel, Champ?" he asks.

"How do I—that's... I don't feel..." I'm about to say I don't feel any different when something tugs at my heart.

Wait.

There is... something.

I close my eyes and focus on the weird tugging sensation.

It's right there, thudding in time with my pulse almost like... a second heartbeat. It's warm and vital and alive. A force, struggling like a caged lion to break free from its imprisonment, courtesy of my ribcage.

Something burning inside me that wasn't there before.

But what?

And then I realise.

Magic.

It's magic.

I draw in a deep breath. "I feel it." My voice is small. I don't want to feel it. I want to claw it out, I want to—

"It's a part of you, now," Mum says. "It'll be with you for the rest of your life."

My stomach plummets. So much for clawing it out. I turn my attention back to my ruined surroundings, and take in the carnage. "The house."

Mum fans her hand like she's shooing a wasp. "Don't worry about it."

"We can fix it." Dad nods at Mum.

They both raise their hands and speak in unison. "*Instaurabo*."

The mutilated fragments of furniture float into the air and spin around, and shards of glass—shining in the moonlight spilling through the busted patio doors—hover outside. Invisible hands sort through pieces of the broken jigsaw and prod them into place. The wood and glass click back together, the cracks in the window panes disappear, and the now fixed furniture—upright and gleaming—floats down to rest on the floor. Something shoots towards me and I duck. The gilt-framed mirror swings onto its hook above the fireplace.

"See?" Mum lets her hands fall so they hang at her sides. "No harm done."

I stare, open-mouthed, at the reformed lounge. "This isn't real. It can't be."

"Tip of the iceberg." Dad hooks his thumbs through his belt loops.

I realise something I should've twigged earlier. "Witches cast spells in Latin. That's why you taught me."

Mum nods.

The mirror shows me my reflection. I stride towards the fireplace, and blink at myself. The guy staring back at me is familiar, but something's off. His eyes. They don't belong to me. My eyes are warm brown. His eyes are emerald-green, with a ring of silver around each iris—a ring of silver, like Primrose's. "What have you done to me?"

My parents appear behind me, one at each shoulder.

Mum says, "You have the Sight."

I tilt my head, and the silver rings wink at me. "The Sight?"

Dad's beaming. "It's rare. I've never met a Sighted witch before."

"Is this what Primrose meant when she said I was like her? Is this what you were so excited about? What does it mean?"

Dad laughs. "Slow down and take a breath. Yes, that's what she meant. She must've been able to sense your aura, because you were about to Manifest. And you must've been able to see Razor under that invisibility spell for the same reason."

"She could see my what now?"

"Your aura. Your magic. It's one of the things the Sight detects."

My head spins. "I don't—this is..."

Dad carries on like I didn't speak. "You'll be able to see through all kinds of illusions, too, not just invisibility spells."

"Illusions?" I ask.

Dad nods. "Glamours, duplications—"

Mum cuts across Dad, a glint in her eye. "Better than that. It means you're powerful. Well, you will be with a bit of training, anyway."

"Training?" The way she says it sends a chill through me. "Training for what?"

Mum and Dad exchange furtive glances.

"What? You guys are freaking me out. What is it?"

"Can I tell him?" Mum's cheeks are flushed pink.

Dad nods.

"Tell me what?"

She smiles. "Dad and I got you an application form for the MID. We might have to wait a bit, until we've got Razor, but you can fill it out, and—"

It takes a beat for what she's saying to sink in, but when it does, my spine goes rigid. "Wait. You did *what*?"

Mum's grin becomes fixed, the sparkle artificial and brittle, like spun sugar. "We hoped you'd want to follow in our footsteps."

"Follow in your—" My voice cracks and I clear my throat, shake my head. "No way."

Dad cocks his head to one side, his mouth turning down at the corners. "Think about it, Champ—"

"No. I'm not a kid anymore. You can't decide my future for me. Chasing after drug dealers and murderers might work for you, but I don't want any of that."

"You still want to be a *writer*?" Mum's mouth twists.

"Of course. This changes nothing."

Dad says, "You're meant for greater things."

"Screw this." I snatch my phone from my pocket.

"What are you doing?" Dad asks.

"Calling Jez. I need to—"

"You can't." Mum's face pales.

"Weren't you listening? I'm an adult now, so I can do whatever I want." I dial the number.

"No." Mum curls her fingers into a tight fist and yanks her arm back. "*Traho*."

The phone jerks out of my hand, flies across the room, and smashes against the wall. It shatters, shards of glass and metal littering the floor. I stare, open-mouthed, at the fragments, heart hammering. Damn. I wish I knew how to cast that fixing spell.

"Yvonne." Dad narrows his eyes at her.

"I didn't mean to pull that hard." Mum's hands go to her mouth, and she takes a step towards me.

"Stay away from me." What was she about to do? Hug me? After what I've just seen her do. No way. I don't know who these people are, but they're not the parents I grew up with. I don't trust them as far as I can throw them.

Mum holds up her hands, a wounded look on her face. "You can't tell anyone about this. It's too dangerous."

"The only danger here is you," I say.

Mum clutches at her stomach like I winded her.

"Mum's right. You can never tell your friends what you really are."

"It's my life. I can tell people whatever I—"

Mum darts forward and seizes my shoulders. "You need to listen."

"Let go. Hey, let, ow—"

She digs her fingers into my skin, hard enough to bruise. "It's against the First Law."

That gets my attention and I stop struggling. "Why?"

"Because of the Trials." She releases me, turns away, and waves her hand through the air. Her fingers flash yellow, and the candle flames extinguish.

"The Trials?"

Dad walks around the circle, stooping to pick up each candle. "Five hundred years ago, give or take, witches lived peacefully alongside mortals. Nobody knows how it started, or why, but they grew to fear us."

Mum takes the candles from Dad and places them into an antique wooden box on the fireplace before closing the lid. "And we all know what happens when mortals fear something they don't understand. They attack it."

Goosebumps prickle along my arms. "My friends would never hurt me."

Mum snorts. "Don't be so naïve. Power threatens all mortals, because they don't have any of their own."

"I'm not naïve, but I know my friends."

Mum slaps the flat of her palm on the mantlepiece. "You know nothing. Six-hundred thousand witches died in the Trials. *Six-hundred thousand.* That's a tenth of our current population. They burned us, they drowned us, they stoned us. Keeping magic a secret is essential. It's why The First and Second Laws exist."

"Threat? We must pose a greater threat to them, though. We've got magic and they don't."

Mum snorts again, louder this time. "You don't know what you're talking about."

"Go easy on him," Dad says. "It's all new."

Mum closes her eyes and pinches the bridge of her nose. "You explain it to him, then."

Dad's lips tug into a half-smile, without any real humour in it. When he speaks, he sounds tired. "It's true. Witches are powerful, but mortals have two distinct advantages over us. First, magical barriers only defend against magical attacks, not physical ones. In The Middle Ages, mortals only had rudimentary weapons. Guns, knives, that sort of thing. Today, they have access to rocket launchers, nuclear weapons, and nerve agents. Can you imagine what modern day Trials would be like?"

A shiver runs the length of my spine. I can imagine, but I don't want to.

"Second," he continues, "witches are allergic to iron. On contact with the skin, it prevents the use of magic, and over-exposure can make us sick, or even kill us. That's why wrist and leg irons were so popular in the fifteen hundreds."

"What happens if you tell someone? A mortal, I mean."

Dad's expression turns grave. "Breaking either the First or Second Law carries the harshest sentence."

"Which is?"

"The permanent binding of your magic, coupled with a life sentence. They call it being witch-bound. If the MID ever found out... you'd have to be stupid, or incredibly naïve to risk it."

That explains a lot: why Razor didn't simply kill Jez and I at the club, why he feared being witch-bound, why Mum and Dad hadn't told me about magic.

I swallow, my mouth dry. "This is—what you're saying's insane. It's the twenty-first century. Some people identify as witches, for Christ's sake."

Mum's nostrils flare. "Wiccans prancing round stone circles and messing about with crystals are *not* witches."

"I get that, but what I'm saying is, people wouldn't care now."

She jabs a finger at me. "This discussion is over. You can't tell anyone, end of."

I clench my teeth. "You can't stop me."

"I think you'll find we can," Dad says.

"What?"

Mum says, "We could arrest you."

"Arrest me? You're joking."

"Wouldn't have a choice."

"This is bullshit."

She crosses her arms with finality. "That's the way it is."

My nails dig into my palms. "I hate you. Both of you."

Dad's shoulders slump. "You don't mean that."

Tears sting my eyes, my voice rising. "No? You've put me in a position where I've got to lie to my friends. You've left me completely unprepared for someone like Razor. And everything I'd planned—writing my novel, my Masters, all of it—it's gone now. I hate you, and I'll never forgive you."

A hulking wraith of silence crouches in the space between my parents and I.

"Wherever you're planning to take me, I'll go, but I need a minute." I spin on my heel, stride out of the lounge and into the entryway.

"Stay right where you are," Mum calls after me.

"Give him ten minutes to cool off," Dad says. "Hear that? Ten minutes."

I stomp over to the front door. "Fine."

"Come on, love," Dad says, "let's put the kettle on."

I yank the door open, step outside, and slam it shut behind me.

CHaPTer 6

I jog across the drive in a diagonal line and crash into the woodland surrounding the house, my arms pumping in tight circles at my sides.

I hate you, and I'll never forgive you.

I pick up the pace, sprinting until my legs ache and my lungs burn. Barbed branches, hooked like Razor's fingers when he slit Primrose's throat, nick the exposed skin on my arms and cheeks. The small grazes sting, and my ears echo with the sound of twigs snapping underfoot. I burst into a vast clearing, slowing to a halt. My hands go to my knees and I bend at the waste, breathing hard. I spit on the ground to clear my mouth of the coppery taste of the run.

I hate you, and I'll never forgive you.

A crow—concealed by the trees—lets out a strong, harsh caw, accompanied by the fluttering of oily, feathered wings.

My head snaps up.

The crow lands on a fallen tree trunk opposite me, its sharp talons scraping against the rough bark. Its sleek head twitches and flickers, and the bird fixes me with a beady, hungry, death-black eye. I recall the collective term for a flock of crows—a murder—and shudder.

I hate you, and I'll never forgive you.

"Fuck off." The words burst from my throat and reverberate round the clearing.

The crow remains still. It caws again, the sound reproachful.

"I said fuck off." I dart toward the crow.

It takes flight, two feathers drifting from its tail. The feathers float down in eddying circles, coming to rest on the bark. They lie there, heavy and shadowed, like the dead things they are.

I howl and kick the mammoth log hard. Blunt deadening numbness spreads up my leg and the howl becomes a pained cry. I sink down onto the tree trunk and rest my head in my hands. The tears come then, hot and wet, against my palms. I don't know how long I cry for, but by the time I finish, my eyes are gritty and my throat's raw.

What am I supposed to do now? My life's over. Razor, my parents. Between them, they've stolen everything—my friends, my place at uni, my plans for the future—*everything* from me. So, what'll I do?

I scan the treeline. I could keep on running. Keep on moving and let the trees swallow me whole. And go where? I could go to Jez's, or to another mate's place, and crash there. No, no, that won't work. They'd notice my eyes. How can I explain their shift in colour? I can't.

The canopy of leaves above me whisper a laugh as they rustle, chiding me, mocking my feeble plans to escape.

"You can fuck off as well," I tell them in a sullen tone.

The trees ignore me, continuing to breathe their papery death-rattle laughs.

I lift my head and swing my gaze left and right.

The sound of the trees is familiar. This clearing's familiar. I know it. I've been here before. My parents used to bring me here when I was a kid. Which means—yes, there, right in the centre of the clearing, that tree, the thick trunk forking at waist height and resembling the letter Y. Moonlight plays around the roots, highlighting flashes of purple.

Anise hyssop.

I stand and trudge across the springy grass until I reach the tree. Crouching down, I balance on the balls of my feet and pluck a sprig of anise from the ground. I crush the violet fuzz flat between my hands and roll it back and forth before dropping the stem. Bringing my cupped hands to my nose, I inhale the strong scent of liquorice, mint, and fennel. It goes deeper than that for me, though. The rich, botanic oils evoke other, long forgotten fragrances. Scotch eggs and childhood picnics; loamy, dead earth and the sugary fizz of cloying lemonade. Happy smells, warm smells, safe smells.

What had Dad said?

Mum and I want what's best for you, you know that.

And I do. I know the truth, despite it all. Despite all the secrets they've kept, despite all the lies they've told, I know they want what's best for me, and I know they love me. I want to hate them. I want to rage at them and never stop. But they had their reasons for keeping things from me.

The First and Second Laws.

Exposure.

The Witch's Council.

Whoever sits on this council, they must be fearsome, if Mum and Dad are afraid of them.

They were only doing what was right. Sticking to the Laws.

A heavy sigh drops out of me. I'll go back and apologise. I'll make everything right, and then my parents will make me safe again, just like they always have.

I traipse out of the clearing and begin a slow walk back to the house.

Chapter 7

NIGEL

"He hates us, Nigel," Yvonne says, twirling one of her crow earrings—the ones I bought her last year, for our silver wedding anniversary—round and round.

Water gushes from the tap as I fill the kettle. "No, he doesn't. He's angry, that's all. It'll pass."

"What if he doesn't come home?"

"He will, love." I turn the tap off, snap the lid onto the kettle, and place it on the side. Crossing the room, I wrap my arms around my wife, hug her close, and breathe in her scent—the sweet fragrance of rose water and honey so at odds with her steel core. She's a sledgehammer gift-wrapped in pink tissue paper. The knot constricting my heart ever since Henry stormed out loosens and falls away. I brush the crown of her head with my lips. "He will. You'll see."

The tension leaves her, and she squeezes me back. "What makes you so sure?"

We mould together when we hug like this, like spoons in a draw. You couldn't slide a slip of paper between us. We fit, just like always. "Because we're family. All families fight, and when they fight, they forgive each other. There's—"

"Nothing stronger than family," she finishes for me. She's rolling her eyes, I can tell. "You always say that."

"Because it's true."

"And Razor Finch. Is he stronger than our family?"

"Not even close, Little Crow. Not even close."

The doorbell rings.

"Here he is now," I say, drawing back.

"He's forgotten his key," she says.

"Again." I walk over to the door. "You make the tea. I want to have a brief word with him. Try to smooth things over."

Yvonne's lips pinch. "I can smooth things over."

I chuckle. "I love you, but diplomacy is not one of your many talents."

She arches her eyebrow in that familiar, sexy, you-'ll-pay-for-that-later, way she does. "I'll give you diplomacy, Mr Stone."

"I'll look forward to it, Mrs Stone." I fall in love with her for the thousandth time that day as I pull the door closed behind me.

The doorbell chimes again.

"All right, Champ, steady on." I pace across the entryway and open the front door.

CHAPTER 8

I fish my keys out of my pocket as I break through the tree-line, the house—standing alone on the landscape—coming into view. Hang on a minute. The front door's open, and the entryway beyond has wrapped itself in a cloak of darkness. That's not right. I closed the door when I left—slammed it, in fact. A chunk of ice sinks into the pit of my stomach. I creep up the driveway, attempting to minimise the sound of my high-tops crunching on the shingle.

I hate you, and I'll never forgive you.

My fingers fumble for the mini torch clipped to my keyring, and I thumb the power button on. I reach the doorway and shine the light inside, swinging the thin beam left and right. The entryway's empty.

Up and down, and—

A scarlet puddle stains the floorboards, and a thick, dark crimson smear leads away from it, curving—like a maniacal clown's grimace—into the music room.

My mind can't process what's in front of me.

What *is* that on the floor?

Blood.

No.

Maybe it's not what it looks like.

It can't be, it can't—

Fuck.

Razor. It's got to be Razor.

My heart pounds, and my mouth tastes rank, like sour milk. Oh shit, oh shit, oh shit. I don't want to go inside. The thought of it makes the hairs on my arms rise, but I've got to. I don't have a choice.

I tiptoe over the threshold and step around the bloody puddle. I take a deep breath in through my nose and wish I hadn't. The air still carries a whimper of linen and soap, but darker scents—the metallic bite of copper and the rotten stench of voided bowels—strangle the airy fragrance.

The satin smear of blood leads me, in a wide arc, to the music room's open door, and the fetid shit-stench grows stronger.

I cram my fist against my mouth to block a scream.

Dad slumps in the corner, his head bent to one side at an awkward angle, legs sticking out in front of him. His eyes are unseeing, dull, and frozen in a glassine stare. His throat gapes open in a fleshy smile, and blood dyes his green jumper red.

I go to him, crouch at his side and—even though I know it's pointless—grab his shoulder and shake him. "Wake up, Dad. Please. Wake up," I whisper.

His head flops forward, chin resting on his chest.

I gag and pull my hand away, and the skin on my palm itches as if it's tainted. Something in me breaks. I shut down. Everything seems distant. "Dad. Wake up. Wake up, come on, wake up." I know he can't hear me. I know he's gone.

Finished.

Out of juice.

Dead.

Snuffed out like the candles Mum extinguished earlier.

Mum.

I need to find her.

I wrench my gaze away from Dad's bowed head and rise on wooden legs. The movement makes my head spin. I've got to find Mum. That's all that matters now.

A crash comes from the kitchen, and I start, the commotion muffling my shout.

Another crash, followed by the sound of Mum screaming.

My heart plummets. My eyes flick around the room, searching. They skim the top of the piano, landing on one of the heavy glass paperweights the size of my fist. I grab it, hefting its dense bulk into my hand, and dart from the office on light feet. I slow my pace when I reach the sharp bend in the hall that leads to the kitchen.

For a moment, the doorway's empty, and then Mum flies into view, her body slamming into the wall just inside the kitchen door.

I freeze—unable to move, unable to think—and hold my breath.

A dark figure appears and stands over Mum.

I can't make out any of their features, but I can guess who it is.

Razor.

I edge along the wall in a series of jerky, halting steps.

He raises his hand.

"No," Mum says. "No, please."

The fear—the sheer terror—in Mum's voice snaps me out of it, and I rush forward, clenching the paperweight.

Clawed fingers swipe the air.

I slam the paperweight into Razor's temple. It connects with a dull thump and he crumples to the floor.

Mum makes a wet, gurgling, bubbling sound.

"No. No, no, no." I drop the paperweight and it smashes into the floor, cracking the quarry tiles. I crash to my knees at Mum's side. "Mum. Mum, tell me what to do. Tell me what I need to do."

She coughs, a long rattling cough, and blood pours from her mouth.

The back of my throat stings. "Mum."

Sweat soaks her forehead, and her eyes bulge.

"Don't die. Please don't die."

Her hand twitches, reaching for mine, and I curl my warm fingers around her cold, clammy ones.

I hate you, and I'll never forgive you.

My stomach twists, silent tears sliding down my cheeks. "I didn't mean it. I'm sorry. So, so sorry."

She wheezes out a breath. Her chest rattles, and her head slumps forward, the light pressure on my hand disappearing.

"Mum." My lip trembles. "Mum? Please, answer me... Mum?"

Her lifeless body leans towards me.

I release her limp hand and scuttle back.

She slumps on her side, blood pooling around her head.

"Fuck." Something sharp stabs into my stomach and twists. "Fuck, fuck, fuck." I gag, haul myself to my feet, and stagger to the sink. Bending at the waist, I heave and heave, but the only thing that comes up—having emptied my stomach earlier—is a thin string of bile that corrodes my throat. I spit the thick acidic liquid into the sink, slurp water from the tap, swill it, and spit again.

A glint of silver catches my eye.

My parents' wedding rings.

I grab them off the windowsill and go to stuff them in my pocket.

No.

I don't want to lose them. An idea comes to me. My fingers find the delicate silver chain around my neck and release the Saint Christopher my parents bought me this Christmas from beneath the collar of my T-shirt. They said it would protect me after—

We regret to inform you...

No. I need to focus. Focus. I unclasp the chain and let one end fall. The medallion clatters to the floor and I thread the rings in its place, refastening the clasp around my neck.

I tuck the rings away, and they rest, cold against my warm, fast-beating heart.

I turn to glare at Razor's crumpled body—only it isn't Razor.

It's a woman. One side of her head caved in where the paperweight struck—short, brown hair caked in blood.

"What the—"

"What have you done?" says a hoarse voice, thick with tears.

My eyes flick to the doorway.

Razor stands there, staring down at the woman, his face carved into a tragedy mask.

"I—I don't—"

"What have you done to my wife?" He flicks his fingers. "*Dis*." An angry red orb of light flashes from his hand—turning his blonde hair orange for an instant—and shoots towards me.

The light smacks into my chest. I soar backwards. My shoulders strike the opposite wall, and the air rushes from my lungs in one long gust. A heavy pressure pins me to the wall, my feet dangling off the floor.

"Cecilia." Razor sinks to his knees beside the woman. "Cis?" He reaches out and brushes her temple—the one that's still intact—trailing his fingertips down over her sharp cheekbone and along the curve of her jaw.

"Why?" I choke out the word. "My parents had nothing to do with this. Why did you have to kill them?"

Razor repeats the brushing motion, tracing the half-outline of Cecilia's face over and over. "I wasn't going to, but when your dad answered the door, I could tell he knew who I was. You shouldn't have told them."

"They knew who you were anyway, you idiot."

His black eyes flash to mine. "How?"

"They worked for the MID."

Razor stands, the motion sinuous, like a cobra weaving its way out of a basket. "It doesn't matter now." He scrubs a hand across his face, scouring his tears away. "I was going to make this quick. Now, I'm going to make you suffer." He stabs a finger in my direction. "*Secare*."

Sharp pain slices into my shoulder. I grit my teeth, straining against the force pinning me to the wall, inching my head to the right. Blood runs down my arm, flows over my wrist, and drips off my fingers, dotting the floor in a pitter-patter of red splotches.

"*Secare*," he whispers again.

Another deep gash crosses the first one, and I scream.

"*Secare, secare, secare.*"

I don't know how many times Razor slashes my arm. I lose count. All I know is that it fucking hurts. Hurt. Such a tiny word. It doesn't do the agony justice, but I've lost my grasp on vocabulary. Time passes in an intense, painful blur, and my limbs go numb with cold. My arm looks like a slab of raw meat, and a pool of blood spreads out beneath my feet. I'm crying, tears streaming down my face. The blood loss makes me dizzy and everything's fuzzy-edged and greying.

Razor's footsteps approach. "Time to die."

"Don't—I don't want to—to die." My words sound far off, like a recording of my voice with the volume turned way down.

"Neither did Cecilia."

I know this is the end. For real this time. Not like back at the club. It's just Razor and I. Nobody's coming to save me. To my surprise—and despite what I just told Razor—I don't mind. After all, I've got nothing left to live for. I've lost everything, and I can't get it back. Plus, I might see them again. Some people believe that, don't they? Fluffy, fuzzy, whipped-cream-white clouds and angels playing golden harps and being reunited with your loved ones.

I believe that.

At least I think I do, don't I?

Don't I?

Don't I?

CHAPTER 9

R azor points his fingers at my throat. "*S*—"

A deafening crash booms around my skull, followed by a loud crunch, and the back door rockets off its hinges and slams into the Welsh dresser on the other side of the room. The wood splinters under its weight, the glass smashes, the earthenware plates, bowls and cups shatter when they hit the floor.

Razor glares at the doorway.

"*Dis*," barks an unfamiliar voice.

A flash of blue light pummels Razor in the stomach and he folds in on himself, collapses, skids across the floor, and collides with a kitchen cupboard.

The force pinning me to the wall vanishes, and I drop. My feet strike the ground hard, and a twinge of pain shoots up my ankle, my knees buckle and my feet whip out from under me. I slam, arse first, onto the floor, and a dull ache spreads up my spine. The pool of blood I land in soaks through my jeans, my underwear, cool on my skin, thanks to the quarry tiles.

My blood.

The thought turns my stomach.

Heavy footsteps thud towards me.

I raise my head, and the room tilts, my ruined arm blazing with fire.

The man who struck Razor peers down at me, slate grey eyes sharp. "You okay?"

"Who—who are you?"

"That's not important right now." He crouches. "Give me your arm."

"What?"

"Your arm." The man slides something out of his coat pocket—a slim black case, like a glasses case. He pops the lid open and takes out a needle and syringe.

Sweat slicks my forehead. "No. No way."

"You're going to bleed out unless you let me help you." He shuffles around me, flicks the syringe once, twice, and depresses the plunger. A shiny, viscous substance spurts from the needle's tip.

"What the hell *is* that stuff?"

"Liquid silver."

Liquid silver? Why does he want to inject me with liquid silver? That has to be toxic, right? I inch away from him. "You're not coming near me with that thing."

"Now is not the time to be stubborn, Henry."

"Don't—wait, how do you know—"

He stabs the needle into my shredded skin and slams the plunger down.

I wince, as biting cold numbs my entire arm, and ice seeps beneath my skin—the same sensation as a general anaesthetic. My arm grows warm and then hot. I stare, eyes wide, as the skin knits itself back together like some bizarre time-lapse video played in reverse. First, thick cords of fleshy red-pink muscle seal over flashes of white bone with wet, sucking sounds. Then, the outer layers of skin tug towards each other, the open wounds zipping closed so they leave a criss-crossed patchwork sleeve of pink-white scar tissue running down the length of my arm, gloving my hand. The throbbing pain in my back, the dizziness, the exhaustion, it all fades away.

"Better?" The man stands and thrusts out a hand for me to take.

I rotate my arm back and forth. I'm scarred from shoulder to fingertip, the sleeve of my T-shirt in tatters. "How's that possible?"

"Silver has remarkable healing properties for witches."

"No kidding." I slap my hand into his, and he yanks me to my feet. "Tell me who you are."

"My name is Dylan Carmichael. I'm a friend of your parents. Your mother called me earlier and told me to get here as quick as I—Oh, my God, no." Carmichael's eyes have locked onto Mum's body, and they shimmer with tears. "Yvonne. Oh, Yvonne." He brings a shaking hand to his mouth. "Where's Nigel?"

I try to speak, but my too-tight throat imprisons my voice, so I settle for shaking my head.

"This can't be happening," Carmichael says, his voice quiet.

"I thought COVEN witches were powerful. You'll have to do better than that, Director."

I jump and twist to find Razor on his feet again. I'd almost forgotten he was there.

Carmichael wears murder like a cloak. "You killed my friends, you sick bastard."

"Sticks and stones. The boy stuck his nose into my business. Saw something he shouldn't have. I had no choice."

Carmichael's gaze drifts over Razor's shoulder to where Cecelia's body lies crumpled on the floor, and his eyes flick to mine. "Did you do that?"

I nod, still unable to speak past the golf ball sized lump in my throat.

Carmichael mimics Razor's scornful tone. "Dear, oh, dear. Cecilia Finch killed by a twenty-one-year-old untrained witch. I thought she was powerful."

Razor's lips pinch tight and spots of colour bloom on his cheeks.

Carmichael flings out a hand. "*Mortem.*"

Death.

A jagged dart of deep blue energy leaps from Carmichael-'s outstretched fingers and zips across the room, heading straight for Razor's heart.

"*Obstructionum.*" Razor holds an arm across his chest, fist closed as if he's gripping the braces of a shield. The air in front of him ripples red.

Carmichael's spell slams into the rippling air and bursts apart in a shower of blinding blue sparks.

I squint against the brightness and something in my head shifts. My eyes burn with a lemon-juice sting and everything in front of me changes. Blinding red and blue lights surround Razor and Carmichael respectively, eddying about them in undulating waves. I shield my eyes. "It's so bright. What's happening?" I ask Carmichael.

"Looks like your Sight has activated," he says.

She must have been able to sense your aura, because you were about to Manifest.

Is this what Dad meant by aura?

"*Fulgur.*" A vein of darker red threads through Razor's... aura—so weird—wraps around his arm and spirals into his hand.

"Look out." I dive towards Carmichael and shove him out of the way.

A jagged fork of carmine lightning arcs from Razor's palm.

An electric jolt of pain lances into my shoulder, flashes through my entire body, and I black out.

I'm shaken awake by the ground rumbling beneath me, and my heavy eyelids crack open.

Razor and Carmichael—devoid of their shimmering auras once more—face each other on the opposite side of the kitchen, and the quarry tiles between me and them have cracked and splintered. Razor stands with his feet spread wide, arms out at his sides, palms up. His lips move. The ground beneath his feet's steady, but everywhere else it rocks and bucks.

The force of the mini earthquake throws Carmichael off his feet. He crashes to the ground and rolls three times in quick succession.

I try to move, but sharp agony surges in my shoulder, right where Razor's lightning bolt struck me. I collapse onto my back and breathe hard.

Razor lowers his palms and the rumbling stops. "You won't have to miss your friends for much longer, Carmichael."

"Makes you feel powerful, does it, resorting to dark magic? Makes you the big man? You won't win," Carmichael says through gritted teeth.

Dark magic? What's Carmichael talking about?

"Oh, please. You're deluding yourself." Razor shakes his head. "I've already won."

My heart slams against my ribcage. No, I can't let Razor do this, can't let him kill Carmichael, can't let him win. I force myself to wriggle onto my front and I cast about for—ah, there it is. The blood-stained paperweight. I inch my good arm forwards and close my fingers around the cool, sticky glass, twisting and propping myself up.

Razor flexes his fingers at Carmichael.

I don't have time to think, so I launch the paperweight at Razor, ignoring the searing pain in my shoulder.

The paperweight *thunks* into Razor's back and he cries out, stumbling away from Carmichael.

Carmichael launches to his feet, shouts a few words of Latin, and a stream of blue light flashes towards Razor.

Razor throws up another barrier, blocking the spell, says, "*Caeli,*" and waves his hand in a circular motion.

A hot gust of red-tinted wind rips through the room, and Carmichael and I are both slammed into the walls.

The preternatural wind dies down and Razor hinges forward, coughing, clutching at his chest. The coughs subside, he spits and blood smeared saliva stains the floor at his feet. Carmichael must have injured him in the fight. He straightens. "I meant what I said, boy. This isn't over." He spins on his heel and darts from the kitchen.

Carmichael and I sprint after him.

Razor stands in the entryway before a glowing disc of red energy, which hums like an overhead pylon, stretching from ground level to head height. A cool-warm breeze blows from the centre of the disc.

"*Mortem.*" Carmichael aims another killing blow at Razor's back.

I pray it finds its mark.

CHAPTER 10

The humming disc vanishes with a sharp snap, taking Razor with it.

Carmichael's spell whizzes through the empty air and skitters off into the lounge. "Shit. Bastard conjured a portal." At my blank look, Carmichael says, "Portals transfer matter from one place to another."

I'm not taking it in. Portals? Magic? What the fuck have I stumbled into? I'm too heavy. Someone's replaced my blood with syrup, and my legs with concrete. It's too real now, in the aftermath. My parents are dead and I'm alone. I don't want to be alone. The last thing I said to them was a spiteful lie.

I hate you, and I'll never forgive you.

My heart detaches from its mesentery and plummets. I crouch down and rock back and forth on my heels, arms crossed tight over my chest. "I can't do this."

"I hate to be insensitive, but we need to leave. Now."

"Leave?" I stand on shaky legs. "I can't leave, not like this. My parents—their bodies, we have to get them out."

"We don't have time."

"No, no, no." My mind sticks on the word and won't budge, and my insides writhe. My breaths come in sharp gasps, and my pulse hammers against my neck. "Can't—I can't—breathe."

"You can."

"I can't." My vision blurs and my fingertips tingle.

Stony-faced, Carmichael grabs my arm and pulls me towards the front door.

"What are you doing? Get off me. I said let go. Hey!"

His grip on my wrist's iron-hard, and he carries on dragging me along until we're outside.

I twist and thrash, craning my neck back towards the house. But it's pointless. I can't break free. "Oh, God. Help, help me. Can't breathe. Can't."

"You're having a panic attack."

"I'm not. I don't have—"

"Look at me, just look at me. Good. Now close your eyes."

"What? No, you're not listening. I can't breathe."

"Just close your eyes. All right. Okay, good. I want you to listen to my voice, and think of nothing else."

"I don't think meditation is—"

"Listen. You're in a field of wheat and the sun is shining, the summer heat beating down on your skin. As you walk through the field, you let your hand trail beside you and the stalks of wheat graze your palm. You come to a tree. You sit against it and lean your head back against the trunk. Birds sing in the trees. Can you hear them?"

"I—I don't—" I can though, can't I? I can sense it all, just as Carmichael describes. The warm sun heating the crown of my head, the stalks of wheat tickling my palm, the birds twittering away. "... Yes."

"Good, that's good. You're doing well. Now, I need you to breathe. Take in the fresh summer air."

My nostrils flare, oxygen filling my lungs, and a knot in my chest loosens slightly.

"That's it, and again."

I draw in more air, my frantic heart slowing.

Carmichael repeats this process several times. The vision of the field's so real, so vivid. It helps me forget where I am and what's happened.

"You can open your eyes now."

I do as he asks, and I'm caught between two worlds, with the ghost-image of the wheat field overlaying reality like a 3D projection. My gaze drops to Carmichael's hands around my arms. Soft blue light spills between his fingers. Of course, it's magic.

He lets go, and the field—my place of safety, of solace—disappears like it never existed. Which it didn't, I suppose.

"Better?" he asks.

I hug my arms to my stomach. "What do you think?"

"I swear to you, I'll find that bastard Razor, and when I do, I'll make him pay. But right now, I have to keep you safe."

"Why are you interested in keeping me safe?"

"I made a promise to Yvonne and Nigel."

The sound of their names makes my stomach buck, and bile sears my chest. I keep hugging myself. If I don't. I swear I'll fall apart.

Carmichael carries on. "I swore to look after you if anything happened to them. Told them I'd do whatever was in your best interests."

"I'm not going anywhere until you tell me what's going on. One minute I've got a normal life, a normal family, and then it all goes to shit. Witches. Supernatural coppers. Now you, claiming you were friends with—"

"Claiming?"

"Yeah, claiming. I don't know you from Adam. Never even met you."

He arches an eyebrow.

"I'm serious. I don't know you. Who are you?"

"Ask me anything."

I speak through gritted teeth. "What?"

"Ask me something about your parents, something only someone close to them would know."

That gives me pause. He must have known them, if he wants me to ask him a question like that. "Okay. What was Dad's nickname for Mum?"

"That's easy. Little Crow. He's called her that ever since they met, and every day since graduation."

"Graduation? Mum and Dad didn't go to university."

"Neither did I. We graduated from the Magical Investigations Department training college together."

"You're with the MID? That makes no sense. Razor. He mentioned COVEN, whatever that is, and he called you Director."

"Correction. I *was* with the MID. You're perceptive." His lips twitch into the hint of a smile. "Like your father."

"Answer me."

"Tenacious, too. Just like Yvonne. That's good."

Nigel.

Yvonne.

Will I ever be able to hear their names again without feeling like I'm choking to death. Carmichael speaks about them with such reverence, such pride, I wish I could have seen them in action at the MID.

It's not—

"What *is* COVEN?" I ask. Anything to drown out these morose thoughts.

"I'm afraid I'm not at liberty to divulge that information." He tilts his head to one side. "Unless—no, forget it. Probably not a good idea."

"Stop talking in riddles."

"Fine, I'll speak plainly. Be warned though, if you decide not to take me up on my offer, I'll erase all your memories of this conversation."

"I—wait, you can do that?"

"Yes."

He can make people forget things. Can he make me forget my parents altogether? If I couldn't remember them, maybe this hollowness in my stomach—as if all the spongy bits have been scraped out with a rusty ice-cream scoop—would go away.

Maybe—

No.

How can I think about forgetting them?

My stomach pinches with guilt and I swallow, hard. "What's the offer?"

"One thing at a time. You asked me about my position as the Director of COVEN—or, to give the organisation its proper title, The Covert Executioner's Network."

The word *executioner* makes my blood run cold. I take a step back, but I dare not move otherwise. "You mean, you kill people for a living?"

"It's not as black and white as that."

"No? Sounds it to me."

"I can assure you it's all perfectly legal and signed off in triplicate by The Witches Council—oh, that's right, you won't know about—"

"I know who they are. They lay down the law, we follow it."

"You're remarkably well informed."

"My parents told me a few things before"—my stomach wrenches—"it happened."

He gives me an appraising look. "The witches we... well, neutralise, are criminals. The worst of the worst. Trust me. Purgatory is too good for these people."

"Purgatory?"

"It's Daxbridge's supernatural prison. The Witches Council lined the entire building with iron. It's the only way to weaken witches. Did your parents tell you about that?" He says it like a challenge.

I nod. "Your offer?"

He scratches at his upper lip. "COVEN has a new cohort of trainees joining tomorrow. We have one space left. I couldn't fill it in time."

"You're asking me to become an assassin?" Even saying the words makes my heart rate spike, my insides turn to jelly. "Are you insane? You've got the wrong guy, mate."

"I don't think so."

"Trust me, I'm not cut out for it."

He gestures towards the house. "When Razor attacked me with that lightning bolt, you jumped in front of it to save me."

My face scrunches up. "That was just a reaction. I—"

"I think you have what it takes. You're smart, perceptive, brave—"

"Ha! I'm not brave."

"Your actions prove otherwise, and I know your parents were eager for you to pursue a career in law enforcement."

They'd said that, told me they hoped I'd follow in their footsteps—they'd even gotten me an application form for the MID—but I can't. Too high-stakes. Too high-risk. The new scars on my thumb-tip find the old scar at my neck and pick, pick, pick. "You don't know me."

His eyes latch on to the movement. "Our scars only define us if we let them."

I stop scratching.

"You want Razor to pay for what he did, don't you?" Carmichael asks.

A flash of heat races through me. "What kind of stupid question's that?"

"Join COVEN, and we'll teach you how to make that happen. You should be the one to do it. For them."

For Mum and Dad. "I—no." I pause, then say, "I don't know."

"It's your choice. Make it once and make it fast."

"What's the rush?"

Carmichael says, "Razor won't lick his wounds for long. I know his type. He'll dose himself up with liquid silver, then he'll be back, and he'll likely bring reinforcements. I can't fight a battalion of witches single-handed."

"You're acting like you're asking whether I want sweet potato wedges on the side. This is a massive, life-altering decision, and you want me to make a snap judgment?"

"I don't mean to sound callous, but your life has altered plenty already."

I hate you, and I'll never forgive you.

Why? Why did I ignore them? I should've left with them after my Manifestation, instead of fannying about, navel-gazing in the woods. If I'd done what they wanted me to, followed in their footsteps—

Crack.

My head whips towards the sound—something breaking underfoot—coming from the woods. "What was that?"

"Razor must be back already."

A murmuring voice—no, voices, plural—reaches my ears, coming closer.

"I was right. He didn't come alone." Carmichael spins away from me and spreads his arms wide. "*Ostium.*"

The sound of tearing fabric rips through the night, and the air two metres in front of Carmichael cleaves in two. A person-sized disc of pale blue light—a portal—appears and the familiar hot-chilly breeze washes over me. In the distance—glowing deep in the woods—several orbs of multicoloured light bob between the trees.

"Last chance, Henry. Either you come with me now, or I wipe your memories and take you to an undisclosed location."

"Undisclosed location?"

"I can't risk taking you to COVEN if you won't be a part of it. It's too dangerous."

What do I do? I can't go along with this. Can't be an executioner.

I hate you, and I can't forgive you.

Those words—those cruel, untrue, unjust fucking words—make my decision for me. My old life's over, and there's no going back. I can only move forwards. By joining

COVEN, I can honour my parents. I can make amends. Maybe even earn forgiveness.

Maybe.

Perhaps I owe it to them.

No, I *do* owe it to them.

I wish I didn't, but I do.

I take one last look at the house, duck my head, and stalk towards the portal.

CHapTer 11

Everything I am disintegrates like soluble aspirin dissolved in water. The disparate parts of me—tiny sub-atomic particles—float in an endless void, an absence stretching into eternity. It's like a vacuum. I'm only half-aware of my consciousness, as if I'm squinting at my distorted reflection through a thick sheet of soap smeared glass. I don't know how long I hover here, suspended in a colourless, odourless, worry-less sea of nothing—maybe seconds, or hours, or days, or months, or years—but I love it. Here, there's no stomach-chewing grief. No boiling, impotent anger. No sting of suffering. Henry Stone's a dream, a figment of my imagination. Here, I'm free, and I could stay like this forever.

A sharp point of pale blue light pierces the null space.

No.

I don't want to go back.

The disparate particles of my being swirl closer and closer. A cloud of swarming locusts. I slam back together. There's a moment of weightlessness, and then I fall, the pinprick of light getting larger, yawing open like some grotesque beast's filthy maw.

The light swallows me in one gulp.

Static crackles over my newly reformed skin, and I stumble into darkness.

A chill wind belches in my face, and I'm enveloped by the melodious stink of brackish water and stagnant piss, too strong after the sensory deprivation of the portal. My head swims and my stomach heaves. I stagger to one side, throwing out an arm for balance. The flat of my palm smacks into something cold and unyielding. A wall, I think. I dry heave, and my stomach constricts. I retch again, but nothing comes up.

The portal snaps shut behind me, followed by the sound of Carmichael's low chuckle.

I lean back against the wall and breathe through my mouth. The faint damp, rotten flavour of the air clings to my taste-buds. "Something funny?" I ask.

"No. Sorry. I shouldn't laugh. It's been a long time since I encountered a witch who suffers from portal sickness, that's all."

"Yeah. It's hilarious."

Carmichael's expression sobers. "Follow me."

"Where are we?"

Carmichael strides past me, clicking his fingers as he goes. "*Lux.*"

A smoky cloud of blue light blossoms in the air above Carmichael's head and the shadows scamper away. Carmichael and I have emerged into a long, narrow underpass—a solid, graffiti-stained wall on one side, and a silky ribbon of soupy, verdigris water on the other. Burned orange leaves and golden-brown cigarette butts float on the water's surface like rough-chopped toasted croutons.

"Daxbridge Canal," I say.

"Yep."

"I thought you were taking me to COVEN."

"I am."

"Hang on a sec. So, you're telling me that your super-secret headquarters for supernatural hitmen's smack bang in the middle of the city?"

"That's right."

My brow furrows. "Not exactly smart. What's stopping someone from wandering straight through the front door?"

We reach the wide mouth of a dark underpass.

Carmichael flings out a hand to stop me from going any further.

"What are you—"

"*Dona accessum ad hiems Henricus*." Carmichael says.

Magic hums through the air, but everything looks the same. I blink at the empty space. "What did you just do?"

"Only members of COVEN can grant non-members access to the compound," he explains.

I shrug his hand away.

He leads me into the underpass. "As for stopping someone, 'wandering straight through the front door,' as you put it, there are two things preventing that. There are hundreds of wards and misdirection spells woven around the area to keep any undesirables from using this stretch of footpath. I'm surprised you can't see them."

My brow furrows. "What do you mean? I can't see anything."

Carmichael halts exactly halfway down the underpass. A large pentagram—stretching from ground level to head height and sprayed in white paint—covers the wall next to him. "You should be able to detect them with your Sight."

A thrill goes through me. "It happens at random. I can't control it."

"It should come pretty naturally. Imagine something covering your eyes, and then imagine it being whisked away."

I do as Carmichael says, picturing thin sheets of gauze draped throughout the narrow tunnel. I envision them floating up and disappearing. My eyes sting, like they had back at the house when I'd glimpsed Razor and Carmichael's auras.

"Holy shit."

Strings of multicoloured light—vibrant red, aqua blue and sunshine yellow—crisscross the entire underpass and bury themselves in the walls, burrow beneath the floor and sink below the water.

"If I hadn't granted you access just now," Carmichael says, "let's just say it would've hurt you to walk any further than the mouth of the underpass."

I reach out a hand to touch one of the glowing threads.

Carmichael shouts a warning. "Don't—"

The tip of my index finger brushes a honey-coloured strand and I jolt as fire and ice and numbing pain race up my arm. I flinch and the neon filaments vanish. My fingertip burns like I caught it on the stove, so I shove it in my mouth to cool it.

Carmichael shakes his head. "Only the most powerful among us can unpick a witch-weave. I wouldn't try that again in a hurry, if I were you."

"What's a witch-weave?" I ask.

"It's the most comprehensive protection ward there is. Only the most powerful witches can undo them."

"Can you?"

"Can I what?"

"Unpick a... witch-weave."

"Yes."

Just how powerful is Carmichael? "What's the second thing?"

"Second thing?"

"Hiding the front door."

"Oh, yes. Well, the, 'front door,' is difficult to find." Carmichael lifts his arm, places his right hand in the centre of the pentagram, and flattens his palm to the wall. His shirt sleeve rides up and reveals the edge of an inky-black tattoo on the underside of his wrist.

"*You've* got a tattoo?"

"Surprised?"

"You don't look the type."

Keeping his hand flush with the concrete, Carmichael yanks his sleeve further up his arm. The tattoo's a mini replica of the pentagram on the wall. "Every executioner has one of these. It's the only way to gain access to COVEN."

"Huh. Like a magical swipe card?"

"Exactly." He narrows his eyes at the wall. "*Vi. Iustitia. Fides.*"

The tattoo on Carmichael's wrist flashes silver, and so does the larger pentagram. The white lines of the five-pointed star fade—leaving only the circular outline—and the wall vanishes with them, revealing a dark passageway beyond.

"No way," I breathe, astonished.

"Impressed?"

"Strength. Justice. Loyalty," I say, translating the words Carmichael used to open the passageway.

"It's our motto." If he's surprised I know how to speak Latin, he doesn't show it. Maybe all witching families teach their children the dead language. "Welcome to the Covert Executioner's Network." Carmichael steps into the dark opening.

Strength.

Justice.

Loyalty.

The words speak to the deepest parts of me, like a sign I'm on the right path.

I hate you, and I can't forgive you.

Maybe I *can* find redemption here.

I follow Carmichael without further hesitation.

Carmichael leads me through a warren of bare concrete tunnels that slope downwards. We sink farther and farther into the earth, and the air gets colder and colder, until goosebumps erupt along my arms. The azure light Carmichael brought with us carves crooked shadows into the featureless, grey walls. I try to memorise the convoluted route we take—right, left, left, right, right, left—but I soon lose track. The air's thick with moisture. Dry with dust. It tastes like powdered chalk.

"This isn't what I was expecting," I say.

"What were you expecting?"

"Something a little flashier, I guess."

The path narrows further, stopping when we reach a sturdy-looking mahogany door with another pentagram and COVEN's motto tooled on its smooth surface.

"There's no handle," I say.

Carmichael doesn't answer. Instead, he strides up to the door and waits.

The pentagram glows brighter and brighter until it purrs with energy.

Something beeps.

The glow fades.

A mechanical voice says, "Access granted. Welcome back, Director Carmichael."

The wooden door swings open, and warm light spills into the corridor.

Carmichael strides through.

I follow, the soles of my high-tops sinking deep into plush red carpet. My eyes adjust to the light, and my mouth drops open.

We stand on a slim landing at the top of a wide, sweeping wooden staircase, thick red carpet hugging every tread. The foyer below could be the reception area at a swanky five-star hotel, the white marble floor threaded with dark veins like rich blue cheese. A sparkling chandelier hangs from the ceiling—surely those aren't genuine diamonds? A cadre of low-backed, dark leather sofas sit in a square in front of a gleaming bank of lifts.

"Fuck me," I say.

"Flashy enough for you?" Carmichael asks, gripping the spotless, polished banister and making his way down the stairs.

With each step, I marvel at how luxurious the carpet is. I can almost feel it through the soles of my shoes. "What exactly does training involve?" I ask when we reach the foot of the stairs.

Carmichael flashes his teeth at me. "You'll find out soon enough."

"But—"

One lift makes a dinging sound and the shiny chrome doors whisper open.

A woman I judge to be in her mid-to-late twenties strides out of the elevator, her pink stiletto heels clicking smartly on the marble floor. Her light blonde hair falls in soft curls to her shoulders. She wears a low-cut pink dress, pink lipstick, pink eyeshadow. The only thing about her that isn't pink is the black COVEN tattoo on her right wrist, and the inky DNA helix spiralling all the way up her left arm. She draws closer to us. Even her eyes are a strange shade of pale pink, the edge of her irises glimmering silver.

My throat tightens. Something about her makes me feel uneasy, and it takes a second to put my finger on it.

It's the silver rings around the iris, and their unnatural colour.

First Primrose.

Then me.

Now this woman.

Whoever she is, she has the Sight, too.

"Ah, Zara." Carmichael breaks into a wide grin, his voice brightening. "I was hoping we would run into you."

Zara stalks closer still. Click. Click. Click. "I thought you were going home." The sharp tone of her voice is at odds with the pretty dress. She tries to hide the way her pink eyes widen when she catches sight of my emerald green ones.

"I was, but I got side-tracked."

"Who the fuck's this?" Zara places a hand on her hip and cocks it to one side.

My cheeks flush.

"Zara White, this is Henry Stone, our newest trainee."

"You said you couldn't fill the sixth trainee post this year."

"Henry's a last-minute addition."

She makes a *tsk* sound. "Since when do you do last minute?"

"There's an exception to every rule."

"Not when I make them."

Carmichael laughs. "Henry's here as a favour to some friends."

Images of the scarlet slash across Dad's throat and the blood pooling around Mum's head flash through my mind. My stomach squeezes and I worry at my scar.

Zara's eyes snap to the movement.

I stop picking.

"Zara's your trainer," Carmichael says.

"Good to meet you." I hold out my hand.

She wrinkles her nose like I've offered her a basket of rotting fish. "You don't know me yet."

"Zara. Play nice." There's a note of pride in Carmichael's voice whenever he talks to Zara.

She snorts.

I drop my arm back to my side. "You're Sighted."

"Top marks for observation," she says, dryly.

"So, what do you think?" Carmichael moves aside.

Zara walks around me once, twice, three times. She squints her eyes and her irises glow vivid pink.

My skin prickles when she looks at me, like snowflakes landing, and I know without being told, she's examining my aura. Do my eyes look like that when I use my Sight? Alien. Wrong.

The circles she turns get tighter and tighter. When she stops in front of me again, her eyes bore into mine like interrogation lamps. She cocks her head to the side, reminding me of the crow I scared off in the woods.

I swallow, hard.

"What happened to your arm? Looks nasty," she says.

My blush deepens, and I hide my arms behind my back, lacing my fingers together. "It's nothing."

Her lips purse into a thin line.

"Well?" Carmichael says.

She steps back, blinks, and her eyes stop glowing. "Sighted, so he's powerful, obviously."

"How powerful?"

She fixes me with a cool stare and admits, "Very."

"Looks like you've got what it takes." Carmichael's eyes crinkle at the corners when he smiles, like Dad's used to.

Dad.

My lower lip trembles.

Zara's rosy lips, in contrast, purse tighter still. "I'll be the judge of that." She strides past me, bumping my shoulder with hers. "Power's useless if you're not strong enough to use it." She stomps up the red-carpeted stairs.

"Nice dress," Carmichael says.

She twirls at the top of the staircase. "Cheers."

"Who's the lucky guy?"

"None of your fucking business."

Carmichael tries for a stern scowl, but the corner of his mouth twitches. "Shouldn't that be 'none of your fucking business, Director'?"

She shoots him the middle finger over her shoulder, strides through the exit door and slams it shut behind her.

"She always so pleasant?" I ask.

Carmichael chuckles. "Zara's a pussycat once you get to know her."

Pussycat? Fearsome tigress would be a more apt description.

"Come on," Carmichael says, walking across to the lifts and pressing the call button. "I'll show you to your room."

"How do you navigate this place?" I ask Carmichael after ten minutes of traipsing along a dozen identical wood-panelled, marble-floored hallways. "It's like a maze designed by a psychotic carpenter?"

He doesn't answer.

We reach a fork in our path.

"What size are your clothes?" he asks.

"Medium on top, thirty-two regular trousers. Why?"

"Wait here," he says, taking the right fork.

"Where are you going?"

"To fetch you a trainee uniform. I'll only be a moment."

I lean back against the wall and close my eyes, instantly wishing I hadn't. Memories flood my brain—all rusty blood, and open throats and clean linen, spoilt by the stench of guts emptied in death.

I hate you, and I'll never forgive you.

The sound of footsteps startles me, and my eyes snap open. Is Zara coming back? I can't face her right now, so I duck around the corner, heart slamming in my chest.

The footsteps come closer.

I hold my breath.

Another hurried set of footsteps catches up to the first. "Syed," says a cultured, sharp-edged, female voice.

"Katya. Are you heading home, too?" Syed replies in a rich, pleasant tone.

"Yes. It's been a long day." Katya pauses. "So, how's Layla feeling about training?"

"Nervous."

"She told you that?"

"Of course. My daughter is honest to a fault."

"Just like her father."

"What about Bianca?"

"She's a wreck. *Honestly*, I don't know where she gets it from. I swear there was a mix-up at birth."

Syed makes a sound in his throat like a choked off laugh.

"You think I'm joking," Katya says, her words sharp.

Their voices grow quieter as they move beyond the fork and travel down the hall in the direction Carmichael and I came from. I inch away from the wall, risk a quick peek.

Syed lopes along with an easy, unhurried gait, the light glinting off the salt in his salt and pepper hair.

Katya's hair's coal black, and she walks like she's balancing a book on her head. "Five trainees, and only one Outsider this year, thank God."

Outsider? What's an outsider? Whatever it is, the term makes me go cold.

"Does it matter?" Syed asks.

Do I detect a hint of reproach in his voice?

Katya makes a huffy sound. "Calls himself Geek. How ridiculous is that? I've told Bianca to stay away from him."

Geek? A strange nickname to adopt. It sounds more like an insult than anything, or maybe that's just the way Katya says it.

"Why on earth would you do that?" Syed asks.

Definitely reproachful.

Katya's tone's still diamond-edged. "She needs to stay on the winning side. You know as well as I do that Outsiders can't cut it. None of them have been successful since..."

Katya's words trail off as she and Syed round a corner.

I release my held breath, pulse pounding.

"Here you go."

Carmichael's voice startles me. I jump, bringing a hand to my chest. "Jesus Christ, don't sneak up on me like that."

"I wasn't sneaking." Carmichael proffers a bundle of folded black fabric, a pair of rubber-soled black trainers balanced on top.

I don't take it. "What took you so long?"

"I got a call from the MID. About you, actually."

"Me?"

He nods. "It was your parents' boss, DCI Kate Denton."

"Kate? Mum was talking to someone called Kate when I got home. They were arguing, I think."

Something passes across Carmichael's face, but it leaves just as quickly. "Kate and your mother had a—shall we say, fractious relationship? I told her we've taken you in and that you'll be training with us. She's fine with it. She sends her condolences."

I hate you, and I'll never forgive you.

I don't deserve anyone's condolences.

"I'm not standing here for fun." Carmichael holds out the pile of clothes again.

I take them.

Carmichael and I walk down yet more twisty hallways, passing various rooms and doorways as we go. A set of tall double doors marked *Dining Hall*, a slim wooden door marked *Training Room* and a dull gunmetal grey door marked *Island Portal: Authorised Personnel Only*, before I work up the nerve to ask, "What's an Outsider?"

Carmichael's nostrils flare. "Where did you hear that word?"

"Couple of people walked past while you were fetching my clothes. They said you only had one Outsider this year."

"Did you see these people?"

"I—" Wait. If I say yes, Carmichael will know who I'm talking about, and he'll reprimand them. I should tell him, but I don't want to make waves. "No, sorry. I ducked behind a wall. Didn't want to draw attention to myself."

Carmichael doesn't answer.

"So, what does it mean?"

He sighs. "The term denotes a trainee who doesn't have family members working at COVEN. Some executioners whose relatives train here look down on them."

My stomach sinks with the realisation that I, too, am an Outsider. "They said Outsiders hardly ever make it through training."

"Like I told Zara, there are exceptions to every rule. She should know. She's one of them."

My eyebrows shoot up. "Zara was an outsider?"

He nods. "I wouldn't have brought you here if I didn't think you could handle it."

We come to a door marked *Trainees' Quarters*.

Carmichael leads me through the door, and we emerge into a bright, wood-panelled atrium. Doors labelled *Q1* to *Q6* line the walls. He stops outside the door marked *Q2*. "Here we are." He hands me a set of keys.

I slide the key into the lock and push the door open.

My 'room' is larger than some flats. The same rich, red carpet from the foyer covers the floor. The dark mahogany furniture—a huge four-poster bed, large triple wardrobe, old-fashioned writing desk, and sweeping bookcase crammed full of books—shines under the spotlights set into the smooth white ceiling.

I dump my uniform on the bed and cross to the bookshelves. There are some familiar titles. Classics mostly, with a few popular novels thrown in for good measure. It's the top shelf that catches my attention, bursting with leather-bound titles like The *Foundations of Magical Theory, The History & Evolution of Combat Magic*, and *Practical Magic for the Modern Witch*. My eyes land on one book in particular. *Myth & Magic: The Truth About Sorcerers, Demons & the Legend of King Arthur*.

I slide the weighty book from the shelf. "King Arthur was real?"

Carmichael shrugs. "Some people think so."

"You don't?"

"There's no evidence to suggest anything written in that book was real."

"I didn't think witches were real a couple of hours ago."

"That's different. The stories in there are fairy-tales. They have a moral, like those old stories mortals read."

"Aesop's fables?"

He nods. "If you like fiction, I'd try it, but take it all with an enormous pinch of salt."

"What does the symbol mean?" I brush my fingers over the strange golden glyph decorating the cover. A circle divided into quadrants, each quadrant housing a unique symbol. In the top left quadrant, a pair of hands cupped like they're waiting to receive something. A golden sun blazes from the top right quarter. In the bottom right's a pentagram. The final quadrant, the bottom left, shows a wickedly curved crescent moon.

"Legend has it the hands represent mortals, and the pentagram represents witches."

"And the sun and the moon?" I ask, tracing the symbol again.

"An old wives' tale. Apparently, the world used to be populated by sorcerers and demons, as well as witches and mortals."

"Really?"

"According to that book, yes, but if so, where are they? Entire races of people don't vanish overnight."

I slide the book back into place. "I guess not."

"Well, I'll leave you to settle in. Try to get some sleep. Training starts tomorrow, and it'll be a busy day."

Sleep. The chances of me sleeping tonight are slim.

Carmichael turns towards the door.

"Thank you," I say in a small voice.

He looks over his shoulder. "What for?"

"Saving me from Razor, bringing me here, keeping me safe."

"It's my job. Besides, I promised your parents."

"All the same."

"Good night, Henry."

"Night." I pat my pocket, searching for my phone to set an alarm, just like I always do before bed.

My phone.

It smashed against the wall.

All my friends' numbers were in there.

My friends.

Jez.

"I need to make a call," I say.

A quizzical expression crosses Carmichael's face. "To whom?"

"My friend, Jez. Once he finds out about my parents, he'll start freaking out. I need to—"

"This Jez is mortal?"

"Yeah, why?"

He crosses his arms with an air of finality. "Then I'm afraid a call is out of the question."

"What? But I need to—"

"It's too risky. If he ever found out what you are..." He lets the words hang there.

He doesn't need to say anything else.

Exposure.

Witch Trials.

The First Law.

Carmichael continues, a note of gentleness in his voice. "I'm sorry, Henry, but your old life is over. You need to let it go and embrace your new life. Here. With us."

I'm hollow.

My old life's over.

The moment the words are out of his mouth I know they're true.

There's no going back.

No return to normality.

This is my new normal.

I—

"And, Henry?"

Carmichael's words snap me out of my reverie "Yeah." Even my voice sounds empty.

"Even if you're petrified tomorrow, don't show it. Don't pick your scar, don't hide behind walls. First impressions count here, and the executioners have high standards. Remember the motto."

The motto.

Vi. Iustitia. Fides.

Strength. Justice. Loyalty.

"We value those three things above all else," Carmichael says, his voice sombre.

My stomach flips. "I'll be fine." I don't believe that for a second.

"I'm sure you will be."

Once Carmichael's gone, I shut and lock my door, and carry out a quick recce of the room. *My* room now. The bed's soft and sinks in the middle when I lie on it. The wardrobe's empty, and the desk contains a selection of basic stationery supplies. A door at the back of the room leads to a cozy, beige-tiled bathroom with a shower cubicle, toilet and sink.

I go through the motions like a robot. Strip. Shower. Towel off. Open the new toothbrush and brush my teeth. Back to the bedroom. Move the bundle of black clothes onto the chair in front of the desk. Lights out. Climb into bed, still naked and damp from the shower.

Only when I'm in bed, alone in the dark, do I allow the tears to come, crying myself into a fitful sleep and dreading what tomorrow will bring.

CHAPTER 12

That night, I dream of blood and pain and sprinting through COVEN's maze-like hallways deep underground.

Razor chases me in the spotlight-punctuated darkness, his soulless black irises devouring the whites of his eyes, the tips of his clawed fingers glowing blood red.

This isn't over.

I dash around a corner, trip over something soft, and tumble to the ground. I twist round.

Oh, God.

I had tripped over a corpse-blue wrist.

Mum and Dad lie dead, slumped against a door bearing the label *Q2*.

The door to my room.

Dad's fingers twitch.

My blood runs cold.

Dad twists his head to face me, the bones in his neck crunching, black ooze gushing from the deep gash in his throat, glassy eyes locking onto mine.

My heart's racing.

His grey lips part and, when he speaks, his voice is a wet rattle, and the strips of shredded flesh at his throat flutter. "Why do you hate us, Champ? Mum and I only want what's best for you, you know that."

I wake with a start and sit bolt upright, breathing hard and bathed in sweat. My knees draw into my chest and I rest my elbows on them, driving the heels of my hands into my eyelids until the ghost of the dream quits haunting me and my heart rate returns to normal.

I lower my hands and open my eyes. Blood stains my fingers where I've gouged my collarbone scar raw in my sleep.

Carmichael's words from last night come back to me.

Even if you're petrified tomorrow, don't show it. Don't pick your scar, don't hide behind walls. First impressions count here, and the executioners have high standards. Remember the motto.

Vi. Iustitia. Fides.

Strength. Justice. Loyalty.

We value those three things above all else.

Strength.

Justice.

Loyalty.

Emphasis on the strength.

Get it together, Henry.

I drag myself from beneath the tangled covers, pad into the en-suite and hop in the shower. The water's warm and comforting, and I scrub the caked-on blood off my hands and throat until the water runs rust coloured.

I dry myself, walk back into the bedroom, and dress in my new black clothes—a round-necked T-shirt and tracksuit bottoms. Perching on the desk chair, I slide my feet into the matching black trainers.

Static crackles through the room. A small speaker clings to the apex of the ceiling. I hadn't noticed it before.

A nasal voice emanates from the speaker. "This is your last call. Could all trainees report to the ring? That's all trainees to the ring."

Another burst of static, followed by an oppressive silence.

Last call? Must've missed the first one. This is it. I get one chance to make a good impression, one chance to prove Zara wrong, but can I do it? Is my desire for revenge enough to get me through training?

My fingers find the chain around my neck and follow it down to my parents' wedding rings. I fold my hand around them and bring the cool metal to my lips.

Dad used to say there's nothing stronger than family.

I don't have a choice. I've got to be strong for them. "This is for you." I tuck the rings away, stand, stride to the door and yank it aside.

I'm greeted by a loud, derisive laugh that echoes off the walls.

The laugh belongs to a blonde guy with cold green eyes the same shade as iceberg lettuce.

The elfin-featured girl he's laughing at tucks a lock of short brown hair behind her ear, ducks her head and tries to squeeze past him.

Like me, they wear black trainee uniforms.

Iceberg Eyes places his hand on the wall, blocking the elfin girl's path. "I can't believe they let *you* in, Bianca."

Bianca.

I know that name.

This girl must be Katya's daughter, the one she'd called a nervous wreck.

Iceberg Eyes continues, "Must've been scraping the bottom of a really enormous barrel." He mangles the word really into a smooth, round, cut-glass *rarely*.

To my surprise, I hate him on sight, something which doesn't happen often.

Bianca says something, her voice so quiet I can't make out the words. She twists a diamond ring round her finger.

I start towards them. "Is everything—"

Something solid slams into my chest, and my back strikes the wall hard. "Problem, Outsider?"

Heart racing, my gaze travels from the gigantic hand pinning me to the wall, up an arm corded with muscle, and fixes on a pair of cool, black, assessing eyes. I try to speak, but no sound comes out.

"Are you deaf, dumb, or just plain stupid?" My attacker's voice rumbles from deep in his core. Cultured, like the other guy's, but with a rough, sandpaper edge. He shoves me again. "Speak."

"Making friends already, Femi?" Iceberg Eyes appears at Femi's shoulder.

Femi growls, and his lip curls into a sneer. "With an Outsider? You must be joking."

"I apologise for my friend's complete lack of manners. He can be a little prickly." He turns those creepy, antifreeze-green eyes on me. "This is the late addition my father told me about this morning, Femi."

Femi's hand leaves my chest. "You have the Sight."

My voice still refuses to work, so I just nod.

Iceberg Eyes sticks out his neatly manicured hand. "Myles Hedges."

My fingers twitch, my natural inclination to shake with Myles. Something tells me I don't want him as my enemy.

Even if you're petrified tomorrow, don't show it... remember the motto.

Vi. Iustitia. Fides.

I pause, hand half extended. The way Myles spoke to Bianca—the mocking tone, the audible sneer—makes my skin crawl and my blood boil. Do I really want to shake hands with someone like him? Someone I already hate?

What would Carmichael do?

What would Zara do?

My throat tightens, and the skin on my scalp tingles, but I resist the urge to take Myles's hand. I fold my arms instead, fighting the temptation to pick at my scar.

Myles's mouth turns down. He clenches his outstretched hand into a fist and lowers it to his side. "Big mistake, Outsider." Myles turns away and strides towards the door. "Come on, Femi. We're going to be late."

"He'll make you regret that, eventually," Femi says, a gleeful note in his voice, before trailing after Myles.

As soon as they're out of sight, I sag against the wall, my knees trembling.

Bianca crosses the hallway and leans against the wall next to me. "Thank you. You didn't have to do that."

Don't show it.

Vi.

Strength.

I lock my knees, push off from the wall and force my spine straight. "No worries. You okay?"

She ducks her head. "I'm used to it."

The silence that follows is too awkward to bear, so I say, "Where are we meant to be going?"

"The ring."

"You know the way?"

She gives a little bob of her head.

We fall into step beside each other.

"Didn't you get a tour of the place during your orientation?"

Why's she talking to me? Katya told her to stay away from Outsiders, and she heard Femi use that word to describe me. Despite her meekness, maybe there's a rebellious streak buried underneath it all. I smile.

She's still waiting for an answer to her question.

"Oh. No. No orientation for me. Late addition."

Bianca's mouth opens like she wants to ask more, but she closes it again and looks away.

We're walking so close together I get a waft of her fresh scent. It's so familiar. But where from?

The answer punches me in the nose.

She smells like soap and clean linen.

Like home.

My stomach clenches and a thin sheen of sweat slicks my upper lip. I don't want to think about home. Not now. If I do, I'll cry, and that wouldn't create the good first impression I need to make.

"Are you all right?" Bianca asks.

"Fine." It comes out sharper than I'd intended, so I soften my tone. "You know Myles and Femi?"

She blinks her wide hazel eyes and sniffs. "Yes, unfortunately. We went to school together. Manor Grange."

My eyebrows shoot up. I used to walk past Manor Grange—a top tier public school in the city, all *Range Rovers* and yummy-mummies and formal dinners—on the way to my bog-standard state school.

"I hated every second," she says. "It thrilled me when I went to university. Thought I'd escaped them."

"What's Myles's problem with you?"

"His parents have more money than mine."

"That's it?"

"That's all it takes at The Grange. The school's motto was, '*Veritas aequitas veremur*'. We respect truth and honesty. More like '*Veremur pecunia postestateque*'. We respect—"

"Money and power," I finish.

"You speak Latin?"

I bristle. "Don't sound so surprised."

"Sorry. I didn't mean it like that. I meant—"

"Hey. Wait up."

I turn and see another trainee with shaggy, dark brown hair down to his shoulders moseying toward us like he's out for a Sunday morning stroll. "You guys know where you're going?"

"She does."

"Sweet. I've been wandering round like a dementia patient who's escaped from the home."

The odd simile forces a bark of laughter from my throat.

He falls into step beside us. "I'm Geek, by the way."

Geek?

The same Geek Katya mentioned.

He's the other Outsider.

"Henry."

"Bianca." She scrunches up her nose. "What kind of name is Geek?"

Geek's sunny expression clouds over. "Nickname." He doesn't elaborate.

We round a corner, and a woman with grey streaks in her hair blocks our path. "Trainees to the end of this corridor," she gestures. "Take the stairs down. Director Carmichael is waiting for you." The way she says, "Waiting for you," implies we're keeping Carmichael from attending to more important business.

"Thank you," Bianca says.

The woman looks at her like she's sprouted three heads.

Maybe manners and strength don't mix at COVEN. I start down the corridor. "Come on. Let's get this over with."

CHaPTer 13

W e reach the bottom of the stairs and walk down a short passageway. The passageway widens out, leading into a bare concrete antechamber, lined with long metal benches.

Carmichael stands in front of a set of wide, black double doors.

The murmur of voices comes from beyond them.

Carmichael's head snaps up when we enter the room. "At last. I was about to send out a search party."

Myles—perched next to Femi on one bench—leans forward, rests his elbows on his knees, and smirks at us.

"We got held up," I say.

"What happens now?" asks an unfamiliar female voice.

I turn.

A willowy woman stands, straight-backed, in the corner. She's roughly the same age as me, but she's not wearing a trainee's uniform. Instead, electric blue leggings show off her slim, toned legs and a tight, bright red sports top stresses her hourglass figure.

Something flickers in my gut, and the warm feeling spreads lower. I blink the sensation away.

"I'm glad you asked, Layla," Carmichael says.

Layla.

Syed's daughter.

So, despite the colourful clothes, she *is* a trainee.

The final trainee.

Layla tosses her waist-length Stygian ringlets over her shoulder, and tilts her chin up.

Bianca scans Layla from head to toe, taking in her bright outfit and her imperious stance.

"Something to say?" Layla asks her, with the quirk of an eyebrow.

Her smooth voice melts over my ears like warm honey.

Bianca responds in a small voice. "No."

"Good." Layla snaps. "Keep it that way."

Layla's sharp tone leaves me cold, dousing the first stirrings of attraction. I can guess what label Mum would've assigned to her. She would've branded her one of 'those girls'. A stuck up cow with a high opinion of herself. Can't say I disagree.

Carmichael says, "Let's keep things civilised, shall we, ladies?"

Layla jabs a scarlet-painted fingernail at Bianca. "She came for me. All I did was—"

"Ignore Bianca." Myles stands and saunters over to Layla. "The rest of us do."

Femi snorts.

"Myles Hedges."

"Layla Jabara."

"Jabara? Jabara? Ah, your father works on my father's execution team, I think."

Ugh. Myles and Layla are perfect for each other. Two snobs cut from the same expensively woven cloth.

An edge of steel creeps into Carmichael's voice. "There'll be plenty of time for introductions later, Myles. Now, if you don't mind, we're on a tight schedule."

Myles walks back to the bench and resumes his perch.

"As you know, my name is Dylan Carmichael, and I'm the Director of the Covert Executioner's Network." Carmichael laces his fingers behind his back. "What you don't know is that five years ago, I was a Detective Inspector with the Magical Investigations Department."

I almost nod, but catch myself at the last minute. I don't want anyone knowing about my connection to Carmichael. If people knew... well, I'd have to explain everything, and I didn't want to talk about my parents with a bunch of strangers.

"Why'd you leave?" Geek asks.

Carmichael's eyes flash.

Geek bites the inside of his cheek and looks down. "Just asking."

Carmichael sighs. "The system was flawed. We all knew it. Too many guilty parties acquitted. Lack of hard evidence." His mouth twists on the word evidence, like he bit into a rotten pear. "The Witches Council created COVEN to mitigate these miscarriages of justice."

The system *was* flawed.

Razor had said as much. Back at the nightclub.

The MID is already building a case against me. It's all circumstantial...

My fists clench. People like Razor need to pay.

Carmichael continues, "In short, we assassinate guilty criminals who slip the metaphorical noose. If you're lucky enough to graduate from training—"

"*If* we graduate from training?" The words fly out of my mouth before I can stop them.

"Yes, Henry. *If*." Carmichael's eyes are cold. He's looking at me like I'm a stranger. "We only select three executioners each year."

Myles stands. "What?"

"Wasn't I speaking clearly enough?"

"My father didn't mention this."

"He wouldn't. That information is sensitive."

"But that's not fair." Myles wears a sulky expression that makes me want to heave.

"I'll be frank with all of you. If the notion of healthy competition scares you, you might as well leave now. We don't want cowards here."

Two spots of colour appear on Myles's cheeks and his jaw works.

"Well?"

Myles reclaims his seat and glowers at Carmichael.

"What happens if we fail?" I ask.

"We erase your memories and send you home."

Interesting how Carmichael forgot to mention this when he roped me into joining COVEN. A flash of heat goes through me. He offers me the chance to avenge my parents, now he's telling me that chance isn't guaranteed. First Mum and Dad—my gut pinches, but my irritation overrides the sadness—now Carmichael.

Why do people insist on wielding lies and half-truths like weapons?

And as for sending me home? My mouth goes dry.

Home.

I don't have a home anymore.

And if I'm going to kill Razor, I need this.

I will get selected.

I *will*.

Beside me, Bianca fiddles with her diamond ring.

"I know," Carmichael says, his eyes flicking to Geek and away again, "that most of you have a lot riding on this, so I'm sure you'll all try your hardest, and I wish you luck."

"Does Zara decide who gets cut?" I ask, hoping the answer's no. I'll never make it through training if it's up to her.

"Who's Zara?" Layla says.

"The trainer," I say.

Carmichael says, "Zara and I both have the power to exclude you from training if you act against COVEN's core principles."

Strength.

Justice.

Loyalty.

"Failing that," Carmichael continues, "selection is a shared decision."

"What does that mean?" I ask.

"At various points throughout training, we hold several collective votes called ratings. Every executioner gets to vote for their preferred trainee. The better you perform, the more likely you are to secure votes."

"What happens after you've voted?" Layla asks.

"We rank you from first to sixth place, based on the amount of votes each of you receives."

"How many executioners are there?" I ask.

"Two hundred, give or take, and they're all out there, waiting for you." Carmichael points at the double doors behind him.

The room's so quiet you could hear a spider crawling up the wall.

My stomach churns.

Great.

Not only do I have to impress Zara, I've got to impress one hundred and ninety-nine other people as well. The urge to pick my scar's almost overwhelming, but I resist, clenching my fists so hard my knuckles ache.

"Any more burning questions?" Carmichael asks.

Bianca stares at her feet. Geek looks bored. Myles and Femi wear determined scowls. Layla ties her hair back with a thin band on her wrist.

"No? Good. Wait here then. When I call your name, walk out into the ring." Carmichael points at his Adam's apple and mumbles something under his breath. The tip of his finger pulses with blue light. He turns and pushes through the double doors behind him.

I glimpse black marble and a flash of silver, then the doors swing shut.

"Right, you rowdy bunch." Carmichael's voice booms, echoing through my head. "I think I've kept you waiting long enough, don't you?"

The murmur of voices rises into a deafening roar.

"What exactly is the ring?" I whisper to Bianca.

She swallows with considerable effort. "It's where they make us fight each other."

Dear Henry Stone...

We regret to inform you...

Frost prickles my skin. "Fight each other?"

Bianca nods, her face pale. "I don't stand a chance in hell."

Fight each other.

Neither do I.

Nobody speaks. Even Myles keeps his mouth shut for once.

Sweat collects in my clenched fists, and the muscles in my neck are tight. I've made a huge mistake coming here. Of course, they'll make us fight each other. It seems obvious now. How else would they decide who to select? I can't do this. I don't want to—

"Fellow executioners." Carmichael's amplified voice reverberates around the suddenly stuffy antechamber.

I start, heart rate spiking.

"Who wants to meet this year's trainees?"

Another roar from the crowd.

The hairs on my arms stand on end.

"I said, who wants to meet our new trainees?"

The roaring gets louder still, threatening to split my skull.

"That's more like it. Can I get a drum roll, please?"

A low rumble makes the ground tremble. The sound of two hundred pairs of feet drumming on the floor.

"First up, we have Myles Hedges."

Myles shoots to his feet and, without hesitation, flings open the double doors, strides through.

The crowd goes mad, the cheering accompanied by catcalls and several ear-splitting whoops.

"I didn't realise they were going to parade us in front of everyone," Bianca says.

"Hey." I rest my hand on her slim shoulder. "You'll be fine."

She places her clammy fingers on top of mine. "Tell that to my stomach."

"Oluwafemi Abimbola."

Femi elbows his way through the doors. He salutes the crowd, playing up to them.

Layla spins a silver bracelet studded with emeralds around her wrist.

"Nervous?" I ask.

"Of course," she says with a bite.

"Next, it's Layla Jabara."

She draws herself up to her full height and sashays towards the door. She pauses. "You are, too. And if you say otherwise, you're a rotten liar." She brushes the doors aside and the cheers—particularly the male ones—increase in volume. Layla blows kisses to several of her admirers.

The doors close again.

I don't think I've ever met someone so full of themselves.

Bianca clutches her stomach. "I don't say things like this often, but I hate that woman."

"Can't imagine why," I say, nudging her with my elbow.

She gives me a queasy smile in return, and says, "Reminds me of this total bitch-queen from hell at Manor Grange. Nicollette Barnes. She used to pull these nasty pranks. Itching powder in my shoes. Crushed stink bombs in my bed. She stuffed a used tampon in my bag once."

"That's horrible," Geek says. "You should have retaliated."

"Oh, I got my revenge, eventually."

"How?" I ask.

"One evening, while she was in the shower, I—"

"Trainee number four. Bianca Yakhontov."

"Ugh, I feel sick," Bianca says.

"You'll be okay." Geek says. "What is it they say? Just imagine everyone naked."

Her lips pucker. "No way. My mother's out there."

"Ah. Okay, don't do that then."

"Good luck," I say.

"I'm going to need it." She takes several small, hesitant steps, and rests her palm against the door. She exhales a heavy sigh, heaves the door open, and trudges into the ring with her head down.

The cheers become less emphatic.

Geek runs a hand through his shaggy mop of hair. "Man, I'm shitting bricks."

"What happened to, 'it'll be easy, just imagine them naked'?"

"I was just trying to make her feel better."

I snort.

"How about you? How are you feeling?"

How am I feeling? Like I swallowed a vat full of battery acid. *Even if you're petrified tomorrow, don't show it.*

"I'm fine."

"Only two left." Carmichael says. "Gareth Townsend, you're next."

"I guess that's my cue." Geek ambles over to the doors.

"Gareth? Seriously?" A dry chuckle scrapes up my throat. "I can see why you prefer the nickname."

"And here I was thinking, 'this geezer's all right'." Geek shoots imaginary finger guns at me before meandering into the ring.

Sweat beads my forehead. As soon as I'm sure I'm alone, I bend forward, bracing my hands on my knees, and hyperventilate. I don't want to do this. I don't want to—

"And last but not least..."

My heart stops beating. "Shit."

"Henry Stone."

I'm standing at the doors before I know it.

First impressions count here, and the executioners have high standards.

I can't appear weak. I've got to be strong. Drawing myself up to my full height, I square my shoulders, set my jaw, shove the doors open and stride into the ring.

CHapTer 14

I'm swamped by bright fluorescent light, the thunderous clamour of stamping feet and muggy, static-charged air. It's like stepping off a plane somewhere tropical.

The ring's a square space roughly the size of two tennis courts. Black marble, veined with white, everywhere—walls, floor, ceiling—and there's a shining silver circle, spanning most of the ground space, set into the floor. Huge plasma screens, currently showing the COVEN pentagram with the three-word motto beneath it, adorn the walls. Execution-ers—all in varying states of euphoria—gather, three rows deep, around the edges of the room. They shout, they stomp, they shake their fists in the air. And they're all looking at me.

Carmichael stands in the ring's centre, geeing up the crowd. The other trainees are spread out around him.

My vision swims, and cold sweat runs down my back, but I force myself to walk in a straight line.

Don't look at the crowd.

Focus straight ahead.

Focus on Carmichael.

I cross into the circle—the ring—and keep going. Nearly there. Chin up, shoulders back. Don't vomit. Whatever you do, don't fucking vomit.

I stop in front of Carmichael.

"Look at his eyes," someone calls above the din.

"Bloody hell," yells another.

"He's got the Sight," shouts a third.

A balmy quiet descends, smothering the cheers, and nothing but whispers rustle through the room.

Eventually, the whispers die out, leaving the ghost of silence behind.

My skin itches with the pressure of two hundred pairs of eyes on me. I wish someone would explain what exactly the Sight is, and why it's so lauded.

Most of the executioners are smiling, some wear expressions of astonishment, and a few sport tight, pinched looks of fear.

Fear?

Because of my Sight?

I'm not sure how I feel about that.

"That's right," Carmichael says, his mouth quirking up at the corner. "Henry here has the Sight."

Myles glares at me.

I try to ignore him.

"Your training begins now. I wish you the best of luck. If you'll excuse me, I have a few urgent matters requiring immediate attention." With that, Carmichael pivots on his heel and strides back towards the antechamber. He pauses before the double doors and says, "I'll leave you in your trainer's capable hands." He pushes back through the doors, disappearing from view.

"Oh, no," I mutter, hardly daring to move my lips. "Zara."

As if on cue, the crowd parts and there she is. She still sports pink lipstick and eyeshadow, but has replaced the dress and heels with leather ankle boots, fitted black jeans and a—pink, of course—vest top. She stalks to the front of the ring. "Line up."

Nobody moves.

"You lot fucking deaf, or something?" she adds, her voice steel-edged. "I said, line up."

I scamper to comply, standing shoulder to shoulder with Geek and Bianca.

Zara struts up and down the newly formed line. "I'm not big on speeches, so I'll keep it brief. I'm Zara White. For the next twelve months, I'm your trainer. What does that mean, I hear you ask? It means you eat when I tell you to eat, sleep when I say you can sleep, and shit when I tell you to shit. It's my job to turn you into executioners." She pauses and smirks. "Though, looking at the state of you lot, I won't hold my breath."

A smattering of laughter breaks out from the crowd.

Zara stops in front of Layla. "Jabara. Where's your uniform?"

"I don't do black." Layla crosses her arms. "I wouldn't wear that hideous tracksuit if my life depended on it."

"That's my girl!" Syed shouts from the back of the room. "Stick to your convictions."

Zara gives Layla a thin-lipped smile and says, "You never know. It just might."

Do I detect a flicker of apprehension in Layla's eyes? Good. She could do with being taken down a peg, or two... or five.

Zara resumes pacing. "I have two very simple rules. One. When I give you an order, you follow it. Without question."

Myles snorts a laugh and nudges Femi in the ribs. "I doubt I'll be taking orders from *Assassination Barbie* for long."

Zara halts right in front of me, preternaturally still, her face blank.

A noxious hush blankets the room, suffocating all sounds.

My skin crawls with gooseflesh.

Around the ring, several pairs of lips form small round 'Os' of surprise. One woman mimes a throat slitting motion to someone across the room and mouths the words, "He's fucked."

Too late, Myles realises his mistake, and his face turns ashen.

Zara whips round and flings out her hand. "*Flagellum*."

A thin stream of pink light springs from Zara's fingertips, coils around Myles's waist in tight loops, and pins his arms to his sides.

"What the—" he begins.

Zara yanks her arm to the side.

Myles soars across the room at waist height, like Zara shot him from a cannon.

The crowd gasps, and those in Myles's path fling themselves out of the way to avoid getting hit.

Myles slams into the marble wall side on with a dull thump, bounces off, and crashes to the ground in a groaning heap, clutching his ribs.

Serves him right.

Zara advances on Myles and crouches beside him, the crowd giving her an even wider berth. "Rule number two. When I speak, you listen."

The steady way she says it encases my spine in ice. It would have been less terrifying had she screamed at him.

"That's enough." A blonde man in a red silk shirt and black trousers shoves his way forward. He races across the ring, the over-polished uppers of his brown leather brogues catching the light as he moves.

Zara's not fazed. She stands. "Your son needs to learn some manners, Nick."

His son? This is Myles's dad?

"There are better ways to teach someone a lesson," Nick says through gritted teeth.

Zara takes three slow, deliberate steps towards Nick.

I hold my breath.

"Are you questioning my methods?" Her voice is low and deadly.

"Yes. I am."

Several people gasp.

My knees tremble. Is this guy insane? He must have a death wish, going up against Zara like this.

"Think you could do a better job?" Zara smirks at him. "You should've applied for the position."

A muscle in Nick's jaw twitches.

"Oh, I forgot, you did."

Myles groans again, pushing himself back onto his knees.

Zara glares at him. "Get up."

"I can't." He sucks in a pained breath through his teeth. "I think you cracked a rib."

"I don't care if I punctured your fucking lung. Get. Back. In. Line. Don't make me ask you again."

"Father, are you going to let her talk to me like that?"

Zara arches an eyebrow.

Nick's fists clench.

Zara shoots Nick a feral grin. "Tell you what, Nicky-boy. You want my job so badly, you can have it."

The executioners mutter, casting confused, sidelong glances at Zara.

Nick's eyes narrow, but not before they gleam at the prospect of taking Zara's position. "What?"

"You heard me. You can have my job... as long as you beat me in the ring."

"You don't scare me, Zara."

"Good. I challenge you to a Trial by Magic. You win, you get to be the trainer."

"And if I lose?"

"You leave COVEN, and you never come back."

Nick clenches one fist, a flicker of turquoise magic playing over his knuckles.

The resulting staring contest between the two witches goes on forever, and the mutters rise to jeers.

My throat's dry, like I've swallowed a boxful of crackers with no water, and sweat slicks my upper lip. Nick's going to fight her. I know it, and I don't want to be around when it happens.

"Well, don't just stand there, accept," Myles pleads with his dad. "You can beat her."

Nick breaks eye contact first. "Do as she says, boy."

"Dad?"

"She gave you an order. Don't embarrass me, just do it."

Myles's entire face flushes red, the colour a vivid contrast to his blonde hair and pale skin. He hauls himself to his feet with considerable effort and limps back into line.

"We'll discuss this later," Nick says to Zara, before he quick-walks back through the crowd and down a dark corridor leading deeper into the compound.

"I wouldn't count on it," Zara calls after him. She turns back to face us. "Director Carmichael explained the ratings to you?"

Geek nods. "Yeah."

"Good. Then we can get on with the first rating."

"You're rating us now?" Bianca asks.

Zara takes a deep breath and releases it to a slow count of five. "Problem?"

Bianca's cheeks redden, and she casts her gaze at the floor. "No."

"Don't look at the floor," Zara says, her voice sharp. "Look at me."

Bianca strains to lift her head, like it's made of cement, but she manages it.

Just.

Zara gets right in Bianca's face, a curl to her lip. "If I were you, I'd stop fiddling with that pretty ring of yours. It gives your weakness away."

Bianca stops twisting her ring.

"We want people made of steel. Not jelly. You need to toughen the fuck up, and fast. Understand?"

Bianca bobs her head.

Zara scans the crowd and raises her voice. "You know what to do."

The executioners move as one, reaching into their pockets and drawing out slender, palm-sized, pointed shards of crystal and clutching them tight.

The crystals glow all different colours.

Zara strides over to one of the large plasma screens. "We'll display the ratings on these screens. This is only an indicator, based on first impressions."

"Nobody's actually explained what training entails," I say.

"Did I say you could speak, Stone?"

I want to look at the floor, like Bianca had, but I force myself to hold Zara's rose-pink gaze.

Zara crosses her arms. "We split training into three components. First, we teach you how to fight."

My heart misses a beat on the word fight.

"Second, we teach you the art of deliberate practice, which involves mastering the four major disciplines of witchcraft, namely: combat magic, illusions and charms, practical magic, and portals. Obviously, we place a higher emphasis on combat—"

"Five," I say, without thinking.

Zara's hand goes to her hip. "Excuse me?"

She's wrong, isn't she? What about dark magic? The way Razor lights his cigarettes with a conjured flame, the way he can make the earth shake, the way he blew Carmichael and I across the room like a pair of discarded crisp packets...?

I cough past a lump in my throat and continue. "There are five major branches of magic, aren't there?"

The room goes still, and I'm standing in the eye of a storm.

Most of the executioners, who were perfectly happy to meet my gaze moments ago, make a concerted effort not to now.

Zara paces towards me, taking her time. When she's so close I can smell fresh mint on her breath, she says, "If you're referring to elemental magic, the Fifth Law forbids it."

I glance at my feet. "I didn't know that."

"What did I tell Bianca about looking down?"

Shit.

I'd forgotten.

My eyes snap back to hers.

Zara lets ten agonising seconds pass before stepping back and regarding each trainee. "For those of you who—for whatever inexplicable reason—haven't been told by your families yet, there are Five Primary Laws of Magic. I'll paraphrase. One. No discussing, performing, or hinting at the existence of magic in front of mortals. Two. Don't tell your kids about magic until the night of their Manifestation. Three. Don't murder anyone using magic. Four. Permanently binding a witch's magic with a liquid iron injection is a gross infringement of magical rights, except if said witch has broken the First and, or Second Law. Five. The Witches Council classify elemental magic as dark magic, and it's a no-go zone."

"How come it's forbidden?" Geek asks.

Zara taps her chest. "Natural magic, the power that lives inside us, is just that. Natural. The five elements: earth, air, fire, water, and lightning are dangerous primordial forces. They're external to us. When a witch casts elemental spells, they have to invoke those primordial forces. Drawing on that power comes at a price. For every elemental spell you cast, you exchange a sliver of what makes you human. Over time, dark magic poisons the soul."

"If that's true," Layla says, with a quizzical frown. "Why would anyone use it?"

Zara shrugs. "It's powerful—some would argue more powerful than natural magic."

I shiver.

It's powerful—some would argue more powerful than natural magic.

I can attest to that. The way Razor caused the earthquake back at the house. The sheer force of that lightning-strike.

It's powerful all right.

Too powerful.

How am I ever going to defeat someone who has that much destructive magic at their disposal? How will I—

Zara continues in a loud voice, jolting me back into the present. "Some witches value power above all else, even their lives. The only thing is, once you start using dark magic, it's almost impossible to stop."

"You mean it's addictive?" I ask.

Zara fixes me with a glare. "No shit."

I wait for someone to laugh, but nobody does. "But—"

"Shut your fucking mouth. If I catch any of you so much as *thinking* about dark magic, I'll erase your memories and kick your arse out of here so fast, you won't know what hit you. Is that clear?"

All the trainees—including me—are stunned into silence.

No-one responds.

"I said. Is that clear?"

"Yes," the six of us say in unison.

"Good. Oh, and speaking of kicking your arses out, we don't tolerate witch-bane in the compound. If I find any hidden in your quarters, it's game over."

"Witch-bane?" I ask.

Zara rolls her eyes. "It's a highly addictive, highly illegal drug." She scrunches up her face in disgust. "Using the bane is shameful. Weak."

Geek shuffles from foot to foot, a scarlet blush colouring his neck.

What's he so shifty about?

Bianca raises a tentative hand.

Zara lets out a heavy sigh. "What now, Yakhontov?"

"You—you said the Third Law forbids killing people with magic."

"Is that a question?"

"Well, it's just—uh, that's what you're teaching us to do, right? Kill people."

"Executioners are a special case. When we kill, we kill for the good of all witches. Anymore stupid questions?"

Nobody speaks.

"Great. As for the third component of your training. You'll face each other in the ring in a series of bouts. Arguably, this aspect is most vital. The more bouts you win, the more likely we'll select you as an executioner."

My chest tightens and another lump forms in my throat.

Zara's eyes rake over the crowd. "What are you doing? I don't have all day. Cast your votes."

People grip their crystals harder.

The COVEN logos on the plasma screens fade to black.

My heart beats too fast, eyes fixed on the blank screen in front of me. I wait and wait and wait.

Wait some more.

"Oh, God." Bianca looks green.

I reach for her hand and give it a light squeeze. "It'll be fine."

She squeezes back.

The screens flash.

The bottom drops out of my stomach. "That can't be right," I say.

The list reads:

Current Ratings:

1. Henry Stone

2. Oluwafemi Abimbola

3. Layla Jabara

4. Gareth Townsend

5. Myles Hedges

6. Bianca Yakhontov

Bianca's grip goes slack before she releases my hand.

The results make no sense. How? How had I rated first?

"Bullshit." Myles steps out of line and jabs a finger at me. "How did he beat me?"

Zara turns an expectant gaze on me, a look that says, "I'm not fighting your battles for you."

I should put Myles in his place. This is my chance to impress Zara and the other executioners. I open my mouth to speak, but my throat's too dry. I can't do it. Snubbing Myles's offer of friendship in private's one thing, challenging him in public's another. I don't want to piss him off. I want him to leave me alone.

"Well?" Myles waits for an answer.

All eyes are on me again. The executioners are like a pack of slavering wolves, eager for me to serve a meaty comeback.

I clear my throat. "I don't know."

Disappointed groans come from all around, and Zara narrows her eyes. Clearly, everyone was expecting something pithier than that.

"I do," Geek's casual slouching demeanour vanishes, and he stands with a straight back and squared shoulders.

I shoot him a look.

He ignores my silent plea. "Because it's based on first impressions, and you're a dick. No wonder your dad didn't bother sticking up for you."

That gets a laugh from the peanut gallery.

Myles is almost puce now, his whole body shaking. "Say that again, Outsider."

"Is that supposed to be intimidating?" Geek says.

Bianca places a hand on Geek's arm. "Geek, don't, he's not worth it, trust me."

He shrugs her off. "No. People like him make me sick."

"People like me?" Myles says.

"Yeah. People like you. Entitled rich brats. All mouth and no trousers."

"Take that back." Myles starts towards Geek.

Geek squares up to him, shouting, "Come on, then."

Zara steps between them, her hands sparking electric pink. "Enough. Finish your pissing contest in your own time. We're done for today. I suggest you all go get some breakfast and cool down. And by suggest, I mean do it."

We're all frozen on the spot.

"Now."

"Fine." Myles points at me again. "This isn't over, Stone."

This isn't over.

The same threat Razor had issued back on the club's rooftop.

I'm overwhelmed by a wave of queasiness and—I can't help it—I pick my scar.

Myles storms out of the ring and back into the antechamber, and Femi and Layla follow him.

"Jabara?" Zara calls after Layla.

She stops and turns.

"Next time I see you, you'd better be wearing your uniform." Layla nods, looking pale, and leaves.

The executioners file out around us, leaving Bianca, Geek, Zara, and me behind.

"You okay?" Bianca asks, her brow creased in concern.

I start towards the door. "Let's just get some food."

"Stone? A word."

Zara.

"Catch you in a bit," Geek says.

"Fine."

Then it's just me and Zara left.

She stalks up to me. "Carmichael said you're here because of a favour to some friends."

I push aside a pang of grief. "Something like that."

"Well, do *yourself* a favour"—she puts her face close to mine and I get a second waft of mint—"and don't fuck it up before you've even started." With that, she brushes past me. "I'll schedule our private sessions. They'll start in a month or so, once you've mastered the basics."

My eyes freeze wide.

Did she just say private sessions?

"What for?" I ask.

She pauses at the door and turns to face me. "For your Sight. What else?"

My brow creases. "Why does everyone act weird about it? The Sight, I mean."

"Weird?"

"Yeah. Some people seem excited, other people seem angry, and a few people seem... afraid."

She crosses her arms. "Didn't your family tell you about it?"

My family.

My throat catches, but I cough past it. "I—erm—a little."

She waits for a further explanation.

"They said I can detect auras and see through illusions, and that it makes me powerful, but they didn't say why."

"Seeing through illusions is only part of it. If you can master it, the Sight allows you to predict what spell another witch might cast against you."

"You mean... what? We can see the future."

She chuckles but, coming from her, it sounds mirthless. "Hardly. No-one can see the future. It's more like... you'll be able to sense the path someone's magic will take a split second before they cast a spell."

I shake my head. "I don't get it. Why does that scare people?"

"Think about it."

I think... nothing jumps out at me.

"Fights can change in a split second."

Dear Mr Stone...

We regret to inform you...

Yeah. Tell me something I don't know.

Zara rolls her eyes. "It gives you an edge, if you can react fast enough. The other trainees will hate you for it." She says this last part with a little too much glee for my taste. "Remember what I said." She pushes through the door and vanishes from sight.

I'm left alone, cheeks blazing with heat, Zara's warning ringing in my ears.

Well, do yourself *a favour and don't fuck it up before you've even started.*

Fingers crossed.

CHAPTER 15

The woman who directed me to the ring earlier points me towards the dining hall, and I catch up to Geek and Bianca fifteen minutes later.

Bianca's expression brightens when she sees me. "What did Zara want?"

I fall into step with them. "To warn me not to mess up."

She tucks her hair behind her ears. "I don't know about you two, but she scares the crap out of me."

"Carmichael reckons she's a pussycat deep down," I say.

Geek raises his eyebrows. "How do you know what Carmichael thinks of her?"

"Oh. I—uh—I overheard him talking to someone about her when I got here last night."

"Right," he says, but I'm not sure he buys it.

I need to change the subject, and fast. "Hey. Speaking of Carmichael, what was he getting at earlier?"

Geek's brow furrows. "Getting at?"

We move aside to let a group of executioners pass and carry on walking. "When he was talking about some of us having a lot riding on this, he looked right at you."

"Did he?"

"Yeah, he did."

He shakes his head, doesn't meet my eyes. "You must've imagined it."

I hadn't, but I also don't want to rock the boat, so I let it slide.

We round a corner and draw to a halt at the entrance to the dining hall.

"Oh, wow," Bianca says.

The dining hall's impressive. It's huge, with vaulted ceilings; pale, smooth, honey-coloured walls, and a flagstone floor. Long oak benches, laid out in six sweeping columns, stretch from one end of the room to the other. Right at the other end, along the back wall, a wide serving hatch, manned by executioners, fills the room with the mouth-watering smells of breakfast: salty bacon, herb-stuffed sausages, fresh baked bread, pastries, and croissants.

My stomach rumbles. I haven't eaten since yesterday morning.

Executioners cluster around the tables in tight knots, and the room's bustling with activity—chattering, laughter, and the clatter of clinking cutlery. It's so noisy here. So bright. Not like home at all. Home's quiet. Safe. Well, it *was* safe, before—

I hate you, and I'll never forgive you.

No.

I can't think about home now. Thinking about home only leads to tears. I'll only make things worse for myself.

We each grab trays and plates from a low table and join the queue for food. We reach the front, pile our plates high with fry-up, and go in search of somewhere to sit.

"Hogwarts has nothing on this place," Geek says.

I chuckle, then a thought comes to me. "Why are they here all the time? The executioners I mean. They don't live on site, do they?"

Bianca shakes her head while we walk. "No. Mother told me there's always a heavy executioner presence on site for security reasons."

"Looks like everyone's here today, though," Geek says. "There's hardly a spare seat."

"Mother said Carmichael makes everyone come in on rating days. Apparently, he wants everyone to have a say on who gets selected. That way, nobody can complain about the results if they pick a dud."

"Makes sense, I guess," I say.

"That's what I—oh, God," Bianca's face pales. "Look who's coming."

Myles struts toward us.

I square my shoulders, balancing my tray in one hand.

Almost past him.

Almost past him.

I'm almost past him when he sticks out his foot.

His ankle hooks round mine, and I trip. My plate flies upward and I crash to the floor. Seconds later, something hot hits my back with a wet splat—gooey baked beans.

All the surrounding chatter ceases.

"Oh, sorry. Didn't see you there, Stone," Myles says.

Like hell he didn't.

The executioners at the table nearest us chuckle and point at me.

My cheeks burn.

Geek steps forward. "What the fuck is your problem?"

Myles shrugs. "I really didn't see him." He holds a hand out to me. "Here, let me help you up."

Like a fool, I take his hand. I'm halfway to my feet when he lets go and I land on my arse in the bean juice.

Laughter spreads around the room, some people standing and craning their necks to get a better view.

Myles leans over me. "You should've shaken my hand. This is only the beginning. I won't let you beat me in the ratings."

Geek slams his tray down on the table beside him. "That's it, dickwad. You've gone too far."

"What did you just call me?"

"You heard me, dickwad."

"You fu—"

Zara appears behind Myles and places a restraining hand on his shoulder. "Is there a problem here, gents?"

Myles shrugs her off. "Yes, this prick—"

"No," I say, pushing to my feet. "No problem."

"Henry, he just—" Geek begins.

I cut across him. "Leave it. Please."

"Move on, Hedges," Zara says.

Myles adopts an expression of pure innocence. "I don't know what happened. He just tripped."

"Move on, before I make you."

Myles slaps me on the back so hard it stings. "Watch your step next time." He walks off.

Tomato juice from the beans fuses my T-shirt to my skin.

"You okay?" Bianca asks.

I can't stand this. Her sympathy. The eyes on me, like a million needles stabbing into my flesh. I need to run. Now. I spin on my heel and bolt, peals of laughter chasing me from the dining hall.

I race through the endless maze of corridors, rounding corner after corner after corner, trainers slapping and squeaking on the smooth marble. The echo of laughter still snaps at my heels. I don't know how long I sprint for, but when I stop, my breathing's ragged and I stand in a deserted stretch of hallway, with only the buzzing of the overhead spotlights for company.

Resting my back against the cool, wood-panelled wall, I slide down it, no doubt leaving a vivid orange streak of bean juice behind. I stare into the darkness behind my eyelids and take deep breaths of the pine-polish-scented air, fighting back tears. Deep breaths. Deep breaths. My heart rate slows, the angry, embarrassed heat gradually seeping away.

Time passes. I don't know how long.

I pick at my scar the entire time.

Footsteps approach.

I stop picking. I don't open my eyes, don't look up, don't acknowledge their presence.

The air stirs as whoever it is sits beside me. "Tell me what happened with Hedges."

Zara. Of course. It has to be Zara.

I sigh, my entire body deflating. "You—you saw what happened."

"I did, and so did everybody else."

I lower my hands, open my eyes.

Zara sits with her legs stretched out in front of her, head tilted back against the wall. "Why did you run?"

"What else was I supposed to do?"

"Fight back." Her words are firm.

I don't answer her. Instead, I scrub the back of my hand across my nose and sniff. Fight back. I almost snort. Fighting back has never gotten me anywhere. It only makes things worse.

Dear Henry Stone...

We write regarding your application...

We regret to inform you...

My eyes trace the swirl of ink spiralling up Zara's arm. "Why the DNA helix?"

She traces the elegant, curving pattern with gentle fingers. Gentle.

That's not a word I'd ever associate with Zara.

Sure enough, when her eyes swing back to mine, they're hard. "None of your fucking business." She gets to her feet. "I warned you not to fuck it up." Her lip curls. "Great job so far." She pivots on her heel, heavy boots thudding away as she retreats.

She only makes it five steps before I say, "You were an Outsider, too."

Her entire body freezes, and she's balanced on the balls of her feet like she's poised to attack.

Sweat breaks out on my upper lip. Why did I say that?

She turns, slowly—really slowly—pink eyes narrowed to slits. "Get up."

I do, but only because I sense now isn't the time to push any boundaries.

She strides over to me and gets right in my face. "Who told you that?"

"I..." I pause. Carmichael told me, but telling Zara that seems like a betrayal. Instead, I shrug, and say, "Just heard it around."

Her eyebrow quirks, and her voice comes out low, almost a whisper. "You repeat that to the other trainees and I swear on my magic I'll make your life a living fucking nightmare."

I gulp.

"You got that?"

I nod.

"Good." She spins away again.

"I don't get it. If you're like me, why are you so—"

She whirls round fast and jams her forearm against my windpipe.

The air's knocked out of me and my back strikes the wall, hard.

Her face is inches from mine, her teeth bared. "Listen to me, you cowardly little wanker. Don't make the mistake of thinking that because we both have the Sight and we're both Outsiders, we're the same. We're not. I'm *nothing* like you."

"Okay, Jesus—"

She presses harder on my throat and my words choke off. "That's my point. It's not okay. Being an Outsider makes getting through training even tougher. The executioners are waiting for you to mess up, for your guard to slip. You need to make them respect you. Make them fear you. You think that scene in the dining hall did you any favours?"

"Myles—"

She shoves me back into the wall and backs away.

I cough and wheeze as the pressure on my trachea abates.

"I'm going to give you the same advice I gave Yakhontov," she says in that same quiet, steely tone. "Toughen the fuck up. If you can't do that, there's no point in you being here."

When I can breathe again, I straighten, and say, "Okay."

Zara gives a short, sharp nod and stalks away from me. When she gets to the end of the corridor, she pauses, but doesn't look back. "When I told Carmichael you were powerful, I meant it. Use it, before it's too late."

Then she's gone.

When I'm sure she isn't coming back, I take my parents' wedding rings from beneath my T-shirt and squeeze them, hard.

Dad's voice echoes through my mind.

There's nothing stronger than family.

I promise you I can do this. My fist squeezes tighter until the metal bands bite into my skin. I promise I'll make Razor pay for what he did to you.

I promise.

CHAPTER 16

The next day, Zara lines all the trainees up in the training room—a boxy, black-marbled space. A row of silver targets sweeps across the back wall. Groups of silver sparing dummies stand off to one side. Three smaller versions of the ring wait in the centre. She strides up and down the line while she speaks, saying, "You all Manifested at different times, so I'd like to start training by working out where each of you sits in terms of magical proficiency."

My stomach sinks. I only Manifested two days ago, so I'm sure everyone here's been a witch longer than me. How much more advanced are they?

Zara's thick-soled boots *thud-thud-thud* on the black marble floor. "Let's start with a simple question. Who's cast a spell before?"

Every hand goes up—every hand apart from mine.

The sinking feeling in my stomach intensifies.

From the corner of my eye, I spot Myles smirking at me.

My cheeks flush.

Zara stops in front of Myles. "You know how to cast a witch-light?"

Myles's lip curls. "Of course. It's the simplest spell there is. Any witch worth their salt can cast one."

Zara arches an eyebrow. "That right? Let's see it then."

Myles rolls his frozen green eyes, holds up his hand—palm facing upwards—and says, "*Lux*." A steamy grey orb of light blossoms two inches above Myles's hand and casts dark shadows on the walls.

Zara nods. Do I detect a flicker of disappointment in her gaze? "Good," she says. "Now extinguish it."

Myles frowns, narrowing his eyes at the smoky sphere. A few seconds pass, a bead of sweat forms on his forehead, and the light fades and disappears.

Zara makes her way down the line, asking each trainee to cast a witch-light.

They can all do it.

Femi casts a violet ball of witch-light so bright I have to squint my eyes. Layla's light's soft and sunshine yellow. Geek's spell glows sunset orange. Even Bianca—although her hand tremors and the word *Lux* comes out shaky—manages to conjure a weak white light.

The air stinks of sharp ozone, which I'm quickly coming to associate with the scent of spent magic.

Zara halts in front of me.

My gut tightens.

"Your turn," she says.

"I've never—"

"Try." Her tone's stern. "Hold out your hand. Visualise what you want your magic to do, then speak the spell."

I swallow.

Zara pitches her voice low. "Remember what I said. Use it."

Oh, that's right. I'm supposed to be powerful.

I set my jaw. "Fine." My hand comes up and, to my surprise, it doesn't tremble. I hesitate. What happens if it doesn't work? What happens if I fail? There's a slight shake in my fingers now.

Zara lowers her voice, but she needn't have bothered because her words still carry. "This is the easiest spell I'll ever ask you to cast. You shouldn't have any trouble with it." The silver rings around her Sighted irises glint in a silent challenge.

She's right.

I *am* powerful. That's what everyone keeps telling me. This should be simple. It will be. I close my eyes and focus on summoning the most brilliant, blinding witch-light I can think of, then I open my eyes and flex my fingers a little. "*Lux.*"

Nothing happens.

Myles sniggers.

A knot forms in my chest.

Any witch worth their salt...

"Again," Zara says.

I take a deep breath and, on the exhale, try again. "*Lux.*"

Still nothing.

Femi gives a long, low chuckle.

The knot tightens.

Any witch worth their salt...

Geek steps out of line and strolls over to me. "Come on, mate. You can do this."

"Back in line, Townsend." Zara says.

Geek bites his tongue and gets back in line.

Zara gets in my face. "One last chance today. Conjure. The. Witch-light."

The corner of Layla's mouth twitches up, then her face goes blank again.

My cheeks blaze with heat. For some reason, Layla's reaction embarrasses me far more than Myles's sniggering and Femi's chuckling. I want to scratch at my scar, but I know that would be a mistake.

Any witch worth their salt...

Zara would berate me for picking in front of everyone.

"Witch-light. Now." Zara says.

I roll my neck to ease some of the tension there, not that it helps much. Come on, come on. I've got to do this. I close my eyes again. A vision of the perfect witch-light forms in my mind. I take my time, enriching the mental apparition until I can almost smell the chlorine reek of ozone pouring off it. My eyelids flicker open. "*Lux*."

A slight tingle starts in my chest, a spark of static flying down my arm. The back of my throat tastes weird, like old pennies, and a sharp tang scents the air.

It's happening.

Yes!

The spell's going to work.

It's going to—

Something catches in my chest, and the odd pins and needles feeling stutters and dies.

A faint green, foul smelling, mist rises off the surface of my outstretched palm, eddies up to the ceiling and dissipates.

"Useless." Myles says.

The heat in my cheeks spreads down into my throat, my chest, my limbs, until my entire body burns with it.

Zara crosses her arms and shakes her head. "Well, that was disappointing. I don't know why I bother." She goes to turn away.

"Wait." The word comes out high and strangled. "I can do it."

She waits.

"*Lux*," I say.

Nothing.

"*Lux*." More desperate now. A slow pressure builds in my head.

Nothing.

"*Lux*." To my shame, the word carries an edge of panic and the pressure behind my eyes builds and builds and builds.

Nothing.

Zara clicks her tongue and makes her way back up the line.

Building and building and building.

Zara says, "I'm going to—"

I cut across her, the pressure morphing into a sharp, stabbing pain. "I said wait."

Snap.

My eyes blaze with malign fire and the world shifts on its axis.

All their auras come into stark relief. Myles sheathed in grey. Femi blazing violet. Layla shining yellow. Geek glowing orange. Bianca wreathed in soft white.

And Zara.

Zara's aura's blinding, the harsh pink light stretching into the corners of the room.

I know what this is.

The Sight.

The multicoloured glow gets brighter and brighter and brighter until I can't make out any other details in the room. My heart hammers, my entire body alive with power—a frantic *buzz* that sets my nerve endings alight and makes my core sing. "Fuck." I breathe. "This is..." I can't think of a word strong enough for what this is.

Incredible.

Amazing.

Fucking fantastic.

A delighted crow of laughter erupts from my throat.

I'm invincible.

I'm shitting indestructible.

It's—I'm—

A sudden wave of all consuming exhaustion sweeps over me. "This... is..." My eyelids grow heavy... and heavier... and heavier. "What—what's happening?" I stagger to the side on weak legs, my hands slamming into the wall.

Zara appears next to me. "You need to switch it off, Stone."

I slide down the wall, still burning like a dying phoenix, sweat pouring off me. "I don't know how."

"Switch it off." Zara's voice sounds distant.

All the aura colours blur together like a smoothie tossed around in a blender, and I say, "I can't. It won't..."

"What is it? What's wrong with him?" Bianca's voice is too loud.

"Switch it off."

Still burning.

Still blurring.

That's when darkness saunters up to me and drags me under.

Someone slaps me hard around the face. "Get up, Stone."

It's Zara.

Of course it is.

I come to slumped against the wall where I passed out.

The other trainees are gone, so it's just Zara and I left in the training room.

"Wha—ugh—what happened?" I shake my groggy head. It's like I went ten rounds with Anthony Joshua.

Zara, still crouched over me, says, "You used too much magic too soon. You weren't ready for it."

My brow furrows. "Magic? But I didn't cast anything."

She rolls her eyes and straightens. "You used your Sight. What do you think it runs on? Pixie farts?"

I push myself further up the wall until I'm standing on wobbly legs. "Will it always be like this."

"Like what?"

"Exhausting."

Zara gives her head a firm shake. "The more you practice, the less tired you'll be when you cast."

"I feel like shit."

She produces a syringe loaded with a thick, viscous substance.

I recognise it. It's the same stuff Carmichael used to heal my arm back at the house.

Liquid silver.

"I don't make a habit of doing this," Zara says, "but you've used up all your power and you'll be no good for days otherwise." She nods towards my arm.

I hold it out for her.

She jabs the needle into my skin much harder than necessary.

I flinch.

"Don't be pathetic. It's just a scratch." Zara jams the plunger down.

The familiar cold spreads through my veins, warming, and warming until it's like my blood's on fire. The odd sensation fades as quickly as it came and my head clears.

I stretch, my limbs full of strength and power. "I feel like I've just slept for days. That's bloody good stuff."

Zara disposes of the needle in a neon-yellow medical waste disposal bin in the corner of the room. When she turns back to me, her pink eyes are hard. "Yeah, well, don't get used to it. Like I said, I don't make a habit of using that stuff."

"Why not? If it makes—"

"I don't want you relying on it. There'll come a day when you're out in the field and there's no liquid silver to hand. What then?"

I remain silent because I don't have an answer to that.

She continues. "You need to get used to pain and exhaustion. That's half of what being an executioner is." She tilts her head towards the medical waste bin. "That stuff makes you soft. I need you to be strong."

Makes sense, I guess. Typical Zara, making us suffer. Making things harder than they need to be. "I—"

"Speaking of which," she cuts across me for the second time, "what the hell was that earlier."

My face scrunches up. "What, the Sight thing? I don't know what happened. I can't control it."

Zara clicks her tongue. "Not that. Your piss-poor performance with the witch-light."

I flush. "I've never cast anything before. What do you expect?" That last bit comes out more coldly than I anticipated, and I regret it instantly.

Zara's entire body tenses and she stalks over to me with slow, deliberate steps. "I *expect* you to be able to cast the simplest spell in the history of witchcraft when I ask you to."

My embarrassment gives way to a flash of anger, the heat coursing through my chest spiking. "Did you cast it first time?"

"Yes." She speaks the word plainly, with no hint of pride or conceit, just stating a simple fact.

Something inside me deflates.

Of *course* she cast it first time.

"I'm only going to give you one chance on this." She narrows her eyes and places a firm hand on her hip. "Either you cast that spell for me by tomorrow morning, or you're done here."

Ice freezes me to the spot.

Done?

No.

She can't.

My knees tremble a little.

I need this.

I hate you, and I'll never forgive you.

I *need* it.

My fists clench at my sides. "You can't kick me out."

She sets her jaw. "Excuse me?"

"You can't do that. I'm top in the ratings. I need—"

"You *need* to toughen the fuck up is what you need to do. Especially if you want to hang on to the top spot. How long do you think you'll stay there if you carry on like this?"

Her words sting like she slapped me round the face again, and I'm stunned into silence.

She brushes past me and, without so much as a backward glance, says, "I'm only going to say this one more time. Get your shit together, or get out. That's how it has to be."

The door to the training room swings shut behind her.

The only thing I can focus on—the only thing echoing through my skull—is Zara's warning.

Either you cast that spell for me by tomorrow morning, or you're done here.

CHAPTER 17

Geek lets out a heavy sigh and strolls across my room until he's standing next to me. "Come on. It's easy. Look." He holds out his hand. "*Lux*." Orange light blooms across his palm. "See?"

I clench my teeth and rub at a sore spot on my neck. "We've been at this for two hours. I'm not getting it."

I'd told Geek about Zara's threat earlier, and he'd promised to help me learn how to cast a witch-light after dinner. Two hours. Two hours, and I hadn't even managed to produce that cloud of noxious steam I'd conjured back in the training room.

Either you cast that spell for me by tomorrow morning, or you're done here.

My heart rate quickens. "What if I can't do it?"

He claps me on the shoulder then backs up a few steps. "You can. Try again."

"What's the point?"

He slashes a hand through the air. "No way. Fuck that. I don't do pity parties. Any witch can cast a witch-light, and you're not just any witch. You're Sighted, for fuck's sake. This should be a walk in the park for someone like you,"

Someone like me.

Primrose's words from the night of her death drift back to me.

Never met someone like me before, that's all.

I've got to do this.

For my parents.

For Primrose.

Geek's right. This should be easy.

"Just focus on what you have to do," he says.

I close my eyes for the hundredth time and visualise a stunning green witch-light.

It's going to work this time. I'm sure of it.

"*Lux*." I say.

I stare at my empty hand.

"Oh, Jesus, come on." Geek rakes a hand through his hair, tousling his already tousled dark curls.

Still staring. "*Lux, lux, lux.*"

Still empty.

I let out a howl of frustration and kick the corner of my desk. Pain—blunt and numbing—spreads through my toes, up my ankle and makes me squeal. I hop around on one foot, swearing like a docker, until the agony abates, then I sink down onto the bed and rest my head in my hands.

When Geek speaks, his voice sounds quiet and flat. "I don't know what else to suggest, mate."

"You tried," I mumble into my fingers.

"There you are. I've been looking for you guys everywhere."

I glance up.

Bianca leans against the doorframe at the entrance to my room.

"Hey," I say, the word hollow.

"What are you doing?" she asks.

I briefly explain what happened with Zara earlier today.

Her eyes go wide. "She can't do that. You're in first place."

"That's what I said, but apparently she can."

Bianca walks into the room and lowers herself onto the bed beside me. "Well, then we'll just have to teach you how to cast it."

Geek, now slouched against the wall with one foot propped up behind him, says, "Good luck with that. What do you think I've been trying to do?"

I shoot him a venomous look.

His eyes flick away from me. "Sorry, pal. It's been a long day."

Bianca gets to her feet again. "What have you tried so far?"

Geek gives her a rundown of our progress—or *lack* of progress.

Bianca laughs.

I've never heard her laugh before, not properly, like this. It's a musical, sweet sound.

"Well, that's where you're going wrong," she says.

Geek frowns at her. "What do you mean?"

Bianca motions for me to get to my feet.

I comply.

"Magic isn't just about the what. It's about the why, too."

"The why?" I ask.

She bobs her head and tucks her short hair behind her ears. "You need to think about *why* you want to use the spell or—more precisely—what's driving you to use the spell emotionally."

"Clap-trap." Geek says in a huffy tone.

She shrugs. "It's how Mother explained it to me on the night I Manifested."

Geek and I share a look. Somehow, the idea of Katya—cold, clinical Katya—discussing emotions is ludicrous.

The corner of Bianca's mouth lifts, like she read our minds. "Ironic, I know. She's not exactly the warmest person."

"You can say that again," I say.

We all laugh.

Bianca sobers first. "Close your eyes, Henry."

I do.

"Now, think about why you're here."

Why I'm here.

This isn't over.

Your mum and I—we're witches, and you're one too.

I hate you, and I'll never forgive you.

"Think about what drives you."

What drives me?

That's easy.

One simple word.

Revenge.

"Now cast."

I open my eyes and splay my clenched fingers. "*Lux.*"

Magic stirs in my chest, and this time, the connection's strong. Pins and needles race down my arm and the hairs there stand on end. My heart beats so loud blood pounds in my ears.

The smell of ozone.

The taste of copper.

A flash—

And then... finally, a bright green, perfectly formed orb of witch-light hovers in the air, just above my palm.

We stare at the soft sphere in silent shock.

Eventually, I say, "I did it."

The witch-light fades.

Bianca beams at me.

Geek punches the air and whoops. "Try again."

"*Lux.*" Another ball of witch-light replaces the first.

Bianca chuckles. "Again."

I cast the spell five more times, then stifle a huge yawn. Remembering what Zara said about casting too much magic being tiring for inexperienced witches—and not wanting to repeat my earlier fainting episode—I say, "I think that's enough for now. Thank you," I yawn again. "Both of you."

Bianca gives me a shy smile, her cheeks flushing pink. "You're welcome."

"At least Zara can't kick you out now," Geek says.

My joy's marred by a slight hint of trepidation.

He's wrong.

If I know anything about Zara, it's that she's unpredictable and unforgiving.

I might have survived this time, but that means nothing.

It would've been more accurate to say Zara can't kick me out *yet*.

Zara calls me to her office early the next morning.

I shuffle through the door, my stomach a tangled mess of nerves.

She's sitting behind a mahogany desk, pink gel pen in hand, marking up some documents.

The sight jars me.

Zara doesn't belong in an office. She belongs on the battle-field.

"You wanted to see me," I say, forcing my voice to remain steady.

She caps the pen and throws it down on the desk before leaning back in her chair and lacing her fingers behind her head. "You figure out how to cast that spell yet?"

I nod, not trusting myself to speak.

Zara smirks, stands, and crosses the room, standing three feet away from me. "Prove it."

I take a deep breath and hold out my hand.

Shit.

Please let this work. Please don't let last night be a fluke.

"Get on with it, Stone. I don't have all day."

I nod again, and focus, like Bianca taught me.

Why am I here?

I hate you and I'll never forgive you.

What's driving me?

Revenge.

"*Lux*," I say. The witch-light roars to life, the emerald-green orb bright and strong.

The ghost of a smile touches Zara's lips.

I extinguish the witch-light.

"Well done," she says.

I can't help my own half-smile. "Was that a compliment?"

"Don't let it go to your head."

"So, you're letting me stay?"

She shrugs. "For now. Piss off and get ready for breakfast."

I turn away, beaming, and head back towards the door.

"It reminds me why I'm here and what I'm fighting for," she says.

I twist back to face her. "What?"

"You asked about my tattoo. That's why I got it."

I don't know what to say to that, so I just leave, still grinning from ear to ear.

I've got a second chance, and I'm not going to waste it.

Chapter 18

"**K**eep your guard up, Stone," Zara says.

A month's passed since I cast my first witch-light for Zara and she agreed to let me stay, "For now." A month of crying myself to sleep, a month of nightmares featuring my parents' animated corpses, a month of waking to bloodied sheets and bleeding scars. And a month of training.

I stand opposite Geek in the training room now. It smells of fresh sweat and the chlorine-sharp ozone scent of spent magic. Every day's the same. Awake at six, breakfast at seven, and we're all in the training room by eight. We train in alternating pairs—throwing kicks and punches at the heavy bags in one corner, or firing spells at the line of silver targets in the area sectioned off for shooting practice—from eight until twelve-thirty. From twelve-thirty until one-thirty we break for lunch in the dining hall. From one-thirty until six, we're back in the training room, sealed inside one of the small silver circles with our training partner, ready to spar.

This is the worst part of the day.

I adjust my stance, bending my elbows at a ninety-degree angle and holding my fists close to my face.

Geek bounces lightly on his feet. "Think you can beat me this time?"

I doubt it. I haven't yet.

"Conjure your witch-gauntlets," Zara says.

Six shouts of "*Eryx*," echo through the space.

I'm still not used to the way magic feels when I use it. The intense prickling sensation that blossoms in my chest, flows down my arms, and into my hands; the way sharp ozone stings my nostrils; the metallic taste of ancient pennies coating my throat. The sensory overload doesn't last long, then shimmering emerald-green light envelops my closed fists from knuckles to wrist.

Geek's raised fists shimmer, too, sheathed in rippling orange energy.

"Ready," Zara says.

No. My fists tremble, but only a little.

"Begin."

Geek darts forward, aiming an uppercut straight at my chin.

I tuck my chin out of the way, pivoting from the hip and slamming a roundhouse kick into his ribs.

He grunts, dancing back.

We circle each other.

Zara strides past. "Are you two going to spar, or piss about all day?"

I lunge at Geek with a double jab-cross combination.

He conjures three small barriers around his gauntlets—blocking my punches—and counters with an elbow strike, smashing me across the jaw.

I see stars and spit blood.

"Thought you were a martial arts expert, Stone?" Zara taunts.

I ignore her. My face, armpits and back drip with sweat. Resetting my stance, I lash out with a swift front kick.

Geek dodges at the last second, grabs my leg under his arm and clamps it to his side. He pummels my stomach with three brutal rabbit-punches.

Pain flares in my abdomen, and I'm forced to clench my teeth to contain a scream.

Geek ducks low and sweeps my other leg from beneath me.

My back slams into the unforgiving marble; and the wind's forced out of me.

"Townsend wins *again*," Zara says, with a little too much emphasis on the again for my liking. She shakes her head and stalks over to the circle next to ours, where Myles has Layla in a headlock, and she struggles to break free.

"Better luck next time, mate." Geek holds out his hand to help me up.

Angry heat boils beneath my skin. I bat his hand away, coil into a ball with my legs overhead, and spring off the floor. I land on my feet, throwing out an open palm. "*Dis.*" A bright burst of green light—which Zara calls a witch-strike—explodes against Geek's chest.

He stumbles back.

I keep up with him, executing a perfect spinning back kick, my heel sinking deep into his stomach.

Geek's feet leave the floor, his body arcing through the air. There's a flash of Zara's rose pink magic as he crosses the seal and lands on his back, his torso sticking out of the circle.

I stare, open-mouthed.

Shit.

I actually won.

Bianca catches my eye. The shiner on her cheek—courtesy of Femi—well, shining. She smiles at me.

I smile back.

"Okay." Zara claps her hands once. "That's time."

Geek clambers to his feet, rubbing his abdomen. "Wouldn't kill you to let us use some liquid silver once in a while."

Zara puts on a simpering tone. "Aw. Did didums get a boo-boo? What, want me to wipe your arse for you, too? Suck it up, Townsend."

Geek grumbles under his breath.

"Besides," Zara says. "Pain's character building. When it's just you and your target in a fight to the death, you won't always have time to inject yourself with liquid silver."

Geek ignores her, and claps me on the shoulder. "Well done, pal."

"About time." There's a hint of a smile on Zara's face. She turns to address all of us. "Right. Your first official bouts will take place in the ring tomorrow at nine o'clock sharp."

My stomach drops.

Our first bouts.

In the ring.

In front of the executioners.

"Everyone at COVEN has voted for who they want to face each other," Zara says. "The results are as follows."

Not Myles.

Please, not Myles.

Anyone but Myles.

"First pair is Abimbola and Jabara."

Femi and Layla. My heart skips a beat. Please let it be Bianca or Geek.

Please.

"Second."

Bianca or Geek. Bianca or Geek.

"Townsend and Yakhontov."

My heart skips a beat.

No.

That means—

"That leaves Hedges and Stone."

My fingers go to my scar and pick, pick, pick.

Zara narrows her eyes at the movement.

My panic's so severe I don't care.

I've got to fight Myles, who hasn't lost a single bout in training. Myles who, the last time we sparred, beat me to a pulp so bloody it looked like someone had spilled a can of red paint on me. Myles, who hated my guts because I refused his offer of friendship.

And what better way to get revenge than to defeat me in front of everyone, likely knocking me off the top spot in the ratings?

Across the room, Myles's face splits into a wide smirk, his frosty, pale green eyes boring into mine. He mouths, "You're going down."

After dinner—a banquet of tender roast beef, crispy golden potatoes, sage and onion stuffing, and all the trimmings—Bianca, Geek and I sit cross-legged on the floor in my room, playing a friendly game of Texas Hold'Em.

I can't stop thinking about food. I'm constantly hungry, and I know it's not just me. All the trainees are feeling it. We're all eating more and sleeping like the dead. Zara was right about magic being draining.

I'm shattered.

Geek does some fancy shuffling manoeuvre, passing the cards from one hand to the other in a blur. He deals two cards and lays out the spread.

The cards swim before my eyes. I can't concentrate. All I can think about—apart from my next meal—is Myles. His smug smirk, his creepy celery-coloured eyes, and the three words he'd mouthed across the training room, full of malice.

You're going down.

"Henry," Geek says.

"What?"

"Your move."

"Oh—uh—" My stomach's doing complicated somersaults and the room's stuffy as hell. "I fold." I place my cards face down on the floor.

"You're not even trying," Geek says.

"Is it really warm in here?" I pull the collar of my T-shirt away from my skin.

Geek shrugs. "It's fine."

"Is it tomorrow?" Bianca asks.

I don't answer.

She leans over and gives my leg a reassuring squeeze. "You'll be fine."

"You think so?"

"I do," she says, brushing her thumb across my knee.

My gaze drifts down to her hand.

She snatches it back, a slight blush colouring her cheeks, before returning her attention to her cards.

Why's she blushing?

Hang on.

No, surely not.

Does she—

"I don't know, mate." Geek considers the spread, and the cards in his hand. "Myles is a machine. I'd be shitting through the eye of a needle if I was you."

Bianca shoots him a glare.

Geek looks up. "What?"

"You don't think I can beat him?" I try to suppress the quiver of hurt in my voice.

"Do you?" he counters.

I bite my lip and let out a heavy sigh.

"Think yourself lucky." Bianca picks up her cards—puts them down again—picks them up. "At least you're not going up against Femi."

She's got a point. What Femi lacks in finesse, he more than makes up for with raw power. I don't want to say it, but Bianca doesn't stand a chance.

The ensuing silence sours the mood.

Bianca throws her cards down. "I don't want to play anymore. I think I'm just going to go to bed."

Geek stifles a yawn. "Me too."

We get to our feet.

Bianca walks from the room without looking back.

When she's gone, Geek nudges me in the ribs. "Reckon you're in there, pal."

My brow furrows. "What?"

"Bianca. She likes you."

"Yeah, I like her too. We're friends."

"No, numb-nuts. I mean, she *likes* you. As in, 'doodling Mrs Stone all over her notebooks and thinking about you in the shower,' likes you."

I don't know what to say to that, so I say nothing. Is he right? She'd blushed when she touched my knee. And I'd wondered. I like Bianca. She's gentle and sweet and kind, and attractive in a girl-next-door kind of way. But even if I did fancy her—and I'm not saying I do—a relationship's a distraction I can't afford. I'm here for one reason and one reason only.

Become an executioner.

Kill Razor.

Avenge my parents.

Bianca's a friend, and that's all she can ever be.

Geek holds up his fist, and I bump it. "Laters, lover boy."

"Piss off."

He shoots me his signature pretend finger guns as he leaves. Then I'm alone, all thoughts of Bianca banished.

I don't know why—because he never used imaginary finger guns—but the banter with Geek reminds me of Jez.

Jez.

My chest's tight.

What's he doing now? Has he found out about my parents? Is he wondering where I am and why I haven't called? I can almost hear his voice, like he's stood right next to me.

Some best mate you are, Henry.

What if—

Stop.

I've got to stop this.

It's like Carmichael said.

Your old life is over. You need to let it go and embrace your new life. Here. With us.

All I can think about is tomorrow, and my bout against Myles.

Can I beat him?

What if I lose?

No.

No, I have to win. I have to. If I want to stay here, if I want to achieve my goal, I don't have a choice.

I curl my fingers around my parents' wedding rings. Please, let me beat him. I will. I know I will.

Zara leads us into the ring from the antechamber.

All the executioners have shown up to watch, like the bloodthirsty Roman spectators of history showing up for the carnage at the Colosseum. As we enter, they cheer, whoop and jeer in equal measure.

The sound hurts my ears, and my heart uses my ribs to brush up on its tap-dancing skills.

Zara strides into the ring while we wait at its edge. She addresses the executioners in a loud voice. "Today's the day you've all been waiting for. The first round of bouts."

The answering cheer's so loud that it vibrates in my chest.

I spot Carmichael at the front of the crowd. My stomach lurches, and bile threatens to choke me, but I swallow it back.

Beside me, Bianca twists her diamond ring around her finger.

Twist, twist, twist.

She catches me staring at her, and I look away. Geek's theory about notebooks and showers is fresh in my mind.

Twist, twist, twist.

Zara says, "The rules are simple. Get knocked out of the ring, you lose. If you're unable to continue, you lose."

Unable to continue.

I imagine myself beaten, bloodied, and laid out on the ring floor, Myles towering over me, gloating.

"No second chances. No best of three. You only get one shot. And in our time-honoured tradition"—Zara pauses and grins up at her colleagues—"you can vote for who you think will win each bout."

Cold creeps down my spine. The baked bean incident hadn't done me any favours. The chances of everyone—any-one—voting for me are non-existent.

"First up, it's Stone versus Hedges."

My legs won't work. I can't walk to the ring if my legs don't work. I can't do this, I can't—

Geek claps me on the shoulder and says, *sotto voce*, "Good luck."

Good luck. That's it? Good luck. Not, "You've got this," or, "You'll smash it," just good luck. My muscles tense. I want to call him out, to tell him I'll prove him wrong, but I don't. Instead, I shoot him a weak smile and say, "Thanks."

The executioners cast their votes.

The TV screens fade to black, then flash.

Poll results:

1. Myles Hedges (91%)

2. Henry Stone (9%)

At least a few people voted for me.

"Stone, Hedges," Zara says. "Let's go."

Myles practically sprints into the ring. He bounces on his feet and cracks his neck. "Scared, Stone?"

I know I should snap back with some kind of witty rejoinder, but I'm sure that if I speak, I'll throw up, so I ignore him. Someone must've replaced my legs with blancmange, because my slow walk into the ring's unsteady.

Myles and I face each other.

He says, "You're looking rather peaky. Sure you're up to this?"

My cheeks burn and I want to scratch my scar. I want to run. Somehow, I hold my ground, resist scratching, plant my feet, and sink into a firm stance.

Zara approaches us. Her eyes flick to Myles, then to me. "You both understand the rules?"

Miles gives an almost imperceptible nod.

"Yeah," I say.

She shoots Myles a sideways glance, narrowing her eyes at him. "I don't reward dirty tactics. Understood?"

Another almost-nod from Myles.

The air pressure shifts. My ears pop, exactly as they had when my parents sealed the chalk circle for my Manifestation.

My Manifestation.

The night I lost everything.

The night of smeared blood.

Searing pain.

Loss.

Death.

Stop.

Focus.

"Ready?" Zara asks.

"Ready," Myles says.

I nod.

"Begin."

I don't have time to think.

Myles's hand shoots out. "*Dis.*"

The dark grey witch-strike smashes me square in the gut, the impact rattling my bones. I collapse and crash to the ground. Hot, sickening pain radiates out from my stomach.

Bianca shouts something from the side-lines, but I can't make it out over the *thud, thud, thud* of blood pounding in my head.

Myles fires again, and another witch-strike barrels towards me.

I roll to the side, narrowly avoiding the rush of speeding air, the heat, the sparks. I rush to my feet, retaliating with a witch-strike of my own.

Myles throws up his arm. "*Obstructionum.*" The air in front of him ripples and curves. A smoky barrier springs up in front of him, and he blocks my attack with ease. He counters.

I conjure an emerald-green shield and block the strike, but the ferocity of Myles's spell forces me back a step.

He fires a fast volley of strikes. One, two, three, zooming straight at me.

Crash.

I stumble back again.

Crash.

My mind's scattered, and my shield wavers, my feet veering dangerously close to the edge of the ring.

Crash.

The effort of holding the spell in place under Myles's onslaught's too much. My barrier crumples like an old tin can squashed by the wheel of an articulated lorry. My arms ache and my body's heavy.

"*Flagellum.*" Myles's witch-whip coils around my ankle, and he jerks his hand back.

The ground whisks out from under me and my back slams against the hard marble floor, all the air rushing from my lungs, the circle's edge inches from my head. The roar of the crowd's loud, but my frantic pulse is louder.

Footsteps approach.

I'm too winded to move.

A long, dark shadow falls across my body.

Myles looms over me and, pitching his voice low, says, "I'm going to make you suffer."

My blood freezes in my veins.

I'm going to make you suffer.

Those words. The same words Razor uttered right before he tortured me. Suddenly, it's not Myles who towers over me, but Razor. I swear I'm staring into his cold, black eyes, not Myles's frozen green ones.

A hair-raising shriek erupts from my throat.

Myles—Razor—laughs, and the room echoes with it as the executioners join in.

He raises his hand.

A flash of bruised grey light.

Searing pain.

Another.

Burning agony.

I scream.

Another.

All the lights go out at once.

Chapter 19

Whenever I think about my bout with Myles, my cheeks burn with shame, and I still hear the harsh echo of mocking laughter. I've fought in two more bouts since then. The first against Layla. She beat me in five minutes. The second against Bianca. I won that one, but everyone beats Bianca, so it doesn't make me feel any better.

The worst part is, my rating's suffered. I'm in fifth place now. Myles is first.

I don't know if I'm imagining it, but every time I'm around the other executioners—passing them in the corridors, sitting near them in the dining hall, when they're watching me in the ring—I'm sure they pity me.

That's why I've spent all my free time outside of training holed up in my room, reading.

I'm about to read now, in fact. The book Carmichael had labelled fiction.

Myth & Magic: The Truth About Sorcerers, Demons and the Legend of King Arthur.

Fiction's always a reliable escape for me when things get tough. Well, things are tough now, that's for sure. Escape sounds good.

I collapse onto my bed and bury my head into the soft, downy pillows. The book's heavy, but its weight's comforting, like a thick duvet in winter.

I crack the cover, breathing in the musty, almost sweet scent of old books. The smell draws a long, contented sigh from me, and all the tension leaves my body.

I settle in to read.

> *In days long past, days of myth and times of legend, four species walked the earth. First were the humans, known for their connection to nature and their sensory acuity. Second were the witches, famous for their ability to transform words into power and bring magic into the world. Third were the sorcerers, lauded for their wisdom, and their affinity with the light. Fourth were the demons, revered for their cunning and their dominion over the darkness.*

> *These species lived in harmony and made their home in the Kingdom of Camelot, where all were welcome and they shunned none.*

> *Shunned none until The Divide, until—*

A loud crash startles me, and the book falls from my hands, landing on the bedspread.

"What the—"

Crash.

Louder this time, like wood breaking against a wall. It's coming from the room next to mine.

Layla's room.

I'm tense, waiting for a third crash, but the only sound is the ticking of my clock. What the fuck's she doing in there?

A scraping sound makes me flinch. Is she dragging something across the floor? All I want to do is read, lose myself in the dry, musky pages, but I won't be able to concentrate on reading now.

Layla screams.

Without thinking, I spring off the bed, throw my door open, and jog to Layla's room. I knock on the door.

The scraping sound stops. A few seconds pass. The door opens.

I almost don't recognise her.

She's usually so groomed, so poised, but not tonight. Tonight, she wears smudged makeup and mascara-streaked tear trails mar her face like thick black veins. She rakes her fingers through her dishevelled hair, across her face, and blurs the mascara trails to a dull grey bruise. "What the hell do you want?" she asks, her voice ragged.

"You were screaming."

"So?"

"I'm trying to read."

"I don't care."

She's such a stuck up—I take a deep breath and tamp down my feelings. She's obviously been crying, and I might detest her, but I don't enjoy seeing anyone upset. "Are you all right?"

"Do I look all right?" She points at her tear-streaked face, sniffs, then says, in a calmer tone. "What's it to you, anyway? We're on different sides, remember?"

I don't respond. I don't know what to say.

Layla's deep red lips purse. "Just go away."

I peek into her room. I'd caught odd glimpses before; the bed made with hospital corners, the endless array of brightly coloured lipsticks and nail polish bottles and powders all lined up like soldiers, and the pressed uniform laid out for the following day.

It doesn't look like that now.

Her room's a swamp of tangled sheets and discarded shoes, the bed dragged away from the wall, the wardrobe doors ripped open and spilling clothes like herniated intestines.

I bend at the waist and pick up a dog-eared copy of Ben Aaronovitch's *Rivers of London*.

The image of Primrose pouring over Jim Butcher's *Storm Front* back at the club flashes into my mind.

What is it with fit girls and fantasy lately?

My cheeks flush.

I shouldn't be thinking of Layla that way. She's an Insider. She's friends with Myles. She might be heart attack stunning, but—heart attack stunning?—where did that come from?

"Take a photo. It lasts longer," Layla snaps. "And put that book down."

Her words block out my irritating internal monologue. I place the book back where I found it. "What happened in here?" I ask.

She sweeps over to the wardrobe and crams the clothes back inside. She slams the door. "None of your business."

I step over the threshold. "Maybe I can—"

"Get out." She lunges for her desk, picks up a heavy-looking stapler, and launches it at me.

I duck, and the stapler sails over my head, crashing into the wall, leaving a crack in the wood panelling. "Jesus Christ. What's wrong with you?" I shout.

Layla puts a hand over her mouth and sinks to her knees. She breaks down, tears streaming from her eyes, her shoulders shaking with great, wracking sobs.

I don't know what to do. Part of me wants to go to her, wants to comfort her—even though she doesn't deserve it and she would probably scratch my eyes out with those long, crimson nails.

Layla's right. We're on different sides. Myles has treated me like shit, and she's aligned herself with him.

I should leave, but her tears and sobs stop me. I approach her with caution, like an unexploded bomb, and crouch beside her. "What is it? What's wrong?"

"Why would I tell you?" She sniffs again. "You and your little friends hate me."

"I don't hate you," I say, and—despite my earlier thoughts to the contrary—realise it's true. "I barely know you. Myles is the one I have a problem with."

Her eyes sharpen. "Don't look at me like that."

"Like what?"

"Like I'm some kind of damsel in distress."

"I'm not. I—"

"In case you forgot, I obliterated you in the ring."

"I remember." Heat floods my neck, and I look away. "I just wanted to help."

She snorts. "I don't need your help. I don't need anyone. Just get out."

"Fine." I get to my feet and turn my back on her, striding towards the door.

"Wait," she says, a slight tremble in her voice.

Despite myself, I do as she says.

She wipes her eyes. "I've lost my bracelet."

"Your bracelet?" I remember the thin silver band she spun round her wrist on our first day. "The one with the emeralds?"

She nods, a sad little bob of her head.

Am I being a mug? Probably. Why should I help her, after the way she's behaved?

When I speak, my voice sounds harder than I'd intended. "Oh, well. I'm sure Myles can buy you another one."

I expect her to yell at me, to scream obscenities. She doesn't. Instead, her face crumples like she's in pain. "It was my mother's."

A vice squeezes my stomach. It'd belonged to her mother. The vice presses tighter and tighter. "Is—is she—"

"Dead? Yeah."

My parents' wedding rings burn a hole into my chest, singeing my heart. "How?"

She stands and crosses to the desk. "Road traffic accident. Humph. Accident. That was the official verdict, anyway." Layla yanks open a draw, tugs out a pack of cleansing wipes and scrubs her face clean of makeup with quick sharp movements. "She was walking home from work when a drunk driver mounted the kerb."

"Did they go to prison? The driver?"

She takes a deep, steadying breath. "No. He got away with it."

"They didn't breathalyse him?"

"They did. The mortal courts considered the results inconclusive." Her words are coated with bitterness.

"I'm so sorry."

"So am I." She lets out a long huff. "To hear Dad tell it, Mum was one hell of a powerful witch, but I never got to see it. All because of that drunk driver. I know he killed her. That's why I'm here. I want to be just like her. Powerful. I want to get justice for people like her. For people who don't deserve to die. For the people left behind."

A gentle warmth blossoms in my chest. Her reasons for being here are so similar to mine. We've both lost a parent—or parents, in my case—and yet, she seems so… strong. How does she do it? "When did it happen?" I ask.

"You sure ask a lot of questions."

"Sorry," I say again.

She dumps the face wipe into the bin, her eyes red-rimmed. "It'll be a year next month."

"Does it—is it—does it ever stop hurting?"

She shrugs. "If I ever find out, I'll let you know."

I tuck my hands into my pockets and stare at the floor.

When I glance up again, her expression's softer. "You've lost someone recently?" she phrases it like a question, but it isn't really.

"I—" My throat's tight, an elastic band of tension cutting off my voice. My thumbnail finds the scar at my collarbones.

Pick.

Pick.

Pick.

"You don't have to tell me."

I swallow and lower my hand again. "I know you said you don't need help, but I think I know how we can find your bracelet."

She brightens. "How?"

"With a locater spell."

Her brow creases.

I stare at the little wrinkle between her eyebrows.

"Brilliant plan, but Zara isn't teaching us how to cast one of those until next week?"

It's my turn to shrug. "I read ahead."

"Oh, my God."

"What?"

"You're a swot." It sounds light, playful.

I chuckle. "I prefer the term studious."

She rolls her eyes. "Whatever. I'm not going to judge. I'm a swot, too. Not as bad as you though, clearly."

Smart, funny, and snarky. I'm learning all kinds of interesting things about Layla Jabara this evening.

"How does it work?" she asks.

"I need some of your hair," I say. "Wait, that sounded creepy."

She laughs—a melodic sound—then reaches up and plucks a strand of hair from her head and hands it to me, her fingertips brushing against mine.

The places where our skin touches tingle.

I loop the end of the shiny, dark hair around my index finger like a Yo-Yo string and pinch it between my thumb and forefinger. "*Layla armillam de invent.*" Pins and needles prickle down my arm and soft, green light pours from the pinch point of my fingers like liquid smoke. The light coats the hair, and it emits a dim, muted glow.

"Now what?" she asks.

"Now we find your bracelet." I concentrate on the glowing hair. "*Domine deduc me*."

The hair pulls taught, pointing like an arrow. I let the spell guide me, lead me out of Layla's room and down the corridor.

Layla falls into step beside me.

We go where the spell takes us; the light coating the hair, glowing brighter and brighter and brighter with every step.

You've lost someone recently?

I raise my free hand and slip my parents' rings from beneath my shirt. "These belonged to my mum and dad."

She doesn't speak, just watches me.

"They—um—they..."

"Really, you don't have to—"

"No. I—I want to, but I've never said it out loud."

Again, she's quiet.

I sniff, and my throat goes tight. "Someone killed them."

She grips my arm as we walk. "That's awful. What happened?"

"You sure ask a lot of questions," I say, mimicking her earlier words and her imperious tone.

She smiles, soft and sombre.

I tell her everything. It's halting, choked and watery, but I tell her. Primrose. Cecelia. Razor. Carmichael. My parents. All of it. When I finish, my cheeks are wet with tears and my body's leaden.

We round another corner in silence, and another.

Eventually, she says, "Hurts, doesn't it?"

"It's like I've got this thing living in my chest and it's clawing to get out."

Our fingers brush, and she gives my hand a single brief squeeze before dropping it again. "I know."

We reach the ring.

The strand of hair burns white, the light so bright that, when I blink, black spots cloud my vision.

"It's in here somewhere," I say.

Layla had fought with Bianca earlier today. It hadn't ended well for Bianca.

"Where?" The naked hope in her voice makes my chest ache.

I pinch the hair tighter. "*Inveniet.*"

The hair pulls me across the room, gives one final, bright pulse, and a corresponding glow answers. There, right in the corner. Layla's bracelet.

The hair disintegrates into nothing.

"Oh, thank God." Layla dashes over to the bracelet and scoops it up. Her fingers shake and she can't get the clasp to latch.

"Here." I take her delicate, warm wrist and fasten the clasp for her.

"Thank you." Her eyes shimmer. "Thank you." She throws her arms around me without warning.

I'm enveloped by her strong, sweet, woody scent, warm and spicy in equal measure. I hug her back, her smooth hair brushing my fingers. Heat spreads through my abdomen. "You're welcome."

She pulls back. "I can't believe you found it."

"It was nothing, really."

The light catches on the silver band of the ring.

The ring.

A reminder. Layla and I really are on different sides.

I back away. "Well, I'm glad I could help. I'm going to head back now."

"I'm sorry," she says.

My eyes widen. She never apologises for anything. "Sorry for what?"

"I know Myles can be... difficult."

"That's one way of putting it."

"He's just driven. He wants to impress his dad, and honestly, I think he's threatened by you."

I laugh at that. "I doubt it."

She lifts her shoulder. "We all saw you as a threat when we met you."

"Why?"

"The first day. The way the executioners reacted to you, because of your Sight—I think it freaked everyone out a bit."

Saw you as a threat. Freaked everyone out. She's speaking in the past tense. "And now you've realised how weak I am, is that it?" Even to my ears, my voice sounds bitter and pathetic.

"Hey. That's not fair. After the accident in the dining hall—"

"*Accident?* Myles tripped me on purpose."

"I told him he was out of order. He swore it was an accident."

"He's lying." I grind the words out.

"He's not what he seems. He's got a lot of baggage. His dad looks down on him, treats him like dirt. Myles just wants to impress him, so he acts tough."

"So, he gets a free pass to act like an arsehole, is that what you're saying?"

She rolls her wide, brown eyes. "Of course not. All I mean is—"

"I'm glad we found your bracelet. I'm going to go now."

"Henry, you don't have to—"

"Like you said, we're on different sides." I stride out of the ring.

What was I thinking, telling her about my parents? I must be mad. I know what'll happen now. She'll run straight to Myles and tell him everything about me, and he'll use it against me somehow.

What am I going to do?

One thing's for certain.

That's the last time I'll ever help Layla Jabara.

Chapter 20

The following evening, an executioner I don't recognise comes to my room and hands me a note from Zara. It reads:

Meet me in the training room. Thirty minutes.

That was half an hour ago.

I push through the door into the training room.

Zara stands in front of the row of silver targets set against the back wall. "Thirty minutes on the dot." She smirks. "Maybe there's hope for you yet."

I'm tired. It's been a long day and training was shit. My natural instinct to keep the peace is overwhelmed by a flash of anger. "If you only called me here to take the piss, then—"

She laughs, and it's genuine. "Holy fuck. So, you do have a little bite in there somewhere. There's definitely hope."

I can't help it. The corner of my mouth lifts. "So, what am I doing here so late?"

"You've mastered the basics. It's time for your first private session."

Shit.

I'd forgotten about these.

"You're going to teach me how to use the Sight?"

She nods.

My mind wanders back to the first time my Sight kicked in at COVEN. The bright lights of everyone's auras, the world swirling together in a sickening blend, the crushing exhaustion of using too much magic too quickly.

"Spit it out," Zara says.

My stomach squirms and I place my hand against my abdomen. "What?"

"Whatever it is that's got you so bent out of shape."

It takes a few moments for my next words to come out. "What... what if I pass out?"

She rolls her eyes. "Then I'll dose you up with liquid silver and we'll go again."

I wrinkle my nose. "I can't go through that again."

Zara's entire face puckers like she's taken a bite out of a particularly sour lemon, and I know it was the wrong thing to say.

"I—"

She cuts across me. "I only agreed to teach you this because I'm the only person that can. And because Carmichael asked me to, but I'd sooner be fucked sideways with a rusty spoon than waste any more time on you."

Again, whether it's tiredness or something else I'm not sure, but my usual passivity gives way to irritation. "You're wrong about me. I can do this."

She raises an eyebrow. "Prove it."

I clench my fists. "What do you want me to do?"

"Do you know how to summon the Sight?"

I hold up my hand and rock it back and forth. I think back to my first night here, in the canal underpass. "Carmichael explained it a little. He said to imagine something covering my eyes, then to imagine it being whisked away."

"Show me."

"I haven't done it since."

"Show. Me."

I bite my tongue, and do as she says, conjuring the image of something gauzy covering the training room. Then I visualise it drifting up and away.

The weird shift in my head and the bright light of Zara's rose-pink aura tells me it's worked.

"Good," she says, walking round me in a slow circle.

"Now what?" I ask.

"We start simple," she says. "I'm going to cast a duplication illusion to create a double of myself, and I want you to use your Sight to spot the real me."

"That's simple?"

She ignores me, muttering, "*Duplici exemplari.*"

Her aura brightens, the air faintly scented with ozone, then her form blurs, splits down the centre, and I'm confronted with two Zaras.

Fuck.

Two Zaras.

It's bad enough when there's only one of her.

"Focus. Imagine layers of the spell peeling away," both Zaras say.

I do as she says, squinting.

Nothing.

"It's not working," I say.

"Try harder," they echo.

I squint again.

Imagine layers of the spell peeling away.

The pink light around both of them fades, then returns to normal.

"Good, almost there," they say. "Again."

I try again.

I get a brighter flash of pink this time, and a negative after-image of the real Zara floating before my eyes, before it fades away and they're both stood there again.

My body's heavy. "I need a breather," I say. "I'm getting tired."

"I don't give two tiny fucks. Again."

I narrow my eyes a third time.

That's it.

I'm sick of this.

I summon more and more magic, ploughing it all into my Sight.

Show me.

Flash.

Zara—the real Zara—appears in front of me, surrounded by a corona of pink light, and she stays put this time.

"Found you," I say, too exhausted to put much oomph into my voice.

"I can see that." The smile she wears is as real as she is.

My head swims and my heart thrums in my chest. A wave of weariness rears its ugly head, threatening to wash me away.

"Turn it off," Zara says.

Thud-thud-thud.

"How?"

"You need to—"

Thud-thud, thud-thud, thud-thud.

My knees buckle and slam into the floor. "I... can't..."

"Stone, listen to me, you need to..."

My cheek hits the cold floor, and I don't find out what I need to do.

Zara doesn't slap me awake this time. Instead, she must wait for me to come to naturally. When I do, she's leaning against the wall, polishing her nails with hot-pink varnish.

I groan.

She smirks. "Enjoy your nap, Sleeping Beauty?"

I'm still half asleep and filter-less, so I say, "Wait. You think I'm beautiful?"

She actually laughs, low and dirty. "I think your full of shit."

I shake my head and stand—or try to—my legs collapse beneath me half way up and I land hard on my arse.

"Here." Zara rushes forward and injects me with liquid silver. She's much more gentle than last time.

Stable and strong, thanks to the liquid silver, I push to my feet.

Stable and strong.

That's a joke.

I'm weak.

I pass out when I use my Sight, I can't win any bouts, I'm tired all the time. Placing a hand to my forehead, I say, "I can't believe I fucked up again."

Zara's brow creases. "Who said anything about fucking up?"

I let out a heavy breath. "I passed out. What else would you call it?"

"Yeah, you passed out, but before that you saw through my duplication spell."

"So what? What good will that do me if the result is unconsciousness."

"You just need more practice, but I think we might have finally found something you're good at."

"Humph. Yeah. Right." I walk over to the edge of the room and sink to the floor, leaning back against the wall. "Maybe..."

"Maybe what?"

"Never mind."

"Don't piss about. If you've got something to say, just say it."

I hesitate.

"Stone." The warning note in Zara's tone's clear.

I sigh. "Maybe you were right about me. Perhaps I'm not cut out for this. The executioners will never accept me anyway."

"Why?"

"Because I'm an Outsider."

She snorts. "So was I, but I made them accept me. Didn't give them a choice."

I lean my head back against the wall and close my eyes.

Vi. Iustitia. Fides.

Strength.
Justice.
Loyalty.

"But you're different," I say in a tired voice. "You're exactly what they want. You're strong."

She's silent for a long time, then she says, "Yeah, well. I had to be strong. Didn't have a choice."

When I open my eyes again, she's running her fingers along her DNA helix tattoo.

She catches me looking.

I glance away.

She crosses the room and lowers herself down next to me. "Last time we sat like this, you asked about the tattoo. Remember?"

"Yeah."

Zara brings one knee up and stretches her other leg out in front of her. When she speaks again, there's a gentle tone to her voice I've never heard before. "I didn't have the best start in life. My parents were, well, they weren't fit to call themselves parents. Mum abandoned me when I was four. Dad blamed me; I think. He was a drunk. A mean one. Quick with his fists."

My lips part. I don't know what I was expecting her to say, but it wasn't that. I can't even imagine what she's been through. My parents hadn't been faultless, far from it, but they'd never laid a finger on me, never beat me. "I'm—I'm so sorry." It sounds lame.

Sorry.

Such an insignificant word.

She shrugs. "School was the worst. People asking about the cuts, the bruises."

"Did you tell anyone what was happening? Friends? Teachers?"

"Didn't tell my friends, couldn't. I told a teacher once."

"And?"

She laughs, but it's bitter. "Didn't go well. Said only nasty children made up stories to get their parents in trouble."

"That's awful."

"Dad put on a good show. Smiles and jokes and loud laughs. My teachers loved him. Wish they could have seen him at home."

"Did you ever fight back?"

She shakes her head. "Put up with it until I was fifteen, then one day, when he was steaming drunk—again—he broke my fingers."

I hadn't noticed before, but the index and middle fingers on Zara's left hand are a little crooked, the fractures badly set. "What did you do?"

"I ran away. Spent the next six years living rough, scared of everything, even my shadow."

I can't imagine that.

Zara?

Scared?

"When I turned twenty-one, I didn't have anyone to guide me through my Manifestation, nobody to set a circle to keep the power in check and I—well, something bad happened."

A chill goes through me. "What?"

"Doesn't matter. But it fucked me up. I tried everything to forget. Drink, drugs, sex. Nothing worked. Just like Dad, I guess, and that scared the living shit out of me, which made me abuse myself more. Anyway, I don't know how, but Carmichael found me, brought me here, got me clean. Gave me a purpose, gave me a home, showed me I'm nothing like my dad. That's another reason why I got the tattoo. It reminds me when I forget: my past doesn't have to determine my future."

She's so brave. I could never do that, wear my fear on my skin like a permanent, open, festering wound that never closes.

"What was it for you?" she asks.

"What was what for me?"

"The thing that fucked you up?"

The ghost of a scent from before.

Old tobacco.

Fruit-flavoured chewing gum.

We regret to inform you...

My fingers go to the scar between my collarbones. "I don't know what you're talking about."

Zara shakes her head at my picking fingers and clambers to her feet. "Know why I told you that story?"

"No."

"Because I wish I *had* fought back. Against Dad. I wish I'd challenged him, stood up to him. Asked him why he drank, why he hit me, why he wanted to hurt me. If I had, maybe he would've stopped. I don't know. It's the one thing I regret, because now I'll never know."

I consider her words, and bite my lip. "You said he blamed you."

"What?"

"You think your dad blamed you for your mum leaving."

"So?"

"It wasn't your fault."

"Yeah, maybe."

Zara looks so... lost that I don't know what to say.

Then she shifts her stance, and I see it. The armour going back on, the tough-as-granite persona enfolding her like an old, comforting, familiar coat. "That's it for tonight. I'm sick of looking at your miserable face."

I raise my eyebrows. "*My* miserable face?"

"Don't push it." Her words are stern, but she's supressing a smile. "Get the fuck out of here. Go get some sleep. And you'd better bring you're A-game to training tomorrow."

I heave myself up and cross to the door.

Zara calls out before I leave, as she so often does. Always one for wanting the last word. "Stone?"

I can predict what she's going to say, so I say it for her. "I know, I know. I tell anyone what you just told me and you'll pull out my kidneys through my arsehole and make me eat them."

"I was going to go with your liver." She smiles.

I leave our private session repeating one clear thought.

My past doesn't have to determine my future.

Things are going to be different from now on.

I'm sure of it.

CHAPTER 21

T he following morning, I make it my mission to avoid
Layla as best I can, and it works for a few hours. I'm
partnered with Geek and Bianca in training, and we sit at
opposite ends of the dining hall at lunch and dinner. The
evening's a different story.

We're not having free time tonight, but I don't know what
we're doing instead.

Zara leads us down a wide corridor that seems familiar, but
I'm groggy from lack of sleep. I can't follow where we're going.

The three stooges—Myles, Femi, and Layla—walk ahead of
us, while Geek, Bianca and I trail along at the back.

Every so often, Layla casts furtive glances at me over her
shoulder.

I ignore her.

"Why does she keep looking at you?" Bianca asks, her voice
uncharacteristically waspish.

"She doesn't."

"She does, pal." Geek scratches his cheek and yawns.
"Where were you last night, anyway? I checked your room,
but you weren't there."

"I wanted to put in a couple of extra hours in the training room," I lie. Why am I lying. So what if I was with Layla last night. It's not like anything happened between us.

Bianca seems to relax, rolling her neck and tucking her hair behind her ears. "You should have told me. I need all the practice I can get."

"You're not that bad," I say.

"I haven't won a single bout. Zara's going to kick me out, for sure."

I nudge her with my elbow. "She'll be kicking us both out at this rate. I'll help you pack if you help me."

This earns me a half-hearted chuckle.

"Jesus, you two are cheery this morning," Geek says, as we descend a set of steep, curving stairs. "Good job there's nothing sharp around."

My brow furrows. "Why?"

"Because I'd be compelled to slit my wrists. Anything to avoid this fucking pity party."

"It's all right for you, Mr Third Place," Bianca says.

Geek's got a knack for finding people's weak spots and exploiting them. He beat Femi in a sparring match yesterday and knocked him down to fourth place.

Geek says, "You need to fight back."

Bianca rolls her eyes. "Gee, thanks. I'll bear that in mind."

"Right." Zara stops outside a familiar door. "We're going to be doing something a little different today."

I recognise the label.

Island Portal: Authorised Personnel Only.

The word portal makes my stomach lurch, the shepherd's pie I'd eaten at dinner threating to come back up. "Oh, no, you've got to be kidding me," I groan.

"What's wrong?" Bianca asks.

I pitch my voice low, ensuring only Geek and Bianca can hear. "I get portal sickness."

"What?" Geek sniggers. "Is that even a thing?"

"Trust me. It's a thing."

His snigger morphs into a full-on belly laugh. "I can't wait to see this."

I punch him in the arm. "Cheers, mate."

Zara waves her hand in front of the door and it creaks open on rusty hinges. She conjures a cloud of pale pink witch-light and orders us to follow her.

We go through the door and troop down a steep slope, even farther underground, and the wood panelled walls give way to rough-hewn rock. The air smells stagnant and Zara's witch-light bobs and weaves ahead of us, turning the shadows into sinister, hulking creatures of nightmare.

"I reckon this is where she flips and kills us all." Geek says.

Bianca shivers against the cold. "Wouldn't surprise me."

Layla's eyes catch mine again.

My stomach flutters.

"She's definitely looking at you," Bianca says. "What's her problem?"

I shrug. "No idea."

I can't believe I let my guard down. I can't believe I told Layla about my parents. She's bound to have told Myles by now. Bound to. Probably why she's looking so furtive. I'm so lost in thought that I don't notice when Zara brings us to a halt and everyone stops walking. I plough straight into Femi's back.

He spins around, getting right in my face. "Watch where you're going."

"It was an accident," I say, glancing away.

He shoves me, hard.

"Back off," Geek says.

Femi squares up to Geek. "You going to make me, little man?"

"I beat you yesterday, didn't I?"

Femi raises his arm and points his fingers at Geek. They pulse with angry violet light.

"Problem, gents?" Zara's voice echoes down the tunnel.

"No," we all say in unison.

Nobody, not even Femi, dares to provoke Zara.

"Watch your back, Stone." Femi sneers, before turning away from us.

Geek gives Femi's broad back the middle finger.

Zara stands before a craggy rock wall. She brushes an open palm against the jagged stone. "*Ostium.*"

The wall shifts, shimmers and dissipates, and the pink light of Zara's portal bathes the passageway. A blast of familiar cool-warm air, like the sickly gust from a broken car heater, hits me full in the face.

My hand goes to my squirming stomach.

"Wonder what this island place is?" Bianca looks almost as apprehensive as me.

"Follow me." Zara steps into the portal and vanishes.

I grit my teeth. "We're about to find out."

The portal chews me up, swills me round, and spits me out like a used piece of chewing gum.

I glimpse a starry sky, dense woodland and a rock-strewn cliff face before the nausea hits me with full force. My head spins. I collapse to my hands and knees, fingers curling in the lush, springy grass, nails digging into the soft earth. My stomach heaves and I lose my dinner.

The sour stench of vomit's overpowering.

I claw my way to my feet and wipe my mouth on the back of my hand. "Ugh."

Geek claps me on the shoulder. "Better out than in."

"Poor thing." Bianca rubs my back, her hand moving in gentle circles.

Myles's nose wrinkles in disgust. "Christ, Stone. What kind of witch are you?" He twists away before I can answer.

"This," Zara says, throwing her arms wide, "is the island."

"Where—" I swallow back a gag. "Where are we?"

"A private island off the south coast."

We stand on the edge of a high cliff. Moonlit waves crash against the rocks below, and the choppy sea stretches far into the distance, all the way to the star-spangled horizon.

"What are we doing here?" Layla asks. She blows on her hands and her breath mists in the frigid air.

Zara gives a wolfish smile. "We're going to play a game."

"A game?" Femi says, his entire face scrunching up as if the concept of playing games is beneath him.

Zara ignores him. "Magical Hide and Seek."

I almost laugh. "What?"

"Sometimes, as an executioner, we'll ask you to recover dangerous magical objects that have fallen into the wrong hands. Somewhere on this island, I've hidden a dummy artefact, and you'll be working in teams to find it. The first team to bring it back to me wins."

On autopilot, I draw closer to Geek and Bianca.

Zara shakes her head. "When I said we were doing things differently today, I meant it. I'm going to mix you all up."

"What?" Myles scowls at us. "I'm not working with them."

"Do I have to remind you of my first rule, Hedges?" The silver rings around Zara's eyes reflect the starlight, glinting like the curved blades of sharpened scythes.

"I'm not teaming up with any of those clowns," Myles insists.

Zara strides to the edge of the cliff and peers down into the churning molten-steel waves. "It's a long way down. Accidents happen."

I shiver, and it has little to do with the chilly wind or the icy droplets of seawater speckling my skin.

"Any volunteers to switch sides?" Zara asks.

A sea bird squawks in the distance.

A beat passes.

And another.

And another.

Layla steps forward. "I don't mind."

Myles's head snaps up. "*What?*"

She shrugs. "I'm not fussed which team I'm on."

Myles's eyes narrow to thin slits. "You're siding with them?"

Layla laughs. "We might end up working together one day. Might as well start now."

"Over my dead body."

She rolls her eyes. "Grow up, Myles."

Colour creeps into Myles's face. "You've made your choice."

Layla tosses her long hair over one shoulder and saunters over to stand at my side.

Zara's watching Layla with something close to approval. "Anyone else?"

Bianca hangs her head.

Geek and I both cross our arms.

Zara says, "Townsend."

"No way." Geek slashes his hand through the air. "I'd rather you kick me out."

Zara raises an eyebrow at him. "I'm surprised. Given how much you've got to lose."

Geek hesitates, a brief flash of panic crossing his pale features. "You wouldn't."

"Try me."

I glance from Zara to Geek. What does she mean, *how much you've got to lose?* "What's she talking about?" I ask.

He ignores me. "I'm not doing it."

Zara stalks up to Geek, her face inches from his. "Remember what's at stake. One conversation with Director Carmichael, and we'll put both of you right back where we found you and, despite all your bravado, I don't think you want that."

We'll put both of you right back where we found you.

A memory surfaces. Carmichael's speech on the first day.

I know that most of you have a lot riding on this, so I'm sure you'll all try your hardest, and I wish you luck.

I knew Carmichael aimed those words at Geek, and Zara's confirmed it. So, I hadn't imagined it. I *knew* I hadn't. What brought Geek here, and why is he being so secretive about it?

Geek lowers his gaze. "Fine."

"I knew you'd see sense," Zara says. "Now that's sorted, we can get the ball rolling." She waves her hand through the air. "*Revelare.*"

Two yellowed pages—printed with gibberish, a *Lorem Ipsum*-style text—appear in Zara's hand.

She passes one page to me and one to Myles.

With a sinking feeling, I realise what Zara's done. She's not-so-subtly nominated me and Myles as team captains and pitted us against each other yet again.

Myles must realise it too, because his thin lips curve into a wicked smirk. "Aren't you tired of losing to me, Stone?"

Something inside me snaps. I've been taking Myles's shit for the last month, and I'm sick of it. It's about time he gets a taste of his own medicine. I remember what Layla told me about Myles on the night I'd helped her find her bracelet.

His dad... he treats him like dirt. Myles just wants to impress him.

"Aren't you tired of being a colossal disappointment to your dad?" I say.

Zara snorts.

Myles's entire body shakes, every muscle and tendon and fibre vibrating with anger. "At least I've still got parents."

The words pummel me like physical blows. "Wh—What did you say?"

"You heard me, orphan boy."

The urge to scratch at my scar's almost too much, but I resist.

Layla steps forward. "Myles, don't."

"Henry, what's he talking about?" Geek asks.

"You told him?" I ask Layla, the words blistering hot.

Her face creases in pain. "No. Of course not. I'd never do that."

Myles lets out a harsh bark of laughter. "She didn't need to. I followed you both on your little treasure hunt last night. No wonder you don't mind being around him, Layla. Now you can be orphans together."

"Take that back," I snap.

Zara steps in front of Myles. "That's enough, Hedges."

Myles laughs again, cold and distant. "I know what happened to you. I heard it all. This Razor character, the one who murdered your parents, you honestly think you stand a chance against him? He'll make mincemeat out of you."

My blood boils. "I'm going to kill you, you smug piece of shit."

"You realise how ridiculous that sounds, coming from you, don't you?"

I lunge for him.

Zara jumps in front of me, slams her hand into my chest, and shoves me back. "I said that's enough. If you two don't knock it off, I swear on my magic and my Sight, I'll kick you both out of COVEN right now."

Ice constricts around my heart and all the fight goes out of me.

"Got it?" she asks me.

"Got it," I murmur.

She fixes Myles with a steely glare. "And you?"

"Whatever. Are we playing this game or not?"

"*Ostium*," Zara points her finger and another portal crackles to life. "Hedges, Abimbola and Townsend. Portal. Now."

"Where does it go?" Geek asks.

"The other side of the island. When you see my witch-light flare, you can start looking for the book. Now get out of my sight."

Myles and Femi stalk straight into the portal and disappear.

"You okay, pal?" Geek asks.

"I'm fine." I'm not.

Zara says, "Townsend. Portal, now."

Geek trudges into the disc of pink light and vanishes along with Myles and Femi.

Zara conjures another portal. "Remember, you go on my witch-light flare."

I nod.

"And, Stone?"

"Yeah?"

"Make him pay for that."

As soon as Zara's gone, Bianca rounds on me, a coldness in her hazel eyes I've never seen before. "You said you were in the training room last night?"

"Bianca—"

"You were with her."

"Yes, but not in the way you're thinking."

"What am I thinking, Henry? Am I thinking, why did he lie about where he was last night? Am I thinking, I wonder why Henry told her about his past when he hasn't even told his friends?"

"I didn't want anyone to know about my parents."

"Why?"

"Because I didn't want anyone to pity me."

"You really think Geek and I would pity you?"

"It's not like—"

She cuts across me. "Why tell her, of all people? That's what I don't understand."

Layla's eyes harden, and she crosses her arms. "'*Her*' has a name; you know."

I can't answer Bianca's question, not without explaining what happened to Layla's mother, and I won't break her confidence. Layla hadn't broken mine, after all. For some reason, Layla's discretion makes my chest warm with happiness. I push the thought aside. "Don't you get it? This is what Myles wants," I say. "He wants us at each other's throats."

Bianca doesn't let it go. "You told her, but you didn't tell us. Why?"

Typical. She picks now to be brave. "We don't have time to—"

"I lost my mother's bracelet and Henry helped me find it." Layla flashes the emerald bangle at Bianca. "A drunk driver killed my mum, and I guess he felt comfortable telling me because we both know what it's like to lose a parent. That good enough for you?"

Bianca sinks in on herself, like a tortoise retreating into its shell, all her strength vanishing in an instant. "I'm sorry. I didn't know."

"Well, now you do," Layla says.

A loud *bang* splits the air like a gunshot.

I flinch.

From deep in the wooded part of the island, a bright pink ball of light arcs high above the trees and explodes like a firework, showering the sky with rose quartz sparks.

We all look at each other.

"Come on," I say. "We need to get that book before Myles does."

The forest's dark, despite the three clouds of witch-light mushrooming over our heads, and the air smells sweet and earthy and green.

"How will we find it?" Bianca asks.

"Locater spell," Layla and I say in unison.

We grin at each other.

Bianca's gaze finds the floor.

"You think it'll work?" Layla asks me.

"Don't see why not. Zara said this page comes from the book we're after, so they're connected, just like your mum's bracelet's connected to you."

"Try it."

I hold up the page. "*Reperio liber.*"

Seconds pass before the soft, green glow of my locater spell suffuses the page.

"Nice job." Layla holds up her hand and we high five.

"Whatever. Let's get this done." Bianca snatches the page from my hand and says, "*Ostende mihi librum.*"

"You know the spell?" I ask.

"You're not the only one who reads ahead." The page pulses and yanks Bianca's arm forward. She follows the bright page deeper into the forest.

Layla and I walk behind her, twigs snapping and cracking underfoot.

"I don't get it," I say, keeping my voice low so Bianca can't hear me. "She never gets angry. I don't know what's up with her."

Layla chuckles a little. "You're joking, right?"

"What?"

"Oh, my God. Why are boys so clueless?"

"What are you talking about?"

She chuckles louder this time.

Bianca glares at us.

"Please. It's obvious," Layla whispers.

Surely, she won't say what I think she's going to say. "What's obvious?"

"She likes you."

I deflate. "Geek said the same thing."

"He's right."

I squint at her. "We're just friends."

"Well, trust me, she wants to be more than friends."

"Geek said that too, in a roundabout way."

I shove my hands deep into the pockets of my COVEN issue tracksuit bottoms. Maybe Geek and Layla are right. Maybe Bianca has feelings for me. What if she does? Am I interested? She's nice enough, and she's attractive in a delicate, feminine way. If Razor wasn't a factor... it doesn't matter. He *is* a factor, and I'm not here for love, I'm here for revenge. Bianca and I are just friends. Good friends. I shake my head. "I think your radar's off."

Layla winks at me.

My stomach does an odd little flip.

"If you say so," she says.

"Come on," Bianca calls from up ahead. "Less chatting, more finding."

Layla and I catch up with Bianca, and we jog through the trees, slipping and sliding on wet patches of mud here and there. We run for fifteen minutes, and my lungs are about to give up on me when the page pulses and glows brighter.

"It must be close," Bianca draws to a halt.

We pick our way through the trees and emerge into a vast, meadow-like clearing. The page flashes like a beacon. In the centre of the clearing, something flashes in response.

The book.

The page in Bianca's hand crumbles to dust.

"There." I point, taking a step into the clearing.

"Wait." Layla grabs my arm.

Bianca glares at the spot where she touches me.

"What?" I ask.

"This seems too easy," Layla says. "The others should be here by now. Where are they?"

"They're probably still stuck in the forest," I say.

"I don't know." Layla's eyes sweep across the meadow. "I know how Myles operates. Something feels off."

"Henry's right," Bianca says, standing close to me. "They're not here. They would've attacked by now. I've known Myles and Femi a lot longer than you, and they don't do subtle."

Layla's grip tightens on my arm. "Trust me. Something doesn't feel right. I think we're being watched."

"You're paranoid," Bianca says. "Trust *me*, Henry. If they were here, we'd know about it."

"You don't know what you're talking about."

I can't concentrate with both of them going at me like this.

"No, *you* don't know what you're—"

It doesn't feel like they're fighting over the game anymore, and it's too distracting. "Stop bickering." I close my eyes and concentrate. Are the others here? Are they watching us right now? How can I tell?

How can I tell?

A memory—a past conversation—tugs at me.

How. Can. I. Tell?

Wait.

Dad said something about my Sight, right after my Manifestation.

It means you can see through all kinds of illusions.

Illusions?

Glamours, invisibility spells...

I open my eyes and cast my gaze over the meadow, squinting until my optic nerves burn with the Sight. At first glance, everything looks the same. The trees sway in the wind; the stars sparkle against the endless black sky, and the grass swishes back and forth in the breeze.

My pulse beats heavy against my throat and a prickling feeling crawls up my neck and into my hair. "There's nothing—"

A flicker of movement makes me jump.

Something looms out of the darkness.

No.

Two somethings—vaguely humanoid shapes.

I squint harder.

Layers of empty air peel away.

Myles and Femi—wreathed in cloaks of grey and violet light respectively—stand thirty feet away from us.

"Shit," I say.

"He's seen us," Myles shouts.

Femi and Myles fire a volley of witch-strikes right at us.

I fling up a barrier and block the spells. Bianca and Layla—blind to our attackers—remain defenceless.

They both fly backwards and bounce along the ground until they lie, unmoving.

I don't have time to worry about my teammates now. I need to grab the book. "Where's Geek?"

"We knocked him out as soon as the portal dropped us off," Femi says.

"What?"

"I meant what I said." Myles curls his lip. "I'll never work with an Outsider."

"You bastards. You—"

They fire on me again, and I dive to the side, landing hard on my knees.

The witch-strikes whizz over my head. I react quickly, slamming my hands together. "*Traho.*"

My spell jerks Myles and Femi off their feet, and they sail towards each other. They collide with a bone-jarring thump, and fall to the ground, motionless.

I push to a standing position. The book's mine. The book's—

A dark shape darts out of the treeline.

I recognise the way he moves.

Geek.

I bolt towards the book in the centre of the meadow. Come on. Come on. I sprint faster, faster, faster, eating up the distance between me and the book, the grass flying beneath me in a green blur.

Geek and I reach the book at the same time. We both grab for it. Tussle for it.

"Let go, pal," Geek pants. "I need—this one."

"Not as—badly—as I do," We're both breathless from the run. "I'm in fifth place. If I don't win, nobody's ever going to vote for me."

His grip doesn't loosen. "I can't let you take it."

I need to make him let go.

No.

I need to distract him.

Dad used to play a stupid trick on me when I was a kid, if he was trying to beat me in a race or something and needed to divert my attention. I doubt it'll work on Geek, but I've got to try. I force my eyes to widen and let go of the book, backing away.

"What are you doing?" he asks, the book clutched to his chest.

I point into the treeline and yell. "Watch out."

To my surprise, Geek whips round, eyes tracking the path of my pointing finger.

"*Eryx.*" My green, witch-gauntleted fist finds its mark, smacking Geek right between the shoulder blades.

He cries out, stumbles forward. Trips.

The book flies from his grip.

I crook my fingers in a beckoning motion. "*Affer mihi, inquit liber.*"

The book changes course in mid-air and thumps into my outstretched hands.

"You tricked me." Geek's eyes simmer with anger.

"I had to."

He goes to flip to his feet.

"*Pedibus nostris.*"

The binding spell locks Geek's muscles in place. He can't move now, but his narrowed eyes still blister my skin.

I can't think about our friendship now. The only thing that matters is getting the book back to Zara and making sure I impress her. If I win the game, it'll go a long way to getting me into her good books.

COVEN's motto floats to the forefront of my mind.

Vi. Iustitia. Fides.

Strength. Justice. Loyalty.

If I was strong, I'd take the book and run.

As for justice and loyalty? The only justice worth anything is making Razor pay. The only loyalty I care about—in this moment—is the loyalty I owe to my parents.

I hate you, and I'll never forgive you.

"I'm sorry, man. I really am, but I have to do this." I tear my gaze away from Geek's and bolt. Back across the meadow.

Back through the woods. I sprint and sprint and sprint and I don't look back. I burst from the forest's edge and find myself back on the rocky bluff of the cliff.

Zara's lips part when she sees me, her eyebrows shooting up.

She's shocked.

Good.

I drop the book into her outstretched hands. "Expecting—someone—else?" I say between breathless gasps.

Her face splits into a huge grin. "Look who finally showed up to the fucking party."

A fierce surge of pleasure and pride courses through me.

I've done it.

I've won the game.

CHAPTER 22

Geek hasn't spoken to me since our trip to the island two weeks ago. Every time I try to catch his eye or strike up a conversation, he ducks his head, or makes out like he has to be somewhere, or pretends he's forgotten something back in his room.

I hit the training room every morning and every evening. Not through choice. It's the only way I can avoid the awkwardness of running into Geek in a social setting. Anything to avoid that. I haven't spoken to Bianca either. One, because she's always with Geek. Two, because something feels off between us.

I'm practicing a new spell. One Zara taught us earlier today, but I've failed to make it work twice already.

The witch-staff.

"Come on. Get your head on the spell." I hold my hands straight out in front of me, close my eyes, draw on my magic—shivering as the now familiar pins and needles cause goosebumps to erupt along my arms—and whisper, "*Baculum.*" A straight, glowing green staff—two metres long and composed entirely of magical energy—flashes into my outstretched hands.

The staff hums, vibrating with power.

It's intoxicating.

I lead myself through the kata Zara showed us earlier; the staff blurs through the air as I strike and block against an imaginary opponent. My heart isn't in it though, my mind fixated on what happened on the island. The way I'd tricked Geek. The rage in his narrowed eyes cutting into me with laser-like focus. My stomach churns with nausea. I shouldn't have done it.

Fides.

Loyalty.

Why shouldn't I have done it, though?

Geek's had loads of successes in training and, whenever he's done well, I've cheered him on and supported him. Now, what? He can't do the same for me? That's what friendship is, isn't it? Supporting each other. If he can't do that, then I don't need him, anyway. I think of Jez. I'm not saying our friendship was perfect, and he could be a right arse, but I could never accuse him of not being supportive.

I could really use my best mate right now.

My stomach sinks. I can wish all I want. Chances are, I'll never see Jez again.

A tide of grief threatens to overwhelm me, so I plough all my energy into the kata, allowing the routine of the movement to soothe me and bring me back into the present. I spin the staff again and lash out at the air with the butt.

"Impressive."

Bianca.

I release the staff, and it dissipates in a swirl of green light. I don't look at her. "Yeah, well, I've had plenty of time to practice since the island."

"You're the one who's been avoiding us."

I cross to the line of silver targets—still avoiding her gaze—and aim a witch-strike at the one in the centre.

The strike misses the target by a country mile, bursts against the wall and leaves a scorch mark behind.

I scuff my shoe. "Geek won't talk to me, so it made sense to keep to myself for a bit."

"He told me what Zara meant."

"What do you mean?" I shift my weight, adjusting my stance.

"When she said he had a lot to lose."

I look at her now. "What? When?" My voice sounds hurt, and I hate myself for it. It makes me sound weak, and weakness is a luxury I can't afford. Especially here, where strength's a vital virtue.

"The night after the island."

Pain stabs beneath my ribcage. "So, why's he here?"

"It's not my story to tell, but I understand why he's annoyed at you."

"How can you—"

"I didn't say he's right, just that I understand. I wish I could bang your heads together. Get things back to normal."

I face the target again, setting my jaw. "I'm surprised you want things to go back to normal."

"What?"

I miss for the second time. "Well, you're pissed off at me, too."

"I'm not pissed off."

"You are. About Layla. Even though there's nothing going on between us."

"Maybe I was. It shocked me you told Layla about your parents and didn't tell us, that's all."

I fire another witch-strike, and a third scorch mark joins the other two.

When Bianca speaks, her voice is tentative. "Myles mentioned someone called Razor?"

The name's enough to send a jolt quivering through my stomach.

"Who's Razor?" she asks, her tone still gentle.

"He—" My throat feels swollen and bruised, and each time my heart beats, my chest spasms with pain. "I can't say it. When I say it... it's real."

"He killed your parents, didn't he?" Her words are so quiet I nearly miss them.

I nod, brushing away the tears misting my eyes.

Her footsteps come closer, and the light pressure of her palm finds the space between my shoulder blades, warming my back through my T-shirt. "I'm so sorry," she says.

I face her, her hand slipping away. "So am I."

Her brow creases in confusion.

I hate you, and I'll never forgive you.

"The last thing I said to them... we got into a stupid row... I told them—I said—" I choke off and let out a long breath. "I told them I hated them."

"Oh, Henry."

I cry then. Really cry. The kind where snot dribbles from your nose and your entire face is a scrunched up, florid mess.

Bianca wraps her arms around me.

My body stiffens.

She squeezes.

I relent, my arms circling her back, my chin resting on her shoulder. "Sorry. I'm so, so, sorry."

I'm not talking to Bianca, not really, but she rubs my back all the same, whispering, "I know, I know you are."

"Carmichael and I made a deal. If I become an executioner, I get to be the one who kills Razor." I pull back, disentangling myself from the hug and scrubbing my palms across my face to get rid of the tears. "Sorry. I'm a mess."

Her hand rests on my arm. "Don't apologise. I understand. I'm sure Geek will, too, if you explain it to him."

When I sniff, it's wet and thick. "Can't go through that again."

She notices her hand on my arm and blushes before removing it. Her fingers find the diamond ring.

Twist, twist, twist.

"What is it?" I ask. "What's wrong?"

"Nothing."

"Hey. You can talk to me, you know that, right?"

"I like you." Her voice is small. She looks up, her hazel eyes bright and wide and honest.

My stomach sinks. Geek and Layla were right. I smile, try for a jovial tone. "Well, we're friends, so I bloody well hope so."

"That's not—" She bites her lip, swallows, spinning her ring faster and faster. Suddenly, she lunges forward, grabs my face, and kisses me.

I freeze.

Her mouth moves on mine, but I don't reciprocate.

Seconds pass, and she draws away. "Oh."

That, "Oh," expresses more than any single syllable should. It speaks of regret and sadness and embarrassment, garnished with a sprig of anger.

I wipe my mouth.

Her eyes harden.

Why did you wipe your mouth, you idiot? "I'm sorry," I say. "I just... I don't feel the same way."

She closes her eyes, arms folding over her chest like a shield of flesh and bone. "It's her, isn't it?"

"Who?"

Her answering laugh's bitter. That sound—coming from her—is completely alien.

I take a step back.

She must read my shock. Her expression softens a little. "Sorry. I'd... rather you didn't play games, that's all. People have played games with me my entire life. My mother. Myles and Femi. That bitch-queen-from-hell, Nicolette Barnes. I'm sick of it."

Playing games? What's she talking about? "Bianca, I'm not—"

"Layla," she says, as if that explains everything. She glances at the floor. "Precious Layla."

Precious Layla? Where's all this coming from? "I don't know what—"

"If you have feelings for her, that's okay, you don't have to lie about it."

"I don't have feelings for her. I've never even thought about it." Liar. That first day—I noticed how attractive she is. But she is. Anyone can see that. It doesn't mean—

"Wouldn't have thought she was your type," Bianca says.

"I didn't say she was."

"Being so stuck up and everything."

A twinge of annoyance. Bianca's never taken the time to talk to Layla. "She's not like that. Not really. She—"

That hard look's back in Bianca's eyes. "So, you do like her?"

"What? That's not what I said."

"You don't find her attractive?"

"Well, yeah. I don't—I mean, it's not that you're not—"

"Oh, my God. You're unbelievable."

I scratch my head, confused about the turn our conversation's taken. "Hang on. I haven't done anything wrong."

"Wow." She backs up a step. "It's just, you've been so supportive. So kind. The way you smile at me. I just thought, maybe..."

I reach out and rest a hand on her shoulder. "I'm supportive because we're friends."

"Friends."

"Yeah. I never meant for you to think anything else."

She shrugs me off. "Right."

"Are you—"

"I'm fine." Something in her face tells me she's closed off, unreachable. "I'm fine."

"I'm sor—"

"Don't, just don't, okay. God I'm such an idiot."

Something gnaws at the pit of my stomach. Guilt? I don't know. Pity? Maybe. But whatever it is, I don't like it. "Hey," I say, "you're not an idiot."

She nods, but it's a half-hearted movement. "I'm sorry I got it wrong." She turns to leave.

"You don't have to."

"I'd rather be alone right now." She fast-walks across the room, heading straight for the door.

"Bianca, wait, please—"

The door doesn't slam behind her. It just closes with a soft click.

What the fuck just happened?

Playing games...

Precious Layla...

I'm sorry I got it wrong...

Is she right? Have I led her on somehow?

No.

But I could've handled that better.

You don't find her attractive?

Guilt pinches my gut.

I'm not here for this... whatever *this* is. I'm here for one reason—and one reason only—to get justice for my parents.

I hate you, and I'll never forgive you.

I'm sorry I got it wrong.

I let out a howl of frustration and pivot back to the target, firing witch-strike after witch-strike after witch-strike—

Crack.

The target splits in two.

Prick.

I'm such a fucking prick. Great. Now I've lost two friends in as many weeks, and I didn't have many to lose.

I'm so tired.

I need to go to bed. I need to sleep. Forget all of it.

I turn into the corridor that leads to the trainees' quarters, and the sound of chattering voices reaches me.

The scene I'm presented with is unexpected.

Myles stands on one side of the hallway, Femi at his shoulder. Bianca, Layla and Geek stand opposite him.

What's going on?

Geek shakes his head. "You're talking out of your arse, Hedges."

"No change there," Layla says.

"Think about it." Myles taps a finger to his temple. "He's manipulating all of us."

Bianca scowls at her feet, saying nothing.

He? Is Myles—are they—talking about me? A bead of sweat trickles down my neck.

Layla crosses her arms. "The only person playing mind games around here is you."

"Oh, come on. What are you, blind?" Femi says, his deep, rumbling voice resounding through the wide atrium.

Geek narrows his eyes at Femi. "What are you on about?"

"One minute he's falling apart in the ring and the next minute he's running around that island like *Rambo* with an axe to grind. Are you honestly telling me you can't see the huge contradiction in behaviour there?"

"Rubbish," Geek says.

"Is it?" Myles says. "Remind me? What's your rating now?"

"You know damn well I'm fourth."

"Exactly. Because of him. He got close to you, pretended to be your friend, and then double crossed you at the first available opportunity."

Bianca's cheeks redden.

The kiss. Oh, God. She's thinking about the kiss. I want to yell at Myles. Get him to stop. Get him to shut up. But I can't. The words shrivel up in my mouth.

Layla steps forward and jabs a finger at Myles. "You're twisting things because Henry's Sighted and you're not, and you're jealous."

"Truth hurts, eh, Jabara?" Myles retorts. "You only refuse to see it because you're so desperate to fuck him after he found your pretty bracelet."

Bianca's blush deepens to a ruddy scarlet.

Layla stomps over to Myles and slaps him clean across the face, the sharp *snap* echoing off the dark wood panelling.

Myles glares at Layla. "I don't even know why I bother." He rubs his reddening cheek. "If you're prepared to let him shove you out of the ratings, that's up to you." He wheels around, sees me. "Oh, speak of the devil."

My mouth's full of sawdust.

"Well?" Myles asks. "What have you got to say for yourself?"

"I—" I run my tacky tongue across the roof of my mouth, trying to generate saliva, staring from face to face.

Femi glowers.

Bianca's gaze remains glued to the floor.

Geek looks away.

Only Layla holds my gaze, eyes shining with sympathy.

I shake my head. "You're not buying this shit, are you?"

"Of course not," Layla says, instantly.

No one else speaks.

Myles saunters across the room until he stands right in front of me. "Everyone finally sees you for what you are. Those eyes of yours don't make you any better than us." He nudges me with his shoulder on his way out.

Femi follows him, black irises flashing like dark chips of obsidian.

"Bianca?" I take a step in her direction.

"Don't." She puts up a hand. "Just don't, okay? You've already made it clear where we stand." Keeping her gaze on the floor, she scurries down the corridor and rounds the corner.

"Geek? Come on, mate. You don't believe him, you can't."

"I don't know what to believe." Geek rakes a hand through his hair, so it sticks out all over the place. "I really don't know." He ambles into his room and shuts the door gently behind him.

I wish he'd slammed it.

Layla and I are the only ones left behind.

I sag against the wall and put my head in my hands. "I've fucked everything up."

"No." She moves closer and I get a waft of her warm, sweet-spicy fragrance. "Myles is trying to stir the pot. They'll see that, eventually."

"What if they don't?"

"They will." She squeezes my arm.

I rub a hand across my mouth, remembering the ghost of Bianca's lips pressing against mine. "Bianca kissed me."

She releases my arm, like my skin burns her. "What did you do?"

"Nothing. I froze."

"Then what?"

"Told her I didn't feel the same way."

"Ah. She didn't take it well." It wasn't a question.

"You could say that."

"What did she say?"

Bianca's accusation rings in my ears.

It's her, isn't it... Precious Layla, who else?

A hot flush seeps up my chest, my neck, my cheeks. "She—she said—it doesn't matter."

Layla bows her head, a lock of dark hair falling over her face.

I itch to reach out and tuck it back behind her ear, to run the glossy strands through my fingers, to—

"It'll get better." She steps in close and plants a soft, feather-light kiss on my cheek.

The place where her lips brush my skin tingles.

She draws back and our eyes lock. "What? Have I got something on my face?"

"No." My eyes trace the sharp curve of her cheekbone, my gaze lingering on her full lips.

"Then why are you looking at me like that?"

My heart barricades itself in my throat. "You asked me what Bianca said."

"I did."

"She accused me of... she thinks I fancy you."

"I see." Layla smiles faintly, a cute dimple piercing her cheek. "And do you?"

On impulse, I reach out and tuck the loose lock of hair behind her ear—soft, and thick, and lush, coiling around my fingers like it doesn't want to let go of me. "What if I do?" I really want to kiss her.

She doesn't move back, but she doesn't move closer either.

I lean forward a fraction.

Still she doesn't move, but there's something in her eyes. A glint. A challenge.

I lean closer still, our faces inches apart now, so close that I can see a tiny patch of green marring the perfect liquid brown of her right iris. "Won't make this easy for me, huh?"

She arches one perfectly sculpted eyebrow. "Where's the fun in that?"

The pad of my thumb caresses the spot just behind her ear, and her pulse beats against the palm of my hand. Steady and strong. My pulse, by comparison, pounds in my neck. Closer, closer, closer, until we breathe the same air.

Layla's eyes drift closed, her thick, kohl-lined eyelashes fluttering against her cheeks like delicate bird wings.

Closer, closer, closer, lips almost touching.

A sound, like a hiccup, from the doorway.

Layla and I spring apart.

Bianca stands in the atrium's doorway, eyes brimming with tears. "I forgot my jacket."

I clear my throat. "Bianca—"

"Never mind." She spins on her heel and vanishes in a rush of quick footsteps.

"Bianca, wait." I start after her, but Layla grabs my arm.

"Let her go. The last thing she needs right now is you chasing after her."

I brush my fingers through my hair. "I'm sorry."

She smiles, a small, disappointed smile. "For trying to—"

"No. No, that would have been—just bad timing, I guess."

"Could've been better."

"What now?"

"Now, it's late, and it's been a long day. I'm going to bed."

I raise my eyebrows.

She chuckles. "Alone."

I laugh.

She plants another soft, tingling kiss on my cheek, fingertips grazing my chest, tickling. "Good night, Henry."

"Night."

When I climb into bed later, I fall asleep thinking of Layla Jabara, imagining her warmth in my sheets, and the feel of her lips electrifying my skin, aching for more of the same.

CHAPTER 23

Bianca and Geek have withdrawn from me completely, barely acknowledging my existence.

I tried to speak to Bianca yesterday, but that didn't go so well...

* * *

I round a corner and walk smack-bang into Bianca.

"Sorry." Her voice is sullen, and she ducks her head, sweeping past me.

"Bianca, wait." I grab her arm, then let go instantly.

She pauses, but doesn't turn to face me.

"Can we..." I rub my scar, then realise what I'm doing and drop my hand. "Can we talk about what happened?"

Her lips press against mine in the training room.

I don't return the kiss.

I wipe. My. Mouth.

Idiot.

My stomach pinches tight.

"We don't really have anything to talk about, do we?" she asks.

I rock back a step, like I'm dodging a witch-strike. "We're still friends. I still care—"

She turns now, a guarded look on her face I've never seen before. She twists her ring round and round her finger. "The only person you care about is yourself." She doesn't even sound angry, just tired.

I suck in a breath through my teeth, the pinching in my gut getting tighter and tighter. "That's not fair."

She sighs, heavy and awkward. "I asked you about Layla and you swore there was nothing going on between you."

"There isn't."

She arches an eyebrow at me.

"There wasn't... I... Look, I don't know what's happening between Layla and I, if I'm honest."

She shrugs. "It's a little late for honesty."

"Bianca, pl—"

"I have to go. I'm sorry, but I can't do this." She turns and drifts further down the hallway.

"I hate seeing you like this," I say.

She doesn't break her stride.

I raise my voice a little. "I just want to move past this and get back to the way things were."

Still drifting, and then she disappears around the next bend in the hallway.

She's gone, just like that.

"I didn't mean to hurt you," I say to the empty corridor.

It's a little late for honesty.

It's a little late for honesty.

Bianca's words have been bugging me for the last twenty-four hours, refusing to leave me alone. Refusing to quit.

I hope she'll come round eventually. Geek, too. I miss hanging out with them already. Although, if I don't get my act together, I won't be hanging out with anyone at COVEN for much longer.

I've yet to win a single bout in the ring.

Whenever I step into the silver circle, my opponent shifts and morphs before my eyes until they resemble Razor. Same artfully tousled blonde hair, same soulless black eyes, the memory of fruit flavoured chewing gum and old tobacco threatening to choke me to death.

It's happening again now.

My back strikes the floor of the ring, hard. The air whooshes out of me in one long gust.

Bianca stands over me, her pure white witch-staff gleaming in her grip.

I can't even beat her anymore.

The crowd of executioners don't boo, they don't cheer; they don't even look in our direction. Whenever Zara says I'm fighting, they chat among themselves. They aren't interested in my bouts, because the outcome's a forgone conclusion.

Zara flashes the current ratings up on the screen.

Current Ratings:

1. Myles Hedges

2. Layla Jabara

3. Oluwafemi Abimbola

4. Gareth Townsend

5. Bianca Yakhontov

6. Henry Stone

"Stone," Zara says.

I scrape myself off the floor, kneading my bruised back. "What?"

"Follow me."

Zara leads me down a familiar hallway.

"We're going to the island?" Oh, no. The island means using a portal. My stomach twinges at the thought and my mouth floods with saliva.

She doesn't answer.

Her silence—a rare occurrence—unsettles my stomach and I want to scratch my scar so bad, my fingers almost ache. But I sense now wouldn't be the right time, with Zara so close and her mood so unpredictable. I clench my fists and keep walking.

We push on, through the *Authorised Personnel Only* door. The wood shifts to rough rock beneath our feet, the air getting cooler and cooler and cooler.

"What's this about, Zara?" I ask.

She's silent, save for reciting the spell to open the portal, heralding its sickening warm-cool breath.

I grit my teeth. "Zara?"

She gestures towards the portal. "Move it."

I know better than to argue, so I brace myself and walk towards the glowing disc of pink light.

My feet touch the rocky outcropping of the cliff, and the salt spray from the crashing waves below stings my lips. My stomach strains and bucks like an angry horse, but I successfully hold on to my lunch. Last time I was here, the air was bitterly cold, and the darkness was all-consuming.

Now, rare winter sunshine burns through the clouds, flashes off the ocean waves, and paints the hardy tussocks of grass poking out of the bluff in shades of vermilion. Seagulls wheel overhead, calling to each other.

My chest expands as I take a deep breath of the fresh, briny sea air. It feels good to be outside again; the sun warming my skin; the icy breeze ruffing my hair.

The portal snaps closed.

"What are we doing here?" I ask Zara.

"I wanted to talk to you in private." She holds her hand up, fist closing. "*Imperium*."

Tight bands of steel close over my wrists, my ankles, my torso.

Zara raises her hand, and I float into the air.

"What are you doing? Put me down." I struggle, and the bands grow tighter.

"Make me."

"What? No. Are you—"

She squeezes her fist tighter.

The steel bands constrict further, and my breath hitches in my throat. "This isn't funny."

"I'm not laughing."

"What's the point of this?"

"Make me let you go."

"Stop messing around."

"Do I look like I'm messing around?" She stalks closer. "Carmichael told me everything. I know what happened to your parents. I know what Razor Finch did, and I know he wants to kill you."

I struggle again, but it's no use. "He shouldn't have told you."

"No. *You* should have told me. How do you expect me to train you if I don't know the truth?"

"Train me?" Sweat runs in rivulets down my back. "What does this have to do with training?"

"You're failing, miserably, but—"

"Thanks for the reminder." My cheeks burn.

"Let me finish."

I press my lips together.

"*But* you could easily be at the top of the ratings if you wanted."

"Ha. Haven't you been paying attention? I'm rubbish in the ring."

"Only because you're letting them win."

"Letting them win? They're better than me. They're more powerful—"

She holds up a hand for silence. "That's bollocks."

"No, it's not."

She points at her baby pink eyes. "I have the Sight too, remember? None of them are as powerful as you, but it doesn't matter unless you're prepared to use that power."

"I've tried—"

"You want to do this for your parents, yeah?"

Sharp pain slices into my stomach like a steel blade dipped in molten lava. "Of course."

"Then fucking act like it."

"I can't—"

"You're letting them down."

"I—" The pain mutates into something else, something fierce that boils and burns, the lava spreading into my chest, my limbs. "What the fuck did you just say?"

"You heard me. Your parents died to protect you, and this is how you repay them?"

"Stop."

"By being a coward."

"I know what you're trying to do."

"What are you going to do when you come face to face with Razor? Cower in the corner like a snivelling sack of shit? Because that's what you are. A snivelling, cowardly sack of stinking shit."

"Shut up."

She glares at me, eyes full of loathing. "Your parents would be ashamed of you."

"Fuck you." I draw on my power fast, syphoning more and more and more, until pins and needles race across my entire body with such force it's as if I'm being swarmed by a cloud of pissed off hornets. "*Fluctus inpulsa*."

A sound like cannon fire booms in my chest, and a wave of green-tinted concussive force explodes from my core.

Zara's unprepared, and the shock wave hits her head on. She shoots backwards, limbs flailing.

The steel bands holding me in place vanish and I drop to the floor like a brick, collapsing onto all fours, breathing hard. I must black out—I don't know how long for—because when I come to, I'm flat on my back, and Zara's standing over me with a huge grin on her face.

Blood trickles from a small gash in her head, glinting red in the early afternoon sunlight.

"You're hurt," I say.

She shrugs. "I don't have the faintest fuck where that came from, but when you go into the ring tomorrow, bring that fire with you." She thrusts out her hand for me to take, and I let her pull me to my feet.

I don't want to go into the ring tomorrow. What if the fire goes out by then?

Zara continues, "I've cut you more than enough slack. I want you to win tomorrow. If you don't, I'm kicking you out."

A lead weight crashes into my stomach. "Wait, what?" It comes out strangled. "Kicking me out? You—you can't do that."

"You can't do that," she mimics, before getting right in my face. "Your arse is mine. I can do whatever the fuck I want."

A swirling cocktail of emotion—anger, fear, denial—twists my stomach into pretzel-shaped knots. If Zara kicks me out... I can't even comprehend what will happen. It's like the cliff has crumbled beneath my feet. My stomach plummets. I'm falling, falling, falling.

Zara catches me, her hand fastening around my arm. "Last chance, Stone. Do it for them."

Them.

My parents.

I don't care how scared I am, how much the idea of going back into the ring makes my knees go weak. I've got to win tomorrow.

I need to.

This is my last chance.

The next day—probably my last day—I stand in the ring and tense the muscles in my legs to stop the executioners from noticing my knocking knees.

Femi stands opposite me, cracking his knuckles. His mouth curves like a blade.

The results of the executioners' poll are still up on the screens.

Everyone voted for Femi.

Not one person voted for me.

Not one.

I scan the crowd, spotting the familiar faces—Nick and Katya and Syed—but no Carmichael. He doesn't come to my bouts anymore.

Can't say I blame him, considering—

No.

I replay Zara's words from the previous day.

I've cut you more than enough slack. I want you to win tomorrow. If you don't, I'm kicking you out.

Kicking you out.

There's a knot in my lungs that no amount of throat clearing can untangle, and dizzying green-blue spots dance before my eyes. I'm floating in space, surrounded by toxic stars. My heart beats—fast, then slow, then fast again—and my stomach hurts.

Kicking you out.

Zara holds up a hand, and the room falls silent. "You two ready?" She flicks her gaze between Femi and I.

Femi grunts an affirmative and cracks his neck, sinking into a low stance.

I nod and bring my trembling hands up to guard my face.

Layla appears in my peripheral vision and mouths, "Good luck."

I give her a weak smile.

Bianca glares at us from the other side of the room.

Zara walks out of the circle and seals it with a now familiar *snap*.

"You're going down, Stone," Femi says.

"We'll see." My voice sounds confident, but my insides writhe.

Zara says, "Begin."

Despite his muscular build, Femi darts at me like a blur, conjuring his violet witch-staff as soon as the word leaves Zara's mouth.

I fling myself to the side, and Femi's staff rushes past me, screaming like the wind.

He swings the staff again.

Searing pain explodes in my shoulder and I spin with the momentum of the strike, trip over my feet, and crash to the floor.

He advances and launches a hissing orb of purple energy at me.

"*Obstructionum*." The spell splatters against my shield with a wet, corrosive fizzing sound, and the barrier sputters and dies.

An acid spell? If he'd hit me—

The crowd cheer, and shouts of, "Fe-mi, Fe-mi, Fe-mi," drown out the sound of my heart pulsing in my head.

Femi salutes before locking his eyes on mine. "You're finished, orphan boy."

I peel myself off the floor and clamber to my feet. The lava bubbles up in my stomach. The fire. "Don't call me that."

"What? Orphan boy?"

I clench my fists. "I swear to God, if you call me that again, I'll—"

Femi shoves my shoulder. "You'll what?" He pauses, cocking his head to the side. "Orphan. Boy."

The volcano in my stomach explodes, and boiling magma floods my entire body.

Femi raises his hand.

I move faster. "*Dis*."

My witch-strike slams into the centre of Femi's chest, and his legs go out from under him. His back slams into the floor with an audible thump.

Femi cries out—a low, guttural sound—and tries to regain his feet.

I conjure my witch-staff and swing it straight at his bent knee like a baseball bat.

Snap.

Femi screams and crumples back to the ground.

The sound's better than sweet, sweet music.

Orphan boy.

Femi lifts his hand, preparing to cast again.

I lunge forward and stamp on his wrist. It crackles like rice paper.

The scream becomes a wail.

Orphan boy.

I kick him in the ribs.

He grunts.

I kick again.

"Stop."

I ignore Zara's command and kick again, my foot colliding with Femi's nose, which buckles with a sickening *crunch*.

Blood spurts from his nose, staining the black marble crimson.

I half-register the burst of static signalling the circle breaking, but I don't stop. Femi's pushed me to the edge—like Zara back on the island—but this time, I've tumbled into the abyss.

I draw back my foot for another kick.

"I said that's enough." Zara wedges herself between Femi and I and shoves my shoulders hard with both hands. It's not the shove that stops me, it's the look on her face, a look of pure, blistering rage.

Silence as dead and as cold as a thousand graves descends, and the executioners stare at me with open mouths.

Geek and Bianca watch me warily.

Even Layla won't look me in the eye.

Myles glares, as usual.

The tension breaks.

The crowd erupts into roaring cheers.

Zara's eyes flash. "Quiet."

They don't comply; the cheers get even louder.

She brings her fingers to her lips and blows out a piercing wolf whistle. "Shut the fuck up."

That gets their attention.

When Zara speaks again, her voice is almost soft. "Everybody out. Now. Someone get him to the medical bay." She motions towards Femi. "Ask the nurse to give him some liquid silver."

The sound of shuffling feet breaks out all around me.

I move to join them.

"Not you," Zara says, a warning note in her voice.

I freeze, muscles locking in place.

Myles helps a semi-conscious Femi to his feet and guides him to the door.

When the room's empty, Zara says, "What the fuck was that, Stone?"

CHAPTER 24

"What the fuck was that, Stone?"

My cheeks warm with a rush of blood. "You told me to bring the fire, so I brought it."

"I told you to stop."

"What?"

"You were kicking the shit out of him and I told you to stop."

I grit my teeth. "He deserved it."

"That's not the point." A few seconds of quiet elapse. "What's my first rule?"

Silence rings in my ears. Silence, and the pounding of my pulse. "I know what the rules are."

She waits, saying nothing.

I sigh. "When you give an order, we follow it."

"I gave you an order."

"I did what you asked. You keep telling me that my power's useless if I don't use it. Well, I used it, and I won, and it felt great. I felt strong. And that's what COVEN's all about, right? What more do you want from me?"

"Strong?" She snorts. "You think what you did makes you strong? He was baiting you—calling you 'orphan boy' like that—and you let him get under your skin. You weren't being strong. You were giving in to your fear."

"I beat him. I won."

She shakes her head, disappointment colouring her tone when she speaks. "You might as well have lost."

I don't have to listen to this shit. I push past her and stride towards the door. "Forget it."

"Go on. Run away. Why break the habit of a lifetime?"

I spin to face her. "That's not fair."

She jabs a finger into my chest. "Remember what I told you yesterday. Your arse is mine."

A shard of ice pierces my heart. "What are you saying?"

"I'm saying I'm done with you." Zara steps back and drags a hand through her hair, ripping out her ponytail, her blonde curls framing her face. It doesn't make her look softer, somehow, just more menacing. "You're out."

"No." My heart pounds. "No. Please. You know how much I need this. You know why."

She shakes her head. "I have to think beyond that. COVEN's mission is bigger than your vendetta."

"I know that, but—"

"Say I let you stay. Say, by some miracle, you become an executioner and you kill Razor. What then?"

My eyebrows knit together. "What do you mean?"

"That's exactly what I mean. You're here for the wrong reasons."

"What?"

"Executioners want justice." She pauses. "You just want revenge."

"It's the same thing—"

"No, it's not. And it worries me you can't see that. What lengths will you go to?" Zara strides over to the puddle of blood left behind by Femi's busted nose. "Any lengths? Beating the shit out of your fellow trainees like some mindless mortal thug?"

"*I'm* a mindless thug? Myles and Femi have been bullying me for months! They're the thugs, they're the—"

"And you sank to their level today. You're no better than them."

Her words are like a backhanded slap to the face. "How dare you?"

She strides towards me and, for once, I hold my ground. "You're an arrogant little prick," she says, hitting every consonant hard. "You're worse than they are. I expected so much more from you."

A sledgehammer pounds into my gut.

"Strength. Justice. Loyalty." Zara says. "That's what we fight for. What was just about your actions?"

My head spins. I'm quiet for a long time. Is she right? Will I do anything for revenge? The answer's an obvious yes. Am I worse than Myles and Femi? Who knows?

I clear my throat and, in a quiet voice, say, "Razor slaughtered my family, for fuck's sake. I need this. Don't you have any compassion?"

She shoots another pointed look at Femi's drying blood. "Don't you?"

I look away, the contents of my stomach replaced with bitter acid.

"Tonight, you can pack up your shit. Tomorrow, you're done."

"Zara, please—"

"I don't want to hear it." She strides over to the door, pausing in front of it. "When you first arrived, I was so excited. Another Sighted witch. The only other Sighted witch I've ever met. I thought, finally, another Outsider who can beat the system. What a fool. You're such a disappointment."

The door closes.

My eyes well with tears.

You're such a disappointment.

I turn on the hot water and steam billows from the shower. Pulling my T-shirt off, I yank the chain holding my parents' wedding rings over my head, placing them by the sink. "I expect you're disappointed in me too." I stare into the mirror.

The green-eyed stranger stares back at me.

I look down.

The light glints off the silver chain. The rings.

My parents' faces float before my eyes and, for the first time since Razor murdered them, I imagine them as they were when they were alive.

Dad sitting at the table, puzzling over *The Times* crossword.

Mum listening to her old forty-five-inch records, dancing around the lounge and singing along, a little off-key.

Another image.

Razor.

It flicks back.

Mum singing *The First Cut is the Deepest*.

And again.

Razor, standing before me—fingers glowing scarlet—preparing to slit my throat.

I'm going to make you suffer.

My fingers go to the scar between my collarbones, and I pick until it bleeds.

I hate you, and I'll never forgive you...

We write regarding your application...

I'm going to make you suffer...

Orphan boy...

You're such a disappointment...

I press my eyes closed, my face wet with tears. "I'm sorry, I'm sorry, I'm sorry."

A scuffing sound comes from behind me and, before I can react, cool fingers brush my temple. "*Somnum.*"

Somnum?

Sleep.

My legs buckle.

And then I'm falling, fading, and the world goes dark.

CHAPTER 25

A fresh scent hangs in the air.
I recognise it.

Soap and clean linen.

The fragrance is familiar, but the haze of the sleep spell muddles my thoughts, and I can't remember why the smell's significant. Whatever. All I know is it shouldn't be here. Wherever here is. I'm slumped against something hard and cold—a chair?—stripped to the waist. I can tell because of the goosebumps pinching my skin tight. My eyelids are heavy, too heavy to lift, so they cover everything in an impenetrable layer of darkness.

Where am I?

I drift back into unconsciousness, float for a while, then bump into consciousness again. Drift, float, bump. Drift, float, bump. I'm a tethered boat, bobbing on the waves, slamming back into the jetty. Over and over.

What the hell happened?

Stay awake.

I need to stay awake.

My eyelids are so heavy. Someone's glued them shut. I strain and strain, a groan escaping me.

"He's waking up."

Do I know that voice? I think so. It's the same voice that put me here, isn't it? Voices. Concentrating on voices is difficult. So much easier to drift at sea.

Drift...

Drifting...

Smack.

My head snaps to the side and my brain rattles around in my skull. I crack my eyes open. Where am I? Semi-dark, uneven rock walls, cold—so cold. My head thumps with a dull ache, my mouth's dry, and my tongue's furry.

"Good. Now we can get started."

I know that deep rumble. It can only be Femi. If Femi's here, then something bad is about to happen. My chest tightens. My eyes adjust to the dingy half-light. Myles stands over me, blank-faced, his palm bright red from where he'd slapped me.

Femi leans against the rough rock wall, trying to appear nonchalant, but it's a façade. He's tense, ready to spring into action at any moment.

Where am I? I still can't place my location. This isn't COVEN, is it? No smooth wood-panelling here. But, wait. I know this place. It's the tunnel leading to the island portal.

Deep underground.

My heart hammers against my ribcage. I'm deep under-ground. I can try to call for help—scream and shout and rage—but nobody will hear me.

No-one even knows I'm down here.

No-one knows... no-one... the remnants of the sleep spell drag my eyelids down and down until I'm floating again.

Another sharp slap. Stinging pain numbs my cheek, and my eyes snap open. Copper coats my tongue. I spit. A thick glob of blood and saliva spatters the floor.

"Wakey, wakey." Myles crouches, bringing his frozen green eyes level with mine. "I've been looking forward to this."

Sweat breaks out on my forehead. "What have you done to me?" My voice is a croak. My tongue flicks over my dry, chapped lips and I move to stand. I'm halfway to my feet when something hard bites into my wrist. My weak legs collapse beneath me. I flop back into the chair.

Myles laughs. "You're not going anywhere, orphan boy."

I tilt my head. One metal cuff binds my wrist, the other's shackled to the back of the chair. "What the fuck is this?"

"I told you once before, I won't let you beat me." Myles stands and brushes his blonde fringe away from his forehead. "I'm going to teach you a lesson."

Teach me a lesson. My blood congeals. I need to get out of here, and fast. I point at the cuff shackling my wrist with my free hand. "*Recludo.*"

Magic rises within me, the pinpricks racing down my arms, warm and welcome, and—

Stabbing pain pierces my heart. I cry out, a tortured yell that echoes around the dull passage. The pain fades. My breathing returns to normal. I point at the cuff again. "*Recludo.*"

The pain's worse this time, like someone's attached live wires to all the tender parts of me and passed an electric current through my body.

My magic won't work.

But that's impossible. Nothing can—

Witches are allergic to iron. On contact with the skin, it prevents the use of magic, and overexposure can make us sick, or even kill us. That's why wrist and leg irons were so popular in the fifteen hundreds.

Dad's words on the night of my Manifestation.

I stare at the cuff, eyes wide.

Femi glances up and a cruel smile curves his lips. "I think he's worked it out."

"No, no, no." I strain against the cuffs, pulling, wrenching, yanking, but it's no good. I'm trapped.

Powerless.

Myles wears a self-satisfied smirk.

My hands shake so hard the cuff rattles against the chair. "Okay. Fine. I get it. You're pissed off. But think about what you're doing."

Femi struts towards me. "Oh, we've thought about it. We know exactly what we're doing."

"What if someone comes looking for me?"

"Like who?" Myles asks.

Think, think, think. My nostrils flare, and there it is again. That smell. Soap and clean linen. Where do I know that smell from? "Zara," I say.

Femi shakes his head. "She's gone home for the night."

"Geek, then."

"I don't think so," Myles snorts. "You two haven't spoken since the island. He wants nothing to do with you."

Soap and fresh linen, soap and fresh linen, soap and fresh linen.

Home.

It smells like home.

Sickness swirls in my belly.

Femi says, "No one's coming to save you."

Soap and fresh linen.

I'd noticed it on the first day of training.

She smells like home.

Soap and fresh linen.

"Why, Bianca?" I say.

Light footsteps approach, and Bianca materialises from the shadows, her arms folded across her chest like she's hugging herself. She trains her gaze on the uneven floor. "Hello, Henry."

A peel of laughter bursts from Myles. He laughs so hard tears stream from his eyes. "I wish you could see your face, Stone."

Bianca fiddles with her diamond ring.

"Why?" I ask in a quiet, cracked voice. "Bianca, why are you helping them?"

Twist, twist, twist.

The diamond winks at me as she spins it round and round.

"Isn't it obvious?" Myles says. "You've been leading her on for months, taking advantage of the way she feels about you, manipulating her. She's seen through you."

My fists clench. "That's not what happened."

"Took her long enough." Femi says. "Then again, she's not the sharpest lime on the tree."

A blood-blush creeps into Bianca's cheeks, but she ignores Femi's jibe. She shifts her weight onto her other foot and releases her ring.

There's a tiny set of keys clutched in her fist.

Hope flares in my chest. The keys to my cuffs. I lean forward.

Bianca's head snaps up, her sad hazel eyes meeting mine.

"Please. Please help me," I say.

"Why should I?" She sniffs, the sound dismissive.

"Because we're friends."

Her answering laugh's derisive. "Friends. Yes, you've made that painfully clear."

"I'm sorry if I've hurt you, but you know I never meant to." She looks away.

Femi stifles a yawn. "Can we get on with this? I'm bored."

Myles nods. "You know what to do."

Femi stalks forward with a slow grin and raises his hand. "*Acidum.*"

I tense up.

Acidum.

Acid.

No.

Femi's hand glows purple, and swirling heatwaves ripple from the tips of his fingers.

The same acid spell I'd deflected in the ring. I gulp.

Femi's grin widens into a full smile that shows all his teeth. "No shield to protect you this time."

I draw as far away from Femi as the chair allows, which isn't very far. My back's slick with sweat and my pulse thunders at my temples. "You can't do this."

Bianca grabs Myles's arm. "What are you doing? Hurting him wasn't part of the plan."

He shrugs her off. "Plans change."

"You said you only wanted to scare him."

"Scare him." Femi's eyes harden. "I'm going to kill him."

Fine tremors wrack my entire body. "Wh—what?"

"This is payback for what you did in the ring." Femi advances on me, brandishing his glowing hand.

"Wait." My voice shakes, but I force the words out. "Think about what you're doing. If you kill me, you'll be breaking The Third Law. When Carmichael finds out about this, he'll have you arrested, you'll go to Purgatory. In fact, you'll be lucky if he doesn't kill you. You—"

A cruel light flickers in Femi's eyes. "Carmichael has to catch us first. We're really good at covering our tracks."

Ice encases my entire body. "You don't have to do this. Zara's kicked me out. After tomorrow, you'll never see me again. You don't have to do this. *You don't have to do this.*"

"What?" Bianca asks. "She's excluded you?"

I nod, hot tears sliding down my face.

"We know," Femi says.

My brow furrows. "How?"

"Father told me," Myles says.

"Doesn't change anything." Femi steps closer, the sickly heat from his spell warming my bare torso. "Nobody makes a fool out of me and gets away with it."

"You can't—"

Femi flicks his wrist.

My side explodes with blistering agony. I scream, drawn out, high-pitched shrieks that scrape my throat raw. The acid eats away at my ribcage, taking huge, hungry bites out of my flesh. I buck and twist in the chair, the iron cuff biting into my wrist, hot blood trickling from my fingers. I don't know how long it lasts, but it feels like forever.

Bianca does nothing, apart from watch—wide eyed—while Femi tortures me. How can she stand by and do nothing? She's weak and, what's worse, I see her weakness reflected in me, and I hate it.

In that moment, I hate her, too.

I scream until my throat's raw and my cheeks are wet with tears.

I'm going to kill him.

A deep sense of regret lowers onto my shoulders like a thick, water-logged cloak. I'm going to die without avenging my parents.

That's my last coherent thought before the agony becomes too much to bear.

Eventually, Femi lowers his hand and the purple light fades.

The pain remains. Tears stream down my face. A series of pitiful sobs rip from my throat. Femi's spell has ruined my skin. Angry red welts blister my side—ribcage to hip bone—and black patches cling to the edges of the wound. The meaty scent of charred pork wafts up my nose and I gag.

Then the lights go out.

CHAPTER 26

LAYLA

"Come on, Layla. You can do this," I mutter to myself. The soft-soled training shoes muffle my strides. Bloody things. I'd give my right arm to wear real shoes—the *Gucci* stilettos—the blue, jewel-encrusted ones with the spiked heels. I miss the *click-clack, click-clack* that alerts people to my presence and lets them know I'm on the warpath. Trainers. Who wears trainers? I hate the itchy, colourless, cheap black uniform Zara forces us to wear. Most of all, I hate the pinch in my stomach every time I think of Henry.

The pinch of uncertainty.

I don't do uncertain. Then again, I didn't do black poly-ester-cotton blends and flat shoes before I came here, either.

Damn Myles and his big mouth.

I haven't spoken to Henry since Myles accused him of playing everyone off against each other. When Henry asked us whether we believed Myles, I leapt to his defence. But I can't stop the questions buzzing around my brain. Particularly after the way Henry attacked Femi today.

The rage in his eyes. The hate.

I shudder.

What if Henry really is playing games? I know how much he wants—no, *needs*—to be an executioner. Is Myles just jealous, because Henry has the Sight? Are Henry's feelings for me manufactured? When will this pinch in my stomach go away? I know the answer to the last question. The pinching—the uncertainty—will only stop when I get some answers, and that's what I'm doing. I'm going to march right into Henry's room and demand the truth.

My mind wonders to other boys. Past boys, boys promising love and roses and happily ever afters. Is Henry one of those boys? If I can look him in the eye, I'll know for sure. The last time was the last time. A promise I made to myself, and one I swore not to break.

No man plays Layla Jabara for a fool.

I draw myself up to my full height as I round the corner into the trainees' quarters, halting at the entrance to the corridor.

Henry's door is ajar.

That's not right.

He never leaves it open.

"Henry?" I hover on the threshold. "Are you in here? We need to talk."

The bathroom door is wide open. Steam billows out and light blazes from within. The soft hiss of shower water splashing against tiles fills my ears.

"Henry?"

I cross to the bathroom door. Hesitate. He's in the shower, dripping wet and naked right now. My cheeks burn, the slow heat spiralling down, down, down. I shake my head. Get a grip. I don't care if he's slathered in chocolate body paint and hundreds and thousands—Mm. That would be such a turn on. There must be a can of whipped cream somewhere—focus, you horny cow. I want answers. That's all that matters. That, and the whipped cream. I poke my head around the door frame.

The shower cubicle is empty, the glass door gaping open, a puddle of water wetting the floor.

I run to the shower and turn it off.

Where is he? Why did he leave the shower running?

A flash of light glinting on silver catches my eye.

There, on the side of the sink. The coiled chain. The wedding rings. His parents' wedding rings. Something tells me he wouldn't go anywhere without those.

My heart flutters.

I almost slip on the wet floor in my haste to flee from the bathroom. Darting through the bedroom and out into the hall, I collide with Geek.

He staggers back. "Bloody hell. Watch where you're going, will you?"

"Where's Henry?"

Geek's jaw tightens. "Don't know, don't care."

"He's not in his room."

Geek shrugs and pushes past me, strolling toward his own room.

"He left these behind." She holds out the rings.

His expression remains blank. "So?"

"They belonged to his parents. He wouldn't have left without them."

"Maybe he forgot."

"He wouldn't." My breath hitches. "Wait, have you seen the others?"

"No, I haven't."

I march along the corridor, throwing doors aside. Myles's room. Empty. Bianca's room. Empty. Femi's room. Empty. "Where the hell is everyone?"

"How am I supposed to know?"

Something with sharp teeth gnaws at my stomach. "Something's wrong."

"You're overreacting," Geek says. There's an edge of doubt in his voice. "He'll be in the training room. That's where he always is."

I shake my head and brush my hair away from my face. "I checked there first."

"The dining hall, then? Maybe he's getting a snack?"

"Looked in there, too."

Geek bites his lip. "I'm sorry, I can't help you."

"Please, Geek. He's your friend."

He snorts. "Some friend. He tricked me."

"I know, but think about it. You know why he's here. All he wants is to avenge his parents. If you were in his position, wouldn't you have done the same?"

Shadows gather in his eyes. "We're all here for a reason." He turns away.

"He's in trouble, I can feel it," I call after him. "If something happens to him, and you did nothing to help, you'll regret it."

Geek goes still. The muscles in his back pull tight and his fists clench. Seconds pass, minutes. Precious minutes I'm convinced we don't have.

So I tell him Henry's story—all of it, even though it's not my story to tell, and Henry will probably hate me for it—and I don't stop until I've finished.

Eventually, he says, "Fine. I'll help you find him, but this doesn't mean I forgive him."

"Okay, whatever you say, but we need to hurry."

We race along the wood-panelled corridor.

Please, please let me be wrong.

CHAPTER 27

W hen the lights come back up, Bianca's glaring at Myles. "I didn't agree to this," she says, her fists balled tight. "You said you wouldn't hurt him."

Myles says, "And you said you wanted to get your own back."

"Not like this."

My side's stopped steaming, but it's gone numb. A bad sign.

Femi lunges forward and digs his fingers into the wound.

The agony flares anew. I clench my teeth, a wounded animal growl emanating from deep in my throat.

"Did you really think I'd let you get away with humiliating me?" Femi asks.

"Stop. Just stop." Bianca rushes to my side, fingers fumbling over the keys.

"What do you think you're doing?" Femi's voice is sharp.

Bianca crouches next to me, reaching for my wrist. "What does it look like?"

Myles barks a harsh command and curls his fingers into a fist.

Bianca jerks upright, and the keys fall from her fingers. They make a soft, tinkling sound when they hit the floor. Her eyes bulge. She clutches at her throat, gasping for air, a cherry red flush creeping up her cheeks.

"Stop it." I thrash against the cuffs, the metal biting into my skin again. "*Mortem*." The burning agony from my side chases the electric pain of my trapped magic. I scream again.

Myles frowns. "Hear that, Femi? He tried to conjure a death-strike."

"I heard."

Bianca makes a choking sound.

Myles tilts his head to the side. "Trying to kill me, Stone? Didn't know you had it in you."

"Let her go," I say.

Ignoring me, Myles creeps closer to Bianca and places his lips right by her ear, his eyes still on mine. "I could kill her, you know. One flick of the wrist and snap." He looks her up and down, cold and clinical. His fist opens.

Bianca collapses, throwing her hands out to break her fall. She gasps, wretches, coughs—violent, hacking coughs rattling her spare frame.

"But she's not worth the hassle," Myles says.

Bianca's eyes flash to the keys, just within reach.

"Bianca." It's difficult to speak, because powdered glass lines my throat. "Please. If you ever felt anything for me, please help me."

She blinks away tears. Her eyes go from me, to the keys and back again.

"Don't even think about it." Femi kicks out. His foot catches on the keys, and they skitter into a dark corner.

Bianca mouths the word, "Sorry," clambers to her feet and bolts, the sound of her footsteps retreating.

I want to scream at her. To hurl obscenities at her. To brand her a traitor and a coward. But I don't have the energy.

Femi cracks a knuckle, the sound like a bullet firing from a gun. "I told you she'd flake out."

"Doesn't matter now," Myles says, a slow smile creeping over his face. "Where were we?"

I'm sick of screaming. My throat's raw, my voice cracking. I'm lost in a world of agony, and I gave up telling them to stop ages ago. My eyes burn with tears, and I bit my tongue at some point. So everything tastes like copper.

"Stop," Myles says.

The searing heat at my lower back recedes. I'm a creature of scorched, tingling, blistering flesh, and the burning-pork smell plugs my nose. My stomach wrenches. I sag, flinching and crying out when my mutilated skin grazes the back of the chair.

"See?" Myles paces in front of me, unable to stand still. "Your eyes don't make you special. Underneath it all, you're just like the rest of us."

I glower at him and find my voice; the words are ragged and strained. "I'm nothing like you."

"No? You were going to kill me a minute ago. I'm going to kill you soon. What's the difference?"

"It's not the same thing."

"Because?"

"Because I was trying to protect Bianca, and you two are psychotic."

Myles laughs.

"You won't get away with this," I say.

"That's where you're wrong." He paces faster and faster, a manic light in his eyes. "When we're finished with you, we're taking your body through the portal, to the island. No-one will ever find you."

Cold seeps into my bones, and my insides turn to liquid. "You can't. You don't know how to cast a portal."

"Don't I?" He strides over to the portal wall and runs his fingers over the rough rock. "*Ostium*."

A dark grey portal whirls into existence with a static buzz.

No way. My scalp pulls tight. "Zara hasn't taught us that yet."

Myles smirks. "My father's been training me in private for weeks. He thinks Zara's methods take too long. He's right."

"No, no, no." I wrench and wrench and wrench at the cuffs, but they hold fast.

Myles slinks towards me like a sly jungle cat.

Predatory.

Inhuman.

"*Mortem*." Bruised grey energy roars to life in his palm. "Bet you wish you shook my hand now?"

"I—" Even now, moments before certain death, my natural inclination's to keep the peace. I want to say, "Of course I wish I'd shaken hands." But that's not true, and I'd rather die speaking the truth than carry on living in fear. "No," I say. "I don't."

His face contorts. "Say hello to your parents."

Mum.

Dad.

Myles's hand shoots out.

See you soon.

I close my eyes and wait for death.

A blinding flash of sunshine yellow light flares behind my eyelids, followed by a muffled *thump*.

Myles screeches, his voice high and strangled.

I open my eyes.

Myles is lying sprawled in a heap on the other side of the passage, clutching his stomach and groaning.

Femi has his back to me, a mauve death-strike hissing and spitting in his palm.

"*Flagellum*."

A yellow-tinted witch-whip streaks out of the darkness and wraps itself around Femi's wrist. His arm jerks to the side, the death-strike skittering off into the shadows. The witch-whip jerks again, dissipating, and Femi spins on tip-toes, round and round, careening off to the side. His head strikes the wall. He stumbles, falls.

"Henry!"

Layla.

She darts down the passage, her dark curtain of hair streaming behind her like bonfire smoke on the wind. She's ten feet away, five feet—

An orb of grey light smacks into her hip and knocks her sideways. She trips, crashing to the ground.

"No." I twist in my seat—ignoring the searing pain that wracks my body—but the cuffs hold fast.

Myles is on his feet now, outstretched fingers still extended towards Layla.

The ozone stink of spent magic permeates the air.

"Stay out of this," Myles says, striding towards Layla. "I don't want to hurt you, but I will if I have to."

She rolls onto her side and fires a witch-strike at him.

He blocks it. "Have it your way." He conjures another death-strike.

"Don't you dare." I thrash against the cuffs, but they won't break.

Myles's eyes flash, reflecting the light from his spell. The world slows and slows and slows, as Myles draws his arm back, preparing to fire.

Blind terror liquidises my intestines. "Stop. Myles, if you hurt her, I swear, I will kill you. I will—"

Snap.

Myles cries out, and his leg crumples as he sinks to one knee. His death-strike stutters and dies.

What the hell? How?

Geek sprints out of the darkness.

Myles lifts his tear-streaked face, narrowed eyes boring into Geek's. "*Mort—*"

Geek's bent knee slams into Myles's temple, and he collapses onto his side.

Layla staggers to her feet and stumbles over to me. "You okay?"

I don't answer her, all my attention on Geek.

He isn't moving. His wide eyes take in my blistered, blackened skin. "Oh, God." His muddy brown eyes meet my emerald-green ones. "I'm sorry, mate. I never should've believed him."

"No," I say, wincing. "You shouldn't."

Layla examines the cuffs shackling my wrists. "Where are the keys?"

"I—ah—I don't know. Femi. He kicked them somewhere."

Layla's brow furrows, and she holds out her hand, palm facing up. "*Claves me adducere.*" Her hand flashes yellow.

A soft, tinkling sound brushes my left ear and a small, sparkling shape flies out of the shadows.

The keys land in Layla's palm. She closes her fingers around them, kneels beside me and takes hold of my bound wrist.

The movement makes me wince.

"Sorry."

"It's okay."

She inserts the key into the lock and turns.

Click.

The cuff falls away.

Geek still hasn't moved.

"Can you walk?" Layla asks.

"I don't know," I say.

Layla looks at Geek. "Help me get him up."

Geek's hands tremble, but he still doesn't move.

"Geek. Help me."

"What?" He blinks, gazes around as if waking from a dream. "Oh, yeah. Sure." He comes forward and places an arm around my shoulders, careful to avoid the burned patches.

Layla grips my arm.

Together, they help me to my feet.

I grit my teeth against the cutting pain of multiple razors being raked down my back and side. The world spins and I'm lightheaded, like a helium balloon bobbing against the ceiling.

"Where are we—"

A scraping sound cuts across Geek, and Femi's low, rumbling voice barks out a spell.

I don't think, just act. I throw Geek and Layla behind me—my body screaming as if someone's ripping me apart, piece by piece—hurl my arm across my body and shout, "-*Obstructionum*."

Something strikes my shield, hard.

A throbbing ache blossoms behind my eyes.

My shield crumples.

I fall.

The cold, damp floor kisses my cheek, the bruising kiss of a desperate lover.

Stars dance on the ceiling.

Light and sound and heat whizz overhead in streaks of yellow, turquoise, grey, violet.

My vision blurs, fades.

Someone—Myles, maybe?—shouts, "Run!"

Two sets of footsteps retreat.

I reach out, trying to brush my hand through the smudged paint adorning the ceiling. Something mutes the pain and turns it down low.

There's a whiff of something in the cool air. What is that? Not the damp, almost stagnant smell of the passage. No. Something else. Warm and spicy and woody and sweet.

Layla.

She says something, but I can't make out the words. Her voice sounds the way she smells. Warm. Like sinking into a hot bath. I laugh, or try to. Stupid. How can a voice sound like a hot bath? Oh. I'd sink into a bath with her any day. I can practically feel my hands roving over her smooth, dusky skin, fingertips stroking, tweaking, parting—

"Henry? Stay with me." There are tears in her melodious voice, making me ache. "Don't close your eyes. Geek. Get some help."

There's an edge of panic in Geek's voice. "Who? Zara's gone home and Carmichael—"

"Anyone. Just go."

"But—"

"Go!"

"No." My voice croaks on the way out.

"Don't talk," Layla says. "It'll be okay. You'll be okay." She's brushing my hair away from my face, stroking my cheek, my lips.

Zara's earlier words swim up from the depths of my mind.

You're such a disappointment.

I take hold of Layla's wrist, my grip weak as a kitten. "Don't—don't tell Zara."

"Henry, we have to."

"No, Layla. Please. Promise me. Promise me you won't tell anyone."

She ignores me, turning to Geek. "Why are you still standing there like a squashed lemon? Go."

Geek says, "But he said—"

"I don't care what he said. I can't lose him."

Geek hesitates for a fraction of a second before—*thump, thump, thump*—he's gone.

I say it like a mantra. "Don't tell anyone, don't tell anyone, don't tell..."

Someone wraps a thick blanket of darkness around me, tucks it in at the edges, and traps my words in the void.

CHAPTER 28

I'm lying on something soft. Warm air, laced with the sharp scent of antiseptic, caresses my skin.

Antiseptic?

That's not right. What a horrible dream. Down in the caves, being tortured. I attempt to wriggle onto my side, but a cool hand touches my bare shoulder, forcing me to stay on my back.

"Careful," Layla says.

Layla.

A memory—or was it a dream? Warm bath water, questing fingers. Why's she in my room? Did she—did we—it's all fuzzy.

I crack my eyelids open. I'm not in my luxurious quarters. Instead, bright light singes my eyeballs. I blink hard three times and my eyes adjust. The bed I lie on isn't mine. It's a hospital bed. A sickly pea green curtain hangs from a rail suspended from the ceiling, and Layla's face hovers above mine.

The medical bay.

I'm in the medical bay.

It wasn't a dream. It was real.

Myles tried to kill me.

I crane my neck down, trying to ignore the way even slight movements make the room tilt.

A wire frame holds the covers off me, and large swathes of gauze cover my sides, the white material disappearing under my back. "It hurts," I croak.

Layla's hair hangs down around her face. I want to brush my fingers through it, so I raise my hand, but something pinches my arm and my eyes flick to the source of the prickling pain.

One, two, three, four, five needles stud my arm. Thin plastic tubes snake away from each needle, attached to five bags of liquid silver suspended from a metal IV pole. I try to speak, but my throat's too dry.

"Here," Layla says, and a plastic cup of water, with a straw poking out, appears in my peripheral vision.

I suck down a greedy gulp of the cool, life-giving liquid.

"Slowly," Layla moves the cup away.

"Where's"—I clear my throat—"where's Geek?"

"I'm here, mate."

I turn my throbbing head.

Geek slumps in a chair by the bed. He's pale-faced. There are bags under his eyes and he's bitten his fingernails down to the quick.

I swallow. "You look like shit."

This raises a half-smile. "Don't look so good yourself."

Silence—the kind that worms its way under your skin and burrows there—fills the room.

I breathe in through my nose. The bedsheets smell like clean linen.

Clean linen.

Bianca.

How could she? How could she have let them hurt me? Something heavy presses down on my stomach and I groan.

"Are you in pain?" Layla asks. "I'll get the nurse."

"No. I mean, yes, but it's not that."

She rests the back of her hand to my clammy forehead. "You're burning up, I'll get—"

"Bianca was there."

"*What*?" Geek's eyebrows knit into a frown.

"She was there. She—ow—she was helping them."

"No." Geek shakes his head. "She wouldn't do that."

"I'm telling you, she was there."

His face falls. He knows I'm telling the truth.

Layla leaps to her feet and slams her hand down on the small bedside table next to me. "Wait until I get my hands on that prissy little bitch."

More silence.

"Listen," Geek says. "About what happened after the island. About what Myles said, I'm sorry—"

"Forget about it," I say.

"No." He shakes his head. "I need to say this. I'm sorry for how I acted. Ignoring you, it—it was childish."

"I deserved it, after what I did."

He flinches like I kicked him in the shins. "Layla told me about your parents. About everything."

Layla jumps in, her words spilling out in a jumbled rush. "It was the only way I could think of to convince him to help. There wasn't time to—"

I wave Layla away. "It's fine." I turn to Geek. "I should have told you before. Still doesn't make us square."

"No, but it explains a lot." A pained expression crosses Geek's face. "You need to be selected as much as I do." He pauses again, chewing over whatever words he's struggling to say. "You were right. Carmichael was directing that comment at me on the first day."

I know that most of you have a lot riding on this...

I roll my eyes, and even that hurts. "I thought you were supposed to be a geek. Tell me something I hadn't figured out already, genius."

The corner of his mouth lifts, but he doesn't smile properly. "Before Carmichael brought me here, I... I—um—"

"You don't have to tell me," I say, my words echoing Layla's on the night I told her about my past.

"No. I do." He pauses, glances away, glances back. "Before this... I... did some bad shit."

My brow furrows. That's not what I was expecting him to say. "Define 'bad shit'?" I go to sit up, but a sharp pain explodes along my side, down my spine, and I collapse back onto the pillows.

"Easy," Layla strokes my sweaty hair with gentle fingers.

Geek says, "I—uh—I grew up in London. A really nice part of London. It was just me and my mum. She's—well, she *was*, awesome."

My lips part. "She died?"

He shakes his head. "Some dickwad defrauded her company and we lost everything. We had to move into this shitty little flat in Newham. I hated it. And Mum... she... she couldn't handle it. Started taking witch-bane."

Witch-bane? Why's that familiar?

Then Zara's words from the first day of training float back to me.

It's a highly addictive, highly illegal drug. Using the bane is shameful. Weak.

"I don't get why everyone's so against it," Layla says. "I know it's illegal but, from what I've read, it has some useful properties."

"Like what?" I ask.

She lifts a shoulder. "Apparently, it produces these visions that allow the user to cast a locater spell without the need for a locus. If that's true, you could find anyone, any criminal. They wouldn't be able to hide. I wonder—"

Geek shoots her a dark look. "Trust me, it's not worth the risk. You'd have to be pretty desperate to use that stuff."

"Sorry," Layla mumbles.

Geek sighs. "Anyway, I enabled her habit. It was the only thing that made her better. I know, I know. It wasn't really making her better at all."

I can't imagine what it must've been like. Geek had to watch his mum suffer. That must've been hell.

"You said your mum lost everything when she lost her company." Layla wears a frown. "From what I've read, witch-bane's expensive. How could you afford it?"

Geek rubs the back of his neck. "Learned a few... tricks."

"What tricks?" I ask.

He bites his thumbnail. "Confidence tricks. Simple stuff, at first. Three-card monte, that sort of thing. I used to go into the city and take money off the wanker-bankers who wouldn't miss it."

"You're a con man?" My tone sounds judgemental, but I don't mean it to.

He doesn't notice, just carries on speaking, his fingers twisting together and untwisting again. "I thought I was good at it. Being a thief. Got braver, or more stupid. Even managed to pull off a spate of burglaries in Knightsbridge." He catches my look. "Hey. Don't look at me like that. I only took money off people who deserved it. I had to, for Mum."

I bow my head. It's easy to understand how he became a thief, to understand the need to do anything for your parents.

Geek blows out a long breath. "Anyway, that's when I met her."

My head snaps up again. "Her?"

"Helena." He looks down, smiles, bites his lip. "Newham Highstreet. Middle of the day. I went out to get milk, and smacked right into her. I didn't know at the time, but she was using a glamour spell, and—humph, that's not important. She—" He pauses, expelling a little laugh. "She picked my pocket. No one had done that for years, but she... well, she was special. I needed extra money, so did she. We started working together."

"You were a couple?" Layla asks.

"No. we weren't together long enough. She was cute, though, so who knows. One day... maybe." A far away look enters his eyes.

"What happened?" I ask.

He jumps, like he forgot we were there. "Roger Reeves."

I shoot Layla a puzzled look.

She seems equally confused, so she mustn't know the name either.

"He was a nasty bastard. Dodgy landlord who treated his tenants like dirt. We stole something from him. He and his henchman came looking for it."

"They murdered her," I say.

Filmy tears cling to Geek's eyelashes. "Ha. I almost wish they had." His face scrunches up in pain. "Fuck. I didn't mean that, but she..." He drags a rough hand across his eyes. "They severed her spinal cord, so *I* killed *them*. She'll never walk again. Because of me. If I'd acted sooner. If I'd... well, doesn't matter now."

I know that feeling. The what if. What if I hadn't run off into the woods on the night of my Manifestation? What if I'd stayed? I could've... I would've... the questions never end.

"What happened next?" Layla asks.

Geek rolls his shoulders, clearly uncomfortable. "The MID showed up. Helena told me to run. She got arrested. I ended up in this fuck-hole dive pub, chugging tequila like water. Carmichael showed up. I thought he was one of those city-slicker pricks. Expensive shoes, tailored clothes."

"He offered you a place here," Layla asks.

He nods. "Struck a deal with the MID, apparently. Helena's charges were dropped, but she didn't want to see me. Carmichael said she was struggling to adjust, which I get." He takes a heavy breath. "He said my skillset would be useful and that, if I joined COVEN, he'd pay for this swanky rehab program for Mum."

I grit my teeth against another wave of pain. When it subsides, I say, "And if you don't get selected—"

"Then Mum and I go back to square one. I won't let that happen." A determined light enters his eyes.

We sit in silence for a long time.

Eventually, Layla asks, "Did Helena give you your nickname?"

He chuckles, but it's flat. "Yeah, that and a massive guilt complex."

Layla raises an eyebrow.

"I was wearing a *Star Wars* T-shirt when we first met."

"Of course you were," she says. "Beam me up, Scotty."

"That's *Star Trek*," Geek and I say in unison.

Layla clicks her tongue. "Boys."

Geek and I chuckle, then my eyelids grow heavy.

Layla says, "We'll leave you to rest." She bends down to place a kiss on my cheek.

She's so close.

I could've died.

She saved me.

Without her, I wouldn't be here.

On impulse, I turn my head at the last moment.

Her lips graze mine, soft and warm. Heat spreads through my entire body. She's all there is. Sweet and warm and spicy and soft-lipped.

She draws away. "There are worse ways you could've thanked me, I suppose."

"I would've died if you hadn't—"

She holds a finger to my lips. "Shush, now."

"I don't want to waste any more time," I murmur against her finger.

She leans down and kisses me deeper this time, her tongue grazing mine. "We've got all the time in the world."

"Thank you—for saving my life."

"Thank you for the kisses."

My gaze drifts to Geek.

His eyebrows draw in, his face stricken with pain.

I know he's thinking about Helena. Why had I chosen that moment to kiss Layla? Selfish. I need to lighten the mood. "What? Disappointed you didn't get a kiss, too?"

Geek snorts, gets to his feet and holds out a fist. "Crushed."

We bump.

They leave.

I'm about to doze off when Carmichael's voice startles me. "What happened?"

He stands by the pea green curtain.

"What did Geek and Layla tell you?" I ask.

Carmichael perches on the edge of my bed. "They said they found you passed out in the tunnels. Didn't see anyone else. I don't believe them."

I look away.

"Tell me what happened, Henry."

"I don't know."

"What do you mean you don't know?"

"One minute I was getting ready for bed and the next thing I know; someone knocks me out." I pause for effect. "Then I wake up here."

"You remember nothing in between?"

"No."

"You're a terrible liar, you know."

That's what Mum used to say.

I hold my tongue, staring at the ceiling.

The bed creaks as Carmichael shifts position. "Was it Myles? Femi?"

"I don't know." The lie tastes bitter, but it's a lie I've got to tell.

You're such a disappointment.

Even though Zara's kicking me out, even though I know I won't be here much longer, I won't let anyone think of me as weak anymore. I can just imagine Zara's face—contorted in disdain—if she were to find out about this. Why didn't you hear them come into your room? Why didn't you fight? I was right about you, Stone. That's what she'd say.

No.

I've got to keep the circumstances surrounding my injuries a secret.

Carmichael's silent for a long time. Eventually, he stands. "Zara spoke to me."

My stomach drops.

"She wants you out."

"I know."

"Is that what you want?"

My eyes lock on his. "Of course not."

"Good, because I talked her round. Just."

Hope flares in my chest. "Thank you, I—"

"This time." Carmichael pauses at the edge of the curtain. "You'll have to convince her you're worth the effort if you want to stay long term."

"How do I do that?"

He shrugs. "Acid wounds heal slowly, even with liquid silver. You've got plenty of time to think about it."

The curtain flutters as Carmichael leaves.

How can I impress Zara? She must hate me now, especially if Carmichael convinced—probably *ordered*—her to let me stay. Wait, maybe there *is* a way. An image of her DNA helix tattoo hovers before my eyes.

Her tattoo.

It reminds me that my past doesn't have to determine my future.

A plan forms as sleep drags my eyelids closed.

Chapter 29

While I'm stuck in the medical bay, autumn freezes into winter, and winter thaws into spring, but it all passes me by. No sunburned orange leaves, no frosty flurries of snow, no budding greenery.

Geek and Layla visit me every day. Layla treats me with kisses—deeper and deeper each time—when she arrives and leaves, and Geek brings playing cards and fist bumps and banter. It makes the situation bearable, but still not ideal.

The first month's the worst, stuck in the medical bay staring at the pea green curtains and grey walls, flinching in pain every time I move and reopening my wounds. Month two's a little better. Scabs form over the blistered flesh. They itch like hell, but the nurses remove two of the drips and let me walk from one end of the medical bay to the other for exercise. The third month passes in a hallucinatory blur of nightmare inducing infections, which leave me dizzy and trembling in fear. When I swim back to consciousness on the first day in March, and the liquid silver drips have disappeared, the gauze covering the twisted lattice of scar tissue decorating my back and ribs is gone.

My first thought's of Bianca. The bitter sting of betrayal that cuts through me every time her name echoes through my mind is almost as painful as my burns.

Almost.

I force myself to forget about her. She made her choice when she sided with Myles. She doesn't deserve any more of my time.

I'm discharged, but weak.

Mercifully, Geek and Layla spend the next four weeks rebuilding me until I'm near peak condition. We get permission to go running every morning, and muscle memory allows my strength to return quickly. I'm still not cleared to return to training, but the three of us sneak into the training room for late evening sessions, where Geek and Layla patiently teach me everything they've learned in my absence.

One particular training session with Layla—about three weeks after I was released from the medical bay—sticks out in my mind.

"Favourite movie?" Layla aims a punch at my head.

I dodge and counter.

She evades the move.

I wipe sweat from my forehead. "*Doctor Strange.*"

She laughs and fires a witch-strike at me.

I bring up a shield and the witch-strike breaks apart against it in a shower of sparks. "What's wrong with that?"

Layla conjures a daffodil yellow portal and flings herself into it.

I call on my Sight and get a split-second view of her appearing behind me and swinging her witch-staff at my face.

I dart to the side as the portal flashes open with a ripping sound, right where I'd predicted.

Layla appears and swings her staff in a wide arc, her brow furrowing when she hits empty air.

I fire my own witch-strike, the harsh green glow carving shadows into the walls.

Quicker than I would've thought possible, Layla throws herself forward—the witch-strike flashing overhead—rolls over her shoulder and flips to her feet. Panting, she says, "You have the entire Marvel Cinematic Universe to choose from and you choose *Doctor Strange*."

We circle each other while we regain our breath.

I chuckle. "Okay, *Captain Marvel*, what's yours?"

She rolls her eyes, darts forward in a feint, backs off again. "Definitely not that one, either. It's all about *GOTG*."

I scrunch my face up. "*Guardians of the Galaxy*? Really?"

"Yeah. Why not?"

"Groot gets on my nerves."

She clasps her chest like I struck her. "Groot's cute. The baby version, anyway."

"It's a tree. What's cute about a tree?"

She arches an eyebrow. "*You* get on *my* nerves."

I shoot her a wicked grin, brace myself for the sickness I know is coming, take a deep breath, and conjure my own portal, hoping to use Layla's own trick against her.

The portal breaks me into a million pieces.

I hover in the comforting void for eternity.

When I re-emerge, I grab Layla from behind and crush her back against my chest, breathing deeply until the nausea passes. "Now, I know that's not true," I whisper into her hair. "You think *I'm* cute."

She barks a peel of laughter. "Not as cute as Groot, though."

I spin her round so she's facing me and, all of a sudden, we're sharing the same air. I tuck a strand of hair behind her ear.

"Good job with the portal," she says.

I smile, a rush of pride surging through me. "I had to get the hang of it eventually."

She gives a soft, sweet giggle that makes my insides flip over and over. "That's true."

I brush her bare arm with light fingers. "You're a one off, you know that."

She rests her hands on my chest. "So I'm told."

Our lips touch.

The kiss deepens, and deepens, and deepens.

I'm lost in it.

Lost in her.

Falling... I don't know.

On the edge of that fall.

Almost certainly.

Man, this girl.

I know I'm in trouble.

I know I'm in trouble.

While that's true, a stronger mantra sustains me throughout my rehabilitation.

Stop running. Stop hiding. Fight back.

Stop running. Stop hiding. Fight back.

Stop running. Stop hiding. Fight back.

And I know I will.

Only when I'm well enough, and only when I feel ready, do I set the first phase of my new plan into action—a plan I hope will catapult me back into first place.

I pace along COVEN's mahogany corridors with ease. Funny. Five months ago, I'd have got lost down here. I can walk to Zara's office with my eyes closed now.

Zara.

She didn't visit me in the medical bay—can't say I blame her—and I haven't seen her since she promised to kick me out. I'm not looking forward to this conversation, but if my plan's going to work, I'm going to need her help.

The question is, can I convince her?

I round a corner and come to a broad archway marked *Alpha Section*—home to COVEN's most elite executioners.

Voices murmur beyond the archway.

I pause. Can I do this? Can I—

Stop running. Stop hiding. Fight back.

Start behaving like an executioner.

I close my eyes, take a deep breath, pull my shoulders back, draw myself up to my full height, and stride through the archway.

The chatter ceases when I enter. The *Alphas*—gathered around a bank of desks—turn to stare at me.

"Enjoy it while it lasts, Stone," one of them says. "You won't see *Alpha Section* again in a hurry."

A smattering of laughter rises from the others.

A hot flush creeps into my cheeks, but I ignore the jibe, my eyes fixed on Zara's office door. When I reach it, I raise my fist and give three sharp knocks.

"Come in."

My slippery fingers press down on the handle and I open the door.

Zara glances up from the paperwork spread across her desk. "What the fuck do *you* want?"

The door clicks shut behind me.

Another burst of laughter erupts from the office.

"Well? I don't have all day, Stone," Zara's eyes are marble-hard.

"I need your help."

"Is that so?" She scribbles something on the page in pink gel pen.

"I'm sorry about what happened with Femi."

She leans back in her chair, caps her pen with deliberate slowness—enjoying making me sweat—and places it on the desk. Leaning forward again, she balances her elbows on the desk and props her chin in her hands. "Just about what happened with Abimbola?"

"What do you mean?"

"Are you sorry for defying my orders? Back-chatting? Behaving like a dick?"

The thermostat on the wall reads a cool seventeen degrees, but I'm sweating. I lower my head. "I'm sorry for all of it."

Silence stretches before me like an empty country road.

If I know Zara, she's weighing up the sincerity of my apology and trying to decide whether she believes me.

She stands and paces round the desk. "Look at me."

I do as she asks.

The pink in her eyes appears darker than usual. "If you ever step out of line again, I don't care who's wing you're sheltering under, it'll be the last thing you do here."

I nod.

She considers me. A wolf considering prey. "What do you need my help with?"

I let out a breath. "I need you to take me into the city."

She folds her arms. "What for?"

"Where did you get your tattoo?"

Zara and I stroll along the canal path until we reach the city proper. The evening air cools my skin and the pale spring sunlight sinks behind the butterscotch-coloured buildings on the High Street, painting them with a soft, golden glow.

She halts. "Here we are."

The tattoo parlour isn't what I expected. The shop's white paintwork's peeling, a tacky neon light flashes *CLOSED* in the window, and a weathered sign above the door reads, *Obsidian Ink*.

I shoot Zara a look. "Is this it?"

She knocks on the door, a flake of white paint sticking to her knuckles. "Didn't take you for a snob."

"I'm not," I say, crossing my arms. "It's closed."

"I know the owner. Whatever you do, don't tell him about COVEN."

A few seconds pass. The door opens. The man standing in the doorway's striking. Angular features. Cropped honey-coloured hair. He's black clothed, with a pattern of vines and wildflowers decorating every patch of bare skin on his arms.

The man smiles, a tender expression on his face. "Zara."

"Bob."

I blink. Zara's tone's... warm.

"I was closing up for the day. You're lucky you caught me." Bob's voice is smooth and light, tinged with a faint Irish lilt.

"You couldn't do me a favour?" Zara asks.

"For you, anything."

Is Zara... is she... blushing?

I laugh.

Zara shoots me a murderous look.

I turn it into a hacking cough.

"Who's your Sighted friend?" Bob's eyes settle on me. He steps out of the shop—barefoot—and offers me his hand. "Bob McRae." The head of an inky black snake emblazons his palm, its coiled body slithering through the vines on his arms.

We shake. "Henry Stone."

"He's... I work with him," Zara says. "He wants a tattoo."

"Well, he's come to the right place." Bob retreats back into the shop.

I glance at Zara. "Are you two—"

"None of your business."

"He seems like a nice guy."

A smile tugs at the corner of her mouth. "He is."

Bob's voice floats out onto the street. "Are you two coming in or what?"

Inside, three of the four walls are painted black. Hundreds of exquisite tattoo sketches cover the fourth.

"I'm making tea, if you want one," Bob says. "I've got chamomile, peppermint, jasmine, ginger."

"I'll take a black coffee," I say.

Bob smiles at me. "Caffeine's bad for you."

"Oh. I'm fine, then. Thanks."

"Peppermint," Zara says.

Bob nods. "Have a browse while I fix the drinks." He brushes aside a beaded curtain and glides from the room.

I narrow my eyes at Zara. "You drink peppermint tea?"

"Shut the fuck up and browse."

I cross to the wall of sketches. "Did Bob design these?"

Zara throws herself into one of the chintzy armchairs by the window. "Yeah."

"They're incredible." I reach out and trail my fingers over the lifelike drawings—animals mostly. A tiger close to the ground, stalking. A wolf, head tipped back and howling. And a—

A crow, wings spread in flight, one beady eye fixed on me.

Mum.

Dad.

Little Crow.

My hand leaves the wall and squeezes my parent's wedding rings through the fabric of my T-shirt. My throat closes.

I'm aware of Bob returning with the drinks, clunking a pair of pastel blue china cups on a low table in front of Zara, but I can't take my eyes off the crow.

"See something you like?" Bob asks.

"That one." I nod at the crow. "I want that one."

"Of course. Come on through." Bob ducks back through the beaded curtain. He leads me down a narrow hallway and into a square room with a reclining chair.

"I need you to make a couple of alterations to the design, if that's okay?"

He nods. "Sure."

A tattoo gun gleams on the side.

"Where do you want it?" he asks.

I point at my left chest. "Here."

"Top off then."

I reach for the hem of my T-shirt, but stop myself.

The scars.

The faint white lines criss-crossing my arm are one thing. I'm used to those, and they're tricky to hide, but the ugly burn scars—

"Whatever you're embarrassed about, bet I've seen worse," Bob says.

I nod, slide my arms out of the T-shirt, and pull it over my head.

If he finds my scars repulsive, he doesn't say, and his expression remains blank. "Hop in the chair for me."

Two and a half hours later, Bob dips his latex-gloved hand into a jar labelled *Silver Ointment* and rubs the thick, cold concoction into my chest. "All done. It'll take a minute to heal."

"How did you and Zara meet?" I ask.

His expression clouds over.

"Sorry, none of my business."

"No. It's okay. We met at a friend's house party a couple of years ago. Some guy was hassling her. I threatened to rip his bollocks off if he didn't leave her alone."

My brow creases.

He laughs. "I know. She's not the type who needs defending. Told me so too. Said she was quite capable of ripping his bollocks off herself. I knew I was a goner, then."

I chuckle at that.

"It's all for show. She's a pussycat deep down," he continues.

Funny. Carmichael said the same thing. "Strangely enough, you're not the first person to tell me that." I say with a wry smile.

"So, you work together?"

Whatever you do, don't tell him about COVEN.

"Oh—um—yeah."

"Aren't you a little young?"

"Young?"

"You don't look old enough to be a detective."

"Detective?"

"With the MID?"

The MID. Right. That must be her cover story. "I'm in training."

"Ah. That explains it. Bet Zara's whipping you into shape?"

"She's whipping me, all right."

Bob's eyebrows shoot up. "That right?"

"Not like—I don't mean—"

He collapses in a fit of giggles. "You English. So easy to wind up. Don't take on. Sure, I'm just pulling your leg."

I laugh.

"Should be ready now." He nods at the silver smear coating my chest. "Want to see?"

I nod.

He snatches a wet-wipe from an enormous pack and cleans the silver ointment away.

I stand and cross to the floor-length mirror. When my eyes land on the tattoo, they sting with tears.

The black ink stands out against my pale skin, the crow's wings spread wide over the left side of my chest. The tip of one wing skims the hollow between my collarbones—covering the old scar—while the tip of the other brushes my left shoulder. And the alterations? Two black tail feathers drifting down between the crow's hooked feet, fluttering right over my heart.

One for Mum.

The other for Dad.

I trace a glossy wing with the tip of my finger, the beady eye, the sharp beak. Silent tears stream down my cheeks.

Bob's face crumples. "Oh, shit. You don't like it."

"Oh, no. No, it's not that." I wipe my eyes. "I love it. It's... personal, that's all."

His warm hand rests on my shoulder and squeezes.

"Stone, you finished?" Zara calls from the front of the shop.

I slide my T-shirt back on, a trace of black ink showing above the collar. "How much do I owe you?"

"This one's on the house."

"No. I've got to—"

"Any friend of Zara's is a friend of mine."

"Thanks." I cross to the door.

"Henry?"

"Yeah?"

"Whoever you lost, it gets easier." Bob nods towards my chest.

"I hope so." I turn away from him.

Phase one of the plan's complete.

Now, on to phase two.

CHapTer 30

A scruffy guy stands outside the tattoo parlour, handing out leaflets. He stuffs one into my hand as Zara and I pass by, saying, "Have you seen this man?" I don't even glance at the leaflet.

"What's up with you?" Zara asks.

"Nothing."

"You've got a face like a spanked arse."

"There's something I need to do."

"Oh, yeah? What's that?"

Phase two. "You'll see."

"Since when did you become so mysterious?"

"I'm learning from the best."

"What is that thing?" Zara gestures towards the leaflet.

"I don't know." My eyes skim the leaflet now. "Some guy was handing them—oh, fuck."

"What?"

I hand her the leaflet. The leaflet with the word *MISSING* stamped across the top in big, bold letters, with a picture of my face underneath. I glance back to the guy standing outside Bob's place. No. It can't be, can it? Shit. It is. His hair's grown out a bit, and he's dropped a few pounds, but it's him all right.

Jez.

"Do you know him?" Zara glares at Jez.

"I—um—"

"Don't piss about. The mortal. Do you know him or not?"

"Yeah. We were friends growing up."

Jez mouths something.

My name.

"Fuck." Zara grabs my arm, spins me round and shoves me through the crowds of late-night shoppers. "We need to move."

"Zara, what are you—?"

"We can't let him catch up to us."

Jez's voice cuts through the hubbub of the city. "Henry? Henry?"

Too late.

Zara grips my arm so hard it hurts. "Get rid of him."

"What?"

"Get rid of him, or I'll wipe all his memories of you."

"You can't—"

A hand closes around my other arm and yanks me round. "Holy Jesus fucking Christ. It *is* you." Jez crushes me in a bear hug.

I pat him on the back. "Hi, mate."

He steps away, releases me and runs a hand through his lank, greasy hair. Up close, he looks ill, pasty, and dark smudges circle his eyes. "I can't believe it."

Jez spots Zara standing beside me, and his eyebrows knit together. "Who's this?"

Simple question. Complicated answer. "I—this is—"

"I'll wait over there." Zara stalks over to a bench close by and perches on the edge. She takes out her phone and scrolls with her thumb, but I know she isn't really looking at anything.

"Who is she?" Jez repeats.

"A friend."

"This is insane." Jez grins. "You're alive. I was so worried after the fire."

My head snaps up. "Fire?"

Jez bites his lip, combs his fingers through his hair again. "Yeah. At the house. Your—your parents."

Fire? What the hell's he talking about?

"The police said it was arson."

Arson? Razor must've set the house on fire when he came back—after Carmichael whisked me off to COVEN—to cover his tracks. To destroy evidence.

Jez says, "They found three bodies, but I knew—somehow I knew—you got out. I knew you were alive."

Three bodies.

Mum.

Dad.

Cecelia.

My eyes sting and tears blur my vision. Just one more reminder I'll never see my parents again. My stomach sinks.

Jez's eyes are full of pain. "I'm so sorry, bud. Your mum and dad, they were like family to me."

A lump lodges in my throat. I look away.

Jez continues, "I've been looking for you ever since..." His brow furrows and his words trail off.

"What?"

"Why are you wearing contacts?"

Bugger.

My eyes.

Ignoring the painful way my heart's thumping, I shrug.

"Is that"—Jez tugs the collar of my T-shirt—"a tattoo?"

I shake him off. "So what if it is?"

His eyes widen. "What happened to your arm?"

Fuck. Think, for Christ's sake. Think. Wait, no. That might work. For the first time, I'm grateful for the acid scars Femi gave me. The scars on my arm look nothing like the burn scars on my torso, but Jez might buy it. I lift the hem of my T-shirt. "The same thing that happened here. The fire."

"Shit." Jez rubs a hand over his mouth. "I—hang on. Where have you been all this time?"

How am I supposed to answer that? Think. "I had to get away."

"Get away where?"

"A friend of my parents' took me in." Technically true.

"And you didn't—you couldn't reach out to any of us?"

A sharp pang of guilt jack-knives into my gut, causing me to flinch. How am I supposed to explain that one? "Lost my phone in the fire."

"You couldn't come to my house?" There's a pained whine in his voice.

I wanted to find you. That's the honest answer... at least, it was for a while. Until training, and my new life took over. In reality, I hadn't thought about Jez for... God, how long is it now? The guilt sours into something darker. "I don't know what you want me to say."

"You didn't even go to their funeral."

"Too painful." I shuffle from one foot to the other, letting the words spill out of me. "After it happened, I felt like I'd lost a part of myself. I thought about calling you, letting you know where I was"—that part, at least, is true—"but every time I tried, it just reminded me of them."

"You thought about calling me?" Jez asks.

"Yeah, a lot."

"You're lying."

"No, I—"

"You said you lost your phone."

My stomach clenches, and I lean back against the wall for support, trying to make it look casual. "What?"

"Why are you bullshitting me?"

Sweat peppers my brow. "I'm not."

"Who is that woman?"

Zara leers at us from her spot on the bench.

He squints. "Wait. She's wearing contacts, too?"

I react out of panic, snapping, "I don't have to explain myself to you."

"Like hell you don't." He jabs a finger at me. "I deferred my postgrad place to look for you."

That stuns me. "You did what?"

"You heard me."

"I didn't ask you to do that," I say, my voice quiet.

He gets in my face, his breath a little sour.

I do my best not to balk at the smell.

"Where have you been?" The question's hard-edged.

"I told you. Friend of my parents took me in."

"Oh my God."

"What?"

"You didn't"—he backs away and shakes his head—"no. You didn't do something stupid, did you?"

My mouth goes dry. Surely, he can't mean what I think he means. "Something stupid like what?"

His face drains of colour. "The fire."

I reel back like he punched me in the jaw, cold anger flaring in my chest. "How can you even ask me that?"

"Mate, I—"

"Fuck you." I wheel around, not wanting to look at his sad, wasted face anymore. I need to leave, or I'll do something I regret.

He grabs my wrist. "I had to ask."

I fling his hand away. "Don't fucking touch me."

He's looking at me like he no longer recognises me. "What's got into you?"

"Nothing."

"You're so angry."

"Oh, you think? I wonder why? My parents are dead, my house burned to the ground, and I've lost everything." I'm shouting, and a few passers-by are giving me the side eye like I'm crazy. "And now I've got you asking me whether I killed them."

"This isn't you."

Zara's words ring in my ears.

Get rid of him, or I'll wipe all his memories of you.

I let the burning rage take over. "I know what this is. You're being a dick because I'm not reacting the way you want."

Jez screws his face up. "What? No."

"Because I normally go along with everything you say."

"That's not—"

"You say, let's go play football. I play football. You say, let's go clubbing on your birthday. I go clubbing on my birthday. You say jump. I say how high. Now I'm standing up for myself, and you can't take it."

"You're talking shit."

"Am I?"

"Yeah."

The anger isn't fake anymore. I can feel it bubbling under the surface. "You were happy when I didn't get into Oxford."

"What? Why would I be happy about that?"

"Because you wouldn't be able to control me from there."

"Control you. I've never—"

"You were never my friend, you just wanted someone you could boss around."

"Stop it."

He's almost at breaking point.

Almost.

He accused me of being involved in my parents' murder. How dare he? How fucking *dare* he? He's close to the edge, and I want to push him over, so I say, "No wonder your dad left."

Wham.

He really punches me in the jaw this time.

My head snaps to the side and stars dance before my eyes.

"You're a prick. I never want to see you again." With that, Jez storms off.

"Feeling's mutual," I call after him, ignoring the sour acid corroding my stomach.

A minute passes.

Zara slides off the bench, smirking, and strides up to me. "That was priceless. What the fuck did you say to him?"

"Doesn't matter." I hate Zara. I hate Carmichael and COVEN. All of it. I hate myself. I've sacrificed my oldest friendship to protect my secret. Rage burns in my gut, yearning to be put to good use. Luckily, I still have my plan, and the rage to fuel me. "Come on. Let's get back to COVEN."

Chapter 31

As soon as Zara and I get back to COVEN, I head to my room and swap my T-shirt and jeans for a pair of black trainee joggers and a black vest that shows off my new tattoo.

What I'm about to do will define the rest of my time here, or cost me everything. I can't afford to screw it up. I brush my fingers over my parents' wedding rings.

This is for you.

I tuck them beneath my vest and set off towards the dining hall, where I know dinner will be in full swing.

When I arrive at the dining hall, the heavy wooden doors are closed.

I flick my fingers and utter a spell, and they fly open, crashing into the walls on either side.

The room beyond falls silent as every pair of eyes lands on me.

Without breaking stride, I march into the canteen. The familiar urge to flee surges through my body, but I shove it deep down and carry on walking.

Layla sits at a nearby table with Geek, looking at me askance, and goes to stand.

I give an almost imperceptible shake of my head.

She remains seated.

Myles is at his regular table, with Femi by his side as usual, and Myles's dad—Nick—sits with them, his back to me. Myles wears his trademark smirk.

I can't wait to wipe it off his face.

When I reach their table, Nick stands, blocking my path. "Can I help you, Stone?"

"I'm not here for you." I glare at Myles.

Nick's eyebrows shoot up. "Who do you think you are? I'm an executioner. You will speak to me with respect."

Whispers blow through the canteen like a cool breeze.

My heart thumps so loud, I'm surprised nobody else can hear it. I need to stand my ground. Voice low, I say, "Unless you want me to tell everyone what your son did to me, I suggest you sit down."

Uncertainty flickers over Nick's features. He glances at Myles. "What's he talking about?"

A scarlet blush floods Myles's entire face, and his gaze fixes on his dinner.

"Sit down," I repeat, loud enough for my command to carry. He sits.

The whispers become murmurs.

Myles looks up. His cheeks are still red, but his smirk's back. "Is that tattoo supposed to make you look tough?"

"No. It reminds me why I'm here."

He leans back in his chair, places his hands behind his head and laces his fingers together—his posture showing everyone he's not intimidated by me. "And why exactly are you here? I assume it's not just to ruin my meal."

"I—" The words catch in my throat. If I do this, there's no going back.

Myles rolls his eyes. "Well?"

My stomach roils and crashes like the waves against the cliffs on the island.

The island.

Myles's threat echoes through my mind.

When we're finished with you, we're taking your body through the portal to the island. No one will ever find you.

Everything in me hardens. I clench my fists. "I challenge you to a Trial by Magic."

The noise erupting from the crowd drowns out Myles's answering laugh. The executioners shout and jeer and exclaim in shock.

Someone grabs my arm. Layla. "What the hell are you doing?"

Geek's close behind her, lines of worry carved into his face.

The noise dies down.

I quirk an eyebrow at Myles. "Well?"

Myles picks up his fork, stabs a piece of chicken, and places it in his mouth.

My pulse beats everywhere.

He takes his time chewing, chewing, chewing. Eventually, he swallows, wipes his mouth with a napkin and sets it down. "What are your terms?"

I remember my first day here, when Zara challenged Nick to a Trial by Magic. I also remember what she demanded should he lose.

It was enough to get him to back down.

Maybe the same will be true in my case.

I'm wound so tight, my tongue fuses to the roof of my mouth. With considerable effort, I unclench my jaw. "If I win, you leave COVEN and I take your spot in first place."

More gasps from the surrounding tables, followed by a scattering of mumbled phrases.

"And if I win?" Myles asks, looking unconcerned.

"Then I'll leave instead."

Layla jumps in front of me, her fingers threading through mine. "You can't."

I squeeze her hand. "I need to. It's the only way to finish this."

"Geek." Layla wrenches her hand out of my grip. "Do something. Talk some sense into him, for God's sake."

Geek shoots me a sidelong glance. "You sure you know what you're doing, pal?"

I nod.

He nods back.

"No." Layla lowers her voice to a whisper. "There's no way you can beat him."

Ouch. That stings. I draw away from her a little. "Thanks for the vote of confidence."

"That's not—" She takes a short breath. "None of us can beat him."

"First time for everything."

"If you lose, if you leave, they'll wipe your memories."

"I know."

"You'll forget me."

My stomach spasms.

"I know."

Her eyes shine with tears. "We were just—we were just..." She shakes her head, turns, and walks out of the canteen without looking back.

I want to chase after her, to tell her I know what I'm doing, to assure her that everything will be okay, but I can't, because I'm not sure myself. Instead, I lock gazes with Myles. "Do you accept?"

He seems uncertain, now.

Good.

I can imagine what he's thinking. He's thinking, I can beat him with both hands tied behind my back, blindfolded. He's an easy target. I bet he's also thinking, but why's he challenging me? What tricks does he have up his sleeve?

His gaze flicks to Nick.

"He can't help you," I say.

The room's silent. Eerie. A held breath underwater. A dark forest in the dead of night.

Myles crosses his arms. "I'll give you one chance to retract. One chance to stop you making a fool of yourself."

I raise an eyebrow. "Scared to face me?"

Myles gets to his feet, resting the flats of his palms on the polished wooden tabletop, and leans forward a little. "I'm not scared of anything, least of all you."

"Prove it."

A muscle in his jaw twitches. "I accept."

The floor drops out from under me. Half of me was hoping, praying, he'd decline the challenge rather than risk his place at COVEN.

"Where and when?" he asks.

When I speak, my voice sounds firm. "The ring. One hour."

"Fine."

I stride from the room.

Fuck, fuck, fuck.

What have I done?

CHAPTER 32

I wait in one antechamber, while Myles waits in another. My heart pounds, my stomach turning somersaults. Beyond the double doors, feet thunder against the marble floor and the noise of the crowd's deafening.

Have I made a huge mistake?

Myles is going to beat me. I know it.

"I just heard." Carmichael's voice startles me.

If my heart was pounding before... "Jesus Christ."

"Why are you doing this?"

"It's the only way I can get Myles to stop."

"So he was the one who attacked you?"

"I didn't say that. I've already told you, I don't know what happened—"

Carmichael holds up a hand, cutting me off. "So you say." He pauses. "Are you really prepared to throw everything away over a petty feud?"

I don't answer.

"I can call this off."

"What?"

"I can call this off," he repeats, "before it goes too far. If Myles wins—"

"I know what happens if he wins," I say, shrugging. "I'm bottom in the ratings. You won't be able to stop Zara from kicking me out forever. I'd rather leave on my terms."

Something crosses Carmichael's face. The ghost of a smile? "Your parents would be proud of you."

My chest tightens. "I doubt that."

Carmichael strides forwards and grips my shoulders. "Remember, you have something he doesn't."

"Oh, yeah? What's that?"

He points at my eyes. "You can use your Sight to predict what Myles will cast."

I nod.

"And do yourself a favour. Attack first this time." He releases me. "I have to go. I'll see you out there."

"Carmichael?"

"Yes?"

"Thanks. For coming to see me."

He bobs his head, and leaves.

Then it's just me, and the roar of the crowd.

Ten minutes pass and, by the time Carmichael's amplified voice echoes around the antechamber, my legs have turned to jelly.

He says, "You all know why we're here. Henry challenged Myles to a Trial by Magic. If Henry wins, he takes Myles's place in the ratings and Myles leaves. If Myles wins, Henry leaves."

The crowd falls silent.

Carmichael continues, "As always, we'll open a poll, and display the results on the screens. You're voting for who you think will win. You can cast your votes now."

My stomach bucks and twists like a wild horse.

"I see," Carmichael says. "Trainees, you may enter."

I shoulder the door into the ring open, my eyes darting straight to one of the plasma screens lining the walls.

Poll Results:

Myles Hedges: 100%

Henry Stone: 0%

Surprise, surprise. No-one voted for me... again.

Zara stands at the edge of the ring. What's she thinking? I don't need to ask. The look on her face says it all. She thinks I'm a fool.

Myles strides towards me from the opposite side of the ring, glaring.

Geek and Layla stand next to each other, across the room.

Layla mouths something to Geek, her lips forming the words, "I can't watch this."

Geek wraps an arm around her shoulders and pulls her close.

Layla hides her face in his shirt.

"Thank you," I mouth to Geek.

He shoots me a thumbs up.

Femi leans against the opposite wall, wearing a snarl.

My legs are as stiff as wooden stilts, and the walk into the ring lasts forever.

Almost there.

Myles and I draw close, standing ten feet apart. Close enough that, when he speaks, I'm the only one who hears him.

"You were stupid to challenge me," he says, voice dripping with confidence.

My knees tremble, so I sink into a low combat stance to disguise my nervousness. "And you should've killed me when you had the chance."

Zara paces around the edge of the circle, preparing to seal it.

Hurry, hurry, hurry.

Sweat beads my brow. How long does it take?

"You can't win," Myles says. "Even you know it."

"We'll see."

Zara's on her second revolution of the ring.

Myles rolls his shoulders. "After I've dealt with you, I'm going after your friends."

I swallow. What had Carmichael said? Attack first. I draw on my magic and hold it ready.

Attack first.

Finally, Zara seals the circle. "Begin."

I fire a barrage of witch-strikes at Myles before the command's fully left her mouth.

Myles isn't expecting it. He ducks the first one, dodges the second. The third catches his arm and he stumbles, but keeps his balance. "You'll have to do better than that." He clicks his fingers, says, "*Invisibilia*," and vanishes.

"Didn't you learn your lesson on the island?" I squint my eyes, waiting for the citrus sting to herald the activation of my Sight.

Bang.

A blinding flash of light.

Everything blurs, multi-coloured spots dancing before my eyes.

I blink and blink, but it's no use. My vision stays fuzzy. "What the—"

Something pummels my side. Splintering pain crackles over my ribs, and I sink to one knee. My leg jerks out from under me and my back slams into the floor. Three hard bruising blows to the chest. I grit my teeth to stifle a scream.

Myles's voice sounds from above me. "I'm going to enjoy this."

My vision clears.

Myles holds his witch-staff aloft, preparing to deliver the final blow.

No.

I kick my leg up and drive it back down. My heel smashes into his foot.

He screams and staggers away.

I roll backwards over my shoulder and regain my footing. I squint my eyes again, summoning my Sight.

Half the audience gasps.

I can imagine why. My glowing green eyes must appear strange to them.

Myles's aura spreads around him like a thick grey fog. He raises his hand and brilliant white courses down his arm.

I step aside.

The witch-strike rockets from his palm and sails right past me, pummelling Zara's barrier.

He fires again.

The spell doesn't even come close to hitting me.

A growl of frustration erupts from Myles's throat. "*Flagellum.*"

I know the path his witch-whip will take before it manifests. He'll sweep low first. I jump over the shining band of light. Then high. I crouch down, and the whip sails over my head with a quick swish.

"Fight back," Myles yells.

He wants me to fight back?

Fine.

I close my fist. "*Suffocant.*"

The spell latches around Myles's throat.

He coughs, clutching at his neck. His head jerks this way and that as he struggles to draw breath.

I clench my fist harder, stalking closer to Myles.

He falls to his knees, his face reddening.

When I reach him, I crouch low. "I'm going to enjoy this." I flick my fingers towards the ceiling. "*Subvolo*." My spell hoists Myles high into the air.

His legs spasm, and he's still clutching at his throat, his face turning puce as he makes gagging, choking sounds.

He's finally at my mercy, after all this time. How long will it take? If I hold on, how long will it take for him to die?

"He's going to kill him," Femi shouts.

"That's enough, Stone," Zara says. "Stop."

Stop.

He would've killed me back in the tunnels if Layla hadn't saved me. He would've killed me and taken my body to the island and buried me in an unmarked grave.

Stop.

Why should I?

CHAPTER 33

I stop because Zara ordered me to, not because I want to. I fling my hand forward, palm open.

Myles flies backwards. Backwards, backwards, backwards, until he sails through Zara's barrier and slams to the ground—outside the ring—in a wheezing heap.

I've done it.

My chest swells with one hundred different emotions—pride, righteousness, and excitement among them.

I've won.

Quiet settles over the room like mist, then the crowd bursts into applause. They stamp their feet, punch the air, chant my name, "Stone, Stone, Stone."

My eyes find Layla, still standing at the edge of the ring, her expression a mask of shock. Her face splits into a wide grin, and she runs at me, launching into my arms and kissing me, hard. "You did it. You beat him." She draws back, eyes brimming with tears.

Geek clamps a hand on my shoulder. "Well done, mate."

"Thanks." My smile's too broad. My cheeks hurt.

Over Layla's shoulder, Carmichael's expression mirrors mine. He winks at me.

Zara holds up her hands for silence. "Knock it off."

The cheers die down.

She continues, "That settles it. Stone's the winner. Hedges is out."

Nick appears at Carmichael's shoulder, his mouth set in a grim line, cold eyes drilling holes into my skull.

A shiver runs through my entire body.

Femi helps Myles to his feet.

Zara clicks her fingers and the screens flash.

Current Ratings:

1. Henry Stone

2. Layla Jabara

3. Oluwafemi Abimbola

4. Gareth Townsend

5. Bianca Yakhontov

6. ~~Myles Hedges~~

Myles—still supported by Femi—glares at me from across the room. "This is bullshit. I'm not going anywhere."

Carmichael's voice is stern. "You accepted the Trial by Magic. You agreed to Henry's terms."

He throws off Femi's arm. "No way. He wins one bout—one—and that's it."

"That's it," Zara says, motioning towards a pair of executioners. "Take him to his room. We'll arrange the memory wipe for tomorrow morning."

Myles shakes his head. "You can't do this."

Carmichael strides across the ring until he's face-to-face with Myles. "I think you'll find we can."

Myles shrinks away from Carmichael, his eyes darting to Nick. "Don't let them do this."

Nick closes his eyes and tilts his head down.

"You never stand up for me," Myles says.

Seconds tick by, the silence oppressive.

Eventually, Nick says, "You lost. Why would I stand up for you?"

A deep red blush swamps Myles's face. "Father?"

Nick shoves his way out of the ring.

I know it's bad, but I can't help it. My mouth curves into a grin.

"What the hell are you smirking at?" Femi growls.

Myles's words to me back on the island swim through my mind.

At least I've still got parents.

I march up to Myles. For once, I don't hold back. "Looks like you don't have a dad anymore, either."

Myles stamps his foot like a spoilt child. "You think this is over, orphan boy?"

I grit my teeth.

He spots my reaction. "Oh, I forgot. Don't like that, do you, orphan boy?"

I turn and stomp away from him. I won't let him get under my skin.

"That's enough," Carmichael says.

"I'm just telling the truth. He is an orphan b—"

Enough. I've had enough of his bullshit. I want to break him. I want to shatter his bones into a million pieces. That's exactly what I'm going to do. I whirl around and fling out my hand, bellowing, "*Intermissum*." A bright green, rippling ball of power explodes from my fingertips and barrels towards Myles.

My spell's two metres from him when he holds out the flat of his palm. "*Deflecto*."

The vermillion orb collides with his outstretched hand with a flash and rebounds, flying right at me.

I dive to the side.

It whistles past my ear.

Crack.

Layla screams.

The room erupts into chaos.

The next half an hour passes by in a blur.

Layla drops to the floor—a marionette with severed strings—unconscious.

Carmichael spends the next five minutes barking orders at everyone.

Someone produces a stretcher, and careful hands lift Layla onto it. She looks so small, despite her willowy height.

Two executioners—one at each end of the stretcher—ferry her off to the medical bay and, before the doors to the ring swing shut, one of them says, "Shit. She's fading, we need to hurry."

On Carmichael's orders, another pair of executioners drag a bucking and twisting Myles from the room. And then Carmichael says something to me, but his words make little sense.

At some point, Geek and I must walk to the medical bay, because the next thing I know, we sit outside the ward on uncomfortable plastic chairs.

For the first time in months, I pick at my old scar.

"Hey." Geek grabs my wrist to stop me from picking. "It wasn't your fault, you know."

I wrench out of his grip. "If I hadn't fired that spell—"

"Myles goaded you. He's the one who deflected it."

"What if she doesn't make it?" I stand and pace, raking a hand through my hair.

"She will."

I slam my hand into the wall so hard my palm stings. "You don't know that. You heard what they said."

Shit. She's fading. We need to hurry.

Bile scalds my throat, but I choke it back. "If she—if she dies—" My eyes prickle with tears.

"She won't die."

I lower myself back into the chair, my knee bouncing up and down. "But if she does—"

Geek claps a hand on my knee. "Will you stop? You're making me edgy."

The doors to the medical bay squeak open and an executioner wearing a green nurse's scrubs pokes his head out.

I bolt to my feet. "Is she okay?"

The nurse smiles. "She will be."

A knot in my stomach unravels. "Is she awake?"

He nods. "She'd like to see you."

The knot tightens again, and my hand goes to my stomach. How can I face her after what I've done?

The nurse says, "No one blames you, least of all her. We all saw what happened."

I nod, but his kind words only make me feel worse.

"Come on. Come through."

I glance back at Geek. "You coming?"

"She asked for you, not me. I'll wait here," he says.

I follow the nurse.

He points down the row of beds to a closed curtain. "She's in there. When you see her, it might be a bit of a shock."

Heavy-legged, I inch through the room until I reach the closed curtain. My hand closes over the material. I can't pull it aside. I can't go in.

"Henry? Is that you?"

Layla.

Her voice sounds so fragile.

I take a deep breath and draw back the curtain. All the air rushes out of me.

She lies on her back, propped up with loads of pillows, and her face is pale. Plaster encases both her legs and one arm, the three limbs suspended in traction by slings. Ten tubes carrying silver solution disappear beneath her hospital gown.

This is my fault, this is my fault, this is my fault.

She smiles, but it resembles a grimace. "Hey, you."

"Hey."

She reaches out with her good arm, blood-leeched fingers stretching for mine.

Numb, I trudge over to the bed, sink into the chair, and take her hand. It's cold. So cold.

"I'm so sorry." My words sound feeble.

She squeezes my hand, tugs it close, and brushes her lips against my scarred knuckles. "There's nothing to apologise for. It was an accident. It's Myles who should say sorry."

I lean over and brush a stray lock of hair off her clammy forehead. "I'll never forgive myself."

My fault, my fault, my fault.

It's all my fault.

I hurt everyone I care about. My parents. Jez. Geek. Layla. Everyone. Everyone would be safer if I kept them at a distance.

I drop Layla's hand. "I love you."

Her lips part, eyes widening. "What?"

"It's... I thought you were going to... I had to tell you."

Her eyes shine with tears. "I love you, too." She goes to take my hand again.

I stand.

Her brows crease. "What's wrong?"

"It's because I love you that"—my voice cracks and I clear my throat—"that I can't be with you."

"What?" She wriggles around, trying to sit up and wincing in pain. She sinks back onto the pillows.

My throat tightens. I want to reach out, stroke her hair, pull her into a tight hug. I don't do any of those things, because I'm not thinking about what I want—I'm thinking about what she needs.

She needs to be safe, which can't happen while I'm around.

"I really am sorry. For everything." I'm already halfway towards the door.

"I don't understand," she says, giving another little mew of pain. "Why are you doing this?"

I owe her some kind of explanation, but the words stick in my throat. What can I say? What can I give her? Empty platitudes? We can still be friends. You deserve better. It's not you, it's me. The last one's trite, but true.

"Look at me."

I can't. It hurts too much, like swallowing bleach.

"Please."

That does it.

I turn.

Silent tears stream down her face. "It was an accident."

A bitter laugh escapes me. "That's me. Accident prone."

"It wasn't your fault."

I shake my head with force. "You got hurt, because of me."

"Because of Myles."

I'm crying now too. "You could've died."

"But I didn't. You're just tired. The last few months have been hell, but that doesn't mean—"

"I don't want to hurt you again."

Her eyes harden. "Don't give up on us."

Sniffing, I say, "I haven't. I've given up on myself."

"Don't do this."

I wrench myself away and stride towards the door.

"Henry."

Keep walking.

"Stop."

Keep walking.

"Henry."

Keep walking.

The nurse gives me a sad look when I pass his station, but I ignore him. I shove through the doors so hard they crash against the walls.

Geek stands. "What happened?"

"I don't want to talk about it."

"Mate, I—"

"Leave it, all right."

Keep walking.

Chapter 34

Sleep evades me that night. On the odd occasion I drop off, I'm jolted awake by nightmares featuring my parents' bloody throats and Layla's broken body and the whiff of fruit flavoured chewing gum and old tobacco.

I know it's morning when the lights in my quarters flick on automatically.

Layla.

I had to do it. Had to break up with her. It doesn't matter whether I love her, or whether she loves me. I hurt her, and she's safer without me. I didn't have a choice. I didn't—

The speaker set into the ceiling crackles.

"All executioners and trainees to the ring. That's all executioners and trainees to the ring."

A frisson of excitement races through me.

Myles is leaving today.

I drag myself out of bed, shower, and change into a fresh trainee uniform.

Geek waits outside my room, leaning against the wall. "I spoke to Layla."

I brush past him and head towards the ring.

He catches up. "You think you're doing her a favour, leaving her?"

"Yeah. I do."

"She said you dropped the L bomb."

I press my lips together.

"Funny way of showing it."

"Can we talk about something else?"

He tucks his hands into his pockets as he paces along. "We're finally getting rid of Myles."

I should feel triumphant, but I don't. I'm numb, hollow. My earlier excitement's fizzled away to nothing. "Yeah."

"I thought you'd be happy."

I shrug.

We don't talk after that.

The executioner who greets us at the forked corridor doesn't point us toward the antechambers. Instead, he guides us towards the hallway leading directly into the ring. "You're up here today, lads."

We join the long queue outside.

A few people smile at me. One shoots me the thumbs up and says, "Good job yesterday."

"About time," says the woman standing next to him.

A ripple of laughter passes down the line.

Rather than embarrassment, I feel a surge of pride.

Geek stares at his shoes. "Guess first place has its benefits, huh?"

Geek's still in fourth.

"Hey," I say. "Training isn't over yet. You've got time to pull it round."

"Yeah, maybe."

The resulting silence cramps my shoulders like an ill-fitting jumper. I change the subject. "No sign of Bianca."

Geek's eyes sweep up and down the line. "Nobody's seen her for a few days."

"Good."

"I still can't believe it. She's so inoffensive."

I can't quite believe it myself, but I don't want to talk about Bianca. "Is Layla coming to this?"

Geek shakes his head. "She's still in the medical bay."

My gut twists. "Right."

"I wonder if—"

Femi barges into the queue, snarling at me. "You've got a nerve showing your face here."

"Leave me alone." I meant it to sound cutting, but the words come out flat and tired.

"Myles deserves to be here. He's a better fighter than you."

Geek rolls his eyes. "He's also a sadistic psychopath."

"Say that again, Outsider," Femi growls.

Geek rubs his thumb across his bottom lip and lets out a short, derisive laugh. "I said—"

Zara appears at Geek's shoulder. "Everything okay here?"

"Fine," I say.

"No," Geek and Femi say in unison.

She quirks an eyebrow. "Stone, Townsend, you're up front with me." Zara leads us to the front of the queue.

Femi's withering glare burns into my back.

I'm surprised my skin doesn't blister... again.

"Thanks," I say to Zara.

She doesn't answer.

Carmichael stands at the head of the queue, his face stern. His eyes go to Zara. "Ready?"

She nods.

We file into the ring.

Coldness radiates off the black marble walls and my pulse beats in my fingertips.

Two burly executioners I recognise—Dickinson and O-'Hara—lead Myles into the ring. He finds me in an instant, narrowing his eyes.

The crowd jeers, shouting insults and profanities at Myles. Clearly, his calling me orphan boy yesterday hadn't gone down too well. Someone even shouts, "Good riddance."

Carmichael, who stands next to me, raises his hand.

The noise dies away.

He taps his Adam's apple with his index finger and whispers the spell to amplify his voice. "You all know why we're here. Myles lost the Trial by Magic. Henry's terms were simple. Upon winning, he goes into first place and Myles leaves COVEN. Myles agreed to these terms. As always, any executioner can contest the outcome."

Contest the outcome? My insides turn to stone. That's an option?

"I contest it," Femi shouts from the other end of the room.

Carmichael indulges him with a slow shake of his head. "Perhaps you misheard me, Femi. I asked if any *executioners* wanted to challenge the result. You don't have that title yet." He casts a level gaze over the crowd. "Well?"

Nobody challenges the outcome. Even Nick holds his tongue.

"I contest it." Myles glares up at Carmichael.

The crowd draws a collective breath.

All the muscles in Carmichael's back pull taught. "You're in no position to contest anything."

He shakes off his burly guards and takes a step forward. "It wasn't a fair fight."

"*What?*" The word explodes from me.

"He knew every move I was going to make," Myles says. "Because of those freaky eyes."

"You were pretty confident when I challenged you," I say.

A chuckle spreads through the crowd.

"You want to discuss fairness?" Carmichael asks, a dangerous edge to his voice. "You might think you're clever, but I know what you did to Henry. You're nothing but a coward and a bully."

Confused murmurs rise from the executioners.

Myles meets Carmichael's gaze head on. "Don't know what you're talking about."

Carmichael snorts. "You're lucky he got to you before I did."

A blush floods Myles's face, and he shrinks away from Carmichael.

"As for you," Carmichael says, shifting his attention from Myles to Femi. "I know you had something to do with it, too."

Femi stares into the middle distance, his mask of indifference unbreakable.

"But I can't prove it, so you're safe for now."

A stocky woman, waist-length dreadlocks piled atop her head in a messy bun, pushes her way to the front of the crowd. Rosie Abimbola. Femi's aunt. "Carmichael? What is this? What are you saying to my nephew?" Her metallic silver lipstick shimmers when she speaks.

"I'm telling him a few home truths, Rosie. He needs to hear them."

"What exactly are you accusing him of?"

Carmichael lifts his gaze to mine. "Show them."

My mouth goes dry. "What?"

"Show them what Myles and Femi did to you."

My hands fly to the hem of my T-shirt and tug it down. If I show them my scars, they'll see how vulnerable I am. "I—I can't."

"Director Carmichael gave you an order, Stone," Zara says. "You're serious?"

Carmichael nods. "Remember what I told you about scars?"

"What? I don't—" Wait. He said something about scars months ago, when he rescued me from Razor. Has it only been months? It feels like years, decades, a lifetime ago.

Our scars only define us if we let them.

Slowly, painfully, I revolve until my back's facing into the room and lift the hem of my T-shirt, exposing the lumpy patchwork of scar tissue disfiguring my lower back and left side.

Cries of shock and outrage burst forth.

I lower my shirt and turn back around.

The executioners nearest Femi draw away from him, the others glaring at Myles.

"Bullies," one shouts.

"Wankers."

"Animals."

Zara sticks her fingers in her mouth and blasts out one of her trademark wolf-whistles. "Enough."

Rosie's eyes bug out of her head. "No. Femi would never do that. He's a good boy."

"Tell her," Carmichael says. "Look your aunt in the eye and tell her you didn't do it."

My knees are trembling, and my face is hot.

"Hold it together," Zara hisses in my ear.

I tense the muscles in my legs, my gaze flicking between Femi and Rosie.

"Femi?" Rosie's voice rises two octaves. She unleashes a torrent of Yoruba, her words clipped and stern, before switching back to English. "Tell them, Oluwafemi. Tell them you didn't do this."

"I didn't do it," Femi says, in a bored tone.

"See, Carmichael?" Rosie presses a hand to her ample bosom. "My nephew would never—"

"He's lying," someone says.

My eyes dart around the room. I know that voice. At least I think I do. It sounds like...

Bianca.

She edges through the antechamber doors and walks across the ring with her head down, a curtain of short hair hiding her face, until she stands next to Carmichael. Bianca's already thin frame appears emaciated and the bones in her wrists stick out at sharp angles.

"Bianca, what the hell are you doing?" her mum—Katya—says.

"Bianca?" Carmichael says. "How do you know Myles is lying?"

Myles's eyes narrow to slits. "Don't say a word."

"Because..." Bianca lifts her head like it's weighed down by something heavy—eyes shining—takes a huge gulp of air and says, in a small, quiet voice. "Because I was there."

Mutters whisper over my ears like a soft breeze.

"You were there?" Carmichael repeats.

She bites her lip. "I was there when they tortured Henry."

All's silent.

Carmichael sets his jaw. "When *who* tortured Henry?"

Femi thumps his fist into his other hand. "Shut up."

"Myles... and Femi... and... and—" Her voice cracks.

"And?"

She brings a hand to her mouth. "And me."

"You little bitch." Myles lunges for Bianca.

The guards grab his arms and wrench him back.

Across from me, Femi spins on his heel, attempting to flee.

"*Traho,*" Carmichael barks.

Femi jerks backward, crashing to the ring floor.

"Restrain him," Carmichael says.

Dickinson releases Myles and sprints over to a groaning Femi. He tugs Femi to his feet, clamping both arms behind his back.

Carmichael zeroes in on Bianca. "Tell me exactly what happened."

She swallows, then more words than I've ever heard her speak in one go burst forth in a rushed torrent. "We—Myles, Femi and I—broke into Henry's room. Henry was in the bathroom. The shower was running. He didn't hear us break in. Myles crept up behind him and knocked him out with a sleep spell. Femi carried him into the tunnels and they handcuffed him to a chair using iron cuffs, and—"

"Where did you get the cuffs?" Carmichael asks.

"Myles stole them from the armoury."

"The armoury? There are guards stationed at the armoury."

"He memorised their shift patterns. When we got there, he cast an invisibility spell and slipped in when the guards swapped over, while they were chatting."

Carmichael says, "What happened once you got Henry down to the tunnels?"

She lets out a shaky breath. "He came to, eventually, and then—oh, God—they told me they just wanted to scare him. I never thought... I didn't know. I didn't know what they were going to do. The acid spell... they went too far."

I shouldn't feel sorry for Bianca, I know I shouldn't, but she looks so small, so breakable, like a thin sheet of blown glass. Despite what she's done, I want to give her a reassuring hug and get her a mug of something hot.

Carmichael's brow furrows. "I thought you and Henry were friends. Why go along with this?"

"I had my reasons." She flushes and ducks her head again. "I tried to stop them, but Myles—he—I couldn't."

"Then what did you do?"

"I ran."

"Ran?" Carmichael spits the word.

She nods, a brief bob of the head. "I'm not proud of it."

"Ran? Ridiculous." Carmichael paces up and down. "What, do you suppose, would Myles and Femi have done if Layla and Geek hadn't intervened?"

"Myles told me what they were planning to do," Bianca says.

Myles's face twists into a feral mask of hatred. "I swear to God, if you—"

Bianca rushes at Myles with whippet-like speed, draws back her arm and slaps him across the face.

The *crack* of skin on skin bounces off the walls.

Bianca clutches her reddening fingers. "That felt good."

"Turn up for the books," Zara mutters.

Carmichael asks, "What were they going to do, Bianca?"

Bianca faces Carmichael again, steeling herself. "They were going to kill Henry."

The crowd attacks like a many-headed Hydra.

"Traitors."

"Throw them out."

"Wait until I get my hands on you."

Carmichael stalks closer to Myles and Femi. "Do you still deny it?"

Myles blinks. "Wholeheartedly."

Carmichael's mouth twitches.

Femi says, "Bianca has a flare for the dramatic. We were just messing around. Things got a little out of hand. Just boys being boys."

Carmichael looks as if he wants to punch Fermi. "Boys being boys?"

Bianca clasps her hands over her ears. "I didn't know. I didn't know."

"What do you say now, Rosie?" Zara asks, hand on her hip.

Rosie's eyes are hard. She won't look at Femi. "That coward is no nephew of mine."

The crowd erupts again.

Zara grabs my arm and squeezes hard enough to bruise. "Why didn't you tell me?"

Vi. Iustitia. Fides.

Vi.

Strength.

I hang my head. "I didn't want you to think I was weak."

"You idiot." She drops my arm.

Carmichael nods at Dickinson and O'Hara.

They flick their wrists.

Myles and Femi's legs buckle and they fall to their knees.

"What are you doing?" Femi asks.

It's the first time I've ever heard a tremor in his voice.

"Wiping your memory, of course," Carmichael replies.

"What?"

"You're both finished at COVEN."

Femi blanches. "You—you can't, I—"

"Do it," Carmichael says.

Dickinson grips Femi's head in his meaty hands, palms covering Femi's temples, and O'Hara does the same to Myles.

Myles throws his head around in O'Hara's grasp. "Get your hands off me."

"Wait," Bianca says.

Carmichael regards her coolly.

"What about me?"

"What about you?"

"Aren't you going to wipe my memory, too?"

Carmichael folds his arms. "You said you tried to save him?"

"I did."

"You really didn't know what they were planning?"

"No. I swear."

Carmichael tilts his chin at me. "What do you think?"

"Me?" My throat tightens. The air in the room's stifling. All eyes are on me. My gaze travels to Bianca. Can I forgive her? Her actions had, in part, led to my torture, but she'd tried to save me. "What am I supposed to do?" I ask Zara.

She shrugs. "That's up to you."

"Um—" I'm paralysed by indecision. Was Bianca any different to Myles and Femi? Did she deserve a reprieve? Maybe. I'd humiliated her, and she made a mistake. A huge mistake, granted, but still a mistake.

"Well?" Carmichael asks.

"I want her to stay."

Some executioners—Katya among them—look relieved, but most look pissed off.

Carmichael's expression's inscrutable. Eventually, he says, "It takes a strong person to offer forgiveness. It's your lucky day, Bianca."

"Thank you." Bianca lifts her shimmering eyes to mine. "I'm so, so sorry, Henry."

"I know you are."

She wipes the tears off her cheeks and says to Carmichael, "What if I still want to leave?"

"Leave?" Katya sounds disgusted. "What do you mean, leave?"

"I hate the way this place makes me feel, Mother. I only agreed to come here because it's what you wanted." She shudders. "I don't belong here."

"Don't say that," Katya says.

"It's true. I'm not cut out for it. I'm not strong like you. God, I wish I was, but I'm not. If I was, I never would've let them…" Bianca gaze flicks to me briefly, before she turns back to Carmichael. "If I leave voluntarily, will you still wipe my memories?"

"Yes," he says.

She nods. "Good."

I shove Zara out of the way, dart up to Bianca, and curl my fingers around the tops of her arms. "You don't have to do this."

"I do." She rests her hand on my cheek. "I hate myself for what I did, for what this place has done to me."

"You won't remember us. Me and Geek."

She lets her hand fall and steps away. "I think that's for the best." She walks into the middle of the ring and kneels beside Femi. "I'm ready."

Carmichael stands behind her and moulds his hands to her temples. "You're sure?"

"I am," she says, eyes finding mine. "I'd say I'll miss you, but I won't, so I'll say goodbye instead."

I want to say it back, but my voice won't work.

Carmichael, Dickinson and O'Hara open their mouths and chant as one.

"*Delebo memoriam ut obliviscar eorum*."

The air goes colder still, like ice crystalising on my skin. Goosebumps erupt along my arms. I need to stop this. I can't let Bianca do this. She doesn't deserve this, does she?

"*Delebo memoriam ut obliviscar eorum*."

Femi fixes his eyes on a point in the distance, face set in a stone mask.

Myles glares at me, a look that makes me shiver.

"*Delebo memoriam ut obliviscar eorum.*"

Flash.

Femi goes rigid.

Flash.

Myles sags in O'Hara's grip.

My eyes go to Bianca's. They're wide, too wide, and her lip trembles. She twists her ring around her finger.

Twist, twist, twist.

"Bi—" That's as far as I get.

Flash.

Bianca's eyes go glassy, her face goes blank, and she disappears.

CHapTer 35

When it's over, Bianca, Myles and Femi wear identical expressions—their eyes still glazed and vacant, lips parted slightly.

Carmichael, Dickinson and O'Hara guide them to their feet.

"Come on, that's it. This way," O'Hara says to Myles, his hand resting between Myles's shoulder blades, his voice surprisingly gentle.

Myles drifts along beside O'Hara like a carrier bag caught in a breeze.

Dickinson and Femi follow.

A thin trail of dribble leaks from the corner of Femi's open mouth, and guilt pinches my stomach, even though I shouldn't feel sorry for him. It's Bianca who hits me hardest, though.

Her wide, innocent eyes seem even wider, even more innocent and, as Carmichael nudges her towards the exit, those wide innocent eyes drift to mine. A faint crease appears on her forehead.

My heart jumps into my throat. She shouldn't remember me.

She moves towards me like she's sleepwalking, almost floating across the black marble, closing the space between us step by soft-heeled step. And then she's standing right in front of me, reaching out and stroking her fingers—which are ice cold—against my cheek. "You look familiar." Her voice is light and breathy.

I swallow, but say nothing. How's this possible?

The crease on Bianca's forehead smooths out. "No. Sorry. I thought you were someone else." Her hand leaves my cheek, and she seems to collapse in on herself.

Carmichael motions to an executioner I don't know. "Take her with the others."

The executioner does as she's told, leading a dazed Bianca from the ring.

I let out a long exhale. I've got the beginnings of a headache.

"She did the right thing," Carmichael says.

"She recognised me."

Carmichael shakes his head. "Only for a moment. Sometimes memory spells take a minute to work."

"That was horrible," I say. "They were like zombies."

"It won't last long. Just long enough for us to collect their things and drop them off somewhere. Then the replacement memories we gave them will surface."

"Replacement memories?"

Carmichael gives a soft, sad chuckle. "Well, we can't erase six months and send them back into the world with a giant gap in their memories, can we?"

The cold spot on my cheek—the ghost of Bianca's fingertips—spreads down my throat, across my chest and deep into my gut. I hate the thought of someone messing about in my mind, implanting false memories, but I say, "I suppose not."

"I need to go to the Admin Centre and destroy their personnel files," Carmichael says. "You going to be okay?"

I nod, mute.

He squeezes my shoulder. "Remember, this was justice."

"What happens now?"

He grins. "Zara?"

"Yes, boss."

"Make the announcement."

"Now? But we've still got—"

"There's no point prolonging the inevitable." Carmichael squeezes my shoulder a second time and leaves.

Zara shakes her head. "Fucking mental."

"What was he talking about? What announcement?" I ask.

She ignores me. "We rarely do it this early." She strides over to the bank of screens along the back wall. "But orders are orders, I guess."

Excited mutters spread through the room.

Geek nudges my arm. "Any idea what's going on?"

"Not a clue," I say.

Zara calls for quiet and she gets it. She takes a deep breath in through her nose and pushes it out again, the diamond in her nose stud sparkling. "As trainer, it's my duty, my responsibility and my honour to introduce our newest executioners."

I blink, trying to compute what she's saying.

"Shit," Geek says.

Zara flicks her wrist at the screen and whispers a spell under her breath.

The screen changes.

My stomach drops.

Final Ratings:

1. Henry Stone (Executioner)

2. Layla Jabara (Executioner)

3. Gareth Townsend (Executioner)

4. ~~Oluwafemi Abimbola~~

5. ~~Bianca Yakhontov~~

6. ~~Myles Hedges~~

Every single executioner in the room—except Zara—erupts into cheers and whoops.

I'm stunned, standing frozen on the spot, staring at my name, and the word *Executioner* beside it.

My name.

Several people slap me on the back and shout congratulations in my ear, but I barely notice them.

I've done it.

I'm an executioner.

Something pulls my face out of shape, stretching my skin and making my cheeks tingle. I reach up, wondering what's wrong. My fingers brush the curve of my mouth. There's nothing wrong. I'm grinning.

"Shit." Geek combs his fingers through his shaggy hair, bouncing on the balls of his feet. "We did it. We fucking did it."

I laugh—a big, hearty laugh—for the first time in ages.

Geek grabs me and pulls me into a bear hug so tight I swear my ribs creak. He shouts in my ear, "We did it. We did it. My mum's going to be okay. She's going to be okay," and jumps up and down, forcing me to jump with him.

When he finally lets go and dives into the crowd for more bear hugs, I massage my complaining ribs, but I'm still grinning.

"Well done," says a quiet voice behind me.

Zara.

Her glossy pink lips quirk at the corners.

"Thanks," I say.

"Don't fuck it up."

The grin slides off my face.

She brushes past me and stalks into the centre of the ring. "Listen up."

All eyes turn to her.

"The graduation party will take place a week from now in the dining hall."

"Graduation party?" I say.

"Yes, a party," Zara says, slowly. "You know, get dressed up, get pissed, celebrate."

A roar goes up all around me.

I bite my lip. Dress up? The only clothes I brought with me—the only clothes I own apart from my trainee uniform—are the T-shirt and jeans I was wearing when I got here. The well of happiness in my chest sinks into my stomach and sours with guilt. In all the commotion, I'd forgotten about my parents. Just for a second. I pull the chain from beneath my T-shirt and rub my thumb over their rings. I should go straight to Carmichael and demand Razor's death instantly, instead of standing here worrying about what to wear to a party.

Bit by bit, the crowd disperses.

I approach Zara. "I need to speak to Carmichael."

"About?"

My fist clenches around the wedding rings. "It's personal."

She catches the movement. "Razor's gone into hiding."

Her words wind me. "What?"

Zara continues, "He's cloaking himself somehow. We can't find him."

"But Carmichael promised. He promised I'd be the one to—"

She cuts across me. "Relax. We're working on it. You'll be the first to know when we find him." She pauses, her eyes flicking to the rings clasped in my hand. "They'd want you to celebrate. It's a massive achievement."

I tuck the rings away. I wish Mum and Dad were here. What would they say? Would they be proud? The thought carves searing pain into my chest, so I shove it away. Zara's right, though. They would want me to celebrate. "I've got nothing smart to wear."

"So buy yourself something," she says, like it's obvious.

"I don't have any money."

She laughs. "Wrong. You *didn't* have any money. Report to the finance department. They'll give you a company card."

My brow furrows. "We've got a finance department?"

"Of course. What the fuck do you think this place runs on, positive vibes?"

"Just seems so... normal."

"COVEN's a business. All businesses need accountants."

"How much can I spend?"

"Whatever you like."

Geek calls out to Zara and waves her over.

She's halfway there when she glances over her shoulder and says, "Oh, and Stone?"

"Yeah?"

"Don't buy off the rack."

I can't help the laugh that escapes me. "Why do you care what I wear?"

"You were one of my trainees. How you present yourself reflects on me, and I've got a reputation to uphold."

"Don't worry," I say. "I won't show you up."

"You'd better not."

A week later, I stand in front of the mirror in my room, admiring the COVEN pentagram tattoo on my wrist. And it's truly something to admire, unlike my new suit. I hate dressing up. The fine black fabric fit like a second skin—the tailor Carmichael sent me to made sure of it—but I still feel confined. I unbutton the jacket, roll my shoulders, fasten the top button again, let out a sigh.

"Ready?" Geek stands in the doorway, looking dapper in a grey three piece.

"What's the point of this, again?" I ask.

He rolls his eyes. "Lighten up. It's a party. Our party. It'll be fun."

"I'll take your word for it." I button my shirt cuffs and follow him across the room, the shiny black loafers pinching my toes. "Don't see why I have to wear this monkey suit."

"Again, it's a party."

I grumble all the way to the dining hall.

"We'll be out of there next week," Geek says, hooking his thumb back at the trainees' quarters.

"Yeah." I say.

The day after Zara announced the graduation party, Carmichael called me into his office and told me I had to move out of the trainees' quarters within the month—my new digs all bought and paid for by COVEN. Every time I think of leaving the compound, my mouth goes dry.

"You find a place yet?" Geek asks.

"Yeah."

"Where?"

"Penthouse flat in the city."

The flat was the second place I looked at. The first was a disaster. A cottage on the outskirts of the city so similar to my parents' house that I took one step inside and vomited all over the welcome mat. The estate agent got all red-faced and flummoxed and said I had to leave, which was fine by me. The reason I opted for the flat was simple. No reminders of the past. Not a grain of oak or a Chesterfield armchair in sight. Open plan. Black and white kitchen, white walls, grey furniture. Cold, clinical, and completely devoid of emotion.

Perfect.

"Nice. We've got a few house warming parties coming up, then," Geek says with relish.

I groan. "I'll be sick of parties after this."

Geek prattles on and on about the townhouse he's bought, and the Audi he's going to buy, and the Alaskan Malamute he's going to rescue.

I zone out until we reach the dining hall. When I walk through the door, my mouth drops open.

Swathes of rich, dark red velvet cover the smooth stone walls. Multi-coloured clouds of witch-light float near the ceiling, casting an ambient, somewhat psychedelic glow throughout the room. The long wooden benches have disappeared, replaced with small, round tables draped in white linen. My ears catch an upbeat melody—a string quartet?—in the background. I spot two violins, a gilded harp and a cello, playing themselves in the corner next to a table overflowing with glasses of champagne.

The room hums with activity. Executioners chat in clusters at tables, tapping their feet in time to the music. A couple of brave souls have taken to the makeshift dance floor.

Zara's dancing—of course she is—electric pink dress swirling, arms above her head, a nearly empty glass of champagne caught between her fingertips. She spins round in time to the music, her blonde hair fanning out around her. She catches me watching her, winks, and raises her glass at me.

"Did she just wink?" Geek says.

"Yeah. I think she's smiling, too."

He shudders. "Talk about *Invasion of the Body Snatchers*. Where's the real Zara?"

"Don't know." I grab two glasses from an executioner carrying a tray full of drinks. I down one glass, then the other. On the last swallow, the fizzy champagne catches in my throat, and suddenly I'm coughing and spluttering.

Geek slaps me on the back half-heartedly, still taking in the room. "Thirsty?"

As soon as I can breathe again, I say, "I hate parties."

The crowd parts, and I see her.

Layla.

She's swept her thick, dark curls up into an elegant bun, a few tendrils escaping to frame her face, and she's done something clever with her makeup. Striking smoky eyes, full lips the colour of port. She spots us and smiles. When she saunters towards us, the diamonds in her ears and at her throat sparkle, and the emeralds on her bracelet shimmer. Her dress sweeps the floor. Green, to match the emeralds, probably. It clings in all the right places.

My mouth's bone dry again, but it's nothing to do with the prospect of leaving the compound this time.

It's because I love you that I can't be with you.

"They discharged you, then?" Geek says when Layla reaches us.

"I discharged myself. No way would I miss a good knees up."

Geek kisses her on the cheek. "Good to have you back. You look hot."

She twirls. The dress is backless.

Don't give up on us.

I haven't. I've given up on myself.

She chuckles and runs her hands over the moss-coloured fabric.

I can't help but follow the path of her fingers down to her waist.

"Thanks." She brushes off Geek's shoulders and checks him over. "Don't look so bad yourself."

I catch Layla's eye.

She clasps her hands in front of her and looks down at the floor.

I glance away as heat creeps up my neck.

"Well, this isn't awkward at all," Geek says. "I need a drink." He strolls towards the champagne table.

I want to yell at him. *Come back!* I don't, because I'd look like a tit.

Seconds that feel like days tick by.

"Nice dress," I say.

Layla says, "I like your tie," at the same time.

I rub the back of my neck.

She smooths out her already smooth skirt.

"It's very... It makes you look... you know..." Shut up. Stop talking.

"We're matching," she says, reaching up and straightening my dark green tie with delicate fingers. "Brings out the colour of your eyes." Then her palms are resting on my chest, warm and soft.

More slow, syrupy seconds pass.

"Would you like to—" she asks.

I step back, and her hands fall away. "I should get—oh."

"No, it's fine."

"What were you going to say?"

Her lip snags between her teeth. "I was going to ask if you wanted to dance?"

It's because I love you that I can't be with you.

I look down at the shiny uppers of my shoes. "I don't think that's a good idea."

"I know we're not—I mean I understand why—oh, for God's sake. This is stupid. I'm not about to rip your clothes off, you're not that irresistible."

The tension finally breaks, and we both laugh.

"So, what are we now?" I ask. "Friends?"

She quirks an eyebrow. "Friends who dance?"

My gaze drifts to the dance floor, and my legs turn to jelly. "I can't dance."

"It's easy," she says, holding out her hand. "I'll show you."

After a second's hesitation, I take her hand and let her lead me through the crowd and onto to dance floor. The champagne hits my stomach and the room sways a little. I haven't had a drink since my birthday, so maybe downing two glasses on an empty stomach wasn't the best idea.

The tempo of the music changes to something slow.

I want to run, but Layla's still gripping my hand, so instead I rest my other hand on her waist.

She draws in close and takes hold of my shoulder.

And then we're moving, half-swaying, half-revolving on the spot.

"What did I tell you?" she says with an impish grin. "Easy."

"For you, maybe," I say. "It's taking all my concentration not to step on your feet."

She chuckles, the movement pressing us together so that our bodies touch. Her face is inches from mine. All I see. The cute bow of her lips, the sharpness of her cheekbones, the tiny splotch of green in her right eye. Then her chin's resting on my shoulder, and the familiar, woody-sweet scent of her washes over me.

Slow heat flares in my gut before spreading lower. I swallow hard and resist the urge to bury my face in her neck. I try my best to ignore my heart pounding and focus instead on turning in time to the music.

Layla's breath tickles my ear when she speaks. "Your pulse is racing."

Sparks of electricity dance across my skin. "Can't help it." Why did I say that?

Her lips brush my earlobe.

I let out a shaky breath.

"Would it really be so bad if—" she starts.

"Yes." Even as I say it, my hand slides from her waist to the small of her back, drawing her closer still.

She plants a soft kiss on the side of my neck and the place where her lips touch my skin burns.

"If anything ever happened to you—"

She cuts across me. "Nothing's going to happen to me."

"You don't know that. Nobody can see the future."

"True. But we can't live for it, either." Her fingers wind into my hair.

I kiss the top of her head. "I hurt you. If I hadn't—"

"Can't live in the past." She draws back and places a finger on my lips.

I reach up and brush a tendril of hair behind her ear. "Easier said than done," I murmur against her finger.

She removes her finger, resting her hand on my shoulder.

We turn and turn and turn, and the room dissolves around us.

"I read this article once," she says. "One of those crappy Top Ten listicles."

My brow furrows. Where was she going with this?

"Top Ten Things You'd Regret Not Doing if the World Ended Tomorrow." She trails a finger down my chest. "Imagine if we only had tonight." Her finger moves down and down and down, and she hooks it in my belt loop. "Is there anything you'd regret? Not. Doing?"

Oh, shit.

I'm in trouble.

My back slams against my bedroom door.

Our lips collide and move together, Layla's tongue sliding over mine.

I shove the door aside, pull her into my room, and slam it closed. Frantically, I tug at my tie, yanking it off. My jacket follows. I've undone the top button of my shirt when a thought hits me through the fizzy fog of champagne. "This is just for tonight?"

A slow smile curves across Layla's lips. She presses me back against the door, her fingers finding my shirt buttons. She flicks the next one open and kisses the hollow beneath my throat, right over my scar. "Just." Another button pops open. Another kiss on my chest this time. "For." She unfastens a third button and plants a long, lingering kiss on my lips.

I groan.

She draws back. "Tonight."

"Okay." I bury my face in her neck now, nipping her earlobe and trailing a line of kisses down her throat. My hands find the zip fastening her dress, easing it down.

Layla dances away, kicks off her shoes and shimmies out of the green fabric. It falls in a satiny puddle to the floor, revealing matching green underwear.

My lips part, and my eyes follow the curve of her breasts, the sleek line of her flat stomach. "You're incredible."

Slinking forward, Layla slides my shirt off. Despite my burn scars, the last thing I want to do is hide my body from her. She rewards me with another one of those slow, deep kisses that make all my nerves fire at once. She bites my lip, and a jolt of pain and pleasure rushes through me. "You don't know the half of it," she whispers against my ear. She unbuckles my belt, sliding a hand under my waistband, and wrapping her fingers around me.

I suck in a breath through my teeth.

Her hand moves. "Well, well. Someone's excited."

I press a kiss to the top of her breast. "You don't know the half of it."

She giggles again, slides my belt out of its loops, chucks me on the bed and straddles me.

My hands are exploring the curve of her spine, sliding down to cup her buttocks...

And that's the moment. The moment Layla whispers, "I love you."

"You—you what?"

She kisses me, moves off me, lips whispering down my chest, over my abs, moving down. "I love you. I want to make love to you."

Through the haze of champagne and hormones, I remember why we shouldn't be doing this.

It's because I love you that I can't be with you.

"Stop!" I shout.

She starts and lifts her head, hurt in her eyes. "What?"

"We need to stop." I sit up, brush her off, and fasten my trousers.

She brushes her hair off her face. "You don't want to?"

"No, it's not—I want to, God, I *want* to—but we can't."

"Just for tonight, remember? We agreed." She inches closer and runs her hand up the inside of my leg.

I bat her fingers away, stand, and pace to the other side of the room. "We both know it won't just be for tonight."

"Henry—"

"You need to go."

"Henry—"

"Please."

She clambers off the bed, snatching her dress off the floor. "You're such an arsehole."

"Layla, you know why—"

"I know," she says, bending to pick up her shoes—I try not to look at her arse. "I know. And that makes it worse. I know why you're doing this. I even understand it, but it's not fair. We should be together."

I sigh. "In a perfect world, we would be."

"But it's not a perfect world, is it?"

"I meant what I said. If anything ever happened to you..."

She stomps over to the door and throws it open.

"Layla."

"Don't." She pauses. "I'm not saying we can't be—we can still—I just need some time."

"I'm sorry."

"You're always sorry," she says, and then she's gone.

She's right. I *am* an arsehole.

CHAPTER 36

???

Henry Stone needs to pay.

I creep through COVEN wearing an ill-fitting trainee uniform. Trainers, tracksuit bottoms and a hooded jacket, hood up. I covered my face with a black scarf before I arrived, so nobody will recognise me. Carmichael will kill me if he finds out what I'm doing.

A shiver runs through me, down my legs and into the cold marble floor.

It doesn't bare thinking about.

I round a corner; the stealth spell does a wonderful job of muffling my footsteps. The murmur of voices comes from up ahead. I freeze. What should I do? I look from side to side. Duck through a door. I flatten my back against the wall. My heart thrashes around in my chest.

The voices come closer.

Closer.

"Still can't believe Stone won that bout," one says.

My clenched fists shake. Stone, that bastard. He's going to get what's coming to him.

"I know. I thought Hedges had him for sure. It's Layla I feel sorry for," the other says.

The voices fade away, footsteps retreating.

I wait until I'm sure I'm alone, and slip from the room. The wall is a cold pressure against my back. I slide along it, crossing one leg in front of the other until I reach the corner. I peek out.

A senior executioner—Hargreaves—guards the Admin Centre, where Carmichael keeps all the COVEN employee files.

I don't want to hurt Hargreaves. I know him. He's a good man. Hopefully, it won't come to that. I click my fingers. "*Corium.*"

Rippling turquoise magic flows over my body, hiding me from view.

I shift around the corner and inch closer to the Admin Centre.

Hargreaves yawns, bleary eyes finding mine.

I halt, pulse rapid in my ears. Did the cloaking spell fail?

A second passes.

Another.

And another.

Hargreaves looks away.

I close my eyes and let out a breath. Halfway through the exhale, I sneeze.

Bollocks.

Hargreaves snaps to attention. "*Revelare.*"

The cloaking spell concealing me falls away with a soft *snick*.

"What the—"

I don't let Hargreaves finish. "*Baculum.*" My witch-staff flashes into my hands, throwing a blue-green glow against the walls. I sweep the staff low, and knock Hargreaves's legs out from under him.

He crashes to the floor with a loud, "Ugh."

I spin the staff and slam the butt into Hargreaves's temple.

He goes limp, but his chest still rises and falls.

"I'm sorry." I release the staff. It dissipates. I grab Hargreaves under the arms, drag him through the doors into the Admin Centre, and prop him against the wall. I survey the empty room.

Row upon row of sturdy metal filing cabinets line the walls, housing employee files past and present. Carmichael has an aversion to storing anything digitally, in case COVEN gets hacked.

I need to be quick. If anyone discovers Hargreaves deserted his post before I get what I came for...

Crossing to the filing cabinets, I run my fingers along the rows of labelled draws.

A to C.

D to F.

G to I.

I stop when I reach S to U and slide the drawer open, flicking through the files inside.

Sampson; Santiago; Sedgwick; Sims—come on. Where are you?

Stone.

I snatch Stone's file from the drawer, flip open the cover and devour the pages one by one. What can I use against him? There must be—

Ah, interesting.

Stone's parents are dead, murdered by Razor Finch, the infamous SOCG boss. That's not the interesting bit. Word had spread like wildfire as soon as Myles overheard Stone's conversation with the Jabara girl. This is the interesting part. Turns out Stone had witnessed a murder committed by Finch. I shake my head and mutter, "Don't do things by halves, do you, Stone?"

A photo of Finch glares up at me from the file, the words *Whereabouts unknown* written beneath it in Carmichael's spidery hand.

I ease the photo from beneath the metal paper clip securing it.

Whereabouts unknown.

Carmichael briefed us about Razor last week. He's cloaked himself so no-one can find him. I need to track him down, but a locater spell will be useless without a locus—a physical object tied to Razor—and I don't have anything like that.

But maybe there's still a way...

Witch-bane.

Even the name of the drug sends a shiver through me and curls my lip.

If there was any other way...

Witch-bane has a peculiar hallucinatory side effect. It allows witches to see lost things—maybe even find those lost things... or people.

But. It's addictive. And it's shameful.

Is it worth the risk?

There's only one answer to that question.

Luckily for me, I know a witch-bane dealer in London who owes me a favour.

It takes a good hour and a half to drive to London.

I arrive on the shabby street a little after midnight.

The bungalow is a shit hole, the windows smeared with filth, the overgrown scrubby lawn strangled by weeds, rubbish bags piled against the grimy brickwork.

No-one in their right mind would choose to live here. Then again, I think Jonesy might be a few strawberries short of a punnet.

I switch off the engine and approach the house with caution. You never know what mood Jonesy's going to be in. I bang on the door with a closed fist and wait, tapping my foot on the dirty doorstep. "Come on, come on, come on."

The door opens a crack, and the smell from the house's entrails—a potent mixture of body odour, must, and witch-bane fumes—assaults my nostrils.

Jonesy peers around the door with a beady eye. "What the fuck do you want?"

"Nice to see you, too." I shove the door open and barge past him. The rank stink gets even stronger, almost making my eyes water.

"Hey. Whad'ya think you're doing, this is my fucking—"

I punch the witch-bane dealer clean across the jaw, my knuckles stinging, and he collapses to the floor. I stoop low and grab a fistful of his lank, greasy hair. "What kind of welcome is that, Jonesy? You still owe me a favour, remember?"

He pushes me away and clambers to his feet, wiping his bloody lip with a grimy hand.

My entire face scrunches up. He disgusts me.

"Whad'ya want?"

"I need witch-bane."

He smiles, a grey-gapped grin. "Oh, ho, ho. How the mighty have fallen."

I narrow my eyes to slits. "I'm not an addict. There's someone I need to find."

"Easier ways to do that." He snorts, a thick, wet sound. "Less risky ways, too."

"Just give me the fucking bane." I inject iron into my tone. "Unless you want the MID to find out about your little set up here."

"All right, all right. Keep your bloody hair on. Wait here."

When Jonesy returns, there's a small vial of forest green liquid clutched in his fist. "Here."

I snatch it from him and stride back to the front door, pausing with my hand on the door handle. "Tell anyone I was here, and I swear on my magic, I'll kill you... slowly."

When he speaks, there's a delicious tremor in his voice. "Not gonna say nuthin', am I?"

I leave without another word, the vial secured in my grasp.

Time to find Razor Finch.

I park in a deserted layby and take the vial of witch-bane out of the glove box, staring at the toxic substance inside with trepidation.

Am I really going to do this?

I uncap the bottle and dip my finger in the vile stuff.

Risk addiction, risk being shunned, just to get revenge on Henry Stone?

My fingertip tingles and goes numb.

I already know the answer to that question.

I rub the witch-bane deep into my gums, my eyes roll back into my head. I'm weightless. It's so good. Weightless, worri-less. Floating, flying, soaring. Then I'm falling, falling, falling... into a utopian world of swirling galaxies and everything is light and dark and bright all at once, shattered stars whizzing overhead, and I laugh, the laugh of the mad and the bad and the bold. A crimson moon bleeds rose petals into a syrupy void and I'm one of those petals, swirling and turning and floating in the milky breeze.

My body—back in the world of men and flesh and blood and bone—lets out a long, contented sigh, while I...

Eye...

Eye of the beholder and I behold beauty in all its forms...

Continue...

To...

f

l

o

a

t...

Mm.

Why did I come here, again?

There was a reason, but reason doesn't belong here.

Reason.

Treason.

Traitor.

Stone.

That's why I'm here. To get Stone. To find Razor. The razor blade that will slit Stone's throat open and spill his blood like these pearly petals.

Razor.

The void wants me to see him, wants me to find him. I know it in my rubbery bones.

Ha. Rubbery bones. That's hilarious.

In the other world, the grey, boring one, my lips move. "*Inveniet, Razor Finch*."

A beat.

Find him.

Pins and needles surge down my earthly arms and into the photo I brought with me from COVEN.

Find him.

The spell catches and the photo glows orange.

"Found you," I whisper, before floating away into the honey-glazed embrace of the witch-bane.

CHAPTER 37

???

B y the time I reach Finch's hideout, the weak dawn sunlight paints pastel shades across the sky, and the inside of my mouth is furry like rough carpet. When I turn off the engine this time, my hands shake a little.

How can anyone get addicted to that stuff if it makes you feel like this afterwards? It's like I've been microwaved and I'm only half-cooked, and I have to wait until the shaking stops.

When my body feels solid again, I climb out of the car.

The fresh air clears the last of the grogginess and I get my first proper glimpse of the place.

I wasn't expecting this.

Finch's hideout is an abandoned building site on the edge of Daxbridge.

The tarnished sign outside reads *Gladeview Mews*. I remember when the local MP first announced the project. The new hub of the city, they'd said. Shopping centre, two cinemas, too many restaurants to count. That was the plan, anyway, until the developer went bust. Something to do with a tax dodge gone tits up. It's a graveyard now, filled with the emaciated skeletons of buildings, all broken steel bones and weathered concrete flesh.

What a place to end up in.

I don't have sympathy for Finch, however. He's a crook, thief and murderer. Under different circumstances, I would've been sent here to kill him. I pick my way across the uneven tarmac, hopping over large cracks in the ground and dodging piles of chalky rubble, anticipation tickling my skin.

A towering concrete and glass obelisk comes into view. It's an ugly thing, disfiguring the skyline, and completely ruining the city's old world charm.

The photo of Finch—still clutched in my hand—flashes.

He's in there.

I rush over to the building and spot a narrow door marking a service entrance. I point at the rusted padlock. "*Recludo.*"

The padlock clicks open, and the door swings out with a loud creak.

My breath catches. I stand there until I'm sure that Finch isn't about to ambush me. I creep inside, and darkness robs me of sight. Somewhere in the distance, the drip, drip, drip of water echoes. "*Lux.*"

A turquoise cloud of witch-light flares to life in my hand. I toss it into the air, where it hangs like a plume of powdered snow. My eyes adjust. Everything is bare—the concrete floor, the plasterboard walls. I press deeper and deeper into the deserted cement mausoleum. The dry, dead air tickles my throat and the hairs on the back of my neck rise.

Finch could be anywhere.

Not that it matters.

I'm not scared of Razor Finch. He should be afraid of me.

I pass under a sweeping arch and into a vast empty room. No, almost empty. A ratty sleeping bag, a small pile of dog-eared paperbacks underneath a camping chair, and a Calor gas stove takes up residence in one corner.

No sign of Finch, though. I wonder if—

Something scrapes against the concrete floor.

"*Baculum*." I spin my witch-staff in a wide arc and come nose-to-snout with a mangy stray dog. Can't stand dogs. Vicious creatures. I strike out with the staff.

"*Pedibus nostris*," says a deep, gruff voice.

The muscles in my arms and legs lock in place.

Shit. A binding spell.

The dog barks, baring its scabby teeth.

"Drop it," commands the same voice.

"I have a proposal for you."

Finch steps into view, a crimson death-strike sparkling between his fingers. "I said, drop the staff."

I can still move my hands, so I do as he says, the staff vanishing in a swirl of green-blue light.

Finch fixes his coal-black eyes on me. "Who the hell are you?"

"I'm a witch," I say.

"Obviously. You know who I am?"

I nod.

"Who sent you?"

"No-one."

"How did you find me?"

"Locater spell."

The light from Finch's death-strike twitches and flickers, like it's desperate to be used. "Impossible. I cloaked myself, and this place is warded to the hilt."

Smirking, I say, "I had a little help."

Finch cocks his head to the side. "I'm getting bored. You'd better tell me why you're here."

"Henry Stone."

His black eyes flash like opals catching the light. "What about him?"

"You want him dead?"

"Yes."

"That makes two of us."

"But it doesn't matter what I want. Stone's protected by a powerful witch."

"Carmichael. I know."

Finch's lips curve into a cruel smile. "You're an execution-er."

My heart skips a beat. "Does it matter?"

He laughs, closes his hand around the death-strike, and beckons to the dog. "Here, boy."

The dog pads over to Finch.

Finch crouches down in front of it, fondling its ears and, when he speaks, his tone is softer than melted butter. "Did the nasty man try to hurt you, eh? Did he?"

The dog whines.

"Yes, I know, I know." He extracts his fingers from the dog's fur and rubs the jagged scar running through his eyebrow, before reaching into his pocket and pulling out a palm-sized toy car. "We both know about nasty men, don't we, boy? My father was a nasty man until I made sure he wasn't. Go on then, go."

An icy chill settles in my bones. What kind of man kills his own father?

The dog runs off.

Finch straightens, tucks the toy car away again, and lights a blunt with a crimson flame.

I shudder at the thought of what the dark elemental magic must do to his insides.

He expels a thin plume of smoke. "Tell me why I shouldn't open you up like a ripe melon."

I fix him with a hard stare. "I know how you can get to Stone."

The smoke makes him cough. "He's at COVEN. I can't get to him while he's there. The wards are too strong. Last chance to think of a better reason."

"He goes running. Same time every day. Has done for a month or more."

Finch's eyes narrow. "You know his schedule?"

"I know a lot more than that. I have his file."

His eyes flash. "Where?"

"You'll let me live?"

"I suppose so."

"Swear it on your magic."

Finch makes an irritated noise in his throat, but says, "I swear on my magic. Where's the file?"

"In my jacket."

Finch stalks over to me, takes another drag on the spliff, and blows the over-sweet smoke right into my face.

I cough.

He laughs again, dry and raspy. He unzips my jacket and extricates the file from the inside pocket.

I wait while he reads it.

"Well, well." Finch glances up and points a nicotine-stained finger in my direction. "Why do you want him dead?"

"We have a score to settle. That's all you need to know."

He rubs his chin, the blunt's burning eye bobbing up and down. "I wonder what Carmichael would do if he found out you'd approached me like this?"

Icy fingers of dread sink into my chest. I know exactly what Carmichael would do. Something involving a pair of cement blocks and a trip to the canal, most likely.

"Relax." Finch snaps his fingers, and the binding spell falls away. "Your secret's safe."

I shift from one foot to the other, rubbing my thighs to get some blood flowing back into my legs.

"Tell me." Finch takes another long puff. "Has Stone made any close connections at COVEN?"

"Why?"

"Answer the question."

I tell him about Stone's allies. Gareth Townsend, the Jabara girl, and that smug bitch, Zara.

"Good to know."

"They aren't important."

Finch flicks the spliff to the floor and grinds it beneath his foot. "On the contrary. They're vital."

"I don't understand. It's Stone you want."

"True." Finch's cruel smile is back. "But I want him to suffer before I slit his miserable throat."

CHAPTER 38

"Come on, pick up the pace." Zara sprints ahead of us, arms moving in tight semicircles at her sides.

Geek, Layla and I run behind her, our feet pounding the dirt path of the canal.

It's been a few weeks since the graduation party, and neither Layla nor I have mentioned what happened. We've fallen into an uneasy friendship. We either talk through Geek, or directly to each other, but in a strained and formal way. This tentative friendship doesn't stop the flicker of desire every time she catches my eye, or the flashbacks. Oh, God, the flashbacks...

"Who—ah—who said Zara could come running with us again?" Geek asks, panting and clutching at his side.

Layla laughs. "It's good to push yourself. Stop moaning."

"Good for me? Since when has a potential hernia been good for me?"

"Less chat, more running," Zara barks from up ahead.

Geek's breath hitches. "She realises—Oh fuck, I want to die—she realises she's not our trainer anymore, right?"

"*She* can hear you, Townsend," Zara says.

We hit a fork in the path.

Zara hares off to the left and we follow.

We startle a flock of birds picking at the grass with their hooked beaks. They take to the air, squawking their displeasure at being disturbed. The iron-grey sky opens, spilling rain on us. The weather does nothing to dull my chipper mood.

I'm an executioner.

Carmichael wants to meet with me later to discuss the 'Razor situation'. I can't wait. Spurred on by this thought, I pump my legs harder, gaining on Zara, then outpace her.

"The student has become the master," I call back at her.

"Cheeky fucker," she says, but there's a smile in her voice.

A bridge looms up ahead, its dark maw gaping wide, and we dart towards it.

I take in a huge lungful of air and taste crisp rainwater mixed with the salty tang of sweat on my lips. Happiness swells in my chest and I revel in it: the pounding of my heart, the aching in my limbs, the way I can't quite catch my breath. Today can't get any better.

The darkness swallows us as we pass beneath the bridge.

"Right. That's it, Stone," Zara says. "The game's—" She cries out.

"Zara." I skid to a halt.

Her body crashes into the wall.

"What the—" My feet fly out from under me and my head cracks against something hard and unyielding.

Everything goes black.

The pain in my head's excruciating. Beneath me, nothing but cold, hard earth. I crack my eyes open.

Zara.

We're still under the bridge, and she's slumped against the wall, hands bound behind her back. The position's so familiar.

Flash.

Mum's body propped against the kitchen wall, a bloody gash across her throat.

Flash.

Layla's head lolls on her chest.

My eyes drift closed.

Flash.

Dad's head bowed, blood soaking his jumper.

Flash.

I'm conscious again, and someone's talking.

"You have Stone. I held up my end of the bargain."

That voice. I recognise that voice, but where from? I glimpse something disappearing close by. The sole of a polished brown brogue. Why are brogues familiar? I don't know. I should, but I don't.

Someone stirs beside me.

Geek.

I croak out his name, raise my voice and try again, nudge him with my trainer. Something binds my hands, too. Well, I can take care of that. "*Recludo.*"

Searing pain wracks my body, and I writhe around on the floor like a slug doused in salt. The pain fades, and I'm awake now.

Fuck.

Iron cuffs.

"Where the hell are we?" Geek asks.

"Still underneath the bridge," I say.

"*Rec—*" he begins.

"Don't. They're iron cuffs."

Zara coughs and slits her eyes open. "Everyone all right?"

Layla shifts into a sitting position. "Peachy."

I roll my neck and am rewarded with a satisfying pop. I glare at Zara. "Is this another one of your psychopathic tests?"

"No," she says.

I arch an eyebrow at her.

"I swear."

Cold laughter echoes off the walls. "Good. You're all awake. Now we can have some fun."

Another voice I know. Ice freezes my blood.

Razor.

He prowls out of the shadows, a lit cigarette caught between his teeth. He's still wearing the blood red suit, but the jacket hangs open, and the white shirt beneath is grubby.

"Shit," Zara says.

"Who the fuck are you?" Geek spits at him.

Razor exhales a puff of smoke and crouches down beside me.

Old tobacco.

Fruit flavoured chewing gum.

I shrink away from him, a whimper clawing at my throat. I hate myself for that whimper. I'm supposed to be strong. I'm supposed to be an executioner, but Razor's appearance is too sudden, the pain of the past too much to bear.

"Stay away from him." Zara's voice echoes off the walls.

Razor ignores her. "Why don't you tell your friend who I am?" he says.

"Oh, my God," Layla says. "I know who you are. You're Razor Finch."

He turns and winks at her. "Give the girl a prize."

Even in the semi-dark, the high spots of colour on Layla's cheeks burn. "You fucking bastard."

My eyes widen.

Layla never swears.

"You must be Layla Jabara." Razor shoots me a lascivious grin, and a laugh that turns into a hacking cough. "She's a feisty one. I can see why she gets your engine running."

My stomach drops. How does he know?

"Bet she's a goer in the sack as well, am I right?"

"You deserve to die for what you've done." Layla gets her legs under her—struggling without her arms free—and launches herself at Razor, screaming. She aims a roundhouse kick at his head.

Razor whips around. "*Dis*."

A flash of red light.

Layla slams against the wall and collapses back to the ground.

Tears sting my eyes, my fear giving way to rage. "Don't touch her, you piece of shit."

Razor smirks at me and strolls over to Layla.

"I said, leave her alone."

He kneels and brushes a strand of hair out of Layla's eyes. "Don't you think your boyfriend deserves to die for what he did to my wife?"

"He was defending himself." She looks down, a blush reddening her cheeks. "And he's not my boyfriend."

"Oh, dear." Razor smirks. "Lover's tiff?"

Geek says, "How do you know her name?"

"I know all your names, Gareth—sorry, you go by *Geek* now, right?—but that's not important."

Geek scowls at him. "No?"

"No. What's important is I know how much you all mean to him." Razor licks his lips like he's savouring a tasty morsel. "You can see where this is heading, can't you, Stone?"

"No." I wriggle around until I'm sitting up. I taste bile. "Leave them out of this."

Zara snorts.

Razor's head snaps round. "Something funny?"

She lifts one shoulder. "A little."

"Come on. Share the joke."

She looks Razor right in the eye. "I've heard stories about you, and I've read your file. The great and powerful Razor Finch, head of a big bad SOCG."

"Your point?"

"I thought you'd be taller."

Razor's hand shoots out. "*Dolor.*"

Zara screams, her body arching away from the wall. Her eyes roll back and she bucks and twists, tears of pain rolling down her cheeks.

"Stop," I say.

He lowers his hand.

Zara's body relaxes, but she's breathing hard, a thin stream of blood trickling from her nose. "You'll... have to do... better than that."

Razor's eyes fix on mine. "You took someone from me. Now, I'm going to take someone from you."

"No." I pull my knees underneath me and sit back on my ankles. "Leave them alone."

"The question is, which one? Eeny, meeney, miney, mo." He points a yellow-tipped finger at each of them. "Mentor, lover or friend?"

"Please." Fear knots my insides. "Please don't do this."

"Which one should I choose?"

"This is between us. If you want to kill someone, kill me."

"No!" Layla shouts. "Zara, do something."

"She can't save you." Razor points at the iron shackles binding Zara's wrists. "I've made sure of that." He focuses his attention on me again. "Which. One?"

I realise, then. The question isn't rhetorical. He wants an answer. Ice coats my spine. "Fuck you. I won't choose."

He scratches at the scar on his eyebrow. "Choose, or I'll kill them all."

"You sick bastard." Layla forces the words between gritted teeth. "What's wrong with you?"

Razor ignores her. "You've got thirty seconds."

Thump, thump, thump. My heart races faster than I've ever known. "Hurt them, and I swear I'll kill you."

"That might sound more threatening, had I not chained you up like a dog. Twenty-five seconds."

The intense cold permeates my entire body. My fingers and toes go numb. "I won't do it."

"Tick-tock."

"I don't want to die," Geek says.

Razor shakes his head. "Hear that, Stone? Your friend doesn't want to die. Are you going to let him?"

"Shut up." I bark at Razor, before turning to Geek and softening my tone. "Nobody's going to die."

"*Mortem*." The death-strike flares to life in Razor's palm, the angry red spark carving shadows everywhere.

"Leave them out of this. Kill me instead," I say. "That's what you want, anyway."

"Oh, I want you dead all right, but I want to break you first. Like a twig. Five seconds."

"Don't."

"Four."

Geek laughs. He actually laughs, high and clear and laced with something close to hysteria. "Oh, for fuck's sake, not this countdown shit, again? How do I get myself into these situations?"

I frown at him. "What are you talking about?"

He shakes his head, his expression sombre now. "Nothing. Blast from the past, that's all."

I turn back to Razor. "When Carmichael finds out about this, you're finished."

"Three."

The death-strike shoots from Razor's hand and smacks into the wall right beside Layla's head, kicking up fragments of stone and dust.

She flinches away from the exploding shrapnel with a yelp.

My heart's still pounding. "Don't you—"

"Whoops." Razor gives a little chuckle. "Butterfingers. Two."

Fine tremors make my hands shake behind my back. I want to scream at him, but the words jam in my throat.

"One."

"Enough." Zara edges up the wall until she's standing.

Razor pauses, a curious smile playing over his lips.

Zara draws herself up to her full height and marches over to Razor until she stands right next to him.

"What are you doing?" I ask.

Razor snorts at Zara. "What's this? Last words?"

She nods. "Only two. Kill me."

"No," Geek, Layla and I say in unison.

"Eager to die?"

"I'm eager to do my job. Protecting my trainees." Her eyes are glassy, and her lower lip trembles, but the tears don't spill over.

"Zara," I say. "You can't do this."

"I have to."

Razor cocks his head to the side, studying Zara like she-'s something interesting he's spotted under a microscope. "You're incredibly brave or incredibly dense."

"A little of both, maybe." Zara sniffs.

"Not her," I say.

"Then who?" Razor conjures another death-strike, and it zooms through the air until it hovers inches from Geek's face. "Him?"

Sweat shines on Geek's forehead.

Razor flicks his wrist and the death-strike darts at Layla and skids to a halt a centimetre from her chest. "Her?"

Hot, fat tears slide down my face. "I'll do anything you want. Just stop this."

"Only you can stop it," he says. "One last chance. Choose."

"Stone," Zara says. "It has to be me."

"I won't let him kill you."

"You're not letting him do anything—" Her voice cracks. "I'm telling you it's okay."

"I can't."

She looks at Razor. "Just get it over with."

"Only if he says so," Razor says.

My gaze travels from Zara, to Layla, to Geek. Can I really do this? Can I sacrifice Zara to save the others? Will Razor actually kill them all if I don't? My stomach twists like someone's wringing it out. I know the answer already. Of course he will. If I do this, what will I become? Why am I thinking about myself?

"Well?" Razor's tone's impatient.

I nod towards Zara.

"Just to be clear, you're choosing Zara?"

I unclench my jaw. "I—I... Yes."

Zara gives the slightest nod.

"No." Layla's handcuffs scrape against the wall.

Razor looks at Zara with something like respect in his eyes. "I really am sorry you got caught up in this."

"Go fuck yourself," Zara says.

He ducks his head. "I'll make this quick."

Everything I am collapses inward. I want to block this out, but I can't. All I can do is stare into Zara's pink, shimmering eyes. "I'm sorry."

"It's okay," she says.

Razor moves to stand behind her.

Zara clears her throat. "Will you do something for me?"

A breath shudders out of me. "Anything."

"After you've killed this prick, find Bob. Make sure he knows I didn't want to leave him. Tell him I love—"

It happens so fast.

Razor flicks his wrist again. The hovering death-strike barrels at Zara. It doesn't stop. The sharp, red dart explodes against her back with a loud crack, and a gush of blood spurts from a hole in her chest the size of a fifty pence piece. Her eyes go wide and her jaw slackens. She tips forwards, her cheek slamming into the floor, her legs flying straight out behind her. She tries to speak, wheezes, and more blood spills from the corner of her mouth. Her head moves to the side, her chin scraping along the uneven, rough ground.

My heart stops. I can't look away.

Her pink irises drain of colour, fading to a pale, periwinkle blue, her magic gone.

Zara's dead.

And I killed her.

CHAPTER 39

I killed Zara.
   I killed Zara.
 I killed Zara.
 The words pound through my head in time with my heart. It's just me and those dead, periwinkle eyes. Someone wedges a crow bar between my ribs and prizes them apart. One by one. The pain's endless, bottomless, all-consuming. Zara. I did this. I chose her. And now she's dead because of me. My body shakes and shakes and shakes until I'm certain I'll fall apart.
 Razor's face looms before mine. "There. That wasn't so hard, was it?"
 My nostrils flare.
 I hate him.
 No.
 I loathe him.
 The loathing, hot and alien, wraps itself around my heart, my stomach, my arms, my legs, until that's all there is. "I'll kill you."
 "Not if I kill you first." He winks at me, like this is all a game, some big joke.

He walks over to where Zara's body lays, careful to avoid the blood pooling around her mouth. He places two fingers to his lips, kisses them, crouches, and presses his fingers to the back of her head. "Blessed be. I'm truly, truly sorry."

"Don't touch her," I snarl, dimly aware of Layla sobbing, of Geek's silence, his body pulled as tense as piano wire. "Don't fucking touch her."

Everyone I care about gets hurt.

Everyone.

Because of me.

Razor straightens and opens his arms wide. "*Ostium*."

A glowing red portal crackles into existence in front of him, its queasy breath washing over me in a rush of light and sound.

He glares at me over his shoulder. "I'm going to let this sit with you for a while. Let your actions really sink in, bone deep. But, I promise you, next time I see you, this ends."

I want to say something cutting, but I don't have it in me.

Razor steps into the portal and it snaps shut.

I'm numb.

Empty.

A soulless void.

Zara's eyes glare in reproach. I know she's not glaring, not really, but that's how it feels.

Geek and Layla are talking. Saying something to me, but I can't hear them. The erratic pulse in my head and the blood rushing in my ears drowns them out.

Time passes. Then I'm staring into a pair of familiar slate grey eyes, and Carmichael's shaking me, talking.

Concentrate.

I need to concentrate.

"Henry," he says. "What happened? Are you hurt? Henry, talk to me."

I shake my head. "I'm fine." Fine. I'm not fine. My body's heavy, and I'm broken.

Dickinson and O'Hara show up, and tend to Geek and Layla.

Layla's cheek's bleeding, slashed open by the chips of concrete Razor blasted from the wall. She catches my eye. "It wasn't your fault."

I don't believe her.

"Get these cuffs off them," Carmichael says.

O'Hara slides a pair of heavy-duty bolt-cutters between my wrist and the iron cuffs and snaps them off.

Carmichael helps me to my feet. "You okay?"

I brush him off and run to Zara, dropping to my knees beside her, blood staining the knees of my tracksuit bottoms. My fingers brush her neck, searching for a pulse I'll never find. Her skin's still warm, her eyes still frozen open.

"Henry." Carmichael's voice is thick with emotion. "What happened? Who did this?"

"I did." I take Zara's slim hand in mine and squeeze it.

"What do you mean?"

"Henry did nothing," Geek says. "It was Razor."

"Razor." Carmichael's voice hardens.

I rub my thumb across the back of Zara's hand in small circles. "He said I had to choose. Zara, she—fuck, she..."

"She sacrificed herself to save us," Layla says.

Dickinson says, "Come on, son. Let go of her hand. We need to examine her."

"No."

"Henry, let go," Carmichael says.

O'Hara steps towards me.

I snap.

The next thing I know, O'Hara has a bloody nose and Dickinson clutches his stomach, coughing.

My witch-staff glows bright green in my hands. I blink and release the staff.

Carmichael's arms go around my chest, pinning my own arms to my sides.

"Get off me."

"You need to calm down."

I kick, I scream, I thrash, but Carmichael's hold doesn't break.

Dickinson and O'Hara paw over Zara like a prime piece of meat, their hands glowing as they scan her body.

"Let me go."

"Stop fighting."

I slam my head back, and my skull collides with Carmichael's cheek. Sharp pain shoots through my head and down my neck.

Carmichael grunts, swears, but he doesn't let go. "I'm sorry," he says. "But I don't have a choice. *Somnum*."

Zara's eyes are the last thing I see before my legs go weak, my eyelids drift closed, and the sleep spell takes hold.

Periwinkle blue eyes haunt my nightmares. It doesn't matter where I run, or how fast. Every time I stop, she's there.

And there.

And there.

I'm surrounded by her.

She dabs her finger in the black blood dripping from the corner of her mouth. "Why?" she asks. "Why did you let him kill me?"

I wake up bit by bit, swimming until I break through the surface of consciousness. I hate consciousness. It's too painful, like being flayed, layer by layer, down to the bone.

Zara's dead.

It's my fault.

I should've died, not her.

Everything hurts. I'm lying on my bed, in my room at COVEN, and I sense I'm not alone. Maybe if I pretend to be asleep, whoever it is will go away.

"I know you're awake," Carmichael says.

Maybe not.

I open my eyes and swing round, perching on the edge of the bed, ready to flee any second.

A bruise darkens Carmichael's cheek.

"What happened to your face?" I ask.

"You don't remember?"

I'm about to shake my head, but it comes back in a rush. "Oh." I remember it all. Beating up Dickinson and O'Hara, slamming my head into Carmichael's cheek. "Sorry."

Carmichael bends forward and places a hand on my shoulder. "You need to tell me exactly what happened."

Everything dissolves around me. I'm no longer in my room, and Carmichael's not with me. Instead, I'm back under the bridge, and the death strike slams into Zara's chest.

Crack.

She falls to the floor. Her eyes turn blue.

I can't breathe. Heat and dizziness swallow me and my stomach performs barrel rolls.

"Henry."

My fault.

"Henry." Carmichael gives me a rough shake.

"I can't. I can't go through that again."

His grip on my shoulder tightens. "You have to. Leave nothing out."

I tell him in short, jerky bursts. It's difficult, and I stop and start a lot, but I get through it. I shed more tears than I'm comfortable with, but I make it to the end, all the same.

Carmichael frowns. "I don't understand. How did Razor find you?"

"Do you even care about Zara?"

He draws back, his eyes narrowing to slits, his mouth twisting. "How dare you? I loved her like a daughter."

"You don't seem that upset."

"Upset? I'm trying to get justice. Would you prefer I fall apart like you?"

That does it—shreds my last ounce of self-control. Great, heaving shudders overtake my body, and I can't stop the torrent of tears. I bury my face in my hands and sob for so many reasons. For my parents, for Jez, for Layla, for Zara. For me. I'm wailing, my throat burning, and then I'm rocking back and forth, slowly fracturing.

Carmichael drags me to my feet and crushes me in a tight bear hug, slapping my back once, twice, three times. "That wasn't fair of me."

We stand like that for a while until the shuddering stops and the tears run dry.

Carmichael releases me. "We need to focus, for Zara."

I nod, putting pressure on the lump in my throat.

"Razor knew where to find you. How?"

I shrug. "Don't know."

"Think, Henry. Your COVEN tattoo conceals your location. There's no way he could have tracked you to the canal."

Something hovers at the edge of my mind. A half-remembered voice and a fuzzy image. I exhale and force a hand through my hair. Think.

Think.

You have Stone. I held up my end of the bargain.

A brown brogue, disappearing from view.

"He had help," I say.

"Help?"

"There was someone else there, but they left before—"

"Who?"

"I'm not sure, I can't remember."

"Try."

"I don't—"

Wait.

Brown brogues.

The bottom drops out of my stomach.

There's only one witch I know who wears brown brogues.
"What is it?" Carmichael asks.
"I know who it was, and you won't like it."

Dickinson and O'Hara drag him into the ring.

Iron cuffs bind his hands—and his magic—and a black cloth sack covers his head. He's still wearing the brogues, and they tap against the black marble floor until he stands in the centre of the ring.

"Did he give you any trouble?" Carmichael asks Dickinson.

"Nothing we couldn't handle, Director."

"Why are we here?" Rosie says, her smudged metallic lipstick glinting, her face swollen and puffy from crying.

"Is this about Zara?" Katya asks. Her makeup's perfect, not a hair out of place. She hasn't shed a single tear.

Carmichael inclines his head, then addresses the crowd. "We're here to get justice for Zara."

"Blessed be," I murmur, along with everyone else in the room.

Carmichael waits until the noise dies down, then he continues. "Razor had an accomplice. An executioner."

"No way!" Syed calls out, tightening his arm around Layla, holding her close.

Layla tucks her face into her father's chest. "Dad, please..."

"No, Layla. None of us would help someone like Finch."

Vi.

Iustitia.

Fides.

Strength.

Justice.

Loyalty.

I glare at the black bag covering the traitor's face.

Loyalty.

Humph.

He's about as loyal as a snake.

"And yet." The winter chill in Carmichael's voice makes me shiver. "One of you did." He nods at O'Hara. "Get that bag off."

Even though I know who's under there, my heart still skips a beat when O'Hara whips the bag away.

Nick blinks several times until his eyes adjust to the light.

Whispers fly through the crowd, morphing into shouts of anger.

"Nick."

"He wouldn't."

"Bullshit."

Carmichael taps a finger to his throat to amplify his voice. "Enough."

I stand right next to him. The word bounces around my skull and I flinch.

When Carmichael speaks again, his voice is back to its normal volume and pitch. "I don't want to believe it either, but it's true, isn't it, Nick?"

Nick forces his eyes wide. "You think I did this? Dylan, I wouldn't—"

"You will address me as Director Carmichael."

Nick sets his jaw. "I didn't do this."

"Liar." I spring at Nick.

Dickinson intercepts me, pushing me back.

Nick looks bored. "Why would I want Zara dead?"

"It's no secret that you didn't get on," Geek says.

Nick looks at Geek like he's something he just scraped off the bottom of his shoe. "When Director Carmichael wants the opinion of someone who's barely had their training wheels taken off, I'm sure he'll ask for it."

Geek clenches his fists.

"This has nothing to do with Zara," I spit, still straining against Dickinson. "It's about Myles."

Nick glares at me. "Watch your mouth, you little shit."

Carmichael strides forward, hands sheathed in shining blue witch-gauntlets. He jabs Nick in the stomach, hard.

All the air rushes out of Nick in a long wheeze, and he collapses to his knees.

I go limp in Dickinson's arms. I wasn't expecting that.

"Where were you at two o'clock this afternoon, Nick?" Carmichael says, his gauntlets dissipating.

Nick looks up, face flushed, breathless. "In the training room."

Carmichael narrows his eyes. "Can anyone corroborate that?"

"No, I was alone."

"Convenient," I say.

"It's the truth," Nick says.

Carmichael brings his hands up. "*Eryx.*" The gauntlets reappear.

"I swear it's the truth."

Carmichael socks Nick across the jaw. His head whips to the side and he spits blood onto the marble floor.

"Do *not* lie to me."

"I'm not."

I'm struggling against Dickinson again. "He's full of shit. I saw you. I saw your shoes."

Nick rolls his eyes. "These shoes aren't uncommon." He looks Carmichael in the eye. "Are you really going to believe him over me?"

The certainty in Carmichael's eyes wavers.

Nick carries on. "When have I ever let you down?"

"You haven't," Carmichael admits. The gauntlets fade again.

"You can't let him get away with this," I say.

Carmichael turns to me. "You already told me you hit your head. Maybe you're confused, maybe—"

"No. He did it. He was there."

"Prove it," Nick says.

I stand there with my mouth open, saying nothing.

"See, he can't, because I wasn't there. I didn't—"

"Two o'clock?" Katya says, while examining her black nail polish.

"What?" Carmichael says.

"You said Zara died at two o'clock?"

Carmichael nods.

Katya lowers her hand. "Nick's lying."

Hope flares in my chest.

Dozens of astonished gasps emanate from the crowd.

"You don't know what you're talking about," Nick says.

"I do." Katya shifts her weight onto her other foot and crosses her arms. "Because I was in the training room at two o'clock, and you definitely weren't."

All the colour leeches out of Nick's face, his jaw going slack.

Carmichael whips round to face Nick. "Is this true?"

Nick regains his composure. "No, of course not, I—" He must sense the game's over, because his words choke off. He ducks his head, lets out a quick breath and, when he glances up again, his face resembles the marble floor he's kneeling on. "Yes."

The stunned silence stretches on and on and on.

The tension brakes.

Cries of, "Traitor," and, "Bastard," and, "Rat," ring out.

Carmichael pinches his lips so tight the surrounding skin turns white. "Yes?"

"Yes," he repeats.

Wait.

Zara voice whispers through my mind.

Razor's gone into hiding... He's cloaking himself somehow.

Layla's voice follows.

Apparently, it produces these visions that allow the user to cast a locater spell without the need for a locus. If that's true, you could find anyone, any criminal. They wouldn't be able to hide.

"You used witch-bane to find him," I say.

Gasps of shock and shouts of disgust fly through the room.

Nick smirks at me in a way that makes my skin erupt in goosebumps. "You were right. It was nothing to do with Zara. My son is ten times the witch you'll ever be. I only wish I'd told him more often. I'll hate you until the day I die."

Now it's my turn to smirk. "I doubt that." In my mind's eye, Myles, Femi and Bianca's eyes go blank under the power of the memory spell. "You won't remember me after today."

"Oh, I can guarantee that." Carmichael holds up his hand. "*Mortem*."

A death-strike? "What are you doing?" I ask.

"As if using witch-bane wasn't disgraceful enough." Carmichael bounces the blue sphere in his palm. "*Vi. Iustitia. Fides.* He's broken all three of our tenants. He's a rat. There's only one way to deal with rats."

Nick says, "No, wait—"

But it's too late.

The death-strike finds Nick's heart.

Crack.

Just like Zara.

A spurt of blood from the back of his shirt and he falls onto his side.

Just like Zara.

Dark blood trickles down his chin.

Just like Zara.

Carmichael glares down at Nick's motionless body.

Dispassionate.

Inhuman.

Forget fractured. I shatter now. I can't take any more blood, any more death. "What the hell is wrong with you people?" The strangled cry tears from my throat before I can stop myself.

Carmichael pivots to face me. I know the venom in his eyes is for Nick, not for me, but the look separates me from myself. "You people? In case you've forgotten, you're one of us now."

My voice comes out strained. "I thought you were going to take his memories. I didn't realise you were going to kill him."

"His death was necessary. A life for a life."

A life for a life.

I shouldn't be shocked. That's what I signed up for, isn't it? An eye for an eye. Razor kills Primrose. I witness it. Razor murders my parents. I kill Cecelia. Razor kills Zara. Carmichael murders Nick.

A life for a life.

I stare down at Nick, a strange feeling blossoming in my chest. What *is* that? Warm and satisfying. It hits me then, like a sucker-punch to the temple.

I'm happy.

Happy Nick's dead, and the only thought that springs to mind?

He deserved it.

My stomach lurches. God, I make myself sick. Is this the price of being an executioner? Smiling at death as death takes another life?

Zara's words about elemental magic—from my very first day of training—ring in my ears.

The five elements: earth, air, fire, water and lightning are dangerous primordial forces. Drawing on their power comes at a price. For every elemental spell you cast, you exchange a sliver of what makes you human. Over time, dark magic poisons the soul.

Dark magic might poison souls, but—even in its absence—my soul feels pretty grubby right now.

With Herculean effort, I hold Carmichael's gaze. "What happed to 'it takes a strong person to offer forgiveness'?"

"Some things can't be forgiven," Rosie says, her beaded dreadlocks swinging as she shakes her head. "He killed Zara."

"No," I say. "Razor killed Zara."

"And he led Razor here," Katya says. "Simple cause and effect."

My eyes find Layla's. "You don't agree with this?"

She looks away.

"Geek?"

He lifts his shoulder. "Sorry, mate."

My head spins, and I have to place a hand on the wall to steady myself. The coldness of the black marble seeps into my skin. What am I becoming? I betrayed Geek on the island. I beat Femi to a pulp without so much as blinking. I almost killed Layla by attacking Myles. This isn't me. The old Henry would never have done those things. Sure, the old Henry had a lot of faults, but he wasn't... ruthless. "This is insane. What the hell am I doing here?"

"You knew what you were signing up for," Carmichael says.

The acrid stench of Nick's voided bowels clogs my nostrils, and I gag. "I came here to get justice for my parents, not to be turned into a thug. A murderer."

"That's what you think we are?" Carmichael asks, a hint of steel in his voice. "Thugs and murderers?"

The executioner's voices rise into a unified jeer, teeth bared, eyes hard.

Animals.

"I can't do this." I stride across the ring, stepping over Nick's body, my stomach lurching.

Dickinson and O'Hara block my path.

"Get out of my way." I say.

O'Hara says, "No."

I'm hyperventilating. The room swirls, the faces of the crowd blurring together into many headed, hideous beasts. I need to get out of here. I need to get out. How? A portal, of course. Nobody can portal into COVEN, because of Carmichael's witch-weave, but there's nothing to stop me from portalling out. I brace myself for the portal sickness. "*Ostium*."

A glowing green disc splits the air in front of me, spewing heat.

"Stop him!" Carmichael barks.

It's too late.

I step into the portal and vanish into nothingness.

CHAPTER 40

T he portal spits me out into a dim alley.

I slip on the greasy tarmac and crash headfirst into a pile of rubbish bags. A pungent waft of bitter, rotten vegetables and too-sweet, overripe fruit smacks me in the nose. The combination of the smell and the portal sickness makes me gag, but my breakfast stays down. I push to my feet, the world spinning around me.

Where the fuck am I? I haven't practised portals much—for obvious, stomach-churning reasons—and I was aiming for the High Street. Guess I miscalculated.

Swallow.

Breathe.

Swallow.

Breathe.

The cloudy spots obscuring my vision clear and the rough brick walls of the alleyway come into focus.

Oh, Jesus. Carmichael killed Nick. Without a moment's hesitation.

I should never have joined COVEN. I don't belong there. Mindless thugs. That's what I called them, and I was right. Murderers and mindless thugs. At least I got out of there. But what now? Carmichael will send people after me, eager to drag me back. I can't let that happen. Where can I go? I don't have any money. All I have are the clothes on my back and my magic. Who can I run to?

There's only one answer to that question.

I jog to the end of the alleyway. Stop. Peek out from behind the wall.

Daxbridge Quays?

I'm sandwiched between a bistro-cum-café and trendy barbers called *Clipz*. The Quays bustle with people. The tables heave with patrons. They chat, they laugh, and one woman cries thick mascara tears into a linen napkin while her friend pats her on the arm and makes cooing noises at her. At a corner table, a man dressed in a slick pinstripe suit barks orders into his phone and—wait. I need a phone.

A waiter dressed in black trousers, a starched white shirt and a burgundy waistcoat glides out of the café, balancing a tray in his hand. He skips up the empty plates, cutlery and mugs and glides inside again.

I smile. Never been a waiter before. How hard can it be? I duck into the alley again, flatten my back against the wall to ensure nobody can see me, and snap my fingers. "*Dissimulato.*"

When the shimmering green light of the glamour spell fades, my clothes match those of the waiter.

Perfect.

I rush over to the café's entrance and almost collide with the same waiter, now carrying a tray full of drinks.

Shit.

"I'll take those," I say. Before he can argue, I snatch the tray off him.

"Wait," he says.

"Yeah?"

"You new? Haven't seen you before."

Oh, I'm new all right. "This is my first shift."

"Paulo didn't mention hiring anyone new."

I shrug. "Just doing my job, pal." I wheel round and practically run back outside before he can stop me, squinting to protect my eyes from the midday sun.

That was too close.

I train my eyes on Pinstripe Guy, making a beeline for his table. I'm halfway there when a braying voice says, "Uh, excuse me?"

"What?" I snap.

"That caramel macchiato's mine."

It's the woman with the mascara-tears. "Right." I slam the macchiato down and a few drops spill over the rim.

"Careful," says her cooing friend.

"Sorry," I say, not looking at them. I move away from their table and carry on walking towards Pinstripe Guy.

From behind me, the mascara woman says, "Ugh. This place is getting a solid one star on *Trip Advisor*. I mean, honestly, where do they find..."

I've forgotten her words by the time they trail off.

Four feet away from Pinstripe Guy.

Three feet.

Two feet.

I fake stumble over my own shoes and the tray tips forward, spilling all the drinks right into Pinstripe Guy's lap.

He lets out a strangled yell and bolts to his feet, moving the phone away from his ear. "What the bloody hell are you playing at? What? No, not you, Gerard."

"I am so sorry, sir." I grab a fistful of napkins off the next table and pass them to him.

He snatches the linen wad. "Idiot. This suit is *Armani*. Do you have any idea what it costs? Gerard, I'll call you back, some fucking buffoon just ruined my suit." He places his phone on the table.

"I really am sorry."

"Sorry. Sorry. You'll be sorry."

While he's busy dabbing at his crotch with the napkins, I slip around him, snag the phone off the table and pocket it.

There's a ten-pound note on the silver tray next to his receipt and I pocket that, too.

"I want to speak to your manager."

Good luck with that. But I have to play the part. I plaster a look on my face that I hope says terror. "I said sorry, can't we just—"

"Manager. Now."

"Yes, sir." I retreat into the café, suppressing a smile, and catch the waiter's attention.

"What is it?" he asks.

"See that bloke over there, the one dressed like an undertaker?"

"Yeah?"

"He's asking for you."

The waiter lets out a heavy sigh and tramps outside.

I quick-walk through the coffee shop, push through a set of double doors into the steamy kitchen, and slip out of the service entrance. I'm alone now. Good. Without breaking stride, I let the glamour drop. I cross the road and disappear into a crowded market, the smell of fresh oranges, fish and leather wrinkling my nose.

The stall holders shout out as I pass, trying to tempt people into buying their wares.

"Get your plums. A pound a punnet."

"Kilo of prime sirloin for a tenner. Won't get it cheaper anywhere else."

"Cabbage, carrots and broccoli, fresh as you like. Perfect for your Sunday roast."

I pass a stall blasting out shitty drum and bass music, grab a baseball cap and sunglasses from a rack outside and shove them on, just in case anyone from the café noticed me slip away. Rounding a corner, I fish Pinstripe Guy's phone from my pocket. Password protected. Would an unlocking spell work? I'd only ever cast it on physical locks before. Oh, well. In for a penny. I wave my hand over the screen. "*Recludo*."

My hand flashes green and the numbers 9, 0, 1, 6, 2 and 3 light up.

The home screen flares to life.

I bring up the dial pad and tap in the number.

It rings and rings and rings.

Come on, come on, pick up.

I'm getting ready to leave a voice mail, and then, "Hello?"

The words stick in my throat. I'm not looking forward to this conversation.

"Who's this?" He clicks his tongue. "No, I haven't been in an accident, entered any competitions, or—"

"Jez. It's me."

Silence.

I dash between one stall selling knock off CDs and another flogging cheap pottery. "You there?"

A breath through gritted teeth, followed by the phone crackling as he moves away from it. "Fuck." The phone crackles again. "You've got a bloody nerve."

"Look, mate—"

"Mate? We're not mates. Not anymore."

"I know I fucked up, but—"

"Fucked up?"

The sharp consonants slice into my belly. I wince.

"What do you want, Henry?"

I emerge onto a residential side road, and glimpse the familiar skyline of Daxbridge High Street—the curved slope of the shopping centre, the sharp spike of the Cathedral tower, the arching dome of the Historical Library—in the distance. "Can we meet?"

"I'm busy."

"*Coach and Horses* on Bridge Street?"

He doesn't answer.

Fingering the ten-pound note in my pocket, I say, "I'll buy you a pint."

He sighs. "When?"

"Fifteen minutes?"

"Fine."

"It's good to—"

But he's gone.

Suppose I deserved that.

Two huge green bins hulk up ahead.

I switch the phone off, pop the back open, slide the battery out and snap the SIM card in two. I fling the phone and the battery into one bin and chuck the SIM card into the other.

Next stop, *The Coach and Horses*. I've got a feeling I've got some serious grovelling to do.

The Coach and Horses is a typical, dingy old man pub—the kind where your feet stick to the floor. The cloying scent of a thousand spent cigarettes still seeps from the walls, and the booze comes in four types: lager and bitter, or red and white. Mention craft ale in here, and you're likely to get glassed. Its only saving grace is that it's cheap.

I pay for two pints of lager and grab a table in the corner. My foot drums the floor while I wait for Jez to show. What will I say to him? I need to apologise properly. Get things back on track. Look him right in the eye, and—oh, shit. My eyes. I let my eyelids drift closed and imagine the soft brown colour they used to be. "*Dissimulato*." I open them again.

Jez stands over me, hands in his pockets. "I should turn round and walk right back out."

"Wouldn't blame you."

He lowers himself into the seat opposite me. "You wanted to see me?"

"I—" I sip my beer to lubricate my dry throat, the rich, malty flavour coating my tongue. "I want to apologise."

Jez slides his beer closer. Slides it away again. Slides it back. Crosses his arms. "What for?"

"You know what for."

He shrugs and gets up to leave. "If you can't even say it—"

"Everything. I'm sorry for everything."

He retakes his seat. "You'll have to be more specific."

"You're going to make me spell it out?"

"Damn right I am."

I take a deep breath. "I'm sorry I said you were never really my friend."

"And?"

"I'm sorry for what I said about your dad. I know he didn't leave because of you."

"Apology noted."

"Not accepted?"

"No. Noted." He picks up his pint and takes a long draft.

I almost smile.

Almost.

I know I'm off the hook.

"You took the contacts out?" he says.

"Yeah. They were stupid."

"No shit. Why were you wearing them, anyway?"

"Just trying to fit in, I guess."

"Where's that woman, Tara, or whatever her name was?"

My chest goes tight, and I have to swallow back tears. When I reply, my voice comes out steady. "Zara. I won't be seeing her again."

"How did you even meet—"

I can't talk about Zara—the pain's too acute, like a knife to the eye. "It's been rough since... I left... it's not an excuse."

Jez's brow crinkles, and I know he's still thinking about Zara, but he must decide to drop it, because he says, "You're right. It's not an excuse. So, what? You want to breeze past it?"

"No." I run a hand through my hair. "But I don't want to ignore years of friendship either."

"Humph. How do I know I can trust you?"

Good question. I can't even trust myself right now. My eyes find the scarred wooden tabletop. "I don't know."

"You could start by telling me where you've been."

I open my mouth. What should I say? I could tell him. It'd be so easy. A relief. What would his reaction be? Surely, he would be okay with it. He knows me. He knows I'm not a threat to him. "I—"

Six-hundred thousand witches died in the Trials. Six-hundred thousand. *That's a tenth of our population.*

That's what Mum said.

Six-hundred thousand.

"Well?" Jez says.

"I...Um—"

They burned us, they drowned us, they stoned us.

I shudder.

"Henry?"

If I tell him, I'll break The First Law. A criminal offence that could expose all of us—all witches—to danger. I shake my head. "I can't."

"Then you can shove your apology, and your shitty beer."

"I can't tell you exactly where I've been. It's all a bit of a blur, to be honest." I reach into my T-shirt, pull out the chain holding my parents' wedding rings, and bring them to my lips. "I—uh—got in with the wrong crowd."

"Are they...?" His eyes drift to the silver wedding bands.

I nod. "They're all I could save."

We sit in silence for ages.

Eventually, Jez rubs his eyes. "I should say sorry, too." At my blank expression, he says, "I know you had nothing to do with it. With what happened to them."

A basketball sized lump sticks in my throat. I gulp down a huge mouthful of beer to clear it, and lift one shoulder. "Thanks."

"So?" He picks at the peeling edge of a beer mat. "This 'wrong crowd'. Was it a gang?"

"Not a gang, exactly."

"Then what?"

"You wouldn't believe me if I told you."

"Try me."

Should I tell him? Could I? I want my old life back. I want my mates back. Kick-a-bouts in the park. Dodgy Friday night kebabs. I could even see about going back to uni. Normalcy. I want it all. I've got to tell him. He'll know if I lie. Besides, it's Jez. I'm being stupid. He's practically family. The only family I've got left. He'd never turn on me. I've got to tell him.

"Okay." I pause.

"Just tell me."

"Yeah, yeah. Fine." My heart races, my breathing shallow. Just say it. Just say, *I'm a witch.* How hard can it be?

"It can't be that bad, unless you've murdered someone." His eyes go wide, half-joking. "You haven't, have you?"

"No, of course not." I picture Cecelia's lifeless eyes, her dented skull. That wasn't murder, though. It was an accident. Self-defence.

His face crumples. "It wasn't some creepy sex cult, was it?"

I laugh at that.

"Then what?"

Oh, screw it. "I'm a—"

Someone crashes into our table and sends our drinks flying.

The rest of my pint sloshes out of my glass and soaks through my jeans. The irony doesn't escape me after what happened with Pinstripe Guy. I leap to my feet. "What the fuck?"

"Oh, shit." A woman appears at the man's side. "Sorry, guys. My boyfriend's had a skin-full. Come on, Dean, let's go."

Dean sways on his feet, points at my sodden jeans, and chuckles. "Looks like he's pissed himself."

The woman mouths, "Sorry," again, a scarlet blush creeping into her cheeks.

"It's fine," I reply through gritted teeth.

"Oh, no. Piss-pants has got the 'ump," Dean says, dropping the H in hump. He claps a sweaty hand on my shoulder. "Don't get the 'ump, piss-pants. S'accident, wazinit." He hiccups and belches in my face.

Piss-pants.

Dear Henry Stone... We regret to inform you...

I hate that phrase. Wincing at the toxic, stale beer fumes emanating from Dean, I say, "Get your hand off my shoulder."

"Whatcha gonna do if I don't, huh?" He pats my shoulder three times.

Pat.

Pat.

Pat.

A flash of heat shoots through me. "You don't want to find out."

Jez stands. "Hey. Let's take it down a notch, yeah, fellas?"

Dean laughs and pats my shoulder a fourth time.

I snap.

I slam a fist into Dean's kidneys.

He coughs and bends double, wheezing, and releases another noxious cloud of beer fumes.

I grab the back of his head and drive my knee into his stomach.

He grunts in pain and his girlfriend screeches.

My snap kick catches him under the jaw and lifts him off his feet.

Dean lands hard on his back, tears streaking his face.

I lunge forward and straddle him. I punch him in the face. And again. And again. His nose crackles and my knuckles come away bloody.

A pair of powerful arms go around my waist and drag me off him.

"Get off me," I say.

"No way," Jez says from behind me. "What the hell do you think you're doing?"

I struggle against Jez's grip, but it doesn't loosen. "He had it coming. He challenged me, I had to—"

"Challenged you? He's drunk. It was an accident."

"I—he—what?"

Everyone in the pub's staring at me.

The barman stalks out from behind the bar, hefting a dinged up wooden baseball bat.

Dean moans on the floor, clutching his stomach, and his girlfriend wipes sweat off his brow and glares daggers at me.

Shit.

What have I done?

The fight goes out of me.

Jez must sense this, because he lets go.

The barman nods at me, then at Jez, his knuckles white around the baseball bat. "That's enough, lads. Off you trot."

Jez says, "I didn't do any—"

The barman cuts him off. "Don't make me use this."

"We're going," I say. "This place is a shithole, anyway."

"What did you say?" the barman asks.

"You heard."

"Probably not the best idea," Jez says, eyeing the baseball bat.

The barman says, "Just piss off out of it, before I smash your kneecaps."

"Whatever." I stride past the bar, ignoring the slack-jawed stares and growled insults from the toothless punters.

Jez grabs my elbow when we reach the street and spins me round. His eyes bulge with... is that—fear? "Have you lost your fucking mind?"

"What do you mean?"

"That Dean bloke wasn't doing any harm, not really."

"He was taking the piss."

"So you beat him to a pulp?"

I set my jaw. "He's a bully. He deserved it."

Jez's voice rises to a shout. "Can you hear yourself?"

An old woman with a blue rinse shambles past, towing one of those fabric shopping trolleys on wheels behind her. She shakes her head at us and says, "Bloody lager louts. Didn't get this in my day."

Jez does something I've never seen him do before. He takes a packet of cigarettes and a *Zippo* lighter from the back pocket of his jeans.

"You smoke now?" I ask.

He struggles to light the cigarette because his hands are shaking so much. "So what if I do?"

Why are his hands shaking? Then I realise. "You're afraid of me."

"No," he says, but he can't meet my eye.

"Your hands are trembling."

The flame catches, and he inhales a long drag. "Maybe I am. A bit."

A strong waft of cigarette smoke makes my eyes sting.

My stomach clenches. "Come on, mate—" I reach out to him.

He flinches. He actually flinches.

My hands ball into fists. He fears me. Mum was right. Humans fear us. It's hard-wired into their DNA. "I can't win with you, can I?"

"What's that supposed to mean?"

"My birthday. That argument in the taxi. You basically accused me of being too weak."

He doesn't answer.

"Now I'm not weak enough, is that it?"

He takes another puff. "No. It's not that. I don't know. You've changed, somehow." He says the word changed like it's contagious.

A passage from *Myth & Magic: The Truth About Sorcerers, Demons and the Legend of King Arthur* comes back to me.

In days long past, days of myth and times of legend, four species walked the earth. First were the humans, known for their connection to nature and their sensory acuity...

Chills shower across my skin.

Sensory acuity.

Can he sense what I am, somehow? Does he know instinctively?

A strange look I can't name passes over Jez's face. "I can't quite put my finger on it, though." He sniffs. "Can you smell chlorine?"

Chlorine?

Chlorine smells like ozone.

Ozone smells like magic.

Can Jez smell my magic?

I'm overcome with a sudden pull in my gut. A sense of longing. Longing for COVEN. What am I doing here? I don't belong here. Not anymore. I belong with my people. "I shouldn't have come here."

He's still wearing that strange look. "Probably not."

A patch of cold sweat forms between my shoulder blades. "Fine." I turn away, pause. "I am sorry, you know."

"Me too."

I walk away without looking back.

Jez is right. I can try to fight it all I want, but I've changed. If someone like Dean had confronted me six months ago, I would've crumpled. Ducked my head. Mumbled an apology. But I hadn't done that. I'd fought back.

Vi.

Iustitia.

Fides.

I can fight back.

Against Razor.

Against people like him.

I'm ready.

I break into a run, heading straight for COVEN.

COVEN.

The smile melts off my face.

Murderers.

Thugs.

I've got so many bridges to build, and I don't know where to start. Getting back to COVEN's my priority. The question is, will I still have a place there when I do?

CHAPTER 41

Mercifully, my executioner's tattoo still lets me access the compound. At least I know Carmichael hasn't kicked me out...

Yet.

Wasting no time, I go straight to his office. I use my Sight at each corner to identify deserted corridors. I don't want to bump into my colleagues right now, because I can imagine the heinous insults they'll hurl at me. The door's closed, which means he's in there. I try to ignore the way the skin around my scalp constricts at the sight of the door, and rap my knuckles against the dark mahogany three times.

"Yes?"

There's a steely edge to Carmichael's voice that causes sweat to collect in my palms. I wipe my hands on my jeans and push the door open.

Carmichael sits in front of a laptop, his fingers whizzing over the keys, striking them with unnecessary force. He notices me, and his fingers halt, his grey eyes narrowing. "I was about to send a team to bring you back in."

I can't meet his gaze. "I can explain."

"You think I'm interested in your explanations?"

The rebuke stings like a plaster being torn off. "Please."

"You're an ungrateful little shit." Carmichael rises from the desk, leans toward me, and braces his hands on the dark wood. "I saved your life. I brought you here, and this is how you repay my generosity, by sulking like a petulant child?"

Speaking now would be a mistake. I sense he's got more to say. I keep my gaze averted and my hands behind my back.

"Do you have any idea how much opposition I've faced since I brought you here?"

"Opposition?"

"Yes, opposition." He slams the flat of his palm down on the desk, a red blush colouring his cheeks.

I flinch at the loud *thump*.

"Ever since you lost your first bout to Hedges, I've had most of my senior executioners in here daily, telling me you weren't good enough. Telling me it was a mistake to let you continue. I defended you. Every. Single. Time."

"I didn't know," I say in a quiet voice.

"Tell me why I shouldn't action this straight away." Carmichael spins the laptop round to face me.

Re: Henry Stone: Formal Notice of Dismissal and Memory Removal.

My blood turns to ice water, thaws, then heats and heats until it burns in my veins. I clench my fists. "You can't do this."

Carmichael's eyes flash. "How dare you? COVEN is mine. If I say you're out, you're out."

"But—" Wait. He didn't say he was definitely going to action my dismissal. He'd asked me to tell him why he shouldn't. Is he still fighting to keep me here? Even when I don't deserve it? Why, though? I'd witnessed Carmichael's single-minded drive first-hand when he killed Nick. I remember what he told me on the night he saved me.

I made a promise to your parents. I swore to look after you if anything happened to them. Told them I'd do whatever was in your best interests.

"You promised Mum and Dad you'd keep me safe," I say.

He jabs a finger at me. "Don't use my relationship with your parents against me."

"Say you throw me out. Erase my memories. What do you think's going to happen? Razor will find me in minutes. I won't stand a chance."

"You precocious little f—" Carmichael closes his eyes, takes a deep breath, and releases it. When he speaks again, he doesn't sound angry, he sounds tired. "You've got one last chance. Tell me why I should let you stay."

My anger drains away. I trudge over to the desk and lower myself into the chair opposite Carmichael's. "I saw an old friend today."

"Who?"

"Jez. He is—was—my best mate."

"A mortal?"

I nod.

Carmichael's lips pinch into a thin line. "You didn't tell him about—"

"No. Of course not." The half-truth burns my throat like a mouthful of scalding tea. I would've told him, if not for Dean's interruption. "Mum and Dad told me about the Trials before they died." I sniff to hold back tears. "They said humans hate witches, that it's part of their DNA. I didn't believe them. I thought some of them would understand. But Jez... he knew I'd changed, that I was different."

Carmichael sinks into his own chair again. "And?"

"He was afraid of me. I could see it in his eyes."

He sits in silence, watching me.

Something else occurs to me. "You said that book was fiction."

"Book? What book?"

"The King Arthur one."

His brow creases. "It is."

I shake my head. "It mentions mortals having sensory acuity."

"It's a myth. That's why it's called *Myth & Magic*."

I shake my head. "He could smell it on me."

"What?"

"My magic."

He lets out a humourless laugh. "Don't be ridiculous."

"I'm not. He could smell the ozone."

"He actually said that."

I think back to my conversation with Jez. "Well, no, but he said he smelled chlorine. It's similar."

"Where did you meet?"

"*The Coach and Horses*, it's a shitty pub on—"

"I know it. I also know what's three doors down."

"What's that got to do with—"

"A swimming pool."

"But—" Of course. The pool. Suddenly, I'm overcome with tiredness. Mortals with powers. What am I thinking? It must be the stress. "I never should've said those things. About COVEN. About you. I'm sorry."

"Thank you," he says.

"I need to find Razor, and I need to kill him. If you kick me out—" I duck my head. "It's not just about my parents anymore. I want to do this for Zara, too."

He's quiet for a long time, the only sound the *tap, tap, tap* of his fingers drumming on the desk.

I fight the urge to squirm, heart in my mouth.

Eventually, Carmichael says, "You can stay."

I leap out of the chair and run a hand through my hair. "Thank you, you won't regret it, I promise, I—"

"*If*," he continues, "the other executioners decide to let you stay as well."

The bubble of elation in my chest bursts. "What?"

"I'm not the only one you need to apologise to. You offended everyone with your outburst."

"I—I don't know if I can."

"You can if you want to stay."

It only takes Carmichael fifteen minutes to assemble all the executioners in the ring.

He makes me stand in the centre.

Everyone glares at me, hatred marring their features. Crossed arms, clenched fists, set jaws. The only friendly faces in the crowd belong to Geek and Layla, but even they seem cool.

"Are you ready for this?" Carmichael whispers at my shoulder.

I swallow back a surge of nausea and bob my head.

Carmichael raises his voice. "Henry has something he wants to stay to everyone." He strides out of the ring and stands at the front of the crowd with his arms folded.

I look from one stony face to the next, and the next. "I—" My voice cracks.

Geek and Layla's expressions soften, but only slightly.

I cough, and when I try again, my voice is steady. "I get it. You all hate me because you think I'm not like you. Because I'm not powerful. And because of what I said before I left. You think I'm a coward."

The shouts of indignation and cries of anger from the crowd are deafening.

"You got that right, Stone."

"You're weak."

"Filthy coward."

"Let him speak." Carmichael's voice booms over the others.

Silence falls, somehow heavier than it was before.

Most of the executioners are looking anywhere but at me, not really listening. Chatting in small groups.

What can I say to make them listen? To make them understand? I take a deep breath, and say, "Zara didn't think I had it in me either."

At the sound of Zara's name, two things happen.

One. A few heads turn in my direction.

Two. A couple of people actually leave the room, one muttering, "Zara would be ashamed of you."

A knife jabs between my ribs and twists.

Zara would be ashamed of you.

Are they right?

Would she?

Carmichael does nothing to stop the dissenters this time. He must know I'm fighting a losing battle.

Well, fighting losing battles is my specialty these days.

I clench my fists and raise the volume of my voice so my words rebound off the walls. "But she changed her mind."

"Ha!" someone shouts.

What should I say next? How can I convince them of my sincerity? I know what Dad would say. Speak from the heart. So that's what I decide to do. "I never should have said... those things. You all know what happened to my parents. You know—"

Katya gets right in my face. "We've all lost people, Stone. You don't have the monopoly on grief."

"I know that."

Rosie steps forward. "You stood right there and insulted COVEN. Sullied everything we stand for. Vilified us. Why should we forgive you?"

Speak from the heart. "You probably shouldn't."

Layla's father, Syed, clears his throat. "Not the best argument." His words sound accusatory, but he makes a small concession, saying, "Go on."

I continue. "You're right, Katya. We've all lost someone. We've all lost Zara."

"Because of you," Katya says.

Her words eat into my skin like the acid spell Femi used on me. I suck in a breath through my teeth, and say, "Nobody blames me for her death more than I blame myself."

Katya's expression shifts. A slight crack in the ice surrounding her, maybe?

I step back and address the entire crowd. "Zara taught me everything I know. She taught me how to fight. Taught me how to be strong. For a moment there, I lost sight of that. We grew close, because we both knew what it was like to be Outsiders here."

I expect someone to shout something along the lines of, "You'll always be an Outsider," but it doesn't happen, so I press on. "Zara was my mentor and, more than that, she was my friend. I loved her, and I know you all loved her too."

No-one makes a sound.

Even Katya stays silent for once.

I scan the crowd. "Zara's death affected me more than I can put into words, and I know it's affected all of you, too. Because... because despite everything, we're family."

Katya snorts.

Guess I spoke too soon.

She says, "You have a strange definition of family, you little—"

"Let the lad finish, Kat," Syed says. "You can have your say when he's done."

Katya opens her mouth, then closes it again.

I nod at Syed in thanks.

His expression remains impassive.

I pull out my parents' wedding rings and squeeze the cool metal in a tight grip. "My dad used to say—" My voice breaks a second time and my eyes sting with tears. "He used to say all families fight, and when they fight, they forgive each other, because there's nothing stronger than family."

I don't care whether anyone's listening anymore. I just need to get the words out before they choke me. "Zara was brave. She was the most courageous person I've ever met. She sacrificed herself to save my friends." My eyes find Geek and Layla, and I let the tears fall. Every single muscle in my body tenses, and when I speak, my voice is strong. "I swear to you—all of you—on my magic, on my Sight, if you let me stay, I'll make that fucking bastard Razor pay for what he did to her. For what he's done to all of us. If you let me stay, I'll prove my strength to you and my loyalty to COVEN. If you let me stay, I *will* get justice for Zara. I *will* end him."

Silence roars in my ears, and time slows to a never-ending crawl.

Nobody moves.

Nobody says anything.

Carmichael gives me a slight, almost imperceptible shake of his head.

My heart crumples like someone squashed it underfoot.

No.

This can't be it.

It can't be over.

It can't.

As a last-ditch attempt—one final push—I punch the air and intone, "*Vi. Iustitia. Fides.*"

Slow minutes pass and, eventually, Syed removes his arm from around Layla's shoulder and saunters up to me, stony-faced.

I hold my breath.

What's he going to do?

Hit me?

Cast on me?

He sticks out his hand. "*Vi. Iustitia. Fides.* I forgive you, Henry."

Relief washes over me, and I clasp his hand in a firm grip. "Thank you."

"But I'm just one person. What about the rest of you?"

Silence.

Executioners look to their colleagues.

"I forgive you," Geek says.

"And me," Layla echoes him.

Slowly—painfully slowly—murmurs of, "I forgive you," spread throughout the room.

Carmichael, Dickinson, O'Hara—even Rosie—they all speak the words that absolve me of any wrongdoing.

Everyone except Katya.

I lock eyes with her. "And you," I say. "Can you forgive me?"

Katya huffs, looks away, and rubs her thumb over her bottom lip. "Why should I?"

I consider this, my gaze going to a now smiling Carmichael, and speak the first words that come to mind. "Because someone wise once told me it takes a strong witch to offer forgiveness. I forgave Bianca for betraying me. Can't you do the same?"

Katya stays quiet for the longest time. After a few minutes, she clears her throat and says, "I'm still pissed off with you. But I forgive you. And I'm sorry for the part Bianca played in your torture."

Gratitude swells in my chest. "Thank you, Katya."

She gives a stiff nod.

A playful tone creeps into my voice. "Does this mean I can call you Kat now?"

She smirks, but it's not unfriendly. "Only if you kill that bastard, Razor."

"I will."

Carmichael's smile transforms into a grin so wide he's shows all his teeth. "Okay, everyone. Show's over. Get back to work."

The executioners disperse, a few of them patting my back or shooting me thumbs up signs.

Carmichael appears at my side.

"Guess this means I can stay?" I say.

He nods, then motions to Geek and Layla. "You three. Come with me," he says.

"Where are we going?"

"You'll see."

Carmichael closes his office door. "I'm giving each of you a solo mission."

"Solo?" Geek says. "Shouldn't we have backup or something? We only just graduated."

Layla nudges Geek with her hip. "Aw. Need someone to hold your hand?"

He flushes. "No, but—"

Carmichael raises his eyebrows. "Layla's right. The time for hand holding is over. You're executioners now. Zara taught you everything she knows. That should be enough. Unless you're questioning her methods?"

A steely resolve hardens Geek's eyes. "Never."

"Very well." Carmichael briefs Layla and Geek on their missions, then turns to me. "Are you ready?"

My heartrate increases. "This is it, isn't it?"

"It is."

And increases. "You've found him?"

"Not yet, but we have a way."

Geek claps me on the shoulder, and says, "You'll smash it, bud," before leaving the room.

Layla gives me a hug, and its only a little stiff. "Make him pay," she whispers in my ear. "For everything."

"I will."

She releases me and saunters to the door.

"Layla?" Carmichael calls after her.

She pauses. Turns back.

"I knew your mother a little," he says, and his voice catches. "You're just like her. She would be very proud of you."

Layla's eyes shimmer with moisture. She blinks, and the unshed tears are gone, her face set into a mask of determination. "I won't let you or COVEN down."

"I know," Carmichael says.

Then she's gone.

Carmichael smiles at the closed door, then walks toward the back wall.

"What are you doing?" I ask.

He waves his hand across the wall and says, "*Revelare*."

The wood-panelling blurs, shifts and vanishes, revealing a boxy safe.

Carmichael holds both hands in front of the safe, his fingers twisting and turning in an odd pattern.

What's going on? I squint my eyes to activate my Sight.

Carmichael's sky-blue aura flares to life. Now, I can see that his fingers are tangled in a web of glowing threads. The threads criss-cross together to form a protective dome around the safe.

It's a witch-weave, and a complex one. I wouldn't even know how to unpick it.

Carmichael makes one last motion—coiling a loop of the shining thread around his index finger—and the ward vanishes.

"What's in there, the crown jewels?" I ask.

"Case-sensitive material." He opens the safe, shielding the interior from view with his body. Carmichael rummages around inside the safe and shuts the door. He's holding a palm-sized model Ferrari.

I snort. "I'm a little old for toys."

"It belongs to Razor."

"A toy car? I doubt it."

"Dickinson and O'Hara combed Zara's murder scene. They found the car there. It's got traces of Razor's aura all over it."

I squint my eyes again and the toy car glimmers with a faint red light. "He dropped it?"

"Must have." Carmichael shrugs. "You know what this means?"

A tingle of anticipation runs down my spine. "We can find him."

He nods and holds the toy out to me. "I'll let you do the honours."

I take the car gingerly, like it's going to bite me. A sheen of cold sweat coats my upper lip. Why am I hesitating? I've been waiting for this for six months. It's all I've wanted.

Carmichael frowns at me. "What is it?"

The air's dense, hard to breathe. "I don't know if I'm ready."

Carmichael comes forward and grips my shoulders. "Zara believed in you. And so do I."

"Right." I nod. "Right."

He releases me. "You know what to do."

I let my eyes drift closed and focus on the weight of the toy car in my hand. An image of Razor floats behind my eyelids: the smarmy smirk, the scar crossing his eyebrow, the nicotine-stained fingertips. Something hot and ferocious boils at my core. I'm coming for you, you smug bastard, and I'm going to kill you. I inhale, drawing on my magic. On the exhale, arms flickering with pins and needles, I say, "*Inveniet, Razor Finch.*"

The spell catches.

My eyes spring open.

Green light shines between my fingers, still clamped around Razor's toy.

"I know where he is."

CHAPTER 42

The portal drops me off next to the chain-link fence bordering *Parkview Mews*, the abandoned building site on the edge of the city.

I clench my teeth together, waiting for the wave of portal sickness, but it doesn't come.

Small mercies.

Even though it's April, it's winter-cold. The air bites my exposed face and arms, and goosebumps prickle down my neck. I wish I'd worn a coat. A burst of static—courtesy of the in-ear Bluetooth headset Carmichael fitted me with before I left the compound—fills my ear, making me jump. "Jesus Christ."

"What's your ETA?" Carmichael crackles, his voice tinny and distorted.

"I'm here."

"Any activity?"

I sweep my eyes across the ruined landscape of the building site. The broken buildings, their exposed steel skeletons twisted into grotesque, arthritic shapes, are silent. "Nothing. It looks empty."

Another burst of static. "He's there somewhere. Proceed with caution."

"Copy that." I creep along the fence, searching for a way in, until I reach a section so rusted the chain-link peels up at one corner. I ease the rough, oxidised mesh to one side. It complains, creaking and groaning. I freeze—pulse racing—my fingers still hooked through the red-brown links, half expecting Razor to leap out of the shadows.

The only sound's the wind whistling through the wreckage.

A breath shudders out of me, and I duck under the fence.

Walking through the building site is like walking through a haunted house. A gibbous moon bleaches everything bone white, turning the shifting shadows into potential enemies. The slightest sound startles me. Cracked sheets of tarpaulin rustle in the breeze. Rubble crunches underfoot. A mammoth, hollowed-out bulldozer creaks as I pass in front of it.

"What's happening, Henry?" Carmichael asks.

I fish the toy car out of my pocket. The green glow of the locater spell's brighter. "I'm getting closer."

Something skitters off to my right.

I spin round and conjure a death-strike, preparing to launch.

A stray dog with bald patches in its fur watches me from atop a pile of rubble, canine eyes glinting in the moonlight.

My heart thunders in my chest.

"What is it?" Carmichael asks.

"Nothing," I tell him. "Just a dog."

The dog barks once, then pads away.

"I know what I told Geek about hand holding, but maybe I should portal down there and—"

"No. I need to do this alone."

"Fine, but if anything goes wrong, I'm coming to help you."

"I'll be fine." I say the words with more confidence than I feel, traveling deeper into *Parkview Mews*.

The path ahead of me narrows and I squeeze between two rusted building skeletons. My back scrapes against something rough and, for one heart-stopping second, I'm convinced I won't fit through the gap. I wriggle my way out, emerging at the edge of a deserted stretch of tarmac overrun with weeds and dandelions poking through the cracks.

The toy car flashes bright green.

A skyscraper towers before me.

"Found him," I say.

"Be careful," Carmichael says.

I scan my surroundings for signs of movement. Nothing. I'm alone, or at least, I appear to be alone. Jogging across the barren stretch of tarmac on light feet, I dart for the skyscraper and flatten my back against the wall. I crouch down, waiting for the barrage of death-strikes that I'm sure will blitz me at any moment, but nothing happens.

The ice-cold concrete at my back makes me shiver.

Only when I'm sure I'm safe, do I edge my way round the building until I come to a service entrance, guarded by a rust-brown padlock. "*Recludo*." The lock pops open and I squeeze my way inside, the door squealing on its hinges.

It's dark in here, but I don't want to conjure a witch-light because Razor will spot it. The air's thick with dust and smells like rotten, sweet leaves. I inch down the inky black corridors. My foot strikes something hard, and the sharp sound of metal bashing concrete rings out.

Fuck.

I hold my breath, blood rushing in my ears, then silence. Razor must've heard me. He *must have*. Why doesn't he attack? I'm more careful as I edge farther in, lifting my feet up higher and walking toe to heel. The corridor widens out, and I slip under a wide concrete archway into a bare room the size of a basketball court. I sink into a low, running crouch, hide behind one of six pillars supporting the ceiling, and peek around the corner.

And there he is.

Razor.

He perches on the edge of a foldaway camping chair, an apple-sized orb of red witch-light hovering above his head. A copy of Nietzsche's *Thus Spoke Zarathustra* balances in this hand.

Nietzsche. Typical. It figures Razor has a Superman complex.

He flips a page, the dry rustle of paper loud in the cavernous space.

I reach up and brush the tip of my finger across the tiny microphone on my ear-piece, a code Carmichael and I devised earlier.

"You've found him?" Carmichael asks. "Once for yes, twice for no."

I brush once.

"Has he seen you?"

Twice.

"Good. That's good. Do you have a clear shot?"

I hesitate. I do have a clear shot, but something feels off. This building's a shell. No carpets, no internal doors, no soft furnishings to soak up sound. Hadn't he heard the squeaky door? The sound of my foot knocking something into the wall? Why's he just sitting there reading? It makes no sense.

Carmichael says, "Henry, do you have the shot?"

I scan the room, a prickling feeling raising the hairs on the back of my neck. Something isn't right. I turn my gaze back to Razor and summon my Sight.

At first, nothing happens, but then the air around him ripples and bends, his form blurring.

I take longer than I should to figure it out.

An illusion.

"Henry?" There's a note of apprehension in Carmichael's voice.

"I'm—"

A low grumbling sound cuts me off, and the whole building shudders.

"It's a trap," I say.

"Bugger," Carmichael says. "Get out of there. Get out of there *now*."

The floor rumbles beneath my feet, hairline cracks splintering the concrete.

"Fuck." I break into a sprint, but it's too late. I've only taken two steps when the cracks widen, the earth bucks and the ground falls away.

I drop like a lodestone, my stomach lurching into my mouth.

CHAPTER 43

M y back slams into something hard, my rag doll body bouncing once, every ounce of air squeezing from my lungs. I claw at my chest, struggling to draw breath. Just when I've recovered enough to take in oxygen, the dust particles swarming overhead hit the back of my throat and I'm coughing so hard I'm sure something vital will rupture.

"Henry," Carmichael's voice is loud in my ear. "Henry, talk to me."

Laughter echoes around the pit.

I know that laugh. Stone grating against stone.

Razor.

Red witch-light flares.

I'm in a deserted underground car park, lying on a jagged pile of rubble.

Razor's smirking face comes into view, scarred eyebrow arched. "I'm surprised you fell for that. See what I did there? Didn't that stupid bitch Zara teach you anything?"

Blistering rage boils in my gut. How dare he? How dare he say her name? I shoot him my most withering glare and, in my peripheral vision, the toy Ferrari—still clutched in my fist—pulses with a flash of bright green light, but—for some reason—doesn't disintegrate like the other locus's I've used. "Wh—"

"Ah," he says. "You found it then."

I finally stop coughing enough to choke out, "Found it?"

"I put a protection spell on it. My mother gave it to me before she... it's very precious, and I didn't want it to get damaged."

What's he after... sympathy?

Well, I'm all out of fucks to give.

Razor covers the distance between us in a few quick strides and stomps on my wrist.

The bones crackle and a savage, searing pain races up my arm. I cry out. I can't help it.

Razor bends over me, putting even more weight on my broken wrist.

I scream, and feel a twinge of sympathy for Femi. I broke his wrist the same way, after all.

Razor plucks the toy from my unresponsive hand. "I'll take that as well." He rips my ear-piece out, and the pressure on my wrist eases.

I cradle my splintered arm, gagging at the shard of bone poking through the skin, the florid, swollen flesh.

Razor inserts the headset into his ear. "You didn't think I'd be stupid enough to drop something by accident, did you, Carmichael?"

"You—ah—you knew I was coming."

He ignores me, listening intently, before barking out another peel of laughter. "Shame you aren't here to carry out that threat."

The faint strains of Carmichael's raised voice reach me, but I'm too far away to hear what he says.

"Don't worry. I'll leave enough for you to bury."

The metallic taste of dread coats my tongue, and my heart clenches with fear.

No.

Fuck this.

I won't lie here and let Razor kill me. I refuse. Wriggling onto my side sends stabbing pain zapping through my wrist. Cold sweat drips down my back. I slip my working hand into my jeans and extract the slim, black case Carmichael insisted I bring with me.

"You're welcome to try," Razor says, still speaking to Carmichael.

A patch of dark air to the left grows darker still, then expands into a faint, shimmering blue circle.

A portal.

Carmichael's portal.

Thank God. Hope sparks in my chest, and while Razor has his back to me, I flip open the case to reveal the syringe of liquid silver. Fumbling the syringe from the box, I wedge the cap between my teeth and wrench it off.

Razor's still watching the burgeoning portal.

I depress the plunger a little, expelling any air—and a tiny amount of liquid silver—from the needle.

Something strange happens to the portal. It twists and distorts and pulls out of shape, before collapsing in on itself.

The last of my hope collapses with it.

Carmichael's tiny, aggressive voice emanates from the ear-piece.

Razor snorts. "Must be my witch-weave. Looks like your little protégé's going to die alone, after all."

Not if I can help it. I stab the needle into the most swollen part of my wrist, biting back a yelp as tears of agony blur my vision and force the plunger down. The bitter, anaesthetising chill of the liquid silver flows up my arm, then my skin grows hot. One last burst of pain. I grit my teeth, and breathe out a sigh of relief as my bones shift and realign, and the swelling goes down.

"No offence, but I'm bored now, Carmichael. Places to be. People to kill, and all that." Razor tears the ear-piece out.

I rotate my healed wrist—painless—and stand on silent feet, conjuring my witch-staff with a whispered spell.

"Now," Razor says, flinging the headset into a dark corner. "Where were we?"

"You want to know what Zara taught me?" I ask through gritted teeth.

"What?" He half-twists toward me.

"I'll show you." I swing the staff in a curving green arc, aiming for his temple.

He swerves at the last second and the staff whizzes past his ear.

The momentum of my swing sends me off balance.

"*Eryx.*" Red witch-gauntlets coalesce around Razor's fists. He lands a punch in my side, following up with a swift side-kick to the gut.

I stumble back, grinding my teeth against the ache in my side, and clutching my stomach.

Razor falls into a sparring stance and brings his glowing hands up to protect his face. "Is that the best you can do?"

Patronising bastard. I draw my arm back. "*Flagellum.-*" When I swing my arm again, the witch-whip I'd conjured speeds toward Razor.

He catches the end in his gauntleted hand and loops it around his wrist—once, twice, a third time—and gives a sharp tug.

I'm jerked off my feet. My chin strikes the floor and the rough concrete peels layers of my skin off as I skid along the ground. I barely notice the sting. I slide to a halt.

"This is for Cecelia." Something whistles through the air.

I roll to the side.

The butt of Razor's witch-staff slams into the floor centimetres from where my head was moments ago, and cracks appear in the concrete. I flip to my feet, re-conjuring my own staff.

Razor swings down.

I raise my weapon overhead and brace my arms.

Crash.

The staffs collide.

Razor swings the other end of the staff up.

I block low.

Crash.

We both draw back.

I reverse my grip on the staff and pivot from the hip, driving power through my arms as I aim straight for Razor's temple.

Razor must expect the move because he blocks it just in time.

Crash.

The force of the impact travels up my arms and into my shoulders, making them shake.

"Pretty good," Razor says, sweat dripping down his forehead. He spins on his heel and lashes out, the red blur of his staff cutting through the air and leaving a ghostly after image in its wake.

I duck, and the staff goes whizzing overhead.

He sweeps low.

I jump, narrowly missing the attack, and land funny, a twinge of pain shooting through my Achilles tendon.

Razor leans back and thrusts the butt of the staff straight at my face without missing a beat.

A burst of agony splinters my cheek, and stars explode before my eyes.

With one powerful strike and a cry of anger, Razor knocks my witch-staff out of my hands, and it vanishes. He darts forward, spinning his staff in a tight figure eight.

Sharp pain blazes in my shoulder, my ribs, my hip.

Razor twirls the staff behind his back, driving an open palm forward. "*Dis*."

The witch-strike slams into my chest, and I'm winded by the blow. I stumble back, my shoulder blades striking a concrete pillar.

Razor flexes his fingers. "*Prohibere*."

My muscles lock in place, my back fused to the pillar.

"But not good enough," he says.

I struggle against the spell.

Razor clenches his fist. "*Caeli.*"

Air.

Dark magic.

Steel bands close around my chest, tightening and tightening until my lungs ache for oxygen. I couldn't scream even if I wanted to, with Razor's power sucking all the breath from my lungs.

"You're an arrogant little prick, aren't you?" Razor says. "Did you really think someone like you could kill someone like me?"

My mouth's as dry as sand. I try to say, "Fuck you," but it comes out as a wheeze.

He just laughs.

Blood from the staff wound on my cheek drips into my mouth, and I taste copper.

"I'm getting the strangest sense of déjà vu." Razor's inhuman eyes trace the lattice of pink scar tissue criss-crossing my right hand, and disappearing up the sleeve of my leather jacket. "Fond memories."

The places where his eyes touch my skin itch like I'm infested with fleas. The edges of my vision darken, the pressure in my head intensifying.

"Carmichael isn't coming to save you this time, which means I get to finish what I start—" A hacking cough bursts from his throat, strangling his words.

His dark magic breaks, but not the spell pinning me to the pillar. My chest heaves as I gulp down huge mouthfuls of air.

Razor fishes out a white handkerchief and presses it to his lips, still coughing. It comes away bloody.

Déjà vu.

Something nags at me. The coughing. Every time I come into contact with Razor, he's coughing. First, with Primrose. He slit her throat and started coughing. At my parents' house, he conjured an earthquake while he was fighting Carmichael, and started coughing. Just before he killed Zara, he started coughing. I'd thought it was the smoking, but he wasn't smoking back at the house.

It must be something else.

"You're sick," I say.

He dabs the corner of his mouth and tucks the stained handkerchief away. "Coming from a trained killer, I'll take that as a compliment."

Another memory surfaces. Zara chewing me out for bringing up elemental magic on the first day of training.

The five elements: earth, air, fire, water and lightning are dangerous primordial forces. Drawing on their power comes at a price. For every elemental spell you cast, you exchange a sliver of what makes you human. Over time, dark magic poisons the soul.

Then it clicks. There's only one common thread tying my meetings with Razor together. Magic. The more magic Razor uses, the worse his condition gets.

"No. You're ill," I say.

His eyes flash. "You don't know what you're talking about."

That confirms it. Razor's prolonged use of elemental magic has poisoned his soul. Performing witchcraft makes him ill. Which means if I have any chance of beating him, I need to make him use more magic, and weaken him to the point he can't cast anymore. Hard to do when I'm pinned to a wall.

Razor's hand steals into his pocket, and there's a flash of silver.

A knife.

"What are you doing?" I ask.

He walks toward me.

Slow.

Savouring every step.

My blood runs cold and a crack forms in my mind. I'm half in the present and half in the past.

Dear Henry Stone... We write regarding your application... We regret to inform you...

The rejection letter from Oxford. The rest of that third line drifts through my mind like toxic smoke.

We regret to inform you that, as you failed to attend your interview...

My interview. The bus ride. Taking a shortcut. The headphones ripped from my ears. The press of cold metal against my neck—

No.

No. I can't relive that day. Not now. Never.

Razor stands before me. He spins the knife once, catching the handle again, the blade's keen edge gleaming. "I want to do this up close and personal. Because it is, isn't it? Personal." He's so close that we share the same air. And the smell...

Old tobacco.

Fruit flavoured chewing gum.

Razor presses the tip of the knife to the hollow in my throat—right over the tiny scar—and my mind fractures, the memories spilling out.

CHAPTER 44

SIXTEEN MONTHS EARLIER: OXFORD

I get off the bus at The Plain—the wrong stop, I realise after the bus pulls away, so I'm not off to a brilliant start. Broad Street. I should have got off at Broad Street. I wish I had driven now. The car would've been warmer than the bus, that's for sure. The frigid, early December breeze tastes fresh, like snow, and my breath mists in the air.

I shiver.

My phone bleeps.

It's a text from Jez.

Good luck today, pal. You'd better be back in time for karate. Sensei Toby wants us to help lead the class.

I thumb a quick reply.

Cheers, mate. I'll be back by five. That's stacks of time.

Another bleep.

Coolio. Laters.

I dig my gloves out, slide them on, and stuff my hands in my pockets. Strolling down the road, I drink the city in like a tall glass of water. The quaint shop-fronts, the yellow stone buildings, the buskers playing guitar and singing. Similar to Daxbridge, but with the added benefit of a top-tier university, relative distance from home, and the opportunity to *read* a Master's in Creative Writing. That's what they say at Oxford—*reading*, never studying. That's what I'll be able to tell people soon.

If I get in.

And I will get in.

Won't I?

What if I don't?

My stomach lurches.

It's true. The odds aren't in my favour. I attend a redbrick university, and I don't have any high-powered connections on the faculty I can tap for any wheel-greasing. However, I'm on track for a first-class undergrad degree in English Literature, I've had short stories published in several major publications—including *Writer's Digest*—and I've already read over half of the books on the masters' syllabus.

If that doesn't impress them, I'm not sure what will.

Yeah. I'll get in. I've made sure of it.

My phone tells me I've still got forty minutes until my interview. I breathe a sigh of relief. Plenty of time. I open my music app, stick my earbuds in, hit play, and whack up the volume.

Paramore's *Daydreaming* blasts into my ears.

Perfect.

Squaring my shoulders, I strut down the High Street, past Magdalen College tower, and Magdalen College Library. I cut down Queen's Lane, admiring the tiny quadrangle outside St. Edmund Hall, and the medieval well at its centre.

A narrow alleyway curves round to the right, and my maps app says I'll reach my destination faster if I take it.

I turn into the deserted alley, running my gloved fingers along the buttery stone as I walk.

The current song ends, and the last track on the album—*Be Alone*—begins.

The winter chill seeps from the walls on either side of me.

I glance down at my phone.

Thirty-five minutes.

A dark shape materialises out of the shadows and slams against my chest, knocking me back into the wall. Pale fingers rip my earbuds out and fasten around my throat.

My mind races through ways to break out of a front choke. What targets are available to me? Eyes, throat, face, armpits, groin, knees, feet. Strike with force, throw them off balance. I drop my phone and punch my attacker in the throat, grab hold of his upper arms and knee him in the groin. I slap his hands off my neck, throw him off balance, and crack my elbow across his chin.

He goes down, whimpering.

Someone else grabs me from behind and wrenches my arms behind my back, holding them in place.

A third man with a buzz-cut, wearing knock-off 'designer' trainers, appears. "Holy fuck, lads. Check it out. Like watching *Crouching Tiger Hidden Dragon*." He swaggers over to me, waving his hands. "Waaaah, waaaah. Wax on, wax off, Daniel san."

"Wrong film, arsehole," I say.

"Oh. Funny man, too, eh?" He punches me in the gut.

I sink forward, a deep ache spreading through my abdomen.

The guy pinning my arms forces me to stand up straight again.

Buzz-cut has something in his hand.

Snick.

A flash of silver.

Shit.

A flick-knife.

"Not so funny now, eh?" Buzz-cut says.

My heart pounds, my entire body fizzing with adrenaline. "What do you want?" My voice is an octave higher than usual.

"World peace." The guy restraining me says. "See? We can be funny too."

"Money," Buzz-cut says. "Now."

"Don't have any," I say.

"Liar." He punches me across the face.

My head whips to the side, and I spit blood.

"Nobody bombs about in gear like that unless their rolling in readies."

"You know how to use that thing?" I tilt my chin at the flick-knife.

Buzz-cut rests the tip of the blade between the hollow at my collarbones.

I freeze.

"I know where the pointy end goes, if that's what you're getting at." He presses in on the handle.

A sharp sting of pain and a trickle of blood accompany the point of the knife pricking my throat. A hot stream of urine spreads down my inner thigh, soaking my jeans.

"Oh, fuck. He's pissed himself, boys. Want us to pop over to the chemist and get you some nappies, piss-pants?"

They all laugh.

Heat floods my cheeks.

"Last chance," Buzz-cut says, leaning in close. "Money. Or I swear to God, I'll do you."

His breath reeks of old tobacco and fruit flavoured chewing gum.

"Okay." I swallow a gag. "Okay. My wallet's in my back pocket. Take whatever you want."

Buzz-cut bends even closer—the stale, smoky fruit scent overpowering—sticks his thin, bony hand into my back pocket and pulls out my wallet. "Let him go."

The vice-like grip around my arms loosens.

Buzz-cut grabs me by the hair and hurls me to the ground, yanking several hairs out by the root, and I scream. My face thwacks onto the cobbled pavement with a crack and blood spurts from my broken nose.

Buzz-cut's mate, the one I'd beaten to the ground, is on his feet now, massaging his crotch. He kicks me—fucking hard—in the ribs. "That's. For. Kneeing. Me. In. The. Balls," he says, each word punctuated by a harder kick.

I'm gasping for air, and the world spins in lopsided circles.

Buzz-cut scoops up my phone. "I'll take this an'all." He crouches over me, says, "Posh cunt," and spits in my face.

Running footsteps pound off into the distance.

The sticky string of phlegm, stinking of old tobacco and fruit flavoured chewing gum, slithers down my cheek.

That was it.

That moment changed the course of my life forever.

I'd missed my interview at Oxford. Somehow, I didn't think it'd be prudent to hobble into one of the world's most prestigious universities with a broken nose and busted ribs.

After my body healed, and my nose reset—badly—Dad suggested I rearrange. But every time I picked up the phone to make the call, my heart galloped and my breathing became erratic. I couldn't face Oxford. I didn't make it to karate that night, or the next, or any other. The thought of sparring—even in a safe and controlled environment—made my skin prickle with goosebumps.

The smell of cigarettes repulsed me.

And as for fruit flavoured chewing gum, no chance.

Old tobacco.

Fruit flavoured chewing gum.

I hated those smells and the memories they evoked.

It's the same smell Razor's breathing in my face right now.

CHAPTER 45

T he memory flashes through my mind in an instant.

"I'm going to enjoy this," Razor says, the tip of the blade still poised at my throat.

I wait for the prickle of fear, the sheen of sweat on my brow, the urge to pick my scar until it bleeds. It doesn't come. Instead, a balmy, sweeping calm settles over me, and I realise something. That twenty-year-old kid—the one who got mugged in Oxford, the one who gave up, gave in and withdrew into himself; the one whose skin I've been living in for the last sixteen months—no longer exists.

I'm a witch.

I'm an executioner.

And I'm powerful.

A huge grin spreads across my face, and I laugh, and laugh, and I don't stop laughing until tears stream down my cheeks.

Razor's brow furrows.

His expression makes me laugh even harder until my stomach aches.

"Stop." Razor reverses his grip on the knife and rests the edge of the blade below my Adam's apple. "Why are you laughing?"

I don't stop, I can't. It's hilarious.

"Why?" he barks, his tone threatening.

But he doesn't scare me now. He's no better than the thugs who beat me up in Oxford. No better than Myles or Femi. No better that Dean, the lager lout who spilled beer into my lap at *The Coach and Horses*. They're all the same. Bullies, the lot of them. Well, my days of bowing down to bullies are over.

"Because." Finally—finally—I stop laughing, my ribs feeling bruised, but I can't keep the smile off my face. "I've just realised how weak you are."

"Weak? I don't know what battle you've been fighting, but I'm not the one pinned against the—"

I draw on more magic than I've ever used in one go before, the prickling pins-and-needles racing through my blood, morphing into something forceful that makes my entire body shudder with power. "*Fluctus inpulsa.*"

The green-tinted shock wave blasts from the centre of my chest and flings Razor away from me.

Whatever spell he'd used to pin me to the wall breaks, and I slide to the floor.

Razor—still hurtling backwards, towards the wall that will split his head open—rotates his wrists and hooks his fingers into claws. Tendrils of air spiral around him, and his momentum slows and slows and slows, and then he's floating to a halt just shy of the wall. He lowers his hands and drifts down until his feet touch the floor. "Why won't you just die?"

I summon my Sight just in time to catch the enormous surge of power flaring in Razor's aura.

Oh, shit.

I whip round and sprint across the car park.

From behind me, Razor unleashes a torrent of magic.

I run in a zig-zag formation, dodging crimson fire balls and death strikes and lightning bolts. A stray witch-strike takes a huge chunk of concrete out of a pillar supporting the ceiling as I dart past it, and chips of the flying debris slice into my forehead, the side of my neck, the gashes blazing with heat.

I can't fight him head on. It's impossible. Sick or not, Razor's command of dark magic makes him powerful and dangerous. Think.

Think.

What can I do? How can I win? A light bulb goes off. That's it. If I can't beat him by force, then I'll have to trick him, like he tricked me with that illusion.

A rush of speeding air screams behind me.

I dive to the side, the edge of Razor's witch-whip catching my elbow. I grit my teeth against the numbing sting that shoots through my funny bone and—mid-dive, picturing the roof of the skyscraper—conjure a portal, and fall into the green light head-first.

I crash onto the flat roof, barrel rolling over and over, grazing my hands, my arms, the back of my neck.

It's pissing it down and thunder rumbles overhead like a mortar round. Fat, icy droplets of rain drum against my skin, plastering my hair to my scalp and easing the pain from the burning cuts covering my body.

I'm battered, bruised and so tired my muscles ache with exhaustion. All I want to do is lie with my back pressed against the freezing rooftop, close my eyes, and let sleep drag me into oblivion, but I can't. I've got to move fast.

Razor will track me. He'll be here any second.

Using all the strength I can muster, I brace my hands against the cold concrete and lever myself to my feet. Stabbing pain shoots through my ankle, and I stumble before I regain my balance.

Please.

Please let this work.

My eyelids close.

I'm so tired, I'm not one hundred percent sure I can pull this off, but I have to try.

Clenching my fists, I whisper, "*Duplici exemplari.*"

For a fleeting second, my magic sputters, and I'm sure the spell hasn't caught, but when I open my eyes again, I'm surrounded by sixty carbon copies of myself. I tip my head back and breathe a silent prayer to whatever higher being powers my magic.

This is it.

This is where it finally ends.

A blinding flash of red light rips through the darkness and Razor appears on the very edge of the rooftop, standing twenty feet away from the first line of my doppelgängers. His head whips from side to side, his hateful black eyes narrowing.

"What's the matter?" I say, and all my clones speak at once, creating a hollow echo of my words. "Don't enjoy being force-fed your own vile medicine?"

Razor's face twists into a mask of rage, clouds of misty air puffing from his nose. "It'll take more than a few illusions to stop me."

"We'll see."

Razor's fists spring open and twin death-strikes appear in his hands. He launches them into the crowd.

Two of my doppelgängers explode in a cloud of green smoke and the acrid whiff of burned ozone rises in the air.

He fires again and again and again.

More clones burst apart, releasing more and more pungent smoke, making my eyes sting.

I weave through the crowd of copies as it thins, keeping my eyes trained on Razor. I can see it now, the sickness polluting his aura, splotches of dark grey marring the healthy crimson, like tumour shadows on an ultrasound.

Three doppelgängers directly to my right blow up, and I dart behind the few remaining apparitions.

Razor cries out in agony and doubles over, collapsing onto all fours. He makes a series of raspy, barking sounds and thick gobbets of blood spatter the concrete and stain his lips. His limbs shake and his back arches high into the air as he struggles to draw breath.

It's time.

I dismiss the remaining clones with a flick of my wrist, and it's just me—the real me—and Razor, and nobody else. I stride towards him, chill runnels of rainwater flowing down my arms and dripping off the ends of my fingers.

Razor's head jerks up at the sound of my approaching footsteps. He leans back, so he's sitting on his heels and raises a trembling hand. "*Mortem.*"

I cast a shield to protect myself from the death-strike, but I needn't have bothered.

The red glow wreathing Razor's fingers stutters and dies. He howls in frustration and tries again. "*Mortem.*"

Nothing, not even a flicker of magic.

I lower my shield.

"No." Razor pounds his fists on the rooftop, splashing bloody, muddy puddles in the rainwater pooled under his knees. "You killed my wife, you bastard. You killed the only woman I ever loved."

I fix him with a hard stare. "And you murdered my family in cold blood. You deserve everything that's coming to you."

He coughs, and another glob of blood splatters the ground at my feet.

I know how I'm going to do it now. I raise a steady hand, index and middle finger extended, preparing to slit. His. Throat.

Justice.

Razor bares his teeth in an animalistic snarl. "Kill me, don't kill me. It won't make a difference. You won't last five minutes as an executioner. Know why? It doesn't matter how many spells you cast, or how many tattoos you hide behind. Underneath it all, you'll always be that scared little boy I pinned to the wall, waiting for death. You're nothing. Less than nothing."

I hesitate. Is he right? Will I always be that frightened kid, cowering at shadows?

"You're pathetic. Just like your worthless father."

I clench my jaw so hard my teeth hurt. "Don't you fucking dare. My dad was ten times the man you'll ever be."

Razor's lips curl into that familiar smirk he wears so well. "He was a snivelling worm."

"Shut up."

"I didn't slit his throat straight away, you know."

A fork of lightning cuts through the clouds, the booming thunder drowned out by the blood rushing around my skull.

"Want to know what he said?"

"I said, shut the fuck up."

He shifts into a mocking, high falsetto. Nothing like my dad's warm, rich voice. "Please. Please don't kill them. I beg you. I love my family. Please." Razor resumes his low, snide tone. "He begged me, like a gutless coward."

I want to pummel him into the ground. I want to tear his limbs from his body and use them to beat him to death, but still I hesitate, my bitter, scalding tears mixing with the cool, fresh rainwater pouring down my face.

Razor laughs, a cruel, hollow sound, staggering to his feet. He takes a wobbly step towards me. "You see? I was right. Never mind five minutes, you won't last two seconds. Weak as a limp handshake. Just like your useless parents."

That's enough.

Enough.

Something alien and seething with unbridled fury unfurls at my centre, and the dam breaks.

"This is for Primrose." I slash my fingers downwards. "*Secare.*"

Razor roars in pain as a deep red gash opens at his wrist, spilling more blood.

"This is for Zara." I slash again, and an identical red line streaks the other wrist. I pull my arm across my body, ready to deliver the fatal blow.

Razor sways where he stands, fingers coated in a never-ending stream of crimson. In a weak, husky voice, he says. "If you're waiting for me to beg, don't bother."

"And this..." He may not beg, but he will die. "This is for my parents, you worthless piece of shit." I whip my arm in a wide arc, the tips of my extended fingers blazing with emerald light and energy.

His body jerks, and his nicotine-yellow fingers grasp at his throat.

Then, I'm standing on another rooftop. Primrose is here, and Zara, and Mum and Dad. And I know it's a figment of my imagination. I know everything I've endured since that unapologetically brazen, unashamedly sexy, absolutely no-fucks-given, bronze-eyed girl put her book down and graced me with just five minutes of her precious, limited time, has carved a scar deep within me that will never really heal. Razor was right. A piece of me will stay here, on this rooftop haunted by ghosts.

Waiting to die.

Waiting to be with them again.

Family.

All of them.

Bonded by blood.

Connected by magic.

Fated by circumstance.

Family.

And like Dad always said, there's nothing stronger than family.

I expect to feel something when Razor topples off the roof. Elation? Ecstasy? The fierce rush of righteous justice only revenge can bring? Instead, I feel nothing. Even when I walk over to the edge of the roof, even when I know he's really dead—limbs contorted into unnatural shapes on the cracked tarmac below, lips peeled back from his teeth in a wide rictus grin, an ever-expanding puddle of blood around his misshapen head—even then, I feel nothing.

I'm blank.

Hollow.

Numb.

An empty shell.

I'm still staring at Razor's mangled corpse when the tearing sound of a portal opening startles me. I spin round, conjuring a death-strike.

The shimmering blue portal closes, and Carmichael appears, wearing a huge grin. "You did it. You killed him," he shouts over the relentless drum of the pouring rain.

I don't disengage my magic. Is it really Carmichael? Is it finally over?

He holds out his hands, palms down, and speaks in a soothing whisper. "You're okay. You're okay now. It's just me. Everything's going to be fine. Lower your weapon."

"You can't be here," I tell him, thinking of Razor's witch-weave. Is this another trick? "How did you get here?"

"Henry, think about it." He takes a step closer.

"That's far enough," I say, preparing to launch.

Carmichael freezes. "Fine. I won't come any closer if you don't want me to, but I'm just asking you to think. Carefully. Razor's dead, and you know, *you know*, when a witch dies, their magic dies with them."

Razor's dead.

I killed him.

I watched him fall.

Saw his body.

"He's really gone?" My voice tremors. "It's really finished?"

"It's really finished."

"You swear?"

"I swear."

"On your magic."

"On every last spark."

I lower my arm and the death-strike fizzles away to nothing.

Carmichael walks forward and clinches me into a tight bear hug. "They would be proud of you."

The emotions come then. The sorrow, the grief, the mis-spent rage.

I let it all out. I'm sobbing, shaking, pounding my fists against Carmichael's chest, but he doesn't complain. Even when my legs won't support my weight any longer and we're both kneeling in freezing cold puddles—the iron sky empty-ing buckets of water on us—Carmichael only whispers again and again that my parents would be proud.

Eventually, the tears dry out and I stand.

Carmichael stands with me and moves back. He pulls out a silver syringe, hands it over.

I inject myself, healing my wounds.

"Thanks," I say, passing the needle back. "What happens to..." I gesture at the roof's edge.

"I'll have someone come and dispose of the body."

I nod.

It really *is* over.

Wait.

No.

Not quite.

I've got a promise to keep.

"*Ostium.*" I open up a swirling green portal.

"Where are you going?" Carmichael asks.

"There's something I have to do."

"Now? Can't it wait?"

"It's for Zara."

Carmichael lets me go.

When I stride into the portal, I don't look back.

The rain's stopped, but it's as cold as ever.

Will he still be here? It's late, and the shop's in darkness. I hope he's not here. I don't want to tell him. Sighing, I rap on the door. I wait two minutes and knock again, louder this time.

Another two minutes pass, and I'm about to leave when light spills from inside.

I want to run. I don't want to do this. What the hell am I supposed to say to him? I've only met the guy once.

A deadbolt slides across, a key scrapes in the lock, and Bob opens the door to *Obsidian Ink.*

He yawns, his short blonde hair tousled with sleep, sticking up at odd angles. He narrows his eyes at me, and I know he's trying to work out who I am. After a few seconds, his expression clears. "Oh. Henry, right?"

"I—uh—I wasn't sure whether you'd be here."

"I live upstairs." Bob rolls his neck and draws his dressing-gown closer. "It's late. Why are you here?"

"I—uh—" I rub the back of my head.

His eyes are suddenly alert. "It's Zara, isn't it? What's happened? Is she hurt? Where is she?"

"She—" My throat's so tight it chokes off my voice. I can't do this. I can't. "She's..."

Bob clutches his stomach like I'd winded him. "No."

I suck my bottom lip in, trying to hold back tears. I'm sick of crying, but I can't help it.

"No." The word comes out in one long wail and, although I'm soaking wet, Bob collapses against me, shuddering.

I take a deep breath, slapping him on the back. "She told me to tell you she loved you, and that she didn't want to leave you."

This makes him shake harder. He's getting snot and tears all over my T-shirt, but I don't give a shit.

I hate that someone like Bob—one of the very few nice and gentle people in this world—is in so much pain, and there's nothing I can do to fix it. It isn't right. It isn't just. I make a vow to myself. For Primrose. For Zara. For my family. For innocents like Bob. I swear—on all the magic I possess—that I *will* destroy anyone who causes this much pain.

I'll make them fear me.

I'll make them pay.

Every single one of them.

CHAPTER 46

THREE YEARS LATER

I stride into the ring.

Geek paces up and down in front of this year's trainees. It's his first year as a trainer, and I know he's shitting bricks over it, but he hides it well. "I'm not big on speeches. So I'll keep this simple. I have two rules."

Zara's words, delivered through Geek, make my chest ache. She gave her life for us, an act of true selflessness that I can never repay. Even now—three years later—her teachings, her death, still impact me.

A crowd of executioners block my path. They're so intent on sizing up the new recruits, they've failed to notice my arrival.

Their mistake.

"Move," I say, the word clipped at sharp angles.

Those nearest me jump. They turn, spot me, and a path opens.

I don't break my stride, keeping my shoulders back, my chin up.

Some mutter. Some point and others whisper behind their hands.

I know what they're pointing at.

The skin around my new tattoo—courtesy of Bob—is still rosy-pink, a further addition to the half-sleeve of black feathers covering my left arm from wrist to elbow.

I have nineteen feathers now.

Nineteen missions.

Nineteen feathers.

One for every kill.

My gaze flicks to the line of trainees and the contents of my stomach sour.

Carmichael shouldn't have called me in today. He knows I don't come in during my birthday week. I was about to doze off on the sofa when his message pinged through.

URGENT MISSION. HAS TO BE YOU. CAN'T SPARE ANYONE ELSE.

One week off per year, that's all I ask for. A bit of time to recover from my latest collection of injuries and nurse my psychological scars. Speaking of scars, the slash wound crossing my back from shoulder to hip, a gift from scumbag number nineteen—a charming serial killer by the name of Tessa Murray, whose *modus operandi* included kidnap, decapitation and dismemberment—still itches. Guess my R & R will have to wait.

"Oh my God." One trainee nudges the young man next to her, a note of reverence in her voice. "You know who that is, right?"

The boy follows her gaze. He shrugs. "No. Should I?"

The girl clicks her tongue. "I keep forgetting you're an Outsider. That's Henry Stone."

Two trainees actually gasp.

I carry on walking, fighting back the laugh bubbling up my throat and forcing my face to stay straight.

"Henry Stone?" the boy says.

The girl nods. "My dad told me about him. He's COVEN's best executioner and youngest *Alpha*. Never failed a mission."

"That right? Doesn't look so tough."

Still battling a smirk, I stand statue-still.

The air in the room takes on a heavy, tight quality, and the assembled executioners cast worried glances at the boy.

I pivot towards him—weasel-faced, a mop of curly black hair shading his forehead—and narrow my eyes.

He doesn't shrink away, even when his fellow trainees do. Instead, he crosses his arms, tilts his chin up, and glares right back at me.

Ah. Someone likes to play Billy Big Bollocks. Two can roll that set of dice.

I take three slow, measured steps towards him, adopting my most cutting tone. "Word of advice? Don't go looking for trouble. If you do, chances are it'll find you."

Billy Big Bollocks laughs. "Don't go looking for trouble," he says, in a poor imitation of me. "Is that supposed to be intimidating?"

I can almost taste the tension in the air, thick and sharp. This boy reminds me of Myles. Cocky. Brash. A bully. There's only one way to deal with bullies. Thank God for Zara. I'd learned from the best. "Mind if I take this one?" I ask Geek, eyes never leaving the young man's face.

"Go for your life, mate."

"I'm not scared of—" the trainee begins.

I flick my wrist. "*Dis*."

My witch-strike explodes against the trainee's chest. He yelps—high and strangled—and tumbles backwards, head over heels, landing hard on his back.

"Anyone else got anything to say?" I cast a hard eye down the line of trainees.

One by one, they shake their heads, looking decidedly green.

"Didn't think so." I approach Geek.

He wears a wide grin. "Thanks for that. I've only known him for five minutes and he's already grating on my last nerve."

"He's got guts though. If he survives training, stick him in *Beta Section*."

"Ha. We'll see." His brow furrows. "I thought you were on your annual leave."

"I was. I've been summoned by the *führer*."

"You don't have to take every mission going, you know."

I crease my face up in mock-hurt. "But I'm so good at them."

Geek rolls his eyes.

"Besides," I say. "He said it was urgent."

"Isn't it always?"

"I'd better go. You know what he's like if you keep him waiting."

"Don't I just."

As is customary, we bump fists before I make my way to the other side of the ring.

Geek's voice is quieter now, but his next words still reach my ears. "Where was I? Oh, yeah. Two rules. First rule. When I give you an order, you follow it, without question..."

With a shudder, I push all thoughts of Zara from my mind and head straight for Carmichael's office.

My fist raps against the dark mahogany door.

"Come in."

The door swings open on silent hinges.

Carmichael looks up from his computer screen and removes his reading glasses—a new accessory—and runs a hand through the fine strands of grey threading through his hair. "Good. You're here."

I bristle. No, 'sorry I had to call you in on your week off.'

Deep breaths.

I shut the door. "What have you got for me?"

"Say hello to your new target." Carmichael slides a blue cardboard folder across his desk.

I snatch it up and flip the cover open to reveal a mugshot of a sallow-skinned man in his mid-forties. His watery blue eyes are ringed with dark circles. "Who is he?"

"Peter Sanderson." Carmichael resumes his seat and laces his fingers together on the desk.

I shrug at the unfamiliar name.

"He was having an affair with his sister-in-law. She called it off, so Sanderson killed her."

"How?"

"A combination of air and water magic. Conjured a dozen icicles and, well, she looked like a voodoo doll when they found her."

"Nice bloke then." I shut the folder and chuck it down on the desk again.

Carmichael doesn't acknowledge my sarcasm. "The MID had to let him go."

I snort. "Let me guess. Lack of evidence."

Carmichael nods. "Unreliable witness. We need to move on this now."

"Where is he?"

"We have it on good authority that he hasn't left his flat since the MID released him. 22E Hemingway Court."

I turn towards the door, but a thought stops me from leaving. Geek's usually my handler in the field, but he's too busy with training right now. "Who's my handler on this one?"

"We're short staffed. Layla will have to do it."

My skin prickles at the mention of her name, and my heart gives a funny little squeeze. Jesus, this is going to be awkward.

Damn funny little squeeze.

It's because I love you that I can't be with you.

Nothing's changed on that score.

She's still better off without me.

Safer.

"Problem?"

Carmichael's question starts me from my reverie and I force my mind back to the matter at hand. "No. I'm fine." I wrench the door open and stalk from the room. "I'll be back when it's done."

Can I Ask You a Cheeky Favour?

Thanks for reading *The Witch's Revenge* and joining Henry on his quest for justice. I hope you enjoyed the book.

Reviews are really important to authors. They help other readers—like you—discover our work.

If you liked the book, and have a couple of minutes to spare, it would be great if you could leave a short, honest review on the book's Amazon or Goodreads page.

Happy reading!

Cheers

Shane

WANT MORE FROM THE MYTH & MAGIC UNIVERSE?

DOWNLOAD YOUR EXCLUSIVE PREQUEL SHORT STORY, THE THIEF'S MAGIC (MYTH & MAGIC, BOOK 0.5), FOR FREE!

Want to read Geek's origin story and follow his journey to COVEN?
You can download The Thief's Magic (Myth & Magic, Book 0.5) today!
Visit: https://bit.ly/thethiefsmagic

Acknowledgments

A lot of people have the misconception that writing is a solitary thing to do (I used to be one of them), but this couldn't be further from the truth. Writing is a team sport, and I have one hell of a team to thank.

First, foremost, and always, thank you to my family and friends for your unwavering encouragement and support. I couldn't do this without you. You keep me grounded and stop imposter syndrome from taking over. I couldn't be more lucky. Special shout out to Mum, Nan and Granddad for always being there. Poppa, I wish you were still here to see my words on the page. Uncle Phil, thank you for showing me that with vats of elbow grease and heaps of sheer, bloody-minded stubbornness, success is achievable despite (and perhaps because of) humble beginnings.

To my editor, the phenomenal Alexa Padou from *Luna Imprints Author Services*. You are a word wizard, a story savant, and an absolute bloody genius. Thank you for taking the rough piece of clay I presented you with and helping me transform it into a novel I can be proud of. Here's to working on many more books together.

Thank you to Damon and the team at *Damonza* for another cracking book cover. You couldn't have captured the essence of the book more perfectly. If pictures paint a thousand words, your covers paint a million.

To all the authors who've mentored me (whether that's from a distance, or through personal interaction), I couldn't be more grateful. You all taught me how to write and what it really means to be an authorpreneur. Special shout outs to Sacha Black, Dan Willcocks, and Jeff Elkins.

Sacha, you always bring it with your brutal feedback and insightful advice. You also helped me decide how to brand this entire series in a way that makes sense. From one high Competition to another, thank you.

Dan, your positive mindset, encouraging nature, and *Terminator*-like production levels inspire me. Cheers.

Jeff, thank you for teaching me how to develop character voice and giving me permission to go crazy with hazard characters. What you're trying to accomplish (and the community you're building) is stellar.

Thank you to my fellow authors, Matt Goodall, Sarah Louise, and C. M. "Cassie" Newell for catching those last few pesky errors. I'm grateful for your eagle eyes.

To all the writers I know (whether that be on Instagram, or from the *Rebel Author*, *Next Level Authors*, and *Dialogue Doctor Patreon* communities), I can't thank you enough. I won't name individuals (because I will miss someone out and feel bad about it), but you are my people, and the author journey is much easier because of you.

Last (and by no means least) big thanks to you, dear reader, for picking up this book and reading all the way to the end. Without you, this brilliant, fulfilling, and occasionally frustrating craft called writing wouldn't be worth my time. Because of you, I know that this is what I want to do for the rest of my life and, for that, I will be eternally grateful.

ABOUT THe AUTHOr

S. W. Millar is the author of the *Myth & Magic* urban fanta-sy thriller series. He is also a *Fictionary Certified StoryCoach*, and is currently working on a series of craft guides for writers.

Shane holds a BA in journalism and is a member of *The Alliance of Independent Authors (ALLi)*. He lives in Bucking-hamshire, England.

He has taken too many writing courses to count and en-joys reading as much as possible. Shane is obsessed with five things: the writing craft, mythology, personal development, food, and martial arts movies.

Connect with Shane on Instagram

https://www.instagram.com/swmillarauthor/

Visit Shane's Website

https://swmillar.com/

ALSO BY S. W. MILLar

Myth & Magic

The Thief's Magic # 0.5 (FREE prequel short story)
The Coven's Executioner # 2
The Fury's Vengeance [Novelette] # 3
The Demon's Shadow # 4 (out in May 2022)
More *Myth & Magic* coming soon...

Printed in Great Britain
by Amazon

82206232R00253